"Hynes sure does give good mean streets, and this is another rough ride that never flinches."

—Toronto Star

"Hynes knows the horrors of a hard-liquor, cocaine-spiked hangover at four o'clock in the morning. But he also understands the ecstasies— a woman with her shirt half-open, the wild plunges of conversation and occasionally, just occasionally, the authentic glimpses of wisdom— that happen while you're getting there."

—DAVID GILMOUR, author of
A Perfect Night to Go to China

"Hynes shows his literary expansion in this novel about a young man burning with the resentment and angst of an abusive childhood. Both the hated villain and comic victim, Clayton Reid blunders through his days, riddling everything with passion and destruction, leaving love and loathing in his wake. Written in the tough language of its hero, *Right Away Monday* is a beautiful, suffering story by a gutsy new novelist."

—DONNA MORRISSEY, author of *Kit's Law*

"A rip-roaring and chaotic down-and-out-in-St.-John's novel about an alcoholic drug-addicted bartender and the women who love him in spite of himself. It's a raw comedy about how lost the lost can get before detox and redemption. Its hero is the Energizer Bunny of self-destruction and the anti-Christ of political correctness. It's the grunge rock of Can Lit."

—DOUGLAS GLOVER, author of *Elle*

Tout le monde peut entrer au ciel et personne a besoin de mourir.

Quand chui monté en amour
avec toi tu m'as hissé jusqu'a la
porte du paradis

Right Away Monday

Also by Joel Thomas Hynes

Fiction
Down to the Dirt

Stageplays
The Devil You Dont Know
(co-author with Sherry White)
Say Nothing Saw Wood

Audiobooks
Down to the Dirt

RIGHT
AWAY
MONDAY

Joel Thomas Hynes

HARPER
PERENNIAL

Right Away Monday
© 2007 by Joel Thomas Hynes. All rights reserved.
P.S. section © 2008 by Joel Thomas Hynes.

Published by Harper Perennial, an imprint of HarperCollins Publishers Ltd

Originally published in a hardcover edition by HarperCollins Publishers Ltd: 2007
This Harper Perennial edition: 2008

HARPER ● PERENNIAL®
is a registered trademark of HarperCollins Publishers

HarperCollins books may be purchased for educational, business,
or sales promotional use through our Special Markets Department.

HarperCollins Publishers Ltd
2 Bloor Street East, 20th Floor
Toronto, Ontario, Canada
M4W 1A8

www.harpercollins.ca

Library and Archives Canada Cataloguing in Publication

Hynes, Joel, 1976–
Right away Monday / Joel Thomas Hynes.

ISBN 978-1-55468-232-4

I. Title.

PS8615.Y54R53 2008   C813'.6   C2008-901819-2

RRD 9 8 7 6 5 4 3

Printed and bound in the United States
Set in Galliard
Text design by Sharon Kish

for Dolores and Gary
and for Ron, of course . . .

With eleven pints of beer and seven small
gins playing hide-and-seek inside his stomach,
he fell from the topmost stair to the bottom.

—Alan Sillitoe,
Saturday Night and Sunday Morning

Contents

Contents

Right Away Monday

1. Balls-deep on Duckworth Street

I says look here girl, I says, I'll fuckin eat you alive I will.

And she blushes at that, goes right scarlet she do. Of course. Cause I'm far from stunned. I knows how to smile when I wants me skin. It's all in the smile. I was crossin on the other side of Water Street when that gangly Philip fucker bawls out and waves me over. Skull-and-crossbones on the front of his girls-size tee-shirt. That pisses me off, cause you gotta earn the privilege to wear that particular badge and you can tell at a glance that he's nowhere near worthy. Wavin like that, with his wrist, and I says to meself—who the Christ are *you* to go orderin *me*, Clayton goddamn Reid, across the street there fucko? Course then I spots *her* alongside of 'im, doin a little twirl on the barstool, sippin at something cold, and even though I aint out on the hunt and really do got better stuff to be at, I cant help makin a grand uproar cuttin across through the traffic, just to show 'em all that I dont give a fuck for nothing or no one. Cause I dont.

At the Gropevine, where the whole front wall is a window that the staff opens to the street in the good weather. Water Street drenched with the panic of the comin fall, all hands bailin back the shooters, tryin to make the best of the rest of the summer. Like we're in fuckin Greece or something. But we're not. No sir.

She there swivelling in them skimpy shorts and I knows fuckin well I seen her around the Hatchet the other night. Out back in the alley. Right, I minds that greasy Jane Neary introducin us in the middle of a dirty big draw.

—Clayton, this is Donna. She's from the Battery.

Jane right fuckin singsong about it too, thinkin I'll swallow the notion that there might be something in common between us just cause where Donna's from, the precious Battery. Besides, I dont buy into that fuck-arsed matchmaker shit, cause if you hits it off with someone you're after bein hooked up with, then whoever did the hookin figures they got some kinda claim over your love life, like they can pick around and ask questions and make fuckin suggestions. I says you're better off fuckin around with strangers, easier to walk away when you have to. Cause when *your* buddies and *her* fuckin buddies are all tangled up with the skin situation, then it's bound to fuck shit up when you starts lookin elsewhere. And we never really stops lookin elsewhere now do we?

There she is anyhow: tight white shorts and a store-bought suntan with her clean blond hair whippin around in the afternoon and that desperate screamin plea way down deep in the back of me head that wants me to please just keep hobblin on up the street with me head fully intact and me cock well tucked into me pants, not bothering no one, gettin on with what I should be at.

And I says I'll fuckin eat you alive girlie.

It just pops out like that.

And she goes red like that and I knows I fuckin got 'er.

I tells her me name then. Fuckin right she remembers me from the other night, but she says she knew me from somewhere else before that too. I tries not to let on I'm as popular as I am. But then she's gotta go and ask me if I'm anything to Valentine Reid. And I gotta say yes, cause he's pretty much the only family I got, see, these days, and I loves him for it. But I aint no fuckin name-dropper either and sure I already got her, so . . . I mean, I cant help it that he's all famous and shit. But I just sees him for *who* he is, and that's a crooked old bastard half the time. But then, next thing, after she goes on a bit too loud and long about how much she likes Val's songs, his older stuff anyhow, I finds meself sayin to her (and well within earshot of that glossy Philip dickhead, who sat there sippin his pissy Corona through a fuckin *straw*), I'm sayin:

—Well girl, why dont you come by and I'll introduce you to Val sometime, how 'bout this evening?

And of course she says yes and wants to know if I got any draws. I shakes me head but gives her a wink to let her know I can hunt some down. She offers to buy me a beer then and me skull almost collapses with how easy it could be to just plank meself down and drink the whole goddamn lot of 'em under the table.

Slay the fuckin works of 'em.

Summertime, sun beatin down and the young ones strollin the streets in their tightest whites for one last August flaunt. Me there, perched on a barstool with the music on bust and me whole life ahead of me.

Christ come fuckin kill me.

It's every ounce of energy in me soul to shake me head, to decline. She seems surprised. I stumbles back a bit then, where I got too much weight shifted onto me fucky foot. Then she wants to know what's wrong with it, by the way. And while I'm writin down me address on her little tropical rum coaster I says:

—I'll tell you in the morning.

And she smiles again like that and goes right red and I knows I fuckin got 'er, that she's been *gotten*, that I'm fuckin well gettin some.

. . .

I gets showered and swipes a decent shirt outta Val's closet. I swabs a bit of polish on me boots, but dont bother to shine 'em up, just leaves 'em a nice dull black. Donna shows up at the door around nine o'clock, all dolled up with a suede purse and the makeup caked on like she's off to some karaoke contest. Big loopy gold earrings I dont have much time for. But it's alright. She looks pretty goddamn good, actually. I watches Val sizin 'er up, head to toe, right obvious and sleazy about it. Then he gives me the Nod right in front of her, a foolish attempt to rile a reaction outta me.

—Well done yourself Clayton my son.

Like I needs his fuckin approval.

—Yeah, thanks. This is Donna by the way.

Val's in one of his better moods. He breaks out the guitar and rigs up a couple of hot whiskeys for himself and Donna. Val is into the Jameson and water these days, hot or cold, depending on the time of day. He reckons the clearer the drink, the clearer the next morning. And I says sure why dont you just drink vodka then? But he says vodka's the last resort for the drownin alcoholic. Him with his nasal cavities on the verge of collapse.

—Want one Clayton?

—No thanks.

—Want one?

—No.

—You're sure now?

He keeps diggin at me to take a drop, even sets one down in front of me with cloves and sliced lemon and sugar and all. The steam fumin up me nostrils, snakin into me heavy, heavy brain like that. Breathe. I takes the mug of whiskey and dumps it into a crusty cereal bowl left on the table since this morning. Val's face drops. He puts the guitar away and turns off the kitchen light before headin upstairs. Me and Donna sittin here in the dark. She gives me a look but I dont know what to tell her. That's just the way he is.

We heads down to the Duke for pool. I'm still scopin her out a bit, tryna make sure she's up for a romp later on and not just lookin to snare me in for the long haul. Fuck that, she'll be lucky if she gets tonight outta me. She tosses a scattered sly glance across the pool table at me and smiles like she's sayin *Let's get the fuck outta here and go have at one another.* Or at least that's how I chooses to interpret things.

After a few clumsy games she goes back to the bar and when I scans the room I sees Val comin in through the side door. He takes a booth in the corner and I goes over to join him. He nods and smiles like he aint seen me in months. That's how it is. He takes a clear glass vial out of 'is coat and taps a little mound of coke onto the table. He dont give a fuck who's lookin, what with bein *the* Valentine Reid and all, living legend. He cuts a few lines and rolls up a five-dollar bill, snorts the works back, then slides a line across the table at me. And BANG! Me head reels with the pressure of a thousand possibilities: me and Donna wacked on coke and fuckin my headboard right through the bedroom wall. I plucks the fiver from Val's hand, leans back in me seat to re-roll it. The end of the summer. Family. Skin lined up. Fuck it once more. I forces all the air from my lungs and leans in over the line.

—Hey? What's going on over here?

Donna. She hands me a glass of soda water, like I asked for, and I'm floored with the insanity of how quickly the tables can turn for me, how easy I can fall when I aint watchin where I'm goin. I grabs the glass and slugs back half the soda water in one go. It erupts in me guts and burbles out through me nose. I tosses the bill back onto the table and tries not to look at the white stuff while I makes a straight cut for the downstairs bathroom. As I rounds the corner I hears Val say:

—Help yourself Miss Donna.

I stares at meself long and hard in the foggy bathroom mirror. It's been two weeks. That's the longest I've gone yet without a drink or a beer. Ten days last year. Me eyes dont look so tired and baggy. I aint so pale as I tends to get. I can remember where I was and what I was up to this time last night, and even the night before that. I conjures up all that old detox jargon, one day, one hour, one moment at a time. Me old man Randy throwin up blood in a bowl next to the woodstove, tryin over and over to keep the liquor down long enough for it to reach his bloodstream and regulate his nerves. And I knows how shit like coke and pills are just lubricants, how they makes your resolve all slippery, opens up the windows in your head, the ones that lets all the booze and subsequent madness flow in. I fuckin *knows* all this. Deep breath. Soda water. Smoke.

Two whole fuckin weeks Clayton.

I leaves the bathroom then, finds Donna at the bottom of the stairs tryna coax some cigarettes outta the machine. She cant get no satisfaction out of it, says it ate her money, so I steps in and gives the machine a solid boot with me good foot like that fucker from *Happy Days* and holy fuck sure change and smokes goes flyin across the floor. I glances up the stairs and then drops to me knees and starts stuffin me pockets. I dont bother with the money. Donna giggling nervous behind me. One of the bartenders clomps down over the stairs so fast I havent got a chance to cover up the situation. He looks at the floor, looks back to me. I'm standin there with a load of smokes cradled in me arms like a newborn youngster, coins still drippin outta the machine behind me. He steps towards me but I'm so blinded now with the free smokes, me nerves seethin from the tease of the coke upstairs and the hot whiskey fumes back at Val's and the cold, cold beer I didnt have not one goddamn drop of at the Gropevine earlier today, that just as he reaches a fuckin hand in my direction I shoulders him hard against the wall. He falls back and slops his leg into the scuzzy mop bucket. Donna grabs the hem of me coat. I turns and sees the look of fright and giddy panic in her eyes and we takes off up the stairs and out through the crowd into the night. Fuck Val I says. He's big and ugly enough to look after himself. That's me though, barred from the Duke I s'pose.

On Water Street I trades a pack of Craven A for a couple of hot dogs while Donna flags down a cab.

• • •

She's in the process of movin into this bachelor apartment on Duckworth. All's there is a mattress and some blankets. We lies down and goes right to it. But I'm feelin a bit low-minded, so we smokes a little pin joint from a bit I swiped outta Val's jacket. I dont see nothing wrong with a little draw. I mean, I'm only workin on the

6

booze, not goin born-again or nothing. It's just mellow shit anyhow. Me and Donna chats quiet and listens to the radio for a while and then konks out. Next morning I makes up for it though. Yes by the fuck. And wouldnt you know but the two of us are carryin poppers? I'd sorta tucked mine away in the back of me head till I was in the clear with the booze and all. They crossed me mind earlier in the day when Donna was on her way to the house, but it's always so much energy and fuckin around tryna convince someone to try 'em out, tryna get it through their heads that you're not tryna poison 'em or render 'em brain dead long enough to rape 'em. So I cant hardly believe it when she whips out her own bottle, that I wont hafta go talkin 'em up like some door-to-door salesman only to have her humour me with a few little sniffs and not really get to experience the force of 'em.

She had her own.

Poppers gets a bad rap if you asks me. Cause people dont like 'em on their own, without the *fucking* part. All they knows is that they got messed up guilty feelings that one time they tried it at the bar. Well, dont do it at the bloody bars, hold out for the fuckfest.

Now, I s'pose it really is a bit peculiar to expect someone to try 'em for the first time in bed. So they typically has a first go at 'em out in some social setting, and gets all fucked up and writes 'em off as some sorta lowlife solvent shit. But see, they aint meant for bein fuckin sociable. They're meant for hidin out, gettin lost. *Worst* thing you can do is take a huff out at some bar and then expect to carry on enjoying your beer. It's too, fuck I dont know, it's a different buzz, self-conscious. Numbs your mind and blows it wide open and it's scorchin fuckin hot. Scorchin. Your heart pounds and the heat rushes to your face and them hazy yellowed blotches, like when you stares at a lightbulb too long, settles on everything you looks at.

I first came across poppers in a shady little porn shop near Harcourt Square in Dublin. Gothic little brown bottles labelled *room incense*. Legal, but not really. I was barely out through the doors of the shop before I opened a bottle and stuck it under me nose. Well fuck, like I said, the heat and the rush, and dont look at me cause I dont wanna be held accountable for your nightmares, dont you fuckin look at me while me eyeballs are explodin like this, just get outta the goddamn way and pretend like I never existed in the first place! I shambled right into traffic with me skin all pins-n-needles and me jaw clamped tight and tires squealin and me eyes to the ground with me whole fucked-up life bubblin up behind me eyelids like that and I thought alright, this is it, I'm never comin back. This is what they taught us about in school, how drugs can *permanently* fuckin alter you. I'll never be the same again. Little Irish beeps and toots from all angles.

—Holy fuck. Ho-ly fuck.

Over and over I said it. And then it was over. Two or three minutes, tops. The fog lifted and I came back, like I was never away. And like the fool I did it again that night at a bar in Clontarf, near where I was livin. Five or six of us passed the bottle around. I was the only one new to it though, and soon as I took a haul I had to get up and leave and they all laughed at me. But I just couldnt sit still with the echo and the heat. I floated over to the toilets and ducked into a stall and hung on for dear life till it went away.

—Never again. Never a-fuckin-gain.

And then I was back. And ten minutes later I did it again. But that's the only way I used 'em for the next four and five months cause it's a cold day in Hell and a hefty-size ring on 'er finger before you'll have an Irish girl go down on you, by fuck. It's all money over there nowadays, so if you got none to flash around you're pretty much fucked for skin.

Course, when I got home from Dublin the women were all over me cause they liked me accent. But a lot of people gets all pissy when you comes home with a nice accent, says you're puttin it on for show. And I'm sure some do. Some people fucks off on vacation over there for a couple of weeks and comes home soundin like they just crawled outta the bogs of fuckin Mayo. But if they comes home from Alberta or Toronto sayin "eh" at the end of every sentence, nobody bats a fuckin eye, they just thinks it's such a sin. Because us crowd, Newfoundlanders, fucks off to Canada and nobody under-fuckin-stands us, we have to slow everything down and pronounce everything *proper*. Overseas though, we can talk as fast as we like and there's no need to dumb it down. We're allowed to relax into it. And besides, I comes from the Southern Shore and we still all got the black fuckin plague in us up there. So it was just a matter of gettin back to me real way a talkin, the way me own grandmother fuckin talked. Granted now, I will admit that I could turn it on and off when it suited me, but still, I lived and drank and worked and fought with Irish fuckers for six goddamn months, I was bound to cozy up to the accent. And fuck anyone who says otherwise.

And, I reckon, maybe the women were sniffin around too when I first got home, simply because I was outta town for so long. Truth. It's like this: what's the quickest way to get your skin around these parts? Leave town for a few months.

Me first two weeks home I holed up at the General's Inn on Elizabeth Avenue. And listen here, I never had one lonely night. I even had two on the go one night. Not the same time, but fuck, I barely had one out the door before there was another one knockin. Mostly Hatchet and Ship girls though. Never a Gropevine girl, where if they gotta pay for their own cab they're slummin it.

But by Christ the poppers, the sex part, I had no clue. This girl named, ahhh, this missus comes around one night and we were hot and heavy for a while there, but then it got kinda awkward so I whips out the poppers and starts sellin 'em to her, how they're s'pose to be good for doin the wild thing. I'm kneelin there with me cock goin soft inside 'er. She gives the bottle a little sniff, then says fuck it and takes a giant huff and closes her eyes. I takes one then and holds it in for as long as I can. I'm fully expectin to go off me fuckin head but then the sweat breaks out on 'er forehead and she starts breathin heavier and pushin at me and then I'm hard as a rock and everything else in the fuckin universe fades away except the walls of her cunt. And I knows that sounds crude but it's fuckin true, there really was nothing else, like our bodies were one and the same. Not like we had some connection of the fuckin soul or that kinda shit, just that we were both in the same place at the same time with the heat and the hearts poundin and the sweat and the smell of hungry, rabid fuckin primal sex.

Never laid eyes on her after.

. . .

So this first morning with Donna, that's the fuckin business alright. She wants me to put on a safe first. We tries it out, but it's like washin me goddamn hands with cotton gloves on, so when it slips off we just keeps right on. Fucking. She wants it every which way too, and she dont need no coaxin. I'll just be gettin a good pace up and the next thing I knows she's flat on her belly with the poppers under her nose and her two hands on the cheeks of her arse tellin me to take me pick of where I wants to put it. I aint long makin up me mind either. That's a rare one, I'll tell ya. Loud too she is. Fuck.

. . .

In the blink of a fuckin eye then, two or three weeks is after rollin by and I'm still knockin around with her. However that happened I've no fuckin clue. I helped her lug in what furniture she had, set up the bed and stereo, slapped on a fresh coat of paint. Everything good and laid-back too for a while, nice place to lay low, watch a bit of porn and eat and fuck. Course, then I shows up one evening and she got all this crowd in for drinks and draws, that greasy Jane Neary, who hooked us up and seems so fuckin proud of herself for it, that shiny Philip dink and a few other faces from the Hatchet. Battered and twitchy Jim McNaughton, older than everybody by at least two decades, sittin there noddin along and smilin in his own world and cant peel his eyes away from Donna's tits. Have a good gawk Jim, I knows I'm s'pose to give a fuck but I dont. I really fuckin dont. Everyone's talkin politics and fuckin art and treatin me and Donna like we're some cute little *item*. Donna with a pack of smokes and

10

a half dozen *non-alcoholic* beer in the fridge for me, fuckin Molson Exel, and has to go announce it to me in front of everyone, like she wants to make bloody well sure they all knows she's *lookin after me* or something. And so I barks at her:

—I got fuckin smokes girl. Think I cant fend for meself or wha?

I yanks open the fridge and sees there's a load of beer, real beer, and wine on the bottom shelf alongside the Molson Exel. Molson fuckin Exel. Same slop old Randy use to cart home every time he'd take the pledge. He'd guzzle cases of it for about two weeks, then slip over to a light beer for a while, then on to "the good stuff" again.

Molson Exel. Lord fuck. Like I aint *allowed* now. Like I aint to be trusted around real beer, like I havent got no mind of me own. If I wanted to drink that fuckin bog water I'd fuckin well hunt it down on me own.

Thinks she knows me now do she? Thinks she got it all sussed out.

I stands at the counter and demolishes five Black Horse in ten minutes flat. Fuckin flattens 'em. One after the other. The second one hits me head like a shot of fuckin morphine and I has to laugh at how foolish I've been to be puttin meself through such stresses. Cause if there's one fucker who can handle his drink it's Clayton goddamn Reid. Donna watchin me outta the corner of 'er eye, askin no questions. I turns John Lennon on crank and then I gets all bloated and saucy with Philip till he fucks off for fear of his teeth. When he's gone everything goes right quiet. They're all starin at the floor and sippin their wine like fuckin youngsters caught at something they shouldnt be at. Too shitbaked to look at me, so I fucks off too, cause I'm in the mood for a good old-fashioned dust-up.

I swipes a near-full bottle of wine from the kitchen counter and closes the front door soft behind me. Never even says goodbye.

Down to the Hatchet then, shit-faced. Open mic on the go. I keeps gettin up singin Bob Dylan and the Doors and gettin free beer. Donna shows up at some point, all pissed off at me for bein a prick and spoilin her little fag-fest. I cant stop laughin at her, with the fuckin gold earrings danglin and the bright red blowjob lipstick and that starved and battered need just drippin from her eyes. She grabs me by the sleeve and tries to drag me out the door, but I breaks away and climbs onto the pool table, keeps jabbin at her with the pool stick so's she cant get near me. Next thing I knows I'm arguing with Mike Quinn while he's shovin me out the front door.

Last goin off I'm out in the back alley smokin a big dirty draw with Petey Thorne, the chunky fucker hostin the open mic, and I'm tellin him about me own songs, how I useta have a band, and he's just noddin at me like I'm some kinda shithead wannabe.

And then someone's pullin us apart.

I wakes up on the floor in me bedroom at Val's with blood on me elbow and the knee tore outta me jeans.

• • •

Val with one of his demos on bust downstairs. I can smell that fishy coffee he makes, with the steam and the milk. I was never much on coffee. We only ever had the instant shit in the house growin up. Tea was it and it still fuckin is. The bottled coffee was only kept on hand for townies. Anne-Marie, me old man's missus, always made a big sarcastic deal of it when she offered someone a cuppa tea and they said they wanted coffee. But that's the way up the Shore, ask for anything outta the ordinary, like a cup of fuckin coffee or skim milk, and run the risk of havin yourself labelled a snob, stuck-up: *That one thinks her shit dont stink like the rest of us.* Honest to fuck, wouldnt know but you'd put in a request for broiled lobster or caviar or an eight ball of coke or something. Anne-Marie. Fuck her. She knows nothing, perfect match for the old man.

• • •

I tumbles down the stairs, hopin against hope there's still a few codeine left in the cabinet, and there she fuckin is, Donna, gigglin over some shit Val's fillin her head with. She looks at me then. Fine fuckin sight, first thing in the afternoon. And she all dolled up again.

—Well mister. Did you get it out of your system or what?

Outta me *system*? Fuck do she know about what makes me tick? Thinks she got me pinned already. Think again little miss. Val lookin at me and shakin his head and smilin, like he got the inside scoop on *my* fuckin life when he barely knows what's goin on in his own.

—Fuck are you doin here?

Right hateful I says it, and she's not expectin that. She goes red and stops smilin and drops her eyes to the floor. Val gets right cunt-ish with me and I tells him to fuck off and he laughs, cause he gets a kick outta how I dont take no shit from no one. Cause I fuckin dont. Then *she* starts laughin and we all has a little draw and that brings me head right around to what I went and done. I was almost five weeks this time. Not a drop. She gets yakkin about the way I got on at the bar last night and the sauce I gave to that sparkly Philip fucker. I starts to turn a bit shy, even guilty, because she seems so delighted with me. And even though I wants her gone, gone now out of my life so I can start again on me own where I belongs, I cant help but notice the way the sun catches on her neck, that soft spot beneath her earlobe and how her stretchy top hooks across her nipples that way. How you can almost see right through them little white shorts and I reasons with meself that maybe she's alright after all, that I just might hang out with 'er for another bit.

—Want to go out for a bite or a drink Clayton? On me.

Fuckin hell, see how they lines up against you? Forces. Go out for a drink. Easy as that. But I dont want to anyhow, cause she had to go and say, right in front of Val, that it was *on her*, like I cant find me own dinner or something, or like the only reason I'd go anywhere with anyone is if I didnt hafta pay. I dont answer her. Val gives me a sharp and sadistic poke in the small of me back with the neck of his guitar. It fuckin hurts. I feels like snappin the guitar in half only for he told me I could have it whenever he kicks the bucket. He might be kickin it sooner than he thinks, if he dont fuck off.

—First two rules of rock-and-roll Clayton: never turn down a free lunch, cause there's no such thing as a free lunch.

—Well now Val, that's only one fuckin rule isnt it?

—What's that?

—Well, if I wrote it down on paper, it'd only come out as the one sentence, one rule.

—Fuck off Clayton.

Me and her went down to the Hatchet then. Me stomach too delicate for anything more solid than a pint of Guinness. Game of pool and a straightener. Or a primer I should say. On her.

2. The Lobster Complex

Been crashin at Val's for near on two months now. I had nowhere else to go after they gave me the heave at the General's Inn. Val insisted I move in though. Massie, his wife, my elusive aunt, is after takin off to Corner Brook with some painter. Val, on his own in the big empty house. He didnt give a fuck about rent and shit like that.

So I said why the fuck not?

Val lived in Vancouver for years and then he got all screwed up with his record company and came home. I was livin in Town nearly six months before I knew he'd moved back. I saw his old snarl on a poster downtown and I showed up at his gig that night and introduced meself. He knew me, but he didnt really. He fuckin well called me Clarence first. I mean, I knew him on and off over the years. He'd show up at the house like a fuckin tornado and leave weed all over the floor and the counter, bang away on the guitar for me. He was around a lot after Mom's accident, come to think on it, maybe cause Randy was so fucked up. They'd stay up and have a few beer. Sometimes they got pretty loud and nasty with each other and I heard shit I knows I prob'ly shouldnt have. Just Randy all stroppy and spoilin for a racket after a few too many, always lookin to point the finger at anyone atall other than himself. Diggin at Val I s'pose just cause he'd gone out into the world and made something of hisself. I never heard many good things about Val over the years. Anne-Marie always sayin to me that he was fucked up and his head

15

was all swole up. I s'pose that's the price you pays for gettin on the cover of the fuckin *Herald*. One time he came up the Shore to play at the folk festival and asked some dickhead to turn off his video camera. Of course they all had to go make a big stink about it, but Val was only lookin out for the bootleggin thing. I asked him about that a few weeks back and he says:

—You dont want tapes out there Clayton, especially amateur video, with that shitty outdoor festival sound that gives people the licence to verify what they want to believe about you anyhow: that your success is unwarranted.

Slick enough. Gotta look out for your own interests I s'pose, cause no one else will. People're just jealous anyhow, cant stand to see one of their own get ahead in the world. That's that whole lobster complex: soon as one makes a break for the top of the tank, the rest gives it their goddamn best to drag 'im back down. But I still always looked up to him for doin what he did. What he does. I had a poster of one of his albums on me wall when I was in high school and I 'members Randy belchin at me about gettin suspended and tellin me I'd end up in jail if I didnt straighten out. I points to the poster of Val and says that that's what I'm fuckin into, that's where I wants to go. And ole Randy clicks his teeth and says:

—Yes now, and fuck over everyone in your path to get there? Some life.

But that's the way you gotta go old man. Let yourself get bogged down with the bullshit, fuckin relationships and money and education, and then where's the goddamn music? Fuck that. I'm goin for it. Not the music part, not no more, not now, but maybe I'm thinkin I might write a play or a movie or some such shit. Dont seem to be much to it. I got a few ideas, I knows a few stories. Just needs to get meself rigged out.

Like I said, I tried the band thing for a few years. Me and a bunch of fellas from the Shore had a decent little setup for a while. We did mostly cover songs at first, but after a while we sorta weeded 'em out and wound up with about a dozen of our own. I did all the writin of course. I'd just kinda be walkin along the roads in the night time and I'd hear a song in me head and I'd start singin it and comin up with the words right there on the spot. It's like that shit is waitin there in the back of your head all along. Course, I could never get the hang of the guitar. I mean, I knows a bunch of chords and a few little riffs, but I could never manage to sing and play the one time. So I'd basically end up bringin a song into the band and singin the melody and then Corey, cousin fuckin Corey, he'd just work out the music parts and Mark'd shove a bass line to it and then Jason'd just come in on the drums. At the end of the day we sounded pretty good. But more often than not it wouldnt turn out to be the song I heard in me head first goin off, and we had a few rackets. Good fun though. We played our first show at the Horseshoe down in Cape Broyle. Teenage dance. Packed. People starvin for it, goin cracked dancin and drinkin and fightin out behind. Some shithead grabbed the mic stand and banged the microphone off me front teeth. I booted him in the guts and then the owner came down and told us all to turn it down a bit. We made nearly seventy bucks each and we were delighted with that. Grand laugh it was. We called ourselves the Lost Weekend, after John Lennon's infamous tear in San Francisco where he smashed that fucker's head in with a cigarette case.

The band was good. I can say that much. I sent Val a demo to his address in Toronto but he never did remember gettin it. The Lost Weekend. And I reckon we coulda done alright in Town. We even got bumped up in the battle of the bands on George Street. But everybody was always off at something more important and we could never get it together to have a jam and there was more drinkin goin on than was necessary. I fucked off to Dublin then, to save me own life. And when I got back the b'ys had a new singer, some flimsy fag-boy from Mount Pearl, a CD in the works. They were called the Cold Shoulder, one of the possible names that *I* was after comin up with when we first started out. Fuckin loyalty for ya. Here I was, fresh home, with all kinds of new ideas and songs and nothing goin on in me life and rearin to start singin again, but they were just a bunch a fuckin detached pricks. Corey even told me that he'd *sell* me a CD at a discount when it was finished. Me fuckin cousin and everything. I wanted an explanation, to know what they were all bein so cunty about, but they couldnt come up with a proper excuse, said I was too hard to handle and that there was too much tension all the time and that I was a bastard with everyone when I wanted to be and that I'd just fucked off overseas and left everybody hangin. But sure they had no clue about the stress and the strain I was under. I saw that program in the paper advertising for Dublin and I knew that if I didnt go for it, I'd die. Had to go, had to just get the fuck outta town. I was livin on me own then, in a little deathtrap on Mullock Street with no fire escape and a bunch of psychos and retards on all sides. Me girlfriend was just after havin a so-called nervous breakdown and she was all the time screamin at me to love her and *be there* and then her grandmother died so everything got worse. I blew me student loan on booze and had no way to pay the rent and I was drinkin night and fuckin day.

I swiped a bike one night on Hayward Avenue and rode it up to the university parking lot and went round and round in circles till I fuckin collapsed with the tears rollin down me face and no one in the world to talk to. The next day I checked into the detox centre down in Pleasantville. I had to. I was there for a few days dryin up before I got a call at the pay phone, cause that's the number I gave out, tellin me I was picked to go overseas. So, who in the fuck are *they*, the Cold fuckin Shoulder, to tell *me* I was too hard to handle and self-centred and shit when they had no idea I was on the verge of death? Fuck 'em. They'll all get theirs. And like I said, if I hadnt got out when I did I'd be fuckin dead now anyhow. That's just it see? I got out, I moved on. From where they were standin I was bettering meself, makin a break for the top of the tank. And by turnin their backs on me, well that was just their way of pullin me back down.

I s'pose I coulda started something up on me own around town when I got home, but I didnt really have the energy to go balancing other people's schedules and shit. Plus I drank so much in Dublin that I was just plannin on layin low for a bit when I got home. Dry out and get me shit in order. See how that's workin out? Anyhow, the way I sees it, if you *really* wants to make a band work, you gotta be all livin under the one roof and all drawin welfare. That's the only way, to have nothing else in your life but the music and a few draws and a bit of skin. Not a girlfriend, mind you, not someone who's gonna want you to go off watchin fuckin movies and hangin out with the family on the weekends and houndin you about watchin your money and puttin on clean clothes, just someone to bang around with on your own fuckin terms every now and then.

Plus I figured by then, where I was the great Valentine Reid's nephew, well that's what I'd have to live up to all the time, and I said fuck that, I aint goin livin in his shadow for the rest of me fuckin days. Valentine Reid's savage little crippled nephew?

Fuck that.

I got a few ideas. Just gotta get meself geared up now.

3. Comeback Special

Jesus Christ. That clock working? What road is this? My car?

Pull over here. Pull over. Here. Park. Lock these doors.

Bandage on my hand?

Alright. Breathe. Cigarette. Light it. Breathe that now. Again.

Glove-locker. Pre-scrip-tion. Two left. Full bottle a week ago. A week ago. No refills remaining. A lifetime. Wait.

Yes, wait. Calm. Settle.

Where was I going? Second time that car passed up. Ghost car.

Focus.

Where did I come from?

Your mother, you foolish lummox. Now focus.

Kitchen. Peeled an orange.

No. That was yesterday.

Was it? Oh yes. Right. Massie. On the phone. Looking to set-tle. Settle. Sign papers. Lawyer. Money. Screaming. Money. Locked Clayton out of the house. Shit. Tack wore through my heel. Blistered. Broke a string. Punched the window.

That's the bandage.

Walter. Dropped by. Exactly . . . how much?

Four hundred.

No.

Yes.

Gone? Cant be. Already? Baking soda. Spoon. Pipe. Ash. Eat my way through the table. Gone. Hove Walter out. Shit. My four hundred in his arse pocket. No friends in this racket, hey Walter? Hey? Walter? Dont come around here anymore. Hey, there's a lyric.

No. Tom Petty.

Not the same though, not exactly.

Same idea.

Right, right. Old Tom always gets there first. Three chords and a decent beat, catchy chorus and a pound of weed. *There's* a lyric Tom. Now bite me.

Reid? Okay Reid? Come back. Feel this? This is the wheel. Rubber and steel. Turns the car this way or that way.

The car!

Right.

Piped the works of Walter's gear and now . . . now . . .

Going back for more, Val.

What's that sign say? Springdale. Patrick Street for Walter. Next one over is it? Okay. How do I . . . what . . . ?

This lever right here Val. P stands for Park. Pull the lever down to the D. That's Drive. Gas. Break. Steering wheel. Red means stop. Green means go. That's it. Are you feeling red or green?

Green, by Christ.

Or you can wait. Wait. Come back. Get it back.

Get it all back.

What's missing Val? Precisely?

Everything. She's . . .

Music?

Fuck. Gone.

Never. The one sure thing . . .

Shoulda checked out fifteen years ago. The heyday. Healthy and primal. No more music. Music.

C'mon Val, give us a song. Every night needs a soundtrack. This button here.

Static. FM never worked right in this shitbox. Try the AM. Here's something. Oh Christ . . . not this one . . . too much . . . too god-damn . . . strange . . . yes . . . and . . .

Fitting?

> *Seems the pressing question on everybody's lips*
> *is when you're gonna come back home again.*
> *When are you gonna come back home again?*

Bad lyric. Bad. That melody, too standard. Everything was A minor then. Too young, too consumed.

—By request that was Valentine Reid with "Come Back Home," a *huge* number from what most consider his breakout album, *High Time in '79*. Over twenty years ago for that one and it's been quite a while since his last release, four, five years? Dare I be so bold to state that the "pressing question" on a lot of lips is—whatever happened to Valentine Reid? What say you Mr. Reid? Is there ever gonna be a comeback? Are *you* gonna come back home to us? Because we're starving here Vally, no food in the cupboards on the best of days and my lawyer says I'm entitled to at least . . .

Jesus! Comeback? Come back?
Yes Reid, come back for fuck sakes. Here in the car now. Go home.
Home? Home.
Home.
Walter. Then home. Home. Go. Red means go . . .
No Reid. No. Red means—
Shut the fuck up! Gas. Steer. Go. Go go go . . . means red . . . fuck . . . red and *blue* means . . . keep going now. Walter. Walter. Go!
No! Reid? Val? Come on. Pull off and get straight. Here they are . . .
Royal Newfoundland Cunnyhoppers.
Glovebox Val. Reach. Root. Breathe. Be nice. Dont talk.

Be nice. Late for a show. Wait till he sees my name . . .

Dont fucking talk.

Step. Out. Of the car. That's pavement.

—I'm late officer . . . p-playing a show . . . I'm Val Reid, Val-en-tine . . . I'm late . . .

This is the pavement now.

Tack in my heel. Blister. Broke a string . . .

Something has been broken . . .

—. . . broke, broke a string officer . . . Vvvval fuckin Reid . . . making a comeback . . . playing at Massie's . . . make some . . . late for a show . . .

The show is over Val. The show is over . . .

4. Darker Corners

Val's growin a big fat mustachio. He got a role in some movie that's gettin done here in St. John's. Although they calls it a *film* around these parts. He looks like the last cop that picked me up. I tells him this and he just stares at me vacant, like I aint even in the room, like he does when there's a crowd around. Fucker. I tells him I wants a part in this goddamn *film* too and he says it was cast ages ago and there was no auditions and it's low budget anyhow. I says fuck, how are they gonna find the *real* stars if they sticks with the same crowd all the time and dont even hold no fuckin auditions? Val looks right through me like that again and I feels like clockin him one. He scratches at a sore spot on the inside of his nostril and it starts bleedin and he's suddenly hoppin around the room lookin for a tissue and holding his neck out like a fuckin broody hen cause he's afraid to get blood on the good white shirt that belongs to the *film* crowd. A horn blows out on the street and there's a big white van down below. That must be his ride cause sure he lost his licence, yet again, last week. He's bleedin all over the windowsill with this sudden shattered expression on his face. I hands him a roll of toilet paper and he stares hard at me for a second with this lost-puppy look, like he wants to say something real to me. And I s'pose I knows just how he fuckin feels alright, cause I needs to tuck meself away too, needs to go underground for a while before this old town breaks me all over again like it's always tryna break him. The horn sounds from

24

the street again and Val pulls away from the moment we coulda had, smiles and laughs with the tissue stuffed into his nose, asks me if I got smokes. Where I only got half a pack left, I says no. He slips me two twenties, tells me not to drink it, when we both knows fuckin well that's the only reason he's givin it to me.

• • •

Down at the Hatchet with me foot up. Mike Quinn behind the bar, which is odd where he owns the place. I asks him about it and he says he's gettin a new bartender shortly, or rather an old bartender that quit months ago and now's come crawlin back. Mike, right pleased with that. That Clyde Whelan cunt, who's s'pose to be on the day shift, is workin on the same goddamn movie as Val, along with half a dozen other fuckers from around the bar. Background work, but still. Some fuck of a casting director came around the night before and chatted people up and got 'em to come in to the set. Fuck me then, the one night I aint out on the go and all hands gets offered paid work on a movie. And here I am thinkin about writin one. See if I misses either other night out.

I sits and swills back the beer and offers Mike twenty bucks to put on me tab. Tab cant be too high cause I'm takin it easy these days. He tells me it's cleared off altogether, that the lovely Donna straightened it out the other night when we were leavin. That pisses me *right* the fuck off.

—You got a good little woman there Clayton. Hang on to her.

—She's not my fuckin woman.

—Never say. That wasnt you then, in the stall with her the weekend?

I has a flash of me and Donna doin lines off the back of the toilet and then goin right at it against the stall door. Someone knockin and laughin and tellin us he can hook us up with a nice tidy apartment if we needs a bit more privacy. I s'pose that was Mike. He got all kinds of property. They says he pretty much owns the west end of Water Street.

Mike slops a dirty pint of Smithwick's down in front of me.

—On the house Clayton. What are you doing for work these days?

—This and that.

I knows what he's askin. I aint that fuckin foolish though. I sees the state of his bartenders. Take Keith, fella I knows from up the Shore: he works the Friday night shift these days, his eyes all dark and tired and sunk in and always stretchin his back and shit. I heard he cracked up a couple of years back and went wandering around doin all kinds of drugs and panhandling. His father had to go up to Halifax and get him off the streets cause he wouldnt leave his missus alone after she fucked off on 'im. Fellas like that makes me sick. All clingy and needy and pussy-whipped to the point where they cant think straight and goes off the fuckin head and winds up in jail or the mental. I just dont understand that shit. She musta been some good fuck, that's all I can say. But then I s'pose you cant believe everything you hears, and he gets on nice enough behind the bar. Mike Quinn got 'im all straightened out now, apparently. Never say to look at him though. They says he's on antidepressants and writin a book or some shit. He dont drink or nothing no more, but he's all the time fried on weed. And he slipped me a couple of wicked painkillers for me foot last week. But he got this lofty smile-and-nod thing on the go for everyone too. And he dont hardly talk to me atall cause where we're both from the Shore I s'pose. That suits me just fine, cause if I didnt have nothing to say to him in high school why should I pretend he's me best buddy now?

But yeah, Mike Quinn owns the works. There's another bar on the second floor called My Place, but everyone calls it the Closet cause it's just a hangout for old displaced queers. And then there's a scuzzy apartment on the top floor where everyone goes to buy and drink their booze after hours. Keith runs that little scam cause he lives there. He makes a good bit of money at it too, as far as I can tell. He picks up a few bottles and a few cases of beer at the liquor store and then he sells it for twice what you'd pay at the bar. And people buys it too, cause they cant get it nowhere else at that hour and they can go on in and sit down and drink at Keith's place till seven o'clock in the morning if they like. And then there's a couple of spots up around New Gower and the far end of Water Street that opens at first light. So you can drink all night and all day if you needs to. I found a pretty good system in Dublin like that. The regular pubs called last call at eleven and cleared out by twelve. Then, if you could handle the racket and the plastic yuppies with their soft leather jackets and Doc Martens, you could go on to the dance bars where it was last call at two and all hands out by three. On from there to the fancy wine bars and be out by five. After that you had one hour to decide whether or not you wanted to pack it all in and go home or hang around on the streets for the early bars that opened at six. There'd be a wobbly, fat lineup outside the early bars from half past five, fellas heavin up warm wine in the gutter, doin all they could to hold out for a fresh pint. I useta go to this one place called Slattery's on the north end and they'd have the windows blacked out and the music on bust and all hands fallin around fightin. After a few minutes it was like you had the night back all over again. Twenty-four seven.

Mike Quinn owns a string of buildings up on the west end of Water Street, like I said. They says he started out in his mid-twenties with a used-furniture shop, that he'd cruise down around Placentia and Conception Bay on the weekends in his truck and load up on outport shit: stained-glass doors, tables, pressback chairs, crystal knobs from busted old cupboards, dressers and sideboards and the like. People thought he was cracked. All junk to the ones who owned it, but worth a fortune really, once they were fixed up. Mike'd pay prob'ly twenty bucks for a truckload and then sell a set of chairs for two hundred. Course, he did a fair bit of work too: scrape, stain, tinker and varnish. They says he sat in the back room of his cluttered little shop day and night, fried outta his head on the fumes, till he managed to put away enough money to buy the building next door. He got outta the furniture business then, and he just started slappin little rooms and apartments together, bangin up a wall here and there to meet the city's regulations, then rentin 'em out to any old fuck-up that came along. And the more fucked up the better, cause they were less likely to complain that there was no fire escape or that the toilet was busted and the ceiling was cavin in or whatever. Mostly crowd on welfare and loons fresh outta the Pen and outpatients from the Waterford. And like I said, the more fucked up the better 'cause he liked to straighten people out by ownin 'em. He craves trouble, Mike do. If the rent is late he adds interest by the day till it costs the poor slobs too much to move out. If he wants people gone, he just boots the front door in and tells 'em to get the fuck out. If they aint home he just fucks their shit out on the road and then maybe smashes up a wall so he can claim damages. Sounds sleazy, but I reckon it's smart business too. And of course I'm only goin by what I hears around town.

A few years back he bought the Awl and Hatchet, that's the full name of the place. It was condemned at the time, so he got it for fuck-all-next-to-nothing, fixed it up. S'pose he wanted to branch out and own people in a different way: with tabs and jobs and shit like that. But that's hardly fair, I mean maybe he was just lookin for a change. He cant be all money, all the time.

He was a big drinker himself back then too, so he knew what people wanted in a bar: cheap booze, dark corners and familiar faces. Location was fuckin crucial. The ground floor of the city, Duckworth or Water or maybe even Harbour Drive, was a given. That's where the real drinkers flocked to. George Street was no good cause people only passed through, too fuckin transient. They just hops from one bar to the next, students and arseholes and ex-cons. Too much competition. And then no one around during the week. But with a little hovel like the Hatchet, people gets to hide out in the afternoons and at least the bartender knows what you're drinkin and there's no big meathead with a headset screamin in your face that you're gonna get it punched in for no reason. Drippin testosterone George Street is. I cant stand even walkin past it on Water Street in the night. Always some arsehole lookin to impress some slut. That's the way George Street works; *she* gets all done up, all sexy and provocative, and *he* thinks he's gonna get his skin right away. He drinks to get his nerve up and suddenly finds himself too drunk to even carry on a sensible conversation. He spends all night tormenting the poor disgusted young one, who dont really want her skin anyways, who was just on the hunt for some dunce stunned enough to buy her booze all night. But then when she finally tells the prick to go fuck off, he's still gotta impress his buddies, still gotta blow his load somehow. So what's the *manly* thing to do to save face in a situation like that? He keeps his buddies good and close while he picks a racket with the fella least likely to know how to defend hisself. Some little guy, drunk and on his own.

At least you can see who you're drinkin with at the Hatchet and get to know people so that when some hot dog comes in and fucks around you knows *someone's* got your back.

Mike did it all the first year, never hired a soul, tended the bar and even mopped the floors seven days a week. Then he started up the open mic shit and there was none of that around at the time. Everything was karaoke back then. So when people found out they could just get up and sing and get a free beer besides, well fuck, they came out in droves. Free pool too, that was a stroke of genius. Pool tournament twice a week where any old fucker off the street could win a couple of hundred bucks or a bar tab. All hands started showin up on a regular basis. Good party music on the stereo. Fuck. A little goldmine. Val useta play the Hatchet too whenever he was in town. Mike's got a picture hung behind the bar of the two of them raising their glasses to the camera. Val's got a lot more hair and Mike's got a lot less belly, but it's them alright. Val'd never play this place now though.

Yeah, I useta go to George Street all the time when I first moved to Town, cause it was all I knew. But I got sick of the ignorance and the aggression and the posing. And I caused a bit of trouble. I'll say I was tossed outta pretty much every bar on George Street, and if I wasnt, it was cause I just never got to 'em all. I stumbled into the Hatchet one night when me face was bleedin and some young one cleaned me up in the women's toilet and then Mike gave me a beer and I just kept goin back. Mike treated me good from day one. I could do what I liked and there was lotsa women around who were up for it. I had the girlfriend back then though, so I had to be careful. She was livin up by the university with her Breezeway crowd and I was down on Mullock, like I said. I never had a phone in, so I never knew when she was gonna show up. That was usually whenever the fuck she pleased. One time she crawled in through me bathroom window and there I was with this young one from the Hatchet. We were just finished up and I'm sure you could smell it in the air. I hears a big racket comin from the bathroom, shit fallin on the floor and I just knew it was *her* by the smell of her bleedin heart and I figured this is it now, thank fuck, we're finished. But she was all loaded drunk. I put her in her place quick enough and she never even remembered it the next day.

So yeah, I was what you'd call a regular at the Hatchet for about a year or so before I went away. Fuck, I knows I talks like I was gone for ten years but you know, considerin I never lived nowhere else other than the Shore and then a couple of years here in Town, six months in another country was a pretty big fuckin thing for me. I got out. And really, the Hatchet was the one thing I missed while I was gone. I looked for a spot like it all over Dublin, but there was nothing quite measured up. Couldnt really hide out in the same way. They didnt put up with much shit over there. But at the Hatchet you could dance on the tables and walk in and out with your beer and fight and bang your head off the bar and never get cut off and still be allowed in the next morning. Mike didnt give a fuck. And I'm sure lotsa fuckers wanted to break my fuckin nose when I first showed up on the scene, but where I was in the good books with Mike people just held back and got to know me and then found out I was the best kind. Cause I really am the best fuckin kind, you know.

But that's the way at the Hatchet: if Mike likes you it's a fine place to drink and be drunk. If he dont like you, and he'd hardly go outta his way to try and hide the fact, then you'd likely find you werent really in the right mood to drink that night or that the beer didnt go down quite as easy as it did at the Rose, that the bartender took too long, or that the cigarettes were cheaper at the Ship. You'd find some quick excuse to mosey on, put it that way.

• • •

—You still livin with Val, Clayton? How's he getting on? He's a good old friend you know.

Yes, I fuckin know. Mike's always gotta remind me that him and Val are old friends, tells me yet again about the time he was involved in some sort of botched intervention to help get Val cleaned up, how Val huddled in the corner of the room and screamed and moaned like a savage for seven or eight hours, made a run at Mike with a hard-shelled guitar case, bawled and begged to be left alone, till finally everyone did. I never did ask Val about that, so it's hard to know if it's true or just some exaggerated account of something else that went down. People has a night on the beer or a couple of draws with Val and they're suddenly old friends. I've never heard Val mention Mike.

—Val? Good, good. He's off on tour soon.

—Oh yeah. And what about the other thing?

Mike taps the side of his nose with his chubby money-stained finger and I says to meself that the next person asks me about *Valentine's* fuckin shit I'll crack their fuckin skull open. Cause what about me? No one ever stops to wonder whether or not *Clayton* might be havin a hard time of it these days. No. I aint fuckin famous enough I s'pose.

But I got a few ideas.

Yes by the fuck, I got a few plans, just gotta tuck meself away somewhere and get to it.

Donna walks into the bar with some tall square-jawed fucker in a clean suit and she's lookin back at him and giggling. He's got his fingers like prongs on her bony hips and I just catches the tail end of what he's sayin to her that's makin her so fuckin giddy:

—But *this* is where it counts, Donna. If you're talking about stamina . . .

Then she sees me tucked in the corner and for a split, blinded second there's this shocked horror flickers across her face like she's behind the wheel of a car and just now sees she's in the wrong lane with a fuckin eighteen-wheeler comin right through the windshield. That'd be me, the transport truck. But she catches herself quick enough, seasoned player that she is, and slaps her two hands on the bar with this wide self-conscious grin and orders a round of Baileys shooters for me and her and the Jaw. She told me the other day that she likes me when I'm drinkin. See how they're all so ready and eager to rake you over the coals? Mike raises his eyebrows at me, like I said something outta line, only cause I aint atall smilin back at her. Not at all.

—Hey there *you*. You know Jeremy?

And Jeremy the Jaw's got his hand out and I'm shakin it while I'm downin the shot.

—Clay-ton! You're supposed to wait for everybody.

—So where are you from Clayton?

And this is the Jaw with his neat-trimmed office-cubical beard askin *me*, Clayton goddamn Reid, where I'm from. His mobile phone goes off before I gets the chance to talk back, slice him down to size. He holds two fingers up to me face while he answers. I looks at Donna. She cocks her head sideways and smiles all intimate, like I'm s'pose to rush into her arms where I havent seen her in a few days, but I just tells Mike thanks and then I limps out the door into the blinding sun.

After a bit she comes after me. I knew she would. I wont stop or slow down for her, even though it kills me foot to motor along like this. Her high heels clickin an awkward rhythm behind me and when I comes to this rusty fire escape near that new shoe shop, I yanks it down and climbs up it cause I knows she cant come after me with them things on her feet. She stands down on the sidewalk, huggin 'er arms around herself and lookin up and down the street and only half laughin.

—Clayton? Clayton he's from work. He's my brother's best friend.

Like I gives a fuck who or what she fucks.

One of the rungs on the fire escape is rusted right through and it gives way when I steps on it. Maybe it's one of Mike's properties. Me foot slips and I hears her yelp with the fright from down on the street. But I dont look down, I just keeps goin up, up and up till her voice is only a distant whine.

With the Baileys burnin in me chest I hauls meself onto the roof of the building. I lies down in the far corner and has a smoke lookin up at the sky. A shadow folds over me like a fuckin mortician's blanket. And I s'pose that's what it'll take, eventually, to get meself a bit of peace and quiet. Donna shouts out to me for a bit, but when I finally looks out over the edge she's gone and I feels a bit abandoned then, with the sun gone behind the clouds like that.

5. Head, Cracked

Home on me own watchin some angry Clint Eastwood flick when Val busts in with a whole crowd from that special *film* he's workin on. I goes to excuse meself cause I cant take the racket. When I'm halfway up the stairs Val shouts to me. I turns around and he's standin there at the foot of the stairs with his bottom lip nearly scrapin the floor cause it's so numb with the coke and he says:

—Are you better? There's someone here wants to talk to you.

—Who?

—Come down. And be nice.

So I hops down to the kitchen then, even though I cant stand the smell of meself. There's a bunch at the table with fancy downtown clothes on, one missus in a fuckin orange suede jacket lined with fake fur. There's the stink of weed and wine and whiskey and a couple of guys holdin fuckin hands across the old wooden table in the corner. Fuck sakes. My table, rightfully. Me mother gave it to Massie years ago, and I'll be takin it outta here whenever I gets me own place to crash.

Val puts a glass in me hand but I dont really feel like drinkin it. Didnt I soak enough up last night to get me through another lifetime? And I went a whole week before that too, with not a drop. I sets the glass down. This hefty missus with a bushy drugstore-blond, just-fucked hairdo and a shiny satin shirt that she thinks should make her look younger and more on the ball she stands up and holds out her hand to me. I takes it. It's embarrassing. Cause who the fuck am I that *she* wants to meet *me*? And I knows I should be puttin more force behind me handshake to show that I aint no fuckin underdog. But I cant.

—Hi Clayton. Ahhh, Val tells me you're looking for some work?

And I realizes then that everyone in the kitchen is gone quiet and watchin. There's the hum of the fridge and the tick of the clock and I knows I aint standin up straight and that if I tried to now I'd come across too self-conscious. Me shirt's too big and makes me look like I have more of a gut than I do, and it's maggoty from where I slopped root beer on it while I was watchin old Clint crackin heads. Nobody cracks heads like Clint fuckin Eastwood. I'm wantin to look this woman square in the face. But I cant. There's a spot of grime on the floor. I cant figure how in the hell I missed it this evening, where I scoured everything in sight for three hours straight. I nods me head and says yes to her, then goes over to the sink and rinses out the cloth. I can feel 'em all starin at the back of me head and I'd love to drink that glass of whiskey. But I cant. I wont. Cause I'll slay the fuckin works of 'em. I manages a quick and mostly laid-back glance at the woman before I drops down and scrubs at that spot of grime on the floor. Val lays his hand soft on me shoulder and when I peeks up at him he's got his head tossed back, laughin hard without makin no sound.

—Clayton. For fuck sakes . . .

And then the woman with the just-fucked hairdo pipes up, but I can only see the tapered cuffs of her baggy leather pants from underneath the table. She crosses and re-crosses her legs like a schoolgirl.

—Well . . . we need a driver for tomorrow if you're . . . available Clayton.

—Clayton cant drive.

And that's Val spillin the beans right away that I got no licence. But it's not like I dont know *how* to drive cause I been rippin around the Shore in people's rigs since I was twelve. I feels like sayin how it's just as fuckin legal for *me* to drive as it is for Val to. But he thinks

35

it's such a big secret he'd likely flip and then all this crowd'd get to see me at me absolute worst cause I'd fly right into him. Show 'im me best Eastwood impression wont I? Not much chance of a job after that though.

Missus clears her throat then in that fake way like people does when they feels put on the spot and shit.

—Ah . . . well I'm sure we can find *something* for you to do then Clayton?

And I knows I'm s'pose to jump up and smile and say yes, thank you, I'd love to and ask what time and all that, but I can still see the outline of that patch of dirt on the floor no matter how hard I scrubs at it. I can feel me eyes well up and that lump in me throat. I knows what's comin so I gotta keep scrubbin cause if I stands up now I'll blow to bits and she wont wanna hire me after all. From the floor I manages to nod and I hears Val sayin to her that he guesses that's a yes. I glances up at him and he's mouthing something across the table to her and then I feels his hand in me hair and he scoops me under the arm. I gets to me feet without lookin at anyone. They're all starin into their drinks anyhow, like that's where the secret of a peaceful existence is.

Tunnel vision to the bottom of the stairs. It takes forever to get there cause me feet are too heavy where the bad one is actin up more than normal. Before I makes it to the bottom step the tears are drippin off me chin and me nose is all stuffed up. Cause I really didnt wanna see people for a while. Didnt really wanna talk to no one either. Me old buddy Brent called me up from somewhere out west, said he was makin his way back home, said something 'bout gettin stabbed in the back. He sounded pretty messed up and wantin to talk. I can barely remember our conversation, just wanted to get off the phone and slip back into me bubble.

Val's got his hand on me back, tellin me to just go on to bed out of it. The racket is startin up again in the kitchen and I hears someone say *What was that all about?* But it's like a faraway echo from someone else's life and I feels like callin up the Shore and checkin in on Randy. Randy, that fuckin wasted cunty-balled . . . . no, no, no. Because blood is blood. Blood is fuckin blood. I dont know his new number anyhow. And it's late. It's always this late.

Me head is on the pillow, the rain slashin at the window and I'm fallin, sinkin deep down into this squeaky old mattress and it feels safe with the door locked and this musty old quilt me grandmother stitched together before I was ever even dreamt of.

• • •

Donna is there at the table with Val the next day. She got no makeup on and with her hair tied back she looks like a skeleton on a crash diet. You could hang your jacket on her fuckin collarbone. She smiles right gentle and mellow at me, talks right soft and motherly, like I was dyin or some shit. Val dont even say hi to me. I hears someone skippin down over the stairs. There's suddenly another human in the kitchen, a woman, over turnin the kettle on like she owns the place. She looks familiar. I knows her from . . . from . . . Big burst of red hair and mascara smudged on her eyes. She's good lookin in a rugged dont-fuck-with-me-just-fuck-me sorta way. She wraps her arms around Val's neck and kisses his cheek, but he keeps starin at me like I'm some sorta shithead.

—Hi Clayton.

Val's redhead waves at me like I'm on a boat headin off to the war. When I meets her eyes I realizes she's one of me flings from the Ship that I took to the General's in a taxi back in August or July. Melanie? Didnt she work at the Hatchet last year? Fuck. And here she is clingin off Valentine Reid, who's old enough to be her father's uncle. And he just might be, considering the state of the Newfoundland gene pool.

—Dont say youse dont remember me Clayton?

With Donna there just starin bug-eyed and jaded into her coffee, chompin on her bottom lip. I cant believe this redheaded impostor is so brazen to go gettin on with this kinda shit here and now. Cause she dont know how delicate me and Val are these days. I glances at the man of the hour, but he's lost in some other world now, twistin up a fat starter joint. I just shakes me head at her, all nonchalant, and determines to get cracked and expose her for the lyin fuckin impostor that she is. If she takes it one step further. I gives Donna's ponytail a playful toss and swipes one of her smokes, then stands behind her with me two hands on her shoulders. Lookin straight at Val's redhead.

—Clayton do you know Monica? Monica, my nephew Clayton.

Monica, right. From down around B—— somewhere. Tryna be a photographer or some such shit. Mike Quinn's new/old bartender, I'll wager. She had blond hair when I saw her last, and some kinda punkish goth thing goin on. I was right taken in with her accent, droppin her *h*'s and addin 'em on all over the place. Val looks back and forth between the two of us, the blood vessels busted and raised on the bridge of his nose. Monica reaches across the table with this brassy, sarcastic smirk and I squeezes her hand good and hard, just to send her the message that she better keep her mouth shut. She winces ever so slightly and juts her jaw forward with the pain. That's my message missus, loud and clear. She raises her eyebrows and nods at me as if to say *Fuck off asshole, your secret is safe,* or at least that's what I'm takin it to mean. She spins around then and goes over to the corner and slides her fingers along the edge of *my* table. I notices there's a black mark burnt into the face of it near the centre, like a scar from a blasting knife. Fuck sakes. Monica rubs her finger across the new scar.

—Wow, this's gorgeous. Where did it come from?

Val perks right up then, actually turns around to see what she's talkin about. Donna tries to cup me face in her hand but I pulls away and wanders over to the sink where I can get a better gawk at Monica. I'm about to tell her the table is mine when Val intercedes:

—Clayton's mom gave it to us when we first got shacked up. Must be twenty-five years? One of the hind legs is loose. There's a false bottom in the drawer.

That's Val's term for marriage, shackin up. He gives his little history lesson then, how the chrome table was likely "the defining symbol of progression" in the average Newfoundland home back in the sixties. How the finest handmade wooden tables "such as the one you see before you" were foolishly tossed off cliffs, burnt for firewood, or relocated to stages and wharves to "bear the scars of every abuse the fishery had to divvy out: salt, iron filings and engine juice, maggots and gurry and gull shit, capelin spawn and the jagged backbones of hundreds upon thousands of bloated cod . . ."

I cuts him off for fear I'll heave up me guts:

—Alright Val. And you saved its fuckin life. It's mine anyhow.

—Is it now? Wants it all dont you Clayton?

—Only what's rightfully mine . . .

He stares at me with that smirk that makes you wanna bash his head in with a blunt object. I tries to mirror it but I knows it'll be years yet before I got it down like him. I walks over to the table and pulls out the drawer to see about this false bottom. I reaches me hand around inside but I cant make head nor tail of it. And I'm hardly gonna ask Val to show me either.

The phone rings then, and I hops into the living room to catch it.

On the phone it's that just-fucked missus from the movie. She calls herself Patty. I says hi and sorry about last night, that I wasnt feelin too good. She says dont bother about it and I says thanks.

—Alright Clayton, we need someone on security tonight if you're interested. Just someone to stay in the building to watch over the set. We have a lot of equipment. We'll send someone to pick you up at eight this evening. It pays a hundred dollars a night. If it works out you might get another couple of weeks out of it. Are you up for that?

—What? Holy Christ. Yeah, that's, that's perfect.

—Bring a good book with you . . .

—Alright then. Thank you. Listen I—

She hangs up on me then, but I dont care cause I'm ten feet fuckin tall. A hundred bucks a night? For two weeks? Holy fuck. That's like a couple of grand! That's me straightened right out for a while. Put it away sure, and get the fuck outta town. Montreal. Back to Dublin. Am I up for it? Fuckin right I am. When I turns around, Val and Donna are standin in the doorway lookin at me. I realizes I must look a bit too fuckin jovial cause they're both smilin at me. It feels right creepy. I pushes past 'em both and heads up to the shower cause I havent had no energy for one in days and days. Val wants to know what *Patricia* said on the phone, but I just says I'll let him know later on. I dont wanna let Donna in on it. She knows enough about my goddamn life now dont she?

On me way upstairs I has a glance into the kitchen at that Monica. She's bent over the centre table scoopin toast crumbs into the palm of her hand and the sharp fall sun is shinin right through her skimpy top. I can see the outline of her big rosy nipples. I stops for a second and she looks up and catches me and smiles at me. I has a flash of the fun we had that night at the General's, her on top and her head thrown back. We had the Pogues on too, for rhythm. Her hair was shorter then. The red suits her now though. I musta been a fuckin fool not to keep shit on the go with her.

In the shower it's scaldin hot and I soaps meself up good, but I dont bother to wack off. When I gets out Donna is sittin on the foot of me bed and she takes the towel off me and sees that I'm already hard. She sucks it into her mouth and before I knows it she's stripped off and face down on the bed with her legs spread wide. She's got a bit of a rash and stubble where she shaves it, but I likes it cause of the way it scrapes at the head of me lad. New job comin up, two grand. How the fuckin tables have turned. Donna's face pressed into me grimy, ashy, drool-stained pillow. I should maybe wash that later on. We're goin right to it but all's on me mind is that big head of red hair downstairs, hard pink nipples and toast crumbs. Maybe I'll drop down to the Hatchet later on for a few easy beer, see if she's started workin yet. I'm poundin harder and harder and I dont care if Donna gets off or not, but I hope Monica can hear us downstairs cause it's gettin pretty loud up here with the bed hammering off the wall and I'm thinkin, yeah Val you old bastard, well done yourself.

6. Hands, Held

How they all come flocking to me. Young Monica, on the run from B——. Daddy's girl. Clayton, so headstrong and pigheaded that he cant even recognize when someone's holding his hand, pulling him along and trying to set him straight.

He's a Reid isnt he?

There's a reason I never had children of my own. Where was I when I was his age? Well clear of this town, holed up on Spadina with that busted Epiphone, borrowing everything from picks to drummers, waiting. Least I knew where I was headed, knew that I'd die trying. And where's he? Scrounging, raiding my CD collection for the price of a few beer. Cant see as far as next week. Randy made a fine mess of that one, didnt he.

Had his own burdens to contend with.

Burdens? Goddamn heavy-equipment operator. The machine does all the work.

Rachel.

Rachel. Yeah. But he made his own choices. Like I made mine. And what have I to show now? Randy shacked up with the finest piece of gear on the Shore, then drank her outta the house.

Nobody's fault Val. Accident. Happens every day.

Still.

Still, what about Massie, no real difference.

She's alive.

Well then let her live. Just sign the dotted line.

Signed away enough already. Years, gutting myself for the right line, a lifetime scraping my soul.

Watch it now, the theatrics . . .

And for what? So some snot-nosed young pup with a pretty smile and flashy pants so tight he looks like he's sporting a muss, some little queer catering to the tourist industry, making a mockery of everything Newfoundland never was, can come along and shove his pointless, self-absorbed mediocrity down our throats? Shove it up your hole young man. Muddying up the radio. Cant sing, cant play, but so long as the camera likes you . . .

Alright Val, alright. Is that really your competition?

Fuck no.

This pipe, here in your hand. That's your only competition.

My only comrade these days.

No.

No. I'll get right on that. Just get myself through this fucking movie now.

And then what?

Cut another record, blow 'em all outta the water, all them muss-boys. Get that song. Tour through the winter, get in the clear.

And Clayton?

Cut him loose. He'll have to go it alone. The only way to get there.

Massie?

Young Monica, for now. Daddy's girl.

Val?

Massie, yes. For fuck sakes.

7. Top-notch Security

Ten to eight and rainin a little harder now. A fancy white van with tinted windows pulls up outside Val's and when I jumps in the driver just nods at me with his fruity sunglasses way down low on the bridge of his nose. I says hi and he barely grunts at me, like I'm scum, but I dont give a fuck cause I'm focused and set to go and he's just a fuckin driver anyhow. I knows the way this *film* shit works.

The wind picks up and the rain busts outta the sky. The van's wipers are doin all they can do as we takes a right on King's Bridge Road towards Quidi Vidi Lake. I minds now, in me half-sleep this afternoon, hearin the CBC weather and something about Hurricane Susan slaughtering the Cape Breton crowd. I s'pose this is the tail end of it.

In Pleasantville, not too far from me old stompin grounds (the detox centre where I spent many a cheery evening learnin about how fuckin weak us humans are), we pulls up outside this shabby, bland old building. There's a faded sign in front hangin from its hinges. I cant make it out cause of the rain. I makes a dash for the front door. Someone opens it from inside to meet me. He says his name is Darren, that all I gotta do is hang out for the night and make sure no one fucks around with the building, inside or out. I tries to get some specifics out of him, like what I should expect, but he seems kinda wiped out and eager to get goin. He asks me if I'm Valentine's nephew and when I nods he says that there's a bucket and mop in the kitchen area in case I gets the urge to wash up. Clever fuckwad. Nosy fuckin town. He hands me a long and heavy black Maglite, like what the cops uses for bustin faces. I feels like bustin Darren's face with it. He goes all serious and businesslike then, when he realizes I aint to be fucked around with, tells me to just make regular checks around the outside of the building and that there'll be crew in around seven in the morning, nothing to it. He shows me a phone in case I needs to make a call, points to a fuckin baseball bat leant against the wall and tells me good luck. And then he's gone, with the door closin in me face and the rain beatin off it and the wind rattlin the battered aluminum siding outside.

I turns around to have a look at me station for the night, and fucked if I dont catch sight of a dirty big hairy rat scootin down the hallway with a piece of bread in its mouth. Long night ahead I s'pose.

. . .

Midnight now, or thereabouts. I cant stand lookin down the corridor at the clock. I've been pacin the main area where I'm stationed for a good half hour now. Something, and I'm hopin it was a furnace, made a brief roar a while back and the lights dimmed and blinked and a couple never came back on. I havent been able to sit down for any length of time since. Been sizin the place up. Listening. It's kinda like a high school. I mean, I knows there's people rents the place out, like bands, and there's the movie set here somewhere. But still, I cant quite figure what the fuckin place *used* to be, only that it reminds me of sneakin around in my old high school in the night time. There's this echo comes with every little move and it's like you can feel that there's s'pose to be people around. It's fuckin spooky.

All night long, as soon as I tries to settle into me writin, there's this scuffle and thump down the hall. I knows it's not the storm cause it's definitely from inside. There's no way in fuck I'm goin down there. I points me light down the hall but that's too fucked-up lookin. Something's not right with this place. I knows it. I can feel it. Maybe. Or maybe it's just leftover anxiety, maybe it's all in me head. I turns on all the lights in the main room where I'm stationed. I needs to piss bad but I dont know where the toilets are.

Fuck sakes, this is ridiculous. I'm a grown fuckin man. There's a smaller corridor to me left. A handwritten sign that says QUIET, REHEARSAL IN PROGRESS. A light down at the end of the corridor. I keeps me eye on the light and pushes the door open. I keeps the bat held out in front of me and the flashlight beamin straight ahead. I walks down to another set of doors and it's like there's someone watchin me from behind but when I turns around there's nothing. Maybe a scurry, the pinkish flash of a tail. I just catches hold of me bladder in time. I shines the flashlight into the darkest corner and catches a set of beady little green eyes. I turns me back on it then, valiant solider that I am.

At the end of the corridor I finds a sink with bottles of water and cereal bars and dried fuckin apricot shit next to it. No toilets in sight. I gotta fuckin go bad. I lays me cock over the edge of the sink. When I pisses, it's bright neon yellow from where I had a couple of vitamins at Val's earlier. It all runs outta the drainpipe onto the floor but I says fuck it, cause I cant stop. I'll look for a mop later on, succumb to Darren's witty prophecy. Prick.

I opens the door to where the movie set is and ho-ly fuck it's like walkin into some mansion on Circular Road. So warm, and there's deep red carpet and thick wooden polished chairs and one of them couches from the thirties and portrait paintings on the makeshift walls and a monstrous grandfather clock that goes off for a second when I smacks it. And then I sees there's a bunch of cigarettes in a silver case and an old-style lighter on a table near the couch. I lies down and lights a smoke, but it's one of them fuckin herbal ones. Story of my life. I thinks back on that night with Donna, when I got all the free smokes outta the machine at the Duke. Seems like ages now, and how in the fuck did she manage to drag me in like that? That's it though, when you're deliberately avoiding the hook, that's when they're at their keenest to reel you in, when the bait is at its most enticing, poppers and shit like that. I'll hafta finish off with her now, get on with it all before I knocks 'er up or something. She's just not the One.

Nice smell off these smokes, but all they does is make me crave a real one. I pockets the lighter. Keepsake.

. . .

Cant hear the storm so much in here. There's a buzzin from the lights and it's warm. Right on. Must be near on two o'clock now. I s'pose that only leaves me with five or six hours before me shift is done. A hundred bucks a night? Fuck. Nothing to it.

Quiet and quick as I can, I creeps back to the main room to get me notebook. There's a light flickering and I stands there at the other end lookin at me desk and lookin at me notebook and me lunch. I cant move. All I can do is stare. The light goes out altogether and leaves a black hole over where I was sittin all night and I'm some glad I wasnt sittin there when it happened cause I woulda shit. The storm seems to be tapering off a bit. I makes a run for the desk and scoops up me lunch and the notebook and then tries not to run back to the set but me heart is beatin like mad and the panic takes over and I starts singin, as loud as I can, some old Black Sabbath tune I havent heard in years and cant remember the name of.

Left me fuckin smokes back out on the desk. Looks like I'm on the herbals for a while.

. . .

There's a plug-in heater near the back of the set. I drags it over to the couch and sets it up at me feet. I pulls a scratchy blanket over meself and tries to have a go at me movie idea but I cant get nowhere with it cause I'm too distracted with what Val might think of it, like he's standin over me shoulder almost. I can just see him shakin his head and laughin at anything I have to say on paper.

All hands came to our house one year when me great-grand-mother died and Val came up in me bedroom to roll a joint away from his brothers, who're cops, and Randy, who was tryin out the sobriety thing for a while. I showed Val a few poems and lyrics I was writin at the time, but I could tell when he was lookin at the page that he wasnt really readin the words, but more or less just findin it funny that I was actually writin. Later on I heard him downstairs sayin to 'em all that it's amazing how Clayton is startin to "scribble down teen-angst songs" already. Then the old man asks him what he's talkin about and Val says *Jesus Randy b'y, dont you even know what your own youngster is up to?* And everything went right quiet then downstairs, cause none of 'em knows how to talk about anything real or how to confront one another. True though, what Val said to the old man. I moved like a ghost through that house for years after Mom died, especially when he had that fuckin Anne-Marie around. Only time Randy ever opened his mouth to me was to bawl me out about something or when he was cockeyed and wanted a real racket. He never had a clue or couldnt give a shit what I was up to, who I was with or where I went. Maybe it wasnt always like that though, maybe it just went that way when Mom checked out. He just hit the booze. I mean, I seen him drunk and stuff before then, like Christmas and shit, Mom givin out to him about it, where all his uncles died drunk or their livers shrunk up or whatever. But he just let go altogether after her accident.

• • •

Yes by Christ I reckon the storm is after passin over alright. With the heater on bust and glowin angry orange at me feet I tucks meself under the blanket and closes me eyes. Easy money. The big break I been waitin on. Lay low for the next couple of weeks, get up outta the downtown, off the beer again. Hit the road then, before the weather gets too cold. I tries to take this kinda comfort in me new-found financial security, but every time I starts to drift off it's like the couch starts shakin and I comes to with the dirtiest black dreams still crisp in me mind. I listens then, and looks around. Could be me heartbeat, where I'm dreamin so heavy and shit. Or maybe just the wind at the building outside. But that's not likely. No, but I cant let me mind get carried away, cause I havent slept proper in days. I never sleeps when me head gets in a bad way, and me head was unravelling steady this past while. I *wants* to be sleepin all the time mind you, but usually I just lies in bed starin at the walls and thinkin bad shit and I cant talk to people and I'm always hungry but the thought of food drains the life right outta me. So if I can gather up another hour's sleep here on the set, I'll be alright for a while, get back on track. Val says I needs to see a doctor or someone to talk to, but I done all that when I was a youngster. It was all bullshit. No one *really* gives a fuck, they wants to get you in and out as quick as they can with a prescription in your hands and off to La-La Land. No thanks. Makes a fuckin zombie outta me and then when I drinks I ends up bawlin in a corner with the party goin mad all around me. So I just waits it out these days and tries to stay clear of people as best I can.

I'm just driftin off again when I hears the worst sound I've ever heard in me life. The same thing as earlier, only it dont let up this time, and it's a whole lot louder. A grindin chorus of maybe two dozen burnt-out incinerators roarin to life for the first time in twenty years. It's comin from the basement. I think. Cant tell. I sits up straight and pounds me two feet onto the floor as loud as I can. I howls at the door facin the main room where me desk is. The noise stops. I listens. I glances at the high window. It's turnin daylight, but it dont do nothing for the room. The old grandfather clock in the corner says quarter to seven but I dont know if it's the right time where it's only a prop. I sits there tryin to hear. Cause maybe I never heard nothing atall. Wait. Crackle from the heater. Heartbeat. Foot. Cant get up. Wait and listen. Listen.

After a while, when I dont hear nothing else, I gets up and shuf-fles towards the door, the Maglite tucked into the waist of me pants. Me foot is asleep. Every wary step I takes is just a hint of the pain that's comin. But it's me own fault cause I'm s'pose to sleep with it up. I goes out to the main room. The glow of the morning is there but it makes the place even creepier where there's no windows. The place is dead. But I can feel something. Not rats. I scoops up the flashlight then and lights up a smoke at the desk. Deep, deep draws, not lookin at nothing and tryin to look casual. Me novel is there. I flips through it but it's so long since I read it last I knows I'd only hafta start right from the top. I cant read much when me head gets bad either and that's the worst cause I loves a good book. But when me head is bad it's like I gotta read the sentences over and over and sometimes whole pages that dont make no sense or wont sink in atall. So I waits it out like I said and . . .

Ho-ly shit.

The fuckin elevator. On the way up. Meaning that it musta been on the way *down* the first time I heard it. Someone in the building. The groan and strain of the old pulley system is suddenly deafening, all-consuming. But even though I'm freaked, and there's a little dribble of piss after leakin out in me drawers, it's like I'm bein pulled towards the sound, like it's reelin me in. I'm draggin me bad foot behind where I'm goin so fast and I'm reachin for another smoke but I knows I should be headin back towards the front doors so I can have a proper standoff with whoever or whatever it is that's gonna come through them elevator doors. But I cant stop. I looks through the glass doors, down that murky corridor. Sure enough, the light above the old elevator is on. I can feel the floor vibrating under me feet. Further on down the corridor I can see two rats runnin for their useless lives, one with an orange peel clamped in its jaws. I s'pose it must feel like a goddamn earthquake to them matted little fuckers.

The sound stops. A bell rings. The light above the elevator goes out. I'm standin just outside the doors to the hallway, looking in on it. The elevator door slides open. From this angle I cant see into it. I got the fuckin big flashlight though, and I'll use it by Christ, in ways it's not meant to be used. Cause I'm fuckin Security now aint I? Yes by fuck, I'm gettin paid a hundred bucks for this and I'm gonna earn me fuckin wages and who gives a fuck if *I* lives or dies cause we're all goin sometime. There's pandemics and tidal waves and fire and brimstone blazin a trail towards all of us, it's just a matter of time and nothing's gonna fuckin happen *here* now and I aint no fuckin gimp it's just a bit of pain and I can still kick with it for fuck sakes cause I come through real shit to get to this point didnt I?

I clears me throat as loud and casual as I can, but with the echo down the corridor it comes out soundin like some beast chokin on a human shin bone.

I waits and listens, tries to quiet me heart. Nothing. No one comes out. But the door stays open and I can feel the damp cold on the tip of me cock where I leaked a bit. Them rats are gone, only friends I had, only witnesses to the pending doom that's mine and mine alone. I stands and stares at the door for what must be a good five minutes, tryna control me breathin and tryna take a step backwards, away from the situation, but me hand is locked tight on the bar of the door and I can feel me arm flex and I certainly dont *want* to open the goddamn door but I am anyway, with me shitty foot draggin behind.

I'm quiet as I can and the rats are gone and it's not like I can hear *breathing* from inside the elevator, just a little drip. I takes a hard breath and lunges in front of the door with the flashlight, ready to swing. But there's no one there.

Just a tiny little . . . ahhh . . . wheelchair.

Hardly big enough for a youngster, rusty and with the cushions from the seat all tore open. Drip drip drip. There's a steady pool of brown water collecting near the left wheel. And there's no one there. Like it came up on its own.

I says fuck it and springs into the mouth of the elevator, grippin the flashlight halfway up the shaft for the uppercut position. Breathe. I peeks into the corners like some cheesy prime-time copper. No one there. I kicks the footrest on the little wheelchair and a shower of rust and dust rains to the floor. A squawk catches in me throat when one of them fuckin rats runs out from underneath the wheelchair. I takes a quick jab at it with the flashlight and misses. It makes the foolish mistake of not goin for the open door, but retreats into the far corner of the elevator. I pulls back and spears the little sleaze with the butt-end of the flashlight, pinning it into the corner. It hisses and screams at me with the greedy disease in its eyes and I'm so fuckin sick of this night that I'm only in the back of me mind aware that the elevator door is slidin closed behind me while I'm squattin that little sleaze into the corner with the heel of me fresh-polished boot. He claws at me laces but that's not no use to him and I keeps the pressure on till I hears a little pop and his guts squirts out through his hole. Sick little fuckers they are. Fuckin useless, no place in the natural order of things. They're just festering little pockets of death and shit. One more twitch of the tail then, and I spits a glob of snot onto it. I turns and pushes the button to open the door. Nothing happens. I pushes it again and holds it in a bit longer. Nothing happens. This whole place is fucked. I tries to keep meself together as best I can, but I bites the inside of me lip too hard and I can feel that damp patch in me drawers and there's black, black violence when I closes me eyes and I cant catch me breath cause I shouldnta come in here and who really gives a fuck if old Clayton Reid lives or dies anyhow? I screams at the door to open:

—Open! Open you useless, cunnyhoppin, cockfuckin little whore!

Nothing happens. I hauls back with the Maglite and slams that ugly, clunky prehistoric button. The plastic casing around the button shatters and the lens to the flashlight ricochets off the wall and hits me square in the forehead. I slams the button again and screams at the door till there's a jolt under me feet and the grind of the mechanics and I says to meself *thank fuck,* cause I aint lettin meself believe that I'm goin down, down into whatever is on the ground floor of this hellhole. The loudest elevator in the history of the world. There's always suicide Mr. Reid. Always.

When we reaches the bottom, and by *we* I means me and the wheelchair and that dead little slut in the corner who're me only friends in the world right now, I'm lookin straight ahead at the door, but there's another one that opens behind me. I whips around and it kinda grudgingly rocks open and then stays open. There's a corridor. Everything dead quiet, except for maybe I hears footsteps for a second. And maybe some sorta whisper. But I aint sure cause this is all too fucked up. I cant trust me mind all that much these days anyhow, like I said. There's the drone and dull glow of a fluorescent light and there's a ripe smell of old and rank musty garbage like the bottom crisper in Val's fridge the other night that wouldnt go away no matter how much I scrubbed with the Javex.

I tries the button to go back up, but the door stays open. I turns a left into the corridor and I'm too riled up to stop and praise meself for not limpin for the first time in over two years. That kinda pain is no good to me now anyhow. I takes a left towards the only light that's workin. The floor, I cant tell if it's concrete or wood or tiling or what. I cant tell. It's all mush, squishy, slippery and rank, like trampsin on the flesh of dead animals. I shines the light on it but cant pick out what it is, some invisible texture.

There's a steady drip as I nears the blue glow of the light and the corridor stops when a room opens up in front of me. I flicks the Maglite around but it dont seem to have much guts left with the lens gone. But I reckons the room is pretty big cause of the way the sound of me footfall changes and the echo of the drip gets louder and you can just tell that shit cant you? The static blue light is flickering a bit and there's freaky shadows and the smell of mould is stronger here now. There's rats down here too of course but I'll kill every fuckin one I lays eyes on. And I still walks on, even though me mind is screamin at me to turn back. But there must be a stairs around somewhere to take me back up where the daylight is, where me notebook and me smokes and the phone and me novel is. The phone. I never thought on the phone when I first heard the racket. How fuckin stunned am I atall not to have called someone? Cause I aint no fuckin security guard . . .

Me foot bumps against something on the floor. I aims the light at it and it's like, it's . . . it's a fuckin plastic doll's arm. Except it'd belong to a bigger doll than I've ever seen. And it dont look like it's made for play. It's got no fingers, but more or less a plastic scoop for a hand. But it's certainly an arm cause I can tell by the elbow. I steps forward then and makes a little splash. I'm in some kinda pool, a drained out swimmin pool, cause the way the tiles on the floor are . . . And ho-ly sweet fuck. I shines the flashlight around the pool and there looks to be the same kinds of arms and tiny legs and little wheelchairs and small wooden chairs like fuckin electric chairs with coarse brown leather straps on the arms for like holdin children in place or some shit and I'm feelin behind meself while I'm backin away cause I'm too fuckin shitbaked to turn me head. When I aims the flashlight up in the corner there's a sign with some kinda toxic fungus and slime growin on it with the word AQUATHERAPY. Beyond that there's more arms and legs hangin from hooks on the walls. I'm slowly edgin me way back to the elevator without takin me eyes off the sign or the busted wheelchairs or the fuckin little abandoned limbs. I'm reachin out in the dark behind me, feelin me way, cause I knows if I turns around I'll just start runnin blind into the corridor and then I'd be fucked altogether. There's footsteps comin behind me and the rustle of nylon and someone, something, some*one* is laughin and me knuckle scrapes off what feels like a zipper and then two hands are squeezin me shoulders and some*one* goes:

—BLAAAAHRRRR!

And I got the heavy steel police-issue Maglite up and I'm screamin something fierce and now the piss is runnin free down me left leg cause that's the way me cock hangs and I can feel the thud of the flashlight on a skull and some*one* goes down and I trains the light and there's blood on some*one's* face and I boots some*one* in the nuts good and hard with me fresh-polished boots and some*one* says:

—Clayton, Clayton I'm only . . .

But I'm off, tearin savage down the corridor. All me fine plans fadin fast, all swallowed up in the shock and terror of that prick Darren's moans. So much for me big break, cause there's no price on the planet could lure me back here tomorrow night.

Me foot is fine. No pain now. But there will be. I'll hafta hunt down some tranquilizers later on. And there's the stairs, there's the fuckin stairs.

I knew I shoulda turned right in the first place.

8. Into the Cold Black Nothing

Down at the Hatchet for me birthday and Donna's all dressed in black with black lipstick in that goth way that she's just too fuckin old for and dont really suit her blond hair atall. I slips over to the bar to collect me head. Same old faces, a few new ones. Some fat bastard with a goatee and one of them French director kinda hats on. He's drawin something on a sheet of paper for this ditzy young teeny-bopper type. I hates them fuckin hats. What's-his-face, that Lawlor fella, he's been slinkin back and forth all night between here and the old queer bar upstairs. I hear he's lookin to buy the place, even asked Mike Quinn if he was interested in sellin the Hatchet. Fuck, that'd be some load of shit, fuckin old queen like that runnin the Hatchet. Another fella on the other end of the bar, I knows his face. Some bigshot actor fucker, some VIP, home from Canada, sulkin into his drink cause there's no lineup for autographs and no one's offerin to suck his cock. That Clyde Whelan cunt is always goin on about how "close" they are. But where's our Clyde to tonight? That Charlene missus, she's after goin downhill since last I saw her too. Her eyes all sunk in and drug-black. She waves across the bar at me and kinda pumps her eyebrows a bit. Fuck, I knows you'd hafta be some hard up for it. I wouldnt fuck her with Petey Thorne's cock.

Me old buddy Brent is s'pose to be hittin town someday soon, on his way back from some jaunt out west. I hope he shows soon. Watch now, when the two of us gets on the go. Drink this town dry.

Monica behind the bar. Tell me I wouldnt bury me face in that again, by Christ. I tells her it's me birthday and she slips me a flaming sambuca. When I brings it to me lips I slops a bit on the back of me hand and grinds me teeth while the thin blue flame eats at me skin. Monica just goes right on talkin, like nothing outta the *h'ordinary* is takin place. She wants to know about Val, or more accurately she wants to know about Massie. Right through the pain, me teeth clenched in a death grip, I tells her Val is a cunt, that I came home the other night and me table was gone. My mother's table. I put the place up. Val just sat there all innocent, said the house was gettin a bit crowded. Said how the leg was busted anyhow, and what do you do with a horse when it breaks a leg? So what could I do? Walk out? And go live where? Donna's? What a prick. Monica goes right red for a second, like maybe I hurt her pride or something and so I tells her no, that Val's *not* such a bastard, just that we've had a bit too much of each other these days. I'll be fucked if I fills 'er in on Massie though. She've no idea what she's in for.

Me hand curls up tight with the pain, but I wont even flinch. Donna jumps in between us then and blows on me hand but it wont go out so she dumps her fuckin White Russian on it, the crazy fucker. She turns on Monica then.

—What's the matter with you?

—What?

Cause the music is so loud with that fat fuckin Petey Thorne mangling yet another CCR tune.

—What the hell is wrong with you?

—'Ow do you mean?

—Well you saw what he was doing . . .

And this pisses me off altogether cause she's goin around these days like she fuckin owns me or got this obligation to look out for me. Like I'm five years old or fuckin retarded and dont know no better. Like I aint allowed to top meself any old time I wants to without *her* fuckin say so. Look at her. Face powdered white. If the man upstairs was gonna send me a guardian angel I doubt very much she'd look like that.

Keith walks into the bar then and Monica drops me like a bag of smouldering shit to serve him. She's suddenly all girlish and flighty. Something goin on there, for sure. Maybe Val's finally met his match. The whole scene throws me into a rage. I leans over and plucks the smoke outta Donna's hand.

—How old are ya Donna?

—What's that sweetie?

—I said how fuckin old are ya, and dont be callin me sweetie.

—You know how old I am Clayton.

—Yeah. So whataya goin around with that shit globbed on yer face like a fuckin youngster for then? What?

Fuckin mean, that's me when I'm feelin cornered. Donna slinks off, tryna look all wounded, but it dont last long cause I watches that Clyde Whelan cunt, who works the bar sometimes and smells like cat's piss, scoopin her into his arms for a slow dance to the tail end of the song. The damp under his arms is enough to gag you from over here. Clyde apparently useta be a bit of a hotshot in the local theatre scene. All hands were expecting him to hit the big time. This is like ten years ago. He even had a part in some TV sitcom shot here in St. John's for a couple of years. Some shit about this family who owned a fleet of school buses. I never did see it but I heard it was alright. But then the network pulled the plug and Clyde's head was a bit too swollen to go back to the stage so he just hung about in the bars and waited for the phone to ring, waited for his call-up to the big league. Ten years and fifty pounds of pure gut later and he's downtown with a fuckin bar growin out of 'is chest. Sad I s'pose, if I could bring meself to give a fuck.

Petey Thorne breaks into some faggy old Elvis tune then and Clyde tries to keep Donna on the floor but I s'pose she's ready to heave. Some tidy bit of gear grabs her by the hand and dangles a little baggie under her nose. Donna's face lights up and they're off to the toilets for a session I s'pose. Poor redundant Clyde slumps back down in his stool. And yes I reckon it's safe to say it *is* his stool where he's after groovin the shape of his own arse into it.

Be nice to get that young one on the go with Donna some night, whoever the fuck she is. Wouldnt take too much coaxin for Donna either, I dont say. She's up for just about anything. Sure, we took a run up to that kink shop on Torbay Road the other day and Donna was like a youngster pickin shit up and gigglin and lookin over her shoulder at the missus behind the counter. Sickening.

—See anything you like Clayton?

So I says to meself yes by the fuck, if she's gonna go for it, and I picks the biggest monstrosity in the whole shop, this colossal rubber shlong called Black Beauty. She laughed when I picked it out, not thinkin I was serious, but I said *Fuck that, you asked girl and this is the one I wants.* I s'pose it was just something bad in me that wanted to put her in her place right? Where she's all the time tellin me to give it to her deeper and harder and that she wants it *all* when I'm fuckin well balls-deep with the sweat drippin off me chin and it's almost like she's mockin me. So I wanted to put her in her place. She bought the Black Beauty and a freaky video I picked out with she-males and midgets with cocks bigger than horses and we headed for her place.

I got her down on the bed and I'm ploughin away, but we both knows what's on the other's mind cause it's all just prep work for the Black Beauty right? She slaps on the video then and I fast-forwards till there's a bit of action on the go, this little guy with a Hitler moustache got some he-whore impaled on his massive dick and I turns the sound way up and rolls Donna over on her belly the way we likes it, greases up the new toy and . . . fucked if she dont take the whole goddamn thing. Now, I'll be straight up to say that maybe I wouldnt mind havin a bit more length on the go, but I dont normally give a fuck about how big me own cock is and sure I'll whip it out anywhere atall. But when I seen Donna there takin the full length of that Black Beauty from behind like that and not so much as a whimper or a flinch out of 'er, fuck, I dont know, it was a bit disheartening. So I pulled it out after a few plunges and she looked back at me, wantin to know what was wrong, what's wrong what's wrong what's wrong? She wanted me to keep goin with it but I just didnt wanna use it no more and so we watched the rest of the video and did poppers but I couldnt really get back into it, didnt bother tryna finish meself off even.

But I got rid of it, the Black Beauty, that night down on the waterfront, I slung it into the harbour. Just too much competition for my likin.

· · ·

Donna comes back over to me at the bar. She's swallowin hard and pullin on her nose so I knows she got a bit of blow on the go in the bathroom. She's all smiles again now and I feels that mean streak settlin over me cause this is where *I* fuckin drinks and I could be gettin all kinds of skin if not for her hangin off me and givin the evil eye to any young one who so much as asks me for a light. She hands me a wad of damp paper towel then, says it's for me hand where it's burnt, but I bats it onto the floor cause fuck that shit. I'm right ready to lace into 'er again then, but before I gets the chance that fuckin Petey Thorne's gotta get everyone's attention to announce a special birthday greeting from Donna to Clayton. Liftin dyin bleedin fuckin Jesus. He breaks into "Wild Horses" and everyone claps and cheers and all eyes are on us, expectin me to get out on the dance floor with her like I'm some kinda faggot. They're bangin their glasses and bottles and ashtrays and I feels this grin stretch across me face cause I fuckin well told her not to dare mention me birthday to no one and she gotta go do something like *this*, the coked-up headcase that she is. She backs out onto the floor with her hand outstretched and the big stoned mushy smile on her face. I walks towards her and I'm smilin back and the place is cheerin like we're newlyweds and Petey Thorne says:

—Oh. Here he comes folks, here he comes.

And I'm hobblin towards her and smilin and she's standin there in the middle of the floor with her arms open and her head cocked like that.

And I walks straight out the fuckin door onto the street.

The hoots and cheers from inside are cut short straight away. Fuck that.

I told her not to mention nothing to no one.

I darts across the street as quick as I can with me foot like it is and ducks into the Hayloft. Once I'm inside I glances out the window. There's Donna with her drink in hand, lookin up and down the street, tryna figure which way I went. Fuck that. After a bit she abandons her search and goes back inside, like I aint even worth the fuckin bother on me birthday or something. There's loyalty for ya.

I passes up to the bar and there's Mike Quinn pumpin his world into them foolish video lotto machines. I never could wrap me head around that shit and I'm delighted to say I've never so much as plugged a penny into one of 'em. Shovin your money into a big black hole. Mike fuckin loves 'em though. He had a few of 'em into the Hatchet when he first got it on the go but he got rid of 'em all one night in a fit. He said he useta feel too guilty all the time watchin fellas blow the phone-bill and the grocery money and some people'd be bawlin at the end of the night, lookin to open a tab. Cant say I understands his double standard, where he's face-n-eyes into 'em hisself, but I knows I cant stand the sight of 'em and I dont even like drinkin in bars that got 'em. Too many fuckin zombies around. Most antisocial inventions in the history of the planet. Not to say I never placed me share of bets. Back in Dublin I'd grab the *Sun* first thing in the morning and pick me horses for the day. But at least with the horses you can take shit into account like the jockey and the trainer and the history of the horse and the conditions of the track. You can actually make an *informed* decision. It's not just blind button pushin. And the fuckin rush. Jesus, there's nothing like it. With your horse goin neck to neck and the pints in the air with all hands screamin and roarin come on! Come on! Come on! Fuck.

Win or lose who gives a fuck? And I had meself under control too, for the most part. I'd walk into the bookies and decide how much I was gonna spend, and if I lost that much then I'd give it up for the day. But if I won, which was a fair bit, then I'd just pocket what I first paid in and bet me winnings for the rest of it. Simple as old fuck. One day I walked outta Paddy Power's with nothing less than eleven hundred pounds in me arse pocket. After payin in twenty. And dont think I never got a good drunk on *that* weekend by fuck.

But them VLTs? Fuck, fellas must see the little cherries and bells in their sleep when they closes their eyes. Oh yeah, I'm after hearin tell of fellas actually dreamin on hittin the jackpot and then wakin up all fucked up and broke and wantin to die. And some even do toss themselves into the harbour or slit their wrists every once in a while. Fuck that shit.

I says hello to Mike when I passes but he dont even look at me. I can see the reflection of them lemons and sevens in his eyes. On me way up to the bar I says fuck, fuck, fuckity fuck cause I dont got no money where Donna's been buyin all night. So it's either go home right now or start up a new tab at the Hatchet. But I dont know how I'll pay it off where I'm pretty much fucked for cash these days. I'm owed a hundred bucks still, for my fuckin aquatherapy session. Cant bring meself to phone 'em up though. I heard a rumour that they're none too pleased with me. Fuck 'em.Val's got a gig at the Ship Thursday night and wants me to lug some gear around, but I s'pose I'm after outgrowin that shit. Could sell off a few of his CDs though, he'd never miss 'em. Fuck.

Back at the Hatchet and Monica gives me a beer. Fuck she's dandy in them jeans, red stretchy ones that fits right up her hole. Nice tight lacy bra. Dandy she is, but if she's fuckin around with yon hippie Keith upstairs, *and* the great Valentine Reid, fuck knows what kinda diseases she got.

Donna over sitting in the corner with her back to me. Talkin to that Clyde Whelan cunt. He looks over at me but he dont let her know that I'm there, cause he's dyin to fuck her now isnt he? That nice little one from earlier is there and greasy Jane and that Philip cocksucker too. I goes over and pulls up a chair next to Donna. Clyde gets up as soon as I sits down. The table goes right quiet, so I knows they were talkin about me. But I couldnt give a fuck cause I'm only passin through, I'm only hangin out around town for a while and these pricks are not goin nowhere no time soon I can tell ya that. Philip with his thick blue earrings and twirlin his straw like he owns the place. It's not too hard to claw yer way to the top of this old town I wouldnt say, 'specially if this crowd is the competition. But I aint stoppin there either. These mopes are content when Petey Thorne dedicates a song to 'em on some odd Saturday night. Makes 'em feel right special. Tucked into their daddy's pockets and suckin back the light, light extra-light smooth baby-blue smokes. Fuckin crowd.

Donna looks at me then. She got all that crappy makeup washed off, just regular red lipstick on now. Her eyes are a bit swole up so I s'pose she was bawlin. Fuck sakes. People got no sense of humour no more. But townies never did I s'pose. You gotta explain the livin shit out of a joke before they finally gets it in their heads and by that time it's not even funny no more and everyone is left lookin at their feet. But I mean it was fuckin priceless, me stormin out like that. Right outta the movies. No harm done. And like I said she had no goddamn business wavin the birthday flag cause if I wants special attention I can fuckin well find it on me own cant I? Yes I can.

Donna turns to me then and it's like she hates me, or wants me to think she does anyhow. I can feel the rest of 'em there wantin her to say what she musta rehearsed in me absence. That Clyde Whelan cunt clutchin his beer over at the bar, watchin our table outta the corner of his eye. Donna lookin at me, just lookin, her lips drawn so tight they're white at the edges.

Come on girl, say what you're gonna say, heave it outta ya.

She gawks at me for a long while and I got me jaw set and me two hands gripped under the rim of the table. Cause I'll flip the cocksucker over if she wants a scene. Not that I really gives a fuck what she got to say to me, just that they'll all be wantin a reaction and I'll give 'em all one they aint fuckin well expectin.

—Clayton . . . ahhh . . . we're all goin out to Middle Cove for a fire . . . if you'd like to come along.

She sips at her drink then and peeks over the top of it towards Philip, but he wont look at her. She shrugs and smiles as if to say she tried her best and that greasy Jane's head drops like there's no hope left in the world atall. Dont go outta your ways to make me feel welcome here people. It's only me fuckin *birthday*. Fuck 'em. I slides me hand far up Donna's thigh.

—Who else is comin? What about your friend, that little one was here earlier?

—Who? Claire?

Philip lookin at her then and shakin his head with this fake baffled little snarky grin like *This is all just too much.*

—What's your fuckin problem?

That makes him jump then cause they aint used to bein talked to like that out here in the big city, tucked away in their cul-de-sacs with the fresh-cut lawns and sprinklers and slidin glass doors and all the fond family vacation pictures gatherin dust in the spare fuckin bedroom.

—Excuse me?

—I said what is your fuck-ing prob-lem?

Donna gives me a little tap then and laughs loud in that jagged whiskey way she got.

—Dont mind him Philip. He's only joking.

She gives me hair a little toss and I catches her hand and lays it down flat on the table without lookin at her. I'm blazin a hole in the centre of Philip's thick townie skull. Donna says:

—Dont be so saucy Clayton.

Oh and I can get saucy alright. I'll show him fuckin saucy to go flutterin his way through the world with his potpourri shit and his swanky salted margaritas. I slams me fist on the table and rattles their fancy drinks and they all jumps.

—So are we goin then or what b'ys? Middle Cove is it?

Philip peelin the label off Jane's beer bottle like it's all he got in the world left to hold on to.

—Cheer up Philip fer fuck sakes. I'm only fuckin around.

—I know. I know, I just . . .

—What's that?

—I just . . .

—Just?

—I . . .

—Yeah, yeah. Come on then if we're goin. You fit to drive Donna?

And that's as close as they'll get to a fuckin apology off me.

9. Killing Time

I gotta stand on my tiptoes and squint through the smoke to read the clock h'on the far wall. Eleven thirty. My spine is like murder, this dull h'ache that's been pulsin and burnin since seven or so. I been squeezin my shoulder blades together, that 'elps h'ease it a bit, but then my tits near pops h'outta my shirt. Why I bothers dressin up for this crowd I do not know. Push-up bras makes me self-conscious any'ow. Felt so bloated and gross 'fore I left the apartment though, I was just lookin to take the h'emphasis off my belly. No matter what I tries I just cant shake the belly, flabby jellied h'ugliness. But then with this bra on I just might as well 'ave "come-hungry fuck slut" stamped across my fore'ead, h'if youse are goin by the looks I'm gettin from these leeches all night. Cant show a bit of cleavage without it bein a h'open summons for slobbers and drools 'cross the bar. Creepy sometimes, this place, some nights. Never know where h'anyone's from some nights. And then 'aving to lock up on your h'own.

Back at the goddamn 'Atchet. Full circle. Four more hours till closin time.

Must be near on six months now since I quit this place. I only 'alf 'members tellin Mike to go find 'isself a replacement. Loaded in the daytime I was, like one o'clock in the day. I was a mess them days, couldnt keep h'anything down, nothing solid any'ow. Faintin spells in the mornings. But I was lookin good. Shed a good fifteen pounds that month. That day I quit though, I minds m'self spewin on to Mike 'bout university and trudgin h'off to take pictures in Europe. Mike just nodding along, not givin no sign whether he cared or not that I was quittin, just nodding and grinning to 'isself like he musta known I'd be comin back. And so I did. Spent the 'ole summer stoned and wandering around downtown, blew what money I'd put away. And then the h'unemployment crowd gouged me for no good reason. Five or six weeks be'ind on the rent. Mike's rent. Back at the 'Atchet. Full circle.

Coulda went servin tables, but I'd rather be h'able to scream at drunken late-night lowlifes than 'ave to bite my tongue and take shit from so-called 'igh society. Tips is better in the bars any'ow. People gets drunk and foolish and stupid with their money. 'Specially h'if youse shows anough cleavage. And when I'm in good form, when I'm feelin good and got all my h'exercise in and I 'avent been bingin in the nights when I'm drinkin, when I'm not feelin like the slob I am and maybe I takes a little something for h'energy, to keep me perky and sharp and 'opefully smilin, that's when the tips start pourin in. And the tips is *right 'ere* too, and all mine. No splittin it up with the kitchen staff and the h'other waitresses and then waitin two weeks for some pimply manager to divvy it out. Tips 'ere is h'all mine and none of h'anyone's business.

This place though, mercy. I've worked lotsa bars over the years, managed to vanish though, when the scene got too 'ard on the 'ead, too familiar maybe, too dangerous sometimes, too pricey, peo- ple tryna get too close. But there's something different about the 'Atchet. It 'as this way of suckin youse back in and in no time at all you've done h'away with the h'outside world again, your h'entire social life revolving around your connection with the place. H'all your friends is h'either staff or regulars and there's not h'often a difference between the two. Gets sometimes 'ard to tell which one you is y' h'own self. This place though, mercy, like it seeps into your pores and suffocates you from the h'inside h'out. Sometimes. The smell 'ere, depravity and desperation. But it's nice to get h'in h'outta the cold I s'pose. One big downtrodden family 'ere, this twisted collection of discards, h'outcasts and fuck-ups from all across the province. Wrenched from the bays and coves and shores like scattered h'iron filings to the big city magnet, desperate for a way h'in, for a h'easy place to rest their jaded 'eads and 'earts. H'all on the run from *something* or *someone,* some darkness, some pain too 'ard to face alone in the clear light of day. And no one h'asks the wrong questions, that's the main thing. Cant say I dont really belong 'ere then. Christ, h'almost good to be back. Not for much longer though, not this time. Maybe h'even tonight. Maybe.

Good place for pictures all the same, the 'Atchet. Camera picks up things in 'ere that none of us can see. Mike says 'e dont like me doin that though, takin pictures of people drinkin. He says it's a "h'invasion of privacy." Which it is, but it's not like I dont h'ask people's permission, not my fault h'if they's too drunk to remember givin it to me. Or maybe it is, sometimes, my fault.

Youse cant believe the phone call I got this h'afternoon. My mother. Wantin me to go back to B——. *Dad's sick* she says. *Youse gotta come home.* Just like that, just 'spects me to up and trod on 'ome h'after nine years just cause that h'old bastard is sick? I says to 'er: *Sure I knows that Mom, 'e was h'always fucken sick.* And she goes right quiet then, just 'er breathin there. Then she goes *Monica my ducky, we thought you'd 'ave that stuff h'over and done with now.* Still see, *still* she dont want it to be the truth. Of course she dont, cause what would that make 'er? A fat, greasy fucken 'oremaster like 'im. Imagine me h'off 'ome just so's 'e can 'ave one last gawk at me afore 'e croaks. Imagine me losin me mind goin down h'over that 'ighway, dredgin h'up all that shit h'after nine fucken years. Sure I'd h'only quicken 'im once I finally showed h'up. I'd h'only just barge h'into wherever he's laid up and choke the shit h'out of 'im. *Dad's sick.* Yes.

Nine years. I lost twenty-five pounds before the court date. Some scandal. Young Monica, h'attention-seekin little 'ore, shit-disturber. The 'ailstorm of gossip and rumour. And me comin h'out on the losin h'end of course, dependin on 'ow youse look at it. But at least I left with my 'ead 'eld 'igh, my dignity h'intact, mostly. Gone h'off to the big city to show 'em all. H'only to wash up at the h'Awl and 'Atchet. Sweet mercy. Then, just when youse think you've come through clean, shed away the bullshit, that you've h'outran that h'other life, the phone rings. *Dad's sick. Come 'ome.* Wrecks my fucken 'ead.

Look at that twitchy Jim McNaughton over in the corner, 'asnt taken 'is eyes h'off me once tonight. He must like 'em 'efty. No 'arm to 'im though, our Jim. I can 'andle an 'ole lot worse than 'im. 'E tips 'is glass to show me it's h'empty and like a robot I 'eads straight for the taps to get 'im another. Time 'e switched h'over to the London Dock now, I wonder should I make that decision for 'im? Naw. Lord mercy though, dont tell me that *this* is what I've been put on this planet to become: a bartender killin time on two sides of the bar . . .

Well I can walk away tonight, this very second, h'if I wants to. H'if I 'ave to.

Oh, here comes Limp-along Reid through the front door, back h'again, just couldnt stay clear. H'if I was Donna I'd 'ave the face smacked h'offa that. H'if I thought 'e wouldnt fall apart. Yeah, for h'all 'is bullshit and tough talk Clayton's a bit lost h'underneath it all. And I'm a good one to talk now isnt I?

I twists h'open a beer for 'im and scribbles it down as spillage, cause I knows 'e got no money. I lets 'im 'ave a good gawk down me top while I swipes at the bar in front of him. Miss Donna dont like that do she? I can feel 'er h'eyes from cross the room. I lifts up the phone to go h'under it with the cloth and something, some little critter, scuttles h'over the rim of the bar just h'outta reach. I couldnt get a good look at it. This place is *h'infested,* in more ways than one. When Clayton 'as 'is fill of beer and boobs he sidles over to the other side of the room to join Donna. Yes Clayton, I knows the story. You're just screwin 'er. She's definitely, h'absolutely *not* your girlfriend. I 'as to laugh at that feller. Relentless. I 'avent the 'eart to tell him about the table Val gave me. I'm not partin with that h'any time soon. Fuck, cant believe I screwed his uncle Val. And then to go h'all but pourin my heart out in the h'aftermath. Christ, I told 'im *h'everything*. Details about B——, about court and my father, details Keith 'asnt h'even managed to drag h'outta me. Keith'd be cracked h'if 'e found out about Val. I should fucken well say it to 'im shouldnt I. Yes. Cant trust 'im any'ow, far as youse can throw 'im. Little imp. Still, cant 'elp feelin a bit guilty. What's it been with me and Keith? Two years h'on and h'off, maybe. And still no sense of nothing steady h'out of 'im, lestwise 'e wants something. And of course 'e showed up at the bar earlier, lookin for some slack, lookin to "take things h'easy" for a while. I never let h'on that I gave much of a shit. But I knows fucken well 'e's back on the phone with that Natasha slut up in 'Alifax and that he's burnin to skip town h'again. Thinkin she'll 'ave 'im back. Slut.

Mercy me, time for a shot now. Tequila. And I dont give a shit 'oo's watchin me.

Clayton makes a big roar from over in the corner. 'E's off 'is 'ead. No need for a smart young feller like that to be wiling away 'is nights in the bars. I've read some of 'is songs and stuff. They's pretty good too, might h'even rival 'is famous h'uncle someday, h'if 'e keeps doin it. Seems like some while ago now that I 'ad 'im at the General's. Mercy, I'm gettin around isnt I? Or it'd look that way h'if h'anyone was lookin. But I'm not like that, no. I never was either. I was drunk and driftin around town and Keith was on the missing list and . . . I dont know, there was just something 'bout Clayton that night. This charm, he was so saucy and cocksure of himself. And so vulnerable too, like he was daring me to reject 'im just to show me that 'e could take it. Or maybe it was his limp I took pity on. Jesus, 'e musta tolt me ten different versions of how he got that limp. But 'e's 'andsome too, not too 'ard on the h'eyes that feller. I mind I was right taken in with 'is accent too, but 'e turned h'out not to be h'Irish the next morning, 'e was just h'over there for a while. The sex got a bit rough at the 'otel. I 'ad little bruises around my nipples.

Not violent or nothing forced, I'da cut the nuts h'off 'im sure, just Clayton like a savage, fried on pills and wantin me to snort h'outta some little brown bottle. I wasnt really there for the sex and I know I kinda just let 'im 'ave 'is way. I just wasnt wantin to be alone that night. And sometimes it's just h'easier with a stranger. But youse know what, when I thinks on what fucken h'action I've seen lately, what with Keith tryna *get 'isself centred*, and Valentine's boozy go at gettin it up, I s'pose a few little bruises wouldnt go h'astray right about now.

Merciful mother, this place is filthy. H'everything is sticky with grime. I runs the 'ot water and lifts up the cruddy old dishrag near the h'edge of the sink. When I'm rinsing the h'ash and booze h'outta the cloth I catches sight of one of them disgusting little h'insects, what's they called, they's like little scorpions with the 'ard shells and spitey pincers on their back h'end. European h'earwigs? Is that what they is? Some h'other name too, something more poetic I think. Vile, depraved little fuckers. I turns h'off the tap and stares at it through the rising steam. It'd been scurrying back and forth, confused, rushing around, but stops dead away when the shadow of my 'and passes h'over it. Feelers probing at the toxic countertop for the first sign of trouble. Like it can sense my repulsion. Sweet mercy, it's lookin right h'at me. Is it? It raises the menacing pincers on its tail as a warning. My skin breaks out, h'inflamed with goosebumps. Creepy little bastard.

I think I 'eard somewheres that people with real 'ouses 'ave started sprayin their foundations with a mix of soap and water, that it works to keep these little cretins h'away. The soap clogs their pores or something. I'll get this gross little fuck 'ere now wont I. Yes. As I moves my 'and towards the dish liquid the little devil turns its body in time with me. Like the little swine can 'ear me too. I pulls the cap h'on the Palmolive, quiet h'as I can, never takin my h'eyes off the h'insect. In one quick movement I tips the bottle and draws a thick circle, about ten centimetres in diameter, around where the creature sits. 'E doesnt move, or h'even recognize the fact that 'e's been trapped. Stays just like 'e was, antennas scrutinizing the h'air, pincers raised and ready to plunge. I grabs a wooden pencil from the jar near the phone and gently nudges the beast with what's left of the h'eraser. 'E dont move. I nudges h'again, this time at the vermin's midsection, and 'e makes a few bold, lighting-fast h'attempts to latch 'is 'ooks into the pencil's rubber. Then, deciding maybe that a strong defence is better with a h'unknown h'enemy, 'e bolts towards the shadows beneath the sink's ledge. 'E dont get far of course, but h'instinctively changes direction the moment 'e meets the dish liquid. Not stupid h'either, these things. My 'eart is pounding suddenly and I dont know why. The blare of the drunken bar, Petey's scratchy voice, just a low static in the background. I leans in for a closer look h'as the fucken fiend tries h'over and h'over to find a h'opening in the circle of dish liquid, searchin frantic for a h'escape that will not come. Only one way out youse little piece of shit. Mercy now, listen to me, what h'am I doin? I could just crush it and be done with it. I dont h'even feel guilty. *Dad's sick. Come 'ome.* Die, youse little fucker.

Lord mercy, what's h'after gettin into me? *Monica sweet'eart h'is that you? It's me, your mother.*

Lookit, round and round 'e goes, retryin h'every possible contact point for a break in the circle of soapy death, like 'e dont h'even trust 'is h'own mind. Does it 'ave a mind? A family somewhere? A family that loves it? That wants it to come home? I can feel the giggles comin on now.

My camera this h'afternoon. I 'ad it in my 'and, put some food in the cat's dish, and then turned to leave but the camera was gone. I retraced my steps from where the cat was h'eating, on through the main room and back to the porch maybe a dozen times. I lifted the same newspaper and my jean jacket every time I passed it, h'expecting the camera to just magically materialize beneath one or the h'other this time round. H'over and h'over I repeated my steps till I was literally spinning in circles like this little creature 'ere now, trapped in a circle of Palmolive. I wasnt likely h'even gonna use the camera, didnt *need* it, but more or less needed to reassure m'self that I wasnt gone mental. I finally had to leave the h'apartment without it. The h'afternoon dull and h'overcast. Perfect weather for black and white.

The h'earwig scuttles back to the centre of the circle and stays there, doesnt move. I nudges 'im once more with the pencil and 'e makes a dash towards the h'edge of the circle, stops just as 'e would 'ave collided with the dish liquid, does a quick U-turn and then charges for the h'other end. 'E digs 'ead-first into the Palmolive, little legs scrambling for traction as the thick gel h'envelopes 'is body. 'E drags 'isself 'bout a h'inch before the convulsions h'overtakes 'im and 'e curls 'isself into what must be a purely h'instinctive foetal position. De-feated. I watches 'im twist 'is last, then I snatches a quarter from my tip jar and lays it h'over the poor dyin creature. I presses down on the quarter, slow and firm, with my thumb, the crunch kinda rewarding, like good boot 'eels on broken glass, but not quite loud anough for my satisfaction. Leaves me feelin kinda drained and cheated, kinda h'empty. My 'ead feels suddenly cloudy again, the clatter of the bar floodin my senses tenfold. That dull h'ache in the middle of my back. I takes a dizzy spell from 'oldin my breath.

As I'm washin h'away the squat mess of h'insect and dish liquid I h'almost jumps h'outta my skin at the sound of Mike's distinct townie brogue shoutin at me above the blare of the music for his usual glass of soda water and lime cordial. I never h'even noticed 'im comin h'in. I scoops some h'ice into a glass. I knows my face is red as a beet. I 'ope 'e wasnt watchin too long. 'E'll think I'm cracked. Maybe I am. A splash of lime down over the fresh h'ice before topping it with soda, as 'e likes it. I know my smile must look so fake as I 'ands 'im the glass. 'E likes 'is bartenders smilin. 'E moves round the h'edge of the bar and leans h'over my shoulder to speak. I moves my h'ear h'upwards to meet 'is damp, smoky voice.

—Clyde had to cancel his day shift for tomorrow. Can you handle a double-up?

Counting my h'own day shift this Friday that'd make it a five-day week. Not bad. Pick up a gram of blow later tonight, h'if tips is good. H'if not I'll just 'ave to 'old h'out till the weekend. Mr. Landlord's been a real nuisance lately. I stands on my tiptoes to shout back h'into Mike's h'ear.

—Not a problem! I'll be 'ere.

—What?

—I said I'll be 'ere!

—Excellent. I like your outfit by the way. You should do good tonight.

Mike snaps a dollar h'onto the bar before swaggering h'off to the pool table. I 'as a glance at the clock on the far wall. 'Leven forty. Jim holds up 'is latest h'empty glass and I starts pourin a double London Dock. There'll be a livelier crowd later on for sure. And the time goes so fast h'after twelve. Clayton winks at me when 'im and Donna and the rest of that bunch walks through the front door. I cant 'elp smilin at 'im. It's good to be winked at.

I grab the h'ash bucket from h'under the sink and a stack of clean h'ashtrays from beside the register. The h'ashtrays on the bar isnt exactly overflowing, but it 'elps kill a bit of time.

Bartending, h'all 'bout killin time . . .

10. Into the Cold Black Nothing—Continued

We meets that Patty missus, the one from the film, gettin out of a cab in front of the Hatchet. She got this flashy gaylord type in tow whose teeth are too fuckin white for my likin. He got granny glasses on with no fuckin lenses. They each got little plastic glasses of red wine and they're laughin together about something that musta gone on in the cab. But when she turns around and I'm standin right there her face drops and she straightens out her sparkly blouse.

—Hello Clayton.

And then the gaylord lowers his glasses, like he cant fuckin well see me proper through the goddamn frames, and gives me the special once-over.

—Oohhh, Patricia, is this our enforcer? Sexy.

He holds out his hand, limp, like I'm s'pose to kiss it instead of break it, but I dont bother either way.

—So ahhh . . . when should I expect to get paid for the other night?

—Clayton, you assaulted, you hospitalized one of my employees . . .

—Well no, not exactly, if someone'd hear my side.

—He had seven stitches above his eye.

—Does no one know what's down in that fuckin basement I wonder?

Donna pulls up to the curb then and toots the horn and I sees that that tasty young Claire is there in the front seat.

—Well, whatever went on, all I know is that Darren might be pressing charges.

—He came at me from behind! I was securing the premises like you said. And a hundred bucks is what I'm owed.

—Well I already gave it to your uncle.

She pushes past me and in through the front doors of the Hatchet.

—What?

—I gave it to Valentine at the wrap party last night. He said he'd pass it along.

—Are you fuckin mental or something?

She disappears inside and the gaylord gives me arm a little squeeze as he's passin me.

—We're all mental in our own little way hey Clayton?

He winks then and gives me arm another pump before he skips inside behind *Patricia*. I knows fuckin well I wont see a cent of that money off Val. What am I gonna do, just come out and ask him for it? Jesus.

Charges. What fuckin next? The world is gone so fuckin backwards. The way I came up was if someone gave you a smack you either struck him back right there on the spot or you squared off out behind the snack bar on a Friday night. Charges. And sure there I was in the line of duty. And he's the very one who handed *me* the bat and the flashlight the night before. What was I s'pose to do with a goddamn baseball bat all night, hunt fuckin rats? And sure what was he expectin, fuckin around and gettin me on the go like that? He got what was comin to him as far as I'm concerned. And he's lucky it was only the flashlight I used. Seven stitches? Sure that's fuck-all.

• • •

Donna the speed freak with greasy Jane in the back beggin her to slow down. We're sluggin back piss-warm wine coolers, takes the turn onto the Middle Cove parkin lot doin about eighty clicks. That'd be just fuckin perfect wouldnt it, to die in a car with this lot, caught dead with a wine cooler drove up me hole. We all piles out and down to the beach with that fat smell of seaweed and salt fillin me lungs. The roar from the waves. There're a few little fires on the other end of the beach with bottles clinkin and the burnt smell of marshmallows on the wind. Donna tries to take me hand but that little Claire, the one with the gear that we snorted off the dash on the way out, I can feel her watchin, so I scoots on up ahead.

After I gets a good fire goin (cause none of these pansies knows nothing about startin one) we all has a toke with some of Claire's good gear mixed in for flavour. The back of me throat goes right nice and numb so I can just pour the coolers down without hardly swallowin. Donna says she's cold and tries to snuggle up next to me. I lets her for a second but then it feels too put on, so I starts to strip down.

—What are you doing?

—Goin for a dip, what's it look like?

—Clayton, it's pitch black. It's freezing out.

—Anybody else?

I gives Claire a slick look then cause I'd love to get her in the bare buff and I wouldnt give a fuck, with Donna right here on the beach, I wouldnt give a fuck. Cause I knows where me heart is *not* alright.

But no one else is gonna bother cause they never heard tell of swimmin in the salt water, unless they were off in Florida on a cozy little family vacation. But I've been jumpin off the wharf and fallin outta boats now since I was yay fuckin high and it's so long since I had a swim I'm just gonna go for it.

I stands at the edge of the water and lets it lap over me toes and yes it's fuckin well cold enough. Me bag pulls right tight. But I can hardly change me mind now with all them fuckin city dwellers watchin, dyin to see me back down. I stands there for a bit, gapin into that enormous black, the seagulls squelchin overhead. Donna says *please be careful Clayton*. A wave laps up over me knees and it's so fuckin freezin it almost guts me, but I just says fuck it and dives straight in before I loses me nerve.

The salty death cold cuts right through to the marrow in me bones. There's a bit of a headache but it'll pass. The swell is rockin me back and forth and pullin me farther away from the beach. I flips onto me back to stare up at the never-ending gloom, me feet just barely touchin the smooth rocks underneath. I stays like that, on me back, till I cant feel the bottom no more and the sounds of the fire and the seagulls are duller now with this pull, this massive strength wantin me to just keep driftin out into the cold black nothing to join to the thousands upon thousands of other lost, unsettled souls.

On the upside of a swell I hears Donna's raspy laugh on the wind and I catches a glimpse of all them people, people I dont know, who dont know me, who'll never know me, standin around pokin sticks at the fire I just made for 'em. And I knows I could go back to that, swim in to shore and wrap meself in Donna's blanket from the car, mosey on back to St. John's and live in that rickety little world I got rigged up. Wait around for the big *something* to happen, for everything to just fall from the sky and be alright, for that *someone* who's out there somewhere who's gonna make it through with me and point me heart in the right direction, rid me of this cold-bloodedness I cant seem to shake no more. I could go back to that.

Or I could drift away and never be heard from again.

Sink into the black till I'm more welcome than I've ever been anywhere.

I hears me mother's laugh in that fine girlish way she had. One more snippet of conversation from the fire, the beach rocks rollin and crashin against the cliff face. There's gonna be a dirty scar on me hand from the sambuca burn cause it's turned bright fleshy white in the dark. I have a vague sense of me legs but it's like they're melding with the water and the black, black night, and then that emptiness coats me over and that sound again, that nothingness, that hard disappointing sense of silence like dust settling on a playground after all the children just abandoned their rides at once cause where they knew *I* was comin.

· · ·

The sand and rocks between me toes and the wind at me chest and
I'm walkin upright again. The fire is there and there's a blanket and
me eyes are burnin and swole up I s'pose from the salt water. I'm
tryin to settle me breath and I can feel everyone not lookin at me
while Donna says right soft, with her hand kneadin the back of me
neck:

—Well, there you are. We thought we lost you for a second.

And yes I thinks yes, I s'pose you did, yes . . .

11. The Arm of God

Mike behind the bar again, huffin and puffin cause Monica never showed up. He slips another beer in me hand before I has a chance to even ask for it. I wonder would I have had another one?

—On the house Clayton.

Yeah fuckin right. First two rules of rock-and-roll. I tips the bottle to me mouth nonetheless and nods me thanks at Mike. The cold froth collides with the fiery acid in me chest and me torso erupts in a spasm of hiccups. A sickly swell of hot bile shoots up the back of me throat and up through me nasal passage. Snot and sin and hangover sludge drips from both me nostrils. I gets this sharp cramp under me ribs and it's hard to take a big breath for a second. Mike slaps a wad of crusty commercial tissues in front of me even though they were well within me reach. I wipes meself and then stupidly dabs at me watering eyes with the same spot on the tissue. Now there's a coating of bile in one of me eyes too. One of them days is it? I lets the tears run free down me cheeks. Fuck it. The clock says half past two. Tuesday afternoon? I was plannin on stayin home today, workin out some shit on paper. Makin a list of shit I gotta get done. Maybe work on me play. I havent really written anything down yet, but I got a fair bit of action bumpin around in me head. I sorta scrapped the movie idea. For now. I brought me notebooks down to the kitchen table this morning, but Val was hangin around too and dead quiet and not fit to look at. Pacin around the kitchen with his guitar, grindin his teeth and scratchin at his neck, the clunky echo of his heels like a mallet beatin at the inside of me skull. The steady creak and crank and pop of the old hardwood floors. He never looked at me. I flew into him a couple of nights ago about the whereabouts of me table and we've barely grunted at each other since. Prick. So I figured it was either the Hatchet or the damp, squat quarters of me bedroom with a pillow wrapped around me head.

Or Donna's place.

No contest.

Mike crouchin beneath the sink with a little Maglite clamped in his teeth. I takes the opportunity to give me nose a good blow, clear the rest of the slop out of it. I holds the tissue to me left nostril and plugs the other with me knuckle and blows as hard as I can. What sounds like a woman's scream mingles with the thunderous crack of me eardrum. Fuckin creepy, my head is sometimes. Mike jumps to his feet from beneath the sink and leans over the bar as far as his big belly will let him, his neck bent towards the front door.

—What in the fuck was that?

The force of his roar and the panicky look in his eyes almost topples me off me barstool. How in the fuck could he hear my eardrum crackin? I've been doin that since I was sixteen. I minds of the first time I done it. I'd had this nasty ear infection for near on two weeks. Everything muffled deep inside meself, me own voice seemed so far away and this incessant, relentless ringing that almost drove me insane. I was stoned on weed, this real potent hyper shit that hadda been laced with something, rat poison maybe. Three o'clock in the morning and I was walkin home past the Ferryland graveyard and I thought I heard a child cryin out for help from way down in the back by the cliff. I stopped and listened hard but it was just that fuckin ringing in me ear and then I got thinkin that it was just the shitty weed and then I got thinkin *other* shit and I started runnin flat out down the long black stretch of highway between the graveyard and the first lights of the Cove. I was nearly sick on the side of the road when I finally stopped. I leaned over and plugged my two nostrils and pushed as hard as I could and when I did I had this fuckin, I dont know, this moment. I felt the pressure liftin in me head and the pop of me eardrums and the ringing slipped away like it'd never been in the first place. Fuckin orgasmic. But then, get this, the very moment me eardrums are crackin I hears the old man's drunken snarl in me head and he's belchin at me:

—I mean that stuff sounds like one big suicide note. You needs fuckin help b'y.

Clear as day, that very line echoing around in me head like that. But with my ears cleared up fine and dandy I never made nothing of it cause I was so relieved to have me hearing back. A few days later I'm tearin the house apart lookin for me journal and finally I hafta have a go at old Randy cause there's no other way it woulda disappeared outta me room. He denies it of course, says he never touched it. Then the big racket gets on the go, only he knows better by the time I'm sixteen not to lay a fuckin hand on me. And finally he comes out with it. He shouts at me:

—I mean that stuff sounds like one big suicide note. You needs fuckin help b'y.

Just like that, the very same line. Like I was already there in my head a few days before. Like it'd already happened in some other time or dimension or whatever, if you believes in that sorta thing. Like my head, in the state it was in with the ear infection and the dodgy weed, had tapped into some other space in time, or had a peek through some window into what was to come. I dont know. Sounds kinda fuckin wacko I s'pose. I nearly crumpled to the floor when he said it though. I shut right up, and so did he, thinkin maybe he'd got the upper hand on me. If he only knew. Me, conscious and aware and alive. All the haze of me childish existence burned away and I was literally and utterly *in the world* for the first time. This blazin fresh awareness, how the things I said and did had an effect on the people around me, that other people had feelings and thoughts and hearts. I was *awake*. And then I went around for about two years with me head hung low and self-conscious and depressed and, to be honest, wishin I was dead and thinkin about ways to top meself. How fucked up is that?

This is all rippin through me head and I'm about to relay it to Mike, when there comes that scream again, only this time I'm sure it's not in me head but from the street outside. Squeal of tires. This undeniable film of panic in the air. Mike darts around the bar and pops his head out the front door, squints up Water Street in the direction of the racket. There's a sudden dark thunder and the shock of what sounds like grinding steel. Maybe the end is finally arrived?

—What is it Mike?

—Cant say for sure. Watch the bar for a second will ya.

Then he's out into the street, half joggin. I wastes no time leanin over the bar and fittin the mouth of me empty bottle beneath the draft tap. I gives the handle a slight tug and manages to fill the bottle a little over halfway before it froths to the top. Satisfied with that, I leans back and sparks up a smoke. Me headache feels better. The cash register is wide open where Mike had been countin out the day's float. I props onto me elbows and leans close to estimate how much is there. There's an envelope near the register with a stack of fifties and twenties inside. Broke as I am though, I aint that foolish. You just dont steal from Mike Quinn.

Sirens blarin from up the street. Something's definitely amiss.

Jim McNaughton trips in his own feet as he comes through the doorway. He barely manages to catch hold of the edge of the bar on his way to the floor. He pulls himself upright but keeps his eyes closed, a deep and disturbing rattle in his chest. He must be up to two packs a day these days. Sweat trickles down his flushed cheekbones and his hand pats habitually at his empty shirt pocket. I sees his dilemma and slides me own cigarettes along the bar. Jim's wild, bloodshot eyes zone in on the package. He reaches his hand out but stops himself midway and jams his eyes shut again.

—N-no, no. I'm quitting. I'm q-quit . . .

—Go on Jim for fuck sakes. You're always quittin. Drink?

He glances at me beer.

—No. I'm good. Stayin clear of that too for a while.

His thirsty, love-parched and barren eyes scouring the empty bar. A full forty of London Dock over on the shelf. I can feel his resolve slacken. Come on Jim. Just one. He tears his eyes away from the bottle and snatches a smoke from my package. The lesser evil. The fuckin smell off him though when he leans near me, this sickly sweet, thick and sour stink enough to choke me.

—I just came in to pay my tab, my ahhh . . . pay my tab. Where's that—where's Mike at?

—Up the road. Accident or something. Left me in charge. Drink Jim?

He tosses three twenties on the bar in front of me.

—I-I dont even know how much I owe. Give ahhh . . . g-give that to Mike.

He tucks the cigarette into his shirt pocket as he's walkin back out the door. I takes his money and slides it into my inside pocket. I goes and stands in the doorway and watches Jim crossin the street and workin the key into the door of his old Jeep. Beyond Jim I sees Val and Monica, hand in fuckin hand, strollin into Bianca's Restaurant. I almost waves. A news van tears up the street and when I turns me head to follow it, there's Mike towering over me, his nose swollen and bulbous, his eyes red raw. He must sense what I'm thinkin cause right quick he goes:

—Fuckin allergies. Dust up the road.

—Fuck's on the go up there anyhow?

Mike dont answer me. He goes behind the bar and splashes cold water on his face. He picks up the envelope of money and sort of weighs it out in his palm as if he could tell by the weight of it whether or not a bill was missin. He prob'ly can too.

—Anybody come in?

I casually slips me hand into me inside pocket and stuffs the twenties right down to the bottom.

—Not a soul. What was the racket Mike?

He stares at me for a long time, till I can no longer meet his eyes.

—The Arm of God Clayton.

—What?

—A fucking crane. Some woman. Just sitting there in her truck. Waiting on her husband. Freak accident they says. It's all a mess up there. She was crushed by a fuckin utility crane. It's a mess, all of it.

I clicks on the radio and tunes it to the station of the news van that just went up. The reporter sounds nervous and excited.

—. . . as of yet unidentified woman. Sources say . . .

I'm tunin the dial for better reception when Mike suddenly yanks the plug outta the wall and the radio goes dead.

—That's just it see Clayton. Everything is fine and grand, life is good, easy bubble of familiarity, cozy little routine cocoon, then BOOM! Dead.

Mike hammers his meaty fist down on the bar in front of me, butts and ash scatter from the ashtray and me beer jumps a bit but thankfully doesnt topple.

—Boom. The Arm of God comes crashing down and . . . and snuffs you out. Quick as that. No warning. No second chance. You forgot to feed the meter. Poor woman, I mean, was she even *there*, at the last moment, in the world I mean? Are any of us? Ever?

Mike's eyes starts to fill up again and he bends down to the tap. I drains the last of me beer, tryna push me mother outta me head, trapped underneath two or three tons of twisted metal and not able to think or talk or *feel*. Asphalt and blood and gasoline.

—I'm fuckin alive.

—Are you now Clayton? Are you really?

I stares straight ahead and nods. He aint goin preachin at me today, I aint got the head for it.

—I think I punched my last season in the bar business Clayton.

—Oh yeah.

—Yeah. Might sell. Move on. Before it snuffs *me* out.

—I'm gonna go on now Mike. Be here all day if I dont get now.

—If I had my time back you know Clayton, I mean if I was your age again . . .

84

—Thanks for the beer Mike.

—Yeah . . .

Mike turns his back on me and stomps off towards the toilets with the mop. He shouts over his shoulder as I'm makin me way slowly through the front door:

—Sees Monica tell her I'm none too fuckin pleased.

Yeah, I'll make that me number-one priority Mike.

I feels heavier than normal when I walks out into the grey street. But it has fuck-all to do with me foot or the hangover or the beer I just drank. Some heaviness, unnamed, inside me, that I cant help resenting. I slips McNaughton's money from me inside pocket, folds 'em neatly before tuckin 'em into me wallet. Almost happy hour at the Ship. Sounds about right. I scrapes me tongue along the ridge of me top teeth and spits a glob of yellowy scum into the gutter. That sharp spasm of pain under me rib cage again. I tries to inhale but cant, the pain steady and clear and wont let me lungs move in or out. I clamps a hand over me heart even though I cant truthfully pinpoint the source of the pain. I reaches out with the other hand and grabs hold of a parking meter for balance. *Do not look up that street.* Close me eyes, breathe in small stages, baby steps, adjust to the pain, will away that blackout. More sirens now. Wait it out. *Do not look up that street. Dont listen.* My heart is beatin regular. I am alive. Awake and alive. In the world. The steady tick of the slowly expiring parking meter. One step forward and then I searches me head for a reason to take the next one. Happy hour.

As I'm climbing the steps to the Ship I'm only dimly aware of a child's whining, a man's muffled voice repeating *Oh my God, oh my God.*

The smell of new death lingering in the air over Water Street.

Nothing atall to do with me.

12. I'm Leaving You. Can I Borrow a Suitcase?

It was alright with Claire. Nothing wild. She wouldnt do the poppers. But it was pretty intense all the same. We hooked up this
morning at Keith's place after the Ship hove me out. Someone told
me at the Ship that a couple of lads from the Shore were down at
Keith's, playin guitar and shit. I got it in me head that it was Corey
and them, from the Cold fuckin Shoulder, and so I reckon I went
lookin for a racket, maybe. But there was no guitars or nothing on
the go when I got there and Keith told me it was just a bunch in
from the Goulds. But that's hardly the fuckin Shore now is it? I
glanced around the room and there was little Claire, sat down at a
very familiar old wooden table. My fuckin table, however it ended
up in Keith's rathole. He told me it was Monica's, that she had no
place else to put it for now. The table my dead mother gave Massie.
Family fuckin heirloom. And Val traded it with Monica for a slice
of skin. See how everything eventually comes out in the wash, how
everything comes back around? Old fucker. I went and checked the
drawer, slid me hand inside and dug around for this supposed false
fuckin bottom, but couldnt find a latch or button or nothing to
indicate it existed. I tries to pull the drawer outta the table altogether, but it was built to stay put. I told Keith to prepare himself
for a visit from the repo man in the very near future. I let it go for
then though, content to know where it was at least. Then I just

went straight for Claire. Had to pry her away from the stench of that Clyde Whelan cunt though and he kept askin:

—Where's Donna, Clayton? She was looking for you earlier.

I told him where to go then and he's a big sulky fucker so there was a bit of tension till Keith drove everyone out. Out in the alley, Clyde had the fuckin gall to go offer to put Claire in a cab. She wouldnt hear tell of it. I linked me arm in hers and nodded at him as we passed up the alleyway.

I wasnt hardly drinkin, just takin it easy. She wasnt fucked up either. I dont like that shit anyhow, when they aint really thinkin straight. I dont know; I dont get the same satisfaction out of it. But if they goes and gets fucked up *with* me, *after* I'm well sure there's a bit of skin on the horizon, well that dont bother me much. Some fellas though, some fuckheads thrives on it, and the more fucked up the young one is the better. That's why that date-rape pill is so rampant on George Street these days. Cause the place is fulla weak, cowardly pricks, drove cracked by their own failures and insecurities. Too socially delayed to converse with a *real* young one by the light of day. Sick shit that is. Fellas like that, sure they'd prob'ly fuck a mattress. What's the difference? I s'pose they thinks it's less work or whatever, a shortcut. But I'd say it's twice the work really, havin to put her in a cab and then lug her into your house and up the stairs while she vomits and bawls. Then sure you gotta get her boots and her pants and top and bra off. Then she's just lyin there while *you* does all the pushin for fuck sakes. And how can ya not feel a little . . . lesser once it's over with, knowin that the only way you could manage to get your skin was to drug her and drag her home like some fuckin caveman? Sick and depraved retards is all they are. Sure that's the way that Dahmer fucko in the States started out, druggin fellas in the nightclubs and gettin off on the notion they were dead bodies and shit. George Street hey?

• • •

Claire snorin soft alongside me. The sun is shinin in on her blue-streaked hair. She's hardly the One, but I likes her all the same. I blows a cloud of smoke on her face and dont she look fuckin dandy. Val downstairs tunin his new guitar. I lies there with me head tucked into the cold feather pillow I swiped outta his room. I does some thinkin about me script, watches Claire sleepin till the door-bell sounds and the cigarette burns into me knuckles. I musta dozed off. Val tromps down the stairs and I hears him at the front door, all surprised and delighted to see you-knows-fuckin-who. I havent laid eyes on Donna in nearly a week now. Fuck her I said there one evening when she called me up at the Hatchet. I wouldnt come to the phone cause I was on a winnin streak at the pool and there was a few dollars on the line. She had the bartender shout out across the bar that me supper was done and on the table. So I said fuck that shit. That's all I needs now is some missus with a contract out on me head every time I takes a piss. When are you comin home? Where were you all night? Let's curl up and watch a movie. Fuck all that. I jumped onto a bus outside the bar and went to Shea Heights for the night. I got a few places to crash up there and be fucked if anyone can track me down.

Val downstairs right loud sayin *Come on in, come in my love.* He fuckin well knows I aint up here on me own cause he was sittin at the table with a bottle of whiskey this morning when me and Claire came in. He never spoke or nothing, just a grunt and a glance at Claire. He gets in his so-called trances when he's workin and I tries to stay out of 'is way. But he fuckin well knows better than to let Donna in now. He knows I dont want her around. She's after get-tin right in with him though, so she comes around whenever she likes, whether I'm home or not. Pretty goddamn slick. Never see her when Monica's around though. Speaking of which, I should fuckin well spill *them* beans shouldnt I? Monica, back and forth between Val and Keith. That'd stir shit up alright. I should tell Val I was there already too. Blow it all wide open.

The chimney runs up the wall just outside me room and when

there's no fire on the go I can pretty much hear anything said in the main room downstairs. I hears Donna askin for me, but not in any kinda sincere way.

—Wheeeere is he?

Like, *ohhh my, whatever are we gonna do with that Clayton, he's such a darn rascal.* Fuck. Cunty-eyed fuck. And then of course Val comes to the foot of the stairs and roars out to me, sayin how me girlfriend is here. I can hear the nuisance in his voice cause he fuckin knows Claire is here with me, the fucker. Claire sleeps through it though. I should just drag her outta bed right here and now and march down the stairs with one hand on her hole, straight into the kitchen just to see the look on Donna's booze-logged snout. Yes by the fuck, that'd put an end to all this shit pretty quick. I nudges Claire and she opens one eye and smiles right shy, like she's only half able to remember the nailin I gave her this morning with the day still barely breakin through the curtains.

—What time is it?

—Time to get up I s'pose. Want coffee?

She rolls on her side towards me and slides her hand down across me gut. I sucks it in outta reflex. She giggles before latchin onto the head of me cock with her long shiny fingernails. She gives it a little tweak and I'm ready to have at her all over again. That's the best time for it, first thing when you opens your eyes. No fuckin around. No better way to start your day, 'specially with a strange bit. I tries to jab it right in her but she's too dry so I slips down under the covers and sucks the nub of her little clit into me mouth. I grabs her arms and pins 'em to the bed. Val bangin on the ceiling downstairs with a broom or something:

—Clayton? You up?

She grabs me by the hair and starts grindin me face off her pussy and buckin her hips and I looks up and she's bitin into the pillow so I knows she's ready to blow and when I feels her thighs shakin and squeezin in on me head I flies up and drives me cock into her as hard as I can with Val back at the foot of the stairs wantin me downstairs to entertain, to hurry up, get up, get up, get off, come on, come on and I am, I'm comin, I'm comin:

—I'm fuckin well comin!

I pulls out, cause I dont know if she's on the pill or not, and shoots across her tacky little unicorn tattoo just above her belly button. She catches some in her hand and wipes it into the bedsheets. I can hear Donna downstairs hackin up a lung and fuck, wouldnt it be nice to get all three of us together some night?

Claire lies there with her eyes closed and her head arched back on the pillow with just the ghost of a grin on her face. I gets up and hauls on me jeans. She dont even bother to stop me and that's fuckin right too, cause I cant stand the first five minutes or so afterwards. Gimme the first five minutes on me own and I'm fine then for chattin and maybe even a fuckin cuddle or so. Cause I'm too fuckin out there, too susceptible, stripped bare. I generally hates meself and anyone who thinks they can see me clear. And I knows it's typical but I'm just sayin if I'm pushed, if she tries to put me on the old guilt trip just cause I dont wanna chat and look into her eyes and fuckin *connect* and that sorta shit, then I'll fuckin lose it. Sure how much more connected can you get? Balls and all is not fuckin enough or what? Five minutes to collect meself, that's not so much to ask.

Val bawls out again and Claire sits up.

—Who's that?

—Me uncle. He's right on though. You can go back to sleep if you like.

—Are you going out?

—No, no. I'll be back up. Go back to sleep girl.

I pulls the curtains closed to make the prospect more appealing to her. She puts her face out for a kiss and I gives her a quick peck and leaves. I meets Donna on the stairs.

—Well now. You're not dead after all.

—Got a smoke?

—Is that all you have to say after almost six days?

She hands me a smoke. I turns her around and leads her back down the stairs. Val is standin near the bottom pickin at his guitar, listenin, waitin to see if I was found out or not. Found out. For the love of fuck. Not like we're a fuckin couple now is it? I can fuckin well do what I like and nothing or no one is gonna say otherwise. Supper on the table. *Come home to your supper!* Fuck that shit.

Donna walks into the living room, but I just keeps on down the hall, grabs me jacket off the floor and pulls it on.

—Where you going now?

—Out.

Val loves it all. He comes into the hallway pluckin away at the guitar, lookin straight at me with his trademark vacant, disconnected smirk.

—Made some racket this morning my son.

—I'm surprised you'd remember . . .

—Ohh I remember. Thought the light fixtures might come smashing onto the floors. Pictures falling off the walls in the hallway.

Donna looks back and forth between us.

—In a state was he?

—State? Yes. But never too far gone, hey Clayton?

—I can hold me own.

—*My* own. I can hold *my* own. Go get a dictionary my son.

—I aint your goddamn son.

—No you're not. Cause it's no trouble to see who you take after.

Well now that's a low fuckin blow. I'm hardly awake and this is the shit I'm expected to take? The reek of sugary booze off him enough to turn me stomach. Donna standin there, shakin her head right along with him, like it's nice to see that *someone's* finally puttin Clayton Reid in his place. I picks up me boots and sees there's still a bit of rat guts dried on the toe. Been too long since I gave 'em a good polish. But I dont even stop long enough in the porch to lace 'em up. I'm out through the door into the dusty dry fall sunshine. Fuck Donna now too. If she wants to stay, and waits around long enough for Claire to get up, then she's welcome to it. And fuck Val.

I knows what he was on about anyhow, just tryin to pick enough of a row with me so's he could rat me out about Claire. But he underestimates me. Or he *over*estimates, thinkin he knows how to hit me where I might give a fuck. But I dont. Give a fuck. I really dont.

I'm halfway down Cathedral Street, near that new massage parlour I'm dyin to check out once I gets the money, when Donna rounds the corner and squawks at me to wait up. Yeah, like I'm really clippin along here with the one good foot. But still I stops and lets her catch up. She's done something with her hair. Coloured it maybe. It seems not so drastically blond. She got them tight white slacks on too and I sees there's no drawers underneath. She's lookin pretty healthy to tell the truth. Must be the sunlight. And then I thinks on Claire up waitin in the bedroom. What's she gonna do when she goes downstairs and meets Val and realizes who he is and where she's to? Fuck. Maybe she'll sleep awhile longer and I'll be back before she's up. Dont have any set direction now anyhow, just wanted Donna outta the house and she's such a sucker I knew she'd come chasin after me. Now all I gotta do is make the right kinda uproar till she fucks off out of it. But she's lookin right wicked and I knows she wants her skin where I havent been around for nearly a week. And it was a few days before that since we had our last romp. Fuck. I'm shockin.

—So, did you get it out of your system Clayton?

That's her little catchphrase see.

—What?

There's a bit of bite to the wind and her nipples goes right hard under her sweater.

—Are you coming home Clayton?

—Home? I just came from home.

—Oh yeah . . .

She smiles outta the one side of her face, shakes her head slow like she's sayin that I just dont get it, like *she's* got a clearer picture, all the answers to *my* fuckin life. But she's the one who dont fuckin get it. I dont bend over for nothing or no one. And I'm gone if I gets it in me head. Gone. I'll find some way to gather up the cash and just hit the highway with what clothes I got on me back. And dont fuckin well look at me like that to tempt me, missus. If that's what it takes to get clear of you, then yes by the fuck I got no qualms about skippin the fuckin country for a while. I done it before didnt I? Yes I did.

—How's your foot? Clayton?

I realizes then that I aint puttin any weight atall on it and I'm leaned up against a construction sign for balance. Always reconstructing something around these parts, rippin up roads and sidewalks that were fine the day before. That's how it works though, they gotta blow their load every year to get a refill for the next.

—Why dont you come down to the apartment and give it a rest? Soak it in the tub for a while. There's wine.

She's got her lips right tight that way, like when she's expecting the worst. I s'pose she's at the end of 'er rope with me and really it must take a lot of self-control for her not to tell me where to fuckin go. But I s'pose she must realize that I dont mean to be such a prick. I really dont. It's just that I have an idea of how I wants me life to be and she just dont fit the picture. And it's not like I'm sayin I'm *better* than 'er, cause I aint. I knows I'm hardly the bee's fuckin knees. It's just that I didnt meet 'er in my world, but more or less she's goin out of 'er way to dig into *my* world. So I cant shake the notion that she's not really bein real, that she's taggin along like a little spoiled cousin up from Town for the weekend. Nor do I see nothing I likes in her world. A couple of weeks ago she pretty much begged me to go hang out with her brother and his friends (one of 'em bein that knobbly Jeremy the Jaw bastard that I felt like bashin), and so we all hooked up at fuckin Bianca's and, honest to fuck, I couldnt last ten minutes with all the hockey talk and real-estate news and how much this one fella is bench-pressin these days and which supplement this fella's takin and watchin 'em choke on them twenty-dollar so-called Cuban cigars when they had no clue whether or not the fuckin things coulda came from Needs on Military Road. My world? I wasnt long dartin across to the Hatchet.

—Full bottle, not even opened . . .

This is fucked, that she thinks she can just lure me into her pants with a fuckin bottle of cheap wine this early in the day. But me foot is fairly killin me and just thinkin about that little Claire back in me bed in the buff. Fuck.

. . .

She got the bath runnin with everything steamin over in the living room. I sucks back a smoke and takes a couple of Tylenol with a drop of wine. White fuckin wine at that. Not exactly what I calls a drink, where it's right cold from the fridge and you can barely taste the alcohol off it. She conned me, sly fucker that she is. She's hummin away to herself in the bathroom, in 'er glory cause she knows where I am and she got me where she wants me. I hops back into the kitchen for a refill, and I notices something fucked that I didnt catch on the way in. That supper she called me home to, the other night at the bar when I was playin pool, is still laid out. There's an upside-down wineglass and a knife and fork all laid out nice with a napkin and shit. And the supper, what I s'pose musta been a pork chop and mashed potatoes and maybe some peas, is there on the plate with an inch thick of white fuzz growin off it. There's even a slice of apple pie on the side that actually still looks fit to eat. What kinda fuckin power trip is this now I wonder? Sick. S'pose she's lookin for an apology or some such kinda *talk* is she? S'pose she wants to know where we fuckin stands and all that? Well she coulda figured that out when I never showed up for supper.

—Clayton, are you getting in? Bring me a glass too.

I grabs another glass and the bottle, tries me best to walk upright to the bathroom. And there she is sunk down in the bubbles with just her face showin and a stick of incense burnin that's enough to suffocate ya.

I sits on the toilet and gets me boots and pants off and then me shirt. Her starin at me cock like it's the first one she ever saw. She sits up straight in the tub when I moves to it, but I gives 'er a little nudge with me knee and she moves down the tub closer to the taps. I slips in behind her so's she tucked in between me legs and I got the bird's-eye view of her rickety spinal cord. Nice and hot though, the way I likes it. Be nice to have the fuckin thing to meself. That's twice she conned me now. Sly? Dont be talkin. Still, at least she's not sayin much. Me head cant handle havin to root around for explanations and comin up with ways to make 'er feel secure and all that heavy shit right now. I've been hard at it again for the past while. Nothing I cant control though. But no wonder I can hardly walk cause I'm way too rough with me foot when I got a few in me. It's throbbin now in the hot bathwater like that's where me heart is after endin up. It feels swollen, but I knows it's not. Some fuckin sick of it I am. Went to the doctor with it about two or three years ago and he found nothing wrong with it, said it was healed up just fine. Said the only thing he could think to do would be to break it all over again. I laughed in his face. Fuck that. Nothing worse than a big clunky fuckin cast on your foot to make you look the proper fool, havin to slice the legs out of all your pants and wrap it in a fuckin garbage bag to get a shower. I wasnt long takin a fuckin hacksaw to it down in Randy's basement. This is what he said to me now, on the way home from the hospital he goes:

—Soon as that cast is off I wants you outta the house. Hear that?

Him sluggin back the port wine in the car, eyes nearly welded shut. And so I does what any normal fucker'd do in that situation, gave it a week or so and then cut it off with a hacksaw, learned how to limp. No fuckin way was I spendin another minute in that house. That's cause Anne-Marie was movin in, that's why he said that. Old bag.

Donna leans ahead and lights a candle on the other end of the tub, one of them scented ones too that're all the rage these days. When she's not lookin I pinches out the stick of incense. She slides back between me legs and nearly crushes me nuts. I yelps a bit and she says sorry and I starts to go hard. She takes me foot in her hand and starts rubbin it and I lays me head back with a face cloth over me eyes while she presses the small of 'er back off me cock. But she's tryin to make it seem like she's not doin it on purpose, like she leans ahead and then shifts to the side as if it's all part of 'er foot-rubbin technique, but we both knows it's just cause she wants 'er skin. That's why she's not sayin nothing too, cause she's afraid she'll get a racket on the go and fuck up her chances of a quick one. That's me she got good and pinned down now dont she? This heartbroke, theatrical sigh out of 'er then. Oh yeah, here it fuckin comes.

—Clayton, I know you're just waiting around for someone better to come along . . . .

—Donna . . . .

—No, just listen. I know you're not really into this as a permanent thing, but cant we just have fun and . . . and be decent with each other while it lasts? Is that so much to ask?

She's all choked up now too, barely able to get that last bit out. Fuck. So much for a nice relaxing dip in the tub. I knew it wouldnt fuckin last anyhow cause that's the first goddamn sign, when they're all pensive and quiet with ya. You knows right away they got some heavy *soul-searchin* shit goin on and they wants you in on it. Fuck sakes.

—Lemme out . . .

—Clayton . . .

—No come on, it's killin me foot . . .

She leans ahead in the bubbles and I steps out onto the cold ceramic floor. She got her head down and lays her hand on the small of me back without lookin at me, like I needs her to steady me or something. I scoops up me jeans and keeps one hand against the wall and hops through to the bedroom.

I flops back on the bed with me gut and thighs beet red from the bath, me heart beatin outta me chest like some battle drum. Donna got the hairdryer goin and hey, maybe she's still in the tub and might just drop it by accident, put 'er out of 'er obvious misery. Fuck, she shouldnt be so fuckin foolish to put up with me. There's lotsa fuckers that'd line up to have a go at her.

I looks around the room and I'm disgusted to see so much of my shit lyin around. Shirts and drawers and socks on a shelf in the corner that she musta had to the laundrymat. A few novels and a book of poetry on the end table on *my* side of the bed. Christ. The poems are from that Robert Dawe fucker who's always hangin off the bar at the Hatchet, spewin shit with the Guinness stained onto the corners of his mouth. They calls him Toddler. Big long silver ponytail. Hardly string a sentence together and the next thing you know he's launchin a fuckin book and an album at the same fuckin time. An actor he is too, they says he's after bein in just about everything that's come off the Island for the past fifteen years. Cant say I'm familiar with much of his work though. Yeah, they're all fuckin actors and writers and singers and fuckin dancers. Val with his nine guitars and the movie work besides, and still scroungin for a smoke half the time. What's the good of that? I'll show all of 'em wont I? Yes I will. When I'm ready.

I picks up Dawe's book and looks it over. It's called *Poetry*. How fuckin lazy is that? None of the poems have titles either, just whatever the first line is, that's what he goes and names it. I was so drunk at his launch, I cant see meself *buyin* it. I musta swiped it off the table in the middle of the madness. Cause it was fuckin cracked alright. Dawe had a full band on the go and he never stopped only to slop Guinness down his chin. Dont know how he managed to keep the crowd hangin around though, with his barefaced fuckin hatred for everybody, spittin and cursin down the mic at people, just cause they were talkin. It's different when you sees a young band actin all savage and angry with the world and badmouthin the audience, but for a fella in his fifties who can barely carry a note? I dont know. They needs their so-called fuckin stars I s'pose. But there was some wicked women on the go too. This one dandy one, Christ, I came that close to makin an arse outta meself. Finest creature I've yet to lay eyes on in this fuckin town. I reckon she mighta worked there too cause she kept goin in behind the bar. I've been up to the Ship a few times since but she hasnt been around. She spent half the night out on the dance floor and I spent half the night watchin her dance, her arms raised in the air and her skirt risin up her thighs, skippin and smilin without a worry in the world, her tight tee-shirt soaked with sweat, plastered to her breasts. Then she'd dart into the backroom, Dawe's fuckin dressing room. My Christ, she's the One, now that I thinks on it. But I'll be sober the next time. I shoulda went on into the backroom meself, cause I do whenever Val is playin there, but I couldnt. I was too fucked up. Slammin that fuckin Hard Lemonade shit. That stuff is potent. Next thing I knows the show is over and there she is fallin out through the doors arm in arm with fuckin Dawe. Toddler. Neither of 'em with a leg to stand on. Fuckin old geezer like that with a fine piece of skin like her? Make ya sick.

. . .

I stretches out on the bed and slides me hand in under Donna's pillow. Something under there, a book maybe. I pulls it out and flips it over. A fuckin *framed* picture of me. Never seen it before, dont know where or when it was took. For fuck sakes. This is gone far enough now. *Supper on the table.*

I flies up off the bed and pulls me jeans and shirt on and starts tossin all me shit in a pile on the floor, all that folded-up shit, mounds of dirty socks and dirtier drawers from under the bed that she mustnta caught, jackets from the closet, me sleepin bag, books and tapes and that empty notepad she laid out for me, pens and pencils and that fuckin framed picture. Nice shot though. I looks pretty fuckin hard, not to be fucked with. I can see why she'd want it. I hauls on a fresh pair of socks and goes through to the kitchen for a garbage bag, but there's none where they normally are. I grabs a handful of Dominion grocery bags and back in the room I starts stuffin me shit into 'em. She comes in behind me and laughs first, wantin to know what I'm up to.

—Makin it easier on ya girl.

She standin there with a towel wrapped around her chest. I can just see the shadow of her puss where the towel stops. A bead of moisture trickles down the inside of her reddened thigh. Fuck. She's lookin around the room all frantic now, realizin I aint fuckin around.

—Are you leaving?

These fuckin bags are that cheap now, the corners of the books digs right through and falls to the floor when I goes to lay it on the bed. Cheap fuckwads with their recycled fuckin plastic. *Made with more than 50% recycled plastics.* Half made up of rotted garbage is what they means. Sure they gotta use twice as much of 'em to bag your groceries. Fuck the environment if you cant even lug a few books around.

—Clayton?

I aint gettin into it with 'er. No way. If I'm quick enough maybe I can still catch Claire and make an evening of it. Down to the last bag now and there's no way I'm fittin the rest of me shit in it. No way I'm comin back for it either.

—Clayton why?

Because I'm sick of it. It's one thing to hang around and get kinky and have a few drinks every now and then, but it's another thing altogether to be shackin up. Not what I had in mind when I came back to St. John's, to go gettin all tangled up and tucked away. I'll get that itch now soon enough and I'll be hittin the road. I'm actually tryna make it easier on 'er. Truth. I knows she's all fuckin smitten with me already and when the time comes I'll only fuckin destroy 'er, to put it mildly. And there's nothing that makes leavin easier than someone screechin and howlin in your face, beggin you to stay. She's better off that I fucks off right now rather than a year down the road. Cause it's inevitable that I will fuck off whenever I gets the notion. She's tough as nails sure. She'll drink her way through the first few weeks and I'll hafta keep a low profile. Then she'll turn on me and start fuckin around with certain people so's I'll get a whiff of it, hopin I'll come stormin back into 'er life to claim what's supposedly mine. But when I fails to put up any protest she'll start hatin herself and realizin how stunned she's gettin on, drivin her friends batty, no fun atall, goin on and on about me and how great I am while they all calls me down to the fuckin dirt. Bawlin on their shoulders and havin to be carried home every night of the week. All the friends in the world'll take a few steps back then cause they'll be sick ta fuckin death of 'er. And then she'll just hafta bite the bullet and get on with her goddamn life.

—Who is she Clayton?

Fuck sakes. So typical.

—Donna, we're not a fuckin couple, we're not goin out. We settled that ages ago. So I just needs to be on me own for a bit. This is too fucked up.

—What is? What's fucked up? Hot baths and wine?

But like I said, I'm hardly gonna weaken me position here by fuckin explaining meself. I does what I like, that's the way it is and always was. Just because we works out well in the sack she cant very well expect me to grind against me own nature. No.

I hooks as many bags over me fingers as I can, but there's still half a dozen on the floor. She goes to pick one up but I sticks out me foot and stops 'er. She stands back against the dresser with her arms crossed and 'er head down and she looks like she'll either screech or bat me across the face. I hope she fuckin hits me. That'd be fuckin wicked.

Her hand vaguely searches the top drawer for a smoke but she's not gonna find none cause I got 'em here in me pocket. Fuck that, she got lotsa money with her fancy cubicle job. It's hard goin, but the bags on the floor I manages to slide along the carpet with me bad foot, while the other ones are almost slicin through me fingers. This is no good. I'll never make it to the top of Prescott like this. I drops the bags and walks through to the back storage room. Nice little tucked-away spot that she told me I could turn into a writin space if I wanted. I said fuck that. I pulls down her big leather suitcase off the ceiling in the storage room and lugs it back out to the bedroom.

—You're not taking that are you?

—Why? You're not doin nothing with it.

—No but, it's expensive. I need it back.

—I'll give it back tomorrow.

—So you're comin back then?

—I'll put it in a cab.

—Clayton please just tell me what's happening! Do you . . . do you . . . ?

No I fuckin dont missy, so dont bother askin. I've been sucked into that scene once too often, cant go out through the door or take a piss without makin sure you're well loved? Fuck all that. It's sad and vicious but I loves nothing and fuckin no one these days. I shoves all the bags into the suitcase without even emptyin 'em out. It's a tight squeeze to get it closed and it weighs a ton but there's wheels on the bottom so it wont be so bad goin up the hill. On me way out the front door I gets a fit of the giggles, cause I realizes what a psycho I must look like, makin off with her leather suitcase. I always wanted one of these. She's standin there now with a bit of a grin on too, like she's turnin things around, tryna see the funny side, lookin to share the moment with me. I cuts 'er queer notions short though, with me trademark steely-eyed Reid stare that should send the message home that no, sorry girlie, me and you have never shared a moment and never will, it was all just . . . fucking.

—Clayton I . . .

Dont you fuckin say it. Dont you fuckin dare.

I'm out then, and I can feel 'er eyes drillin into the back of me head and like I said I knows I'm a little prick, but this is fuckin preservation of the self we're talkin about and that's gotta take precedence over whether or not some missus gets 'er feelings hurt. I mean, fuck, gimme a break.

I'm hardly gone twenty feet from the door before one of the wheels on the suitcase gives out and cracks off. That makes it near fuckin impossible to roll the clunky fucker up the hill. I tries pullin it by the strap but it topples over on its side so I just drags it like that. Dandy tough leather suitcase too, hope it dont rip through cause I can put it to good use pretty soon once I hits the road. Me foot is gone again, sorta numb on the inside but with the skin all ablaze and itchy. I'm puttin most of the weight on me heel by the time I cuts across Gower Street. Shoulda soaked it in the tub for another while longer. A sharp stabbing pain in me chest now. I feels like goin the way of the suitcase and just floppin over on the pavement, only who's gonna fuckin well drag *me* home out of it? Worst thing I could do now is stop.

I cuts up a pathway between Gower and Bond with the suitcase draggin behind and when I trundles onto the street I'm nearly run down by some fuckin maniac in a . . . fuck, that's Val. No licence or nothing. With fuckin Claire in the passenger seat. He leans on the horn and she sticks 'er arm out the window and waves without lookin back at me. They got the music on bust. One of Val's albums. Of course. The sun catches on Claire's shiny red nail polish as the car rips past a stop sign, narrowly missin some matted and filthy old tabby tomcat, out on the prowl and not hurtin no one, just tryna make his way home.

13. Skin Out While You Can

Halloween. Donna wanted to go out as Sid n Nancy, only *she* wanted
to be Sid. I said fuck that, she's lucky I came out as meself. There's a
costume contest at the Ship but I couldnt be bothered. Halloween
is for youngsters. Still, when she called me up I was kinda glad to
hear from her, despite meself. I been layin low these days, tryna
figure out what the fuck I'm gonna do with the rest of the year.
Winter comin on and not the most stable of a home life have I got.
And of course since I no longer have Donna's place as an alternative hideout, me and Val are in each other's faces a bit more than's
necessary. He's been makin digs about rent and shit too. There's
a rumour that another chunky movie is gonna be shot here in the
New Year. I've been thinkin about auditioning for that. Scrape up
a few dollars and tell Val to go fuck himself. He was already in with
some producers for a reading of the script. I had a glance at a couple of scenes that he left on the table. Cant be much to it. I'll give
it a go. Make some real cash and skin outta town. That leaves the
next couple of months with fuck-all though. Christmas. Gonna be
a rough go if I dont figure something out. Stay off the beer for a
while too. Gonna have to.

When Donna knew for sure I wasnt gonna dress up for Halloween
she decided on that Morticia character, that witch from the *Addams
Family*. Typical. Even with the stringy black wig though, she's only
gone and made herself even more recognizable, like she's merely

enhanced herself. We hooks up at the Darkroom with that Clyde Whelan cunt and his good friend Philip. I dont normally come to the Darkroom. It's kinda creepy with a lot of red lights and all the walls done black and everybody sort of lurkin in the corners. I like it. It's a bit pricey, but at least it's not George Street. Clyde's done up like the Joker from *Batman* and he looks pretty freaky, 'cept he gotta make a special point of gettin up in my face with his eyes right wide and his teeth bared so there's nearly a racket right off the bat. But I told Donna I'd at least try to have a decent time, not to be a fucker with everyone. As if I'm out to please her or something. But that's just the way I'm feelin lately. There's something in the air, pressin on me. I cant breathe. Like when Randy, me old man, use to push me face into the pillow when I was young, just wrestling like, but I'd go mad and lose it, kickin and screamin like a bloody retard. One time I bawled for me mother and ole Randy gave me a good crack across the face for it. I s'pose he was in the right though, where she's dead and all. But that's exactly what it feels like now, here in Town, like someone's got this giant pillow held in front of me face every corner I rounds. Not pushin into me, but just holdin it there, lettin me know that any minute now they could suffocate me with it. And so I've been lashin out in advance. I s'pose.

And, surprise of all surprises, Philip is done up in women's garb. 'Cept he's gone right conservative with it, like he's on his lunch break from the office: sleek black tweed skirt with a matching jacket and white blouse underneath. Not bad lookin really. Some fellas across the bar been glancin over at him and he dont seem to mind one little bit. Keith comes up the stairs and makes a straight cut to our table. He dont even look at me but zeroes in on Donna. Something concealed in the palm of his hand. He holds it out for her to inspect, looks around the bar, nervous, in case anyone is looking. I wouldnt blame him either; this bar is always chock full of busy, self-important, delicate types who only comes to a place like this in the hopes of catchin a glimpse at the so-called underbelly of the city that their otherwise cozy Monday-through-Friday lives have been deprivin 'em of. They'd get some fright if they saw where he lived though.

Once he decides it's safe, Keith holds up a little film bottle, one of those black Kodak ones with the grey cap. Big shady grin. He's gone all stoner these days: everything is *cool* and *sweet* and *whatever man*. I cant stand that shit.

—Trick or treat?

He's focused on Donna, completely ignores the rest of us. She seems right smitten with him.

—Treat please.

I can nail that fucker though. And he knows it.

Donna whips out a few twenties and they makes an exchange, film bottle for the cash. Keith winks at Philip and fades away into the crowd. Philip looks quite impressed with himself.

—What's that?

—A little Halloween treat.

She opens the bottle and taps four bluish pills into her palm. She gives one to each of us. Mine has a muddy impression of a teddy bear on it. I drops it under me tongue and lets it melt for a second before sliding it to the back of me throat. It sticks there for a bit and I'm tryna dry-swallow but it wont budge. Missus arrives with our drinks then, pina colada for me, and I fuckin devours it. I orders another before she's even got the last drink unloaded from her tray. Best fuckin girlie drinks in St. John's. I can feel the tablet still caught halfway down me throat on the way to me gut. That happens with cold drinks sometimes though. Best way to go about the pills is with a nice hot cuppa tea.

I gets up and makes me way to the toilet. Keith is standin in the doorway, talkin pretty close with Miss Monica. Val gets wind of this and he'll shred the two of them. She looks like she's been bawlin. She's got a cheapish Halloween makeup kit and some kinda black robe or dress tucked under her arm. Keith's talkin at her with this real coldness on his face. That's what always happens though: the women gets all dramatic and passionate and the fellas goes right

105

cold and rational to balance it out, and that drives the women even more cracked. When they sees me passin, Keith stops talkin to her and turns to nod at me. She looks down over the stairs so's I wont see her face all puffed up. Keith says to me:

—Feel it yet?

—No.

—You will man. Wont be long.

Be nice to feel anything atall these days, drug induced or not. I goes for a piss, a long, burnin, disappointing piss like when you're just after comin and your bladder feels fuller than it really is. Has a look at meself in the mirror. Feels a bit sleepy, a bit weak in the knees. Love to go lie down.

Back at the table and Clyde's after takin my chair next to Donna. He's got his arm around her shoulder in a sleazy, we're-just-such-great-friends-that-we-can-be-close-like-this-and-it-doesnt-*mean*-nothing kinda way. I stands behind the chair and gives it a playful bump with me knee. Clyde gets up and goes back to his own chair without acknowledging that he's gettin up because I told him to.

Donna slides her smokes to the middle of the table. Me and Clyde reaches for the package at the same time. Clyde's always on the bum these days. Every cent he makes bartending goes right back on his tab. I heard that it's somewhere in the five-hundred range. That's a bit much, if you asks me. Most mine ever was was seventy-five and I'll be fuckin well dryin up before I lets it go over that.

I leans back and lets Clyde take the first smoke. He pulls one from the pack, lights it and then holds it out to me, like I'm gonna just puff away on it after him slobbering all over the fuckin butt. I looks past the cigarette he's holdin out and I reaches for the pack. They all starts snickering together, some inside joke that I aint quite privy to.

—What? What's so fuckin funny?

Clyde gets right up in me face with that hideous Joker getup, the cheap green hair dye runnin down his forehead in buckets.

—You. You wont even share a cigarette.

—I likes to light me own, anything wrong with that?

—You're paranoid. Here.

He snorts and holds out his drink, a brilliant blue concoction called an asskicker.

—Here, have a sip of this.

I takes the drink and eyes it. Sniff. Vodka and something. The rim is smudged with Clyde's sweaty lipstick. I puts it to my lips, turns it around so the smudge is on the opposite side of the glass. There's a bit of ash or dirt froze onto an ice cube. They're all watchin me. I smells it again, then hands it back to him. He laughs triumphantly.

—What?

—You.

He looks at Donna.

—See? He wont drink after anyone either.

—I wont drink after *you* is all. That dont make me paranoid, that's just common fuckin sense.

Donna puts her hand on me shoulder.

—Calm down Clayton. He's only sayin you're—

—He's lookin for it.

Clyde stands up then. I stands up too and feels the first hint of the pill, a tiny teddy-bear giggle, a heat, a tingling new spring in me knees and shoulders. I holds me drink casually to me chest, tucks it in the crook of me arm just so. Friend of mine in Dublin showed me that. It makes you look nervous, like you're covering up some weakness, and at the same time it draws the other fella's attention away from your other hand. But my other hand right now is a tight-curled ball of barely contained rage and loathing, waitin patiently by me side, waitin for one false move.

Clyde cant keep me eye so he focuses on me drink. Precisely.

—And what is that, exactly? Lookin for what?

—A poke in the face, ya fuckin overgrown ape.

—Now see Donna? A fucking asshole of the highest order.

Clyde's had it out for me ever since I hooked up with Donna. Not hard to tell he's mad over her. He's just dyin to expose me in front of her, like I'm hidin meself or something. But that's one thing I never fuckin bothers with, hidin away, gettin on like I'm something or someone I aint. And I never fuckin will. Drink from *his* glass? If for some reason I ever needs to infect meself with a good dose of herpes, then maybe. Until then I dont fuckin think so. I glances at Donna, then back at Clyde. Philip pushes his chair back outta the way of what's comin. I nods down at the top of Donna's head.

—You want her Clyde?

Donna splutters into her drink. Clyde looks down at Philip. They both laughs, but they aint so cocky now. Neither one of 'em wanted me along tonight and figured they'd get rid of me right off the top. Not a bad idea really, but I'm gonna go once *I'm* fuckin well ready to go, not before, and not for them.

—Fuckin answer me. That's what it's all about isnt it? Cant stand to see me with her, or her with me? Figure she can do *so* much better, right?

—You're embarrassing yourself Reid. Sit down.

—Sit me the fuck down.

I aint fuckin embarrassed, that's one thing I dont get. That's just an admission. That means we're not responsible for what comes out of our own mouths. I aint no fuckin townie. Besides, what he's really sayin is: *You're embarrassing me.* Because it's fuckin true. He's dyin about her. Me and him, we mighta been great drinkin buddies if not for the fact that I hooked up with her. But that's a stretch.

I sees he's not gonna back down because all he knows is pettiness and rage. Big fellas like this are dangerous if you lets 'em get ahold of you. They'll squeeze you and knee you and smash your nose in with their hard, thick foreheads. Push 'em to the point of confusion and that's where they snaps. Because he's right fuckin stunned. Sure, he can talk books and make fancy, regurgitated statements about the local arts scene and quote Dylan till the cows comes home, but when it comes to knowin what he's all about, what his real strengths are and how they applies to the world around him, he's a fuckin retard. You gotta be some quick with these types of fuckers. Hit first and hit fuckin hard, that's the only way. Go for the nuts then and give him another crack on the way down. At least then he'll be damaged when he finally does get ahold of you. I reinforces the grip on me pina colada glass. I'll smash it off his face I s'pose, after I gives him a good right hook to the throat. That'll fuck 'im up. He looks at me and I sees the squint fall from around his eyes, his shoulders drops back just a little bit. He knows. He knows I aint some fuck he can bully around. I'm after havin it out with every arsehole and his dog back home on the Shore and the scars are right here in plain sight. I can live through this big monkey the same as any of the rest.

I keeps staring at him. He stares back, but I sees he's not into it so much now. He was more interested in seein me back down in front of Donna. He fuckin failed now didnt he? I flattens the rest of me pina colada then slams the glass into the corner. It shatters and a sliver of glass ricochets and pricks me hand. Heads turn from the bar. The blood wells up on me knuckle. Donna's sitting calmly, smoke curlin up through her wig, like it's all on television and she can change the channel any time she wants to. Which is kinda true I s'pose.

I straightens me jacket, wipes glass dust off me cuff.

—Well, thank you all for the lovely evening. I'll be on my way now.

Donna looks up and smiles. Clyde sits down. I let him save enough face I s'pose. Now that the moment is gone it dont matter much anyhow. I pushes me way past the bodies. The waitress walks past me with a broom, asks me where the glass broke. I points at Clyde.

—It was that big nuisance over there, look, he's fucked up.

I gets out to the street and takes a few deep, clean breaths. Me legs are shaky. I counts to five and sure enough Donna comes out behind me. I sees her reflection in the window of a car that's parked in front of the bar.

—Clayton?

I turns to face her. She rummages through her big black witch's satchel and comes up with a little grey box. It's tied with a yellow ribbon. She hands it to me.

—What's this?

—Just . . . I dont know. I feel kind of silly but . . . .

I pulls the ribbon and opens up the box. A black leather case. That's always a good sign. I pops open the snap. Something silver. A knife. A good knife. Compact and solid, no markings, a one-piece handle, thick blade. I looks at Donna and she's smilin, delighted with herself. Her teeth are bright white under the blue light of the doorway.

—It's our . . . ahhh . . . third-month anniversary.

She giggles then, but she's far away somewhere.

—Anniversary of what?

—Us . . . our . . . .

—Donna. How many times have I gotta say it?

—I know, I know. I just . . . I saw it and I wanted to get it for you, that's all.

—For our anniversary?

—No. Well yes. But . . .

—Thanks girl. It's dandy.

Her face lights right up then and I almost leans in to give her a peck on the cheek. Cant send her the wrong message though. I unhooks me belt buckle and slides the case on. Perfect. A bit stiff, but it'll soften up.

Then I turns to leave.

—Where are you going?

—For a walk. I'm feelin sick. That pill . . .

—Arent we going home together?

—Donna, I said I'd come out for a few drinks. We're not together, we're just hangin out, remember? I might come back, but if I dont then that's all there is to it.

—But, the pill, I thought we'd . . .

I turns and hops across the street, right out into the traffic. A cop car screeches to a stop and blows the horn at me. I glares at the young pup in the driver's seat and, very slowly, winds up the middle finger for him. He stares back. He's dyin to shoot someone. I walks on. I dont give two fucks. Donna shouts across the street:

—I'm sorry about the dinner Clayton!

No response from Mr. Reid. Scoot down the alleyway behind the Zone. There's a bunch of drama queens huddled in a corner with a big fat joint and, when I floats past, one of 'em whistles. At me. He's done up like that Ron Jeremy fella from the skin flicks, big moustache and afro, stuffed gut and bell-bottoms. I stops and glares at him, dirty like, with me one eyebrow scrunched down over me eye. He tries to keep his good mood intact, but I can tell he's gettin right self-conscious the harder I stares. I've busted his bubble. He cant remember the punchline. The circle goes quiet, none of 'em wants to have a go at me. There's two Draculas, one Madonna, from around her "Like a Prayer" phase, one Grim Reaper and one who may or may not be Joey Smallwood. There's a clown. I feels like sluggin him out, stompin his face into the concrete till he's nothing more than a sludgy mess of brains and bone fragment and lipstick. Me head goes reelin back, back to that day, the day before the accident. We'd all gone to the circus in Renews. Elephants and horses and that sad, angry tiger and the sword swallower. And clowns, lotsa bouncy, jittery, annoying clowns. Popcorn. My mother laughin, Randy sober, not yet a real drinker, and holdin each of our hands. Two of them singin along to Bob Seger's "Against the Wind" in the pickup on the way back up the Shore. Me half asleep across her lap. Her hand strokin me hair. Fuckin clowns.

Ron Jeremy holds out the joint. I plucks it from his hand without takin me eyes off his. I dont smile, but I nods, good-natured like, and walks away with the joint. None of 'em have the balls to protest. That's always the way too. If you wants something, take it. He who hesitates is fucked.

Fuck, I'm lovin this pill, this Halloween mystery treat.

Down past the Crossroads and there's a chaotic lineup outside. All hands freezin their holes off to get a glimpse at some band that fucked up and failed ten years ago but thinks they're still in their prime. You can tell by the crowd, the big nostalgia trip. *Please make me young again. We were the In Crowd. We* were *the scene.* Singer's gone fat and balding, hasnt done fuck-all since the band fell apart. Everybody treats him like he's still actually got something worth payin to see, when in fact in the back of their mushy heads they all knows he's now just a front man for their own failed and miserable lives. And they're bitter, and the bitterness comes through, no matter how much age-defying makeup they cakes on to try and hide it. I knows that scene. I been fucked outta the Crossroads more often than I can remember. Well, to be truthful, I dont remember much of any of it.

As I'm pushin through the crowd to get down to Water Street, there's a vaguely identifiable Gene Simmons on his way outta the club. He's got a can in his hand and he takes a slug. A bouncer grabs the can and tries to pull it away from him. Mean Gene holds on to the beer.

—Hey? What the fuck man?

—Bring beer into my club?

The bouncer gives the can a twist and yanks it outta Gene's hand. Warm beer squirts across my face, in my eyes. I'm blinded. Someone slams into me from behind, the Elephant Man. I tries to catch me balance with me bad foot but it wont offer no support. I goes down. Gene Simmons tumbles on top of me. Someone bends down and snatches the joint outta me mouth. Ron Jeremy. He laughs. It's all numb. I'm jelly. Gene jumps up again and makes a run at the bouncer. Bad move. He'll be dragged out behind and pounded by three or four of 'em and it'll never, ever go anywhere in court. Halloween night. Drunk and up against a pack of sober bouncers who're so tight they prob'ly had a circle jerk in the backroom together before the bar opened. Good luck Gene.

I tries to roll further down the steps to get clear of the crowd and keep from gettin trampled, but someone's standin on the sleeve of me jacket. I pulls and hears the threads let go a bit. I looks up. Dracula, one of 'em. A big one. He's lookin down at me, cold and bloodthirsty. Joey Smallwood and the Clown hovering beyond his shoulder. I'm down. I'm fucked. They'll kick ten shades of shit outta me before I can make it to me feet. I pulls again and this time the sleeve rips free and I rolls down the slop-stained concrete steps, crackin me head hard on the sidewalk at the bottom. Dracula jumps the steps and I can see him in the air, his huge black cape filling the night behind him. He's aiming for my throat. I rolls backwards and flips over onto me feet. He lands where I was lying. He starts for me and stops. He's lookin at me hand. He backs away. I looks at me hand. Me brand-spankin-new knife is in it, gleamin beneath the streetlight. Dracula turns and scoots back up over the steps.

I slips the knife back into the case, brushes off me pants and coat, then heads up Water Street, lighter than I've felt in years. Crazy Clara is sittin outside the Rose. She makes to stand up when she sees me. I offers her me hand and she pulls herself to her feet. Big gummy smile, her teeth ground down to the nerves. She sorta rocks back and forth on her heels, pulls away and tilts way back like she's fillin her lungs for what she got to say:

—Hello there Mr. Reid. Would you like a cigarette?

Poor old girl. I takes the cigarette she offers and flips her a loonie, the only one I've got. She misses it and it rolls under the table. I shuffles on up the street while she scrambles for it. God love 'er, someone said she useta be a teacher or a nurse or some such thing. Now she just wanders the streets.

Val is playin at the Ship. I can just hear him when I'm passin by the Hatchet.

> *I can still taste the gutter in the back of my throat*
> *And some days it hurts me to swallow.*

I saw him earlier at home, tryin on an old Elvis suit in the mirror, swingin his hips and pointin, curlin his lip. He does an Elvis set every year at Halloween, although I've never seen it. Must be finished with it by now though, gone over to his own tunes.

Some days I'm so full I might bust at the seams
Some days are so empty and hollow.

Fuck man, I minds the first time I got ahold of one of his albums when I was in high school. I was right into the Skid Row and Metallica and that sorta stuff back then and granted Val's music wasnt as heavy, but, I dont know. It was wicked. To think that here's my old man's brother, my uncle, pumpin out these crunchy tunes and actually makin a name for hisself. It made shit seem a bit more doable for me back then, in that boring little dead-end harbour. I needed to get outta there some bad, by fuck.

There's a sun up, a sun down, a great chance to skip town
I cant lead the way, you wont follow
There's a blast and a handshake, a backstab for an old face
Who might drop by sometime tomorrow.

Some of his stuff is a bit vague, like he's after just slappin the lyrics in without givin it much thought. But like with any music that you likes, you can always find ways to personalize Val's stuff. He's up on bust tonight, the door handle of the Ship vibrating in me hand. I checks me pocket and finds a ten-dollar bill. That's enough for a few beer. I got Donna's smokes here too, made sure of that before I left the Darkroom. Cover charge at the Ship, but not for me. Val said he'd leave me name on the door. The entrance is blocked with all sorts of ghouls and cowboys. Strawberry Shortcake, a dead zombie bride and one fella dressed like a toilet. I dont fuckin get it. He had to've put some fuckin hours' work into that, and in the end what's he sayin exactly? Shit here. Shit on me. I hope he wins something for it though, all the same. I slides past the crowd and gives a quick nod to the little chicky-chick on the door. I hafta get right up in her face and shout over the blare of the music.

—Clayton Reid! Val said he'd write me in!

114

To say get up off of that cold hard floor
And put it all back to the way it was before . . .

Loves that chorus I do. The whole bar is singing along. Chicky-
chick does a little scan of her book. I sees that Monica is first on
the list, but when I passed the Hatchet just now I seen her dartin
up the alley towards Keith's, her face painted bone white. Make up
your fuckin mind missus. Her and Val are wearing pretty thin now
anyhow, not that they seemed all that thick in the first place. Thick
enough for him to give away me table though, cunty-balled old
whoremaster. I heard him talkin on the phone to Massie the other
night, Aunt Massie. He was screamin first, about some phone bill
she's got, but after a while he went right quiet and he might even
have been chokin up a bit. That's fucked, that whole situation. Me
with Monica when she was with Keith and now she's with Val, me
uncle, while she's still with Keith. And Val on the phone every other
day with Massie, half the time gettin back together and half the time
settin out to kill her. I s'pose I should go to Corner Brook and fuck
Massie meself, just to balance it all out. I needs a good road trip.

The young one on the door is wearin that fuckin dandy hippie oil,
what's it called? Petunia? Patchouli? I gets right off on that. I could
love her, if she always smelled like that. I hovers around her neck
while she flips the page on her clipboard. She shakes her head and
chews her lip and flips open the cashbox.

—Sorry, he said no one gets in who's not on the list. It's six
dollars.

And I'm about to say, he's me uncle, I lives with him, but I dont
go in for that name-droppin shit, like I said. I feels the ten-dollar bill
in me pants pocket, crispy and new, right outta some bank. S'pose
I shoulda come in through the back door, like I normally would.
Some Hugh Hefner type is next in line. He's got two wicked young
ones in bunny ears hangin off each arm. He holds out a twenty
and when Miss Petunia takes the bill I backs into the sweaty, manic

115

crowd towards the bar. She sees what I'm up to but she doesnt make a move towards me.

Leave it alone, you'll only make it sore . . .

It's not worth her while to come after me cause *everybody'd* just walk in then. The crowd swallows me up while I pushes and elbows me way to the bar. I'm dyin with the thirst.

And there's not much left if you'd like a little more.

Val's on his own tonight. He makes more money that way, where he aint gotta pay no other musicians. But still, you hafta hear him with a full band, drums and bass and another guitar. Piano sometimes. That's his sound. That's what his songs call for. But he always goes it alone towards the end of the month, when the rent is due. You'd think by now he'd own his own house somewhere, with all the money he's after generating over the years. But no. Rent and sublet and fuckin squat, that's his way. Dribs and drabs, feast and famine, that's how he lives. I mean, he was on his way for a while, but he fucked it up. I cant say for sure how, just I knows something went down at some awards show one year and some stupid reporter got the story wrong on purpose. At least that's what I've heard. Val dont talk about it.

By the time I gets a good spot at the bar his set is ending. He says good night and thanks for comin out. Someone shouts:

—"Gun Shy!" "Gun Shy!"

One of his earlier songs. His old record label is s'pose to be releasing a greatest-hits album sometime next month. About time too. I tries to catch his eye before he slips into the backroom. He sees me but he dont nod or smile or make any motion towards me atall. Fucker. He's like that when he's out in public. Home too. Everybody starts bangin their glasses and ashtrays and cheerin and shoutin for an encore but I can tell by the way Val's luggin himself to the backroom that he's all-in for the night. He never does an encore no more.

I reaches the bar then, and I can feel me life shiftin, changin, me whole approach turnin inside out and upside down. For good. Or bad. I dont give a fuck. I wants what I sees more than anything I've wanted for as long as I can remember. And this is not some passing infatuation sorta wow-I'd-love-to-fuck-*her* kinda situation. This is the *real* fuckin thing. There she is again. The one who was with Robert Dawe that night, at his release party. The One. Behind the bar, working. Fuckin drop dead gorgeous. Just like I remembered her. Full lips and messy black hair, about my height, maybe a little shorter. Maybe my age, maybe a little older. She fuckin floats. High leather boots and skin-tight black pants that only comes down a little past her knees. She pulls a pint and shakes her head at some arsehole when he lays his hand on hers. She's above the whole racket. She pouts and bounces to the cash register.

She's mine.

I wants her.

She's the One.

14. Encore

Young Clayton hey? Some gall he have. Wants to be on the guest list? Fuck. Cause I really *gives* a shit if he gets in to see me play or not. Two-faced little snot. Thinks this town got no ears, no eyes . . .

Remember that night in Winnipeg? What was that place called?

Fifteen years ago that was. Couldnt beat the women away. Massie, gorgeous. Crowd like that wouldnt stand for this either. They'd drag me back out to the mic.

Listen to 'em out there . . .

This lot? They dont want no encore. Just a courtesy now isnt it.

Well then return the courtesy.

That Isabelle, or fuckin Isadore, there behind the bar, she'll slap on some CD and it'll be like I was never here tonight at all.

Good show tonight Val. Good sound.

Yeah, get the sound guy to do an encore then. I'm just filler, some kinda freak show, relic . . .

Shut it. Listen to 'em out there. You were on fire out there. Packed the place, made the rent. Give 'em one more. "Gun Shy." Give—

Give, yeah. What for? I made the rent, two solid hours. That's it. The night is done and they all know it. Broke a string anyhow.

They're not going to keep it up all night Reid. You know all this, so easy.

Different with no band though. Different with this getup on. Just a buffoon, some kinda clown old enough to be their—

Fizzling out. You're losing them. Make your move.

See how I feel after this now. Get the blood pumping again.

C'mon Reid, you dont need—

Slay 'em all then, big head full of Walter's gear, stay on for another hour . . .

I think we lost 'em Val . . .

Maybe we did. May-be.

15. Still the One

I stands starin at her until she sees me. She smiles from ear to ear like she was expecting me all along. In one movement she lunges from the cooler to the edge of the bar where I'm standin. She lays her two hands flat on the bar as if to say, anything you want, it's yours. Her breasts.

Some precious dyke in a long black coat standin next to me shouts:

—Hey? I've been standing here for twenty minutes!

But my new flame doesnt even look her way. She keeps starin at me. She's lookin at me. And for the first time in a long time I dont know who or what I am. Because she's all there is and I knows I'd give over to her in a flash. I'd let her break me and reshape me any way she sees fit. I would. She keeps starin, her bright grey eyes.

I'm fuckin well in love.

—What'll it be?

—Ah . . .

And I catches meself then, tryna figure what's the best thing to order to give her a good impression. But that's not me. I just wants to be meself.

—Pint. Guinness. Please.

—Water?

—No, Guinness.

—Last call for alcohol! Last call!

She shouts this across the bar and people groan and you can see 'em flatten their drinks so's they might get another one in before the night is up.

Every move she makes causes me an awful distress. The pulsing flex of her calf when she reaches for a glass on the top shelf. Her shirt rises over the waistline of her pants, the flash of her belly with the fading hint of a late-summer tan. She whirls around on her heels and bats the tap down playfully with the palm of her hand. She fills the glass halfway and looks over at me, not smilin, her cheek restin on her shoulder and her hips keepin time to the stereo. Paul Simon. This song burned into me head for the rest of time. She resets the tap when the pint is three-quarters full, to let it settle. And she turns away then, while it's settling, the head slowly swellin and the under-belly blackening, as it does. But she's turned away, plucked a twenty from an outstretched hand, leanin in, ear first, to better decipher the drunken patter from yet another slippery, gap-toothed mouth that wants, wants, wants. Always. And who doesnt? I cant stand it. I hates her. I just wants her here, serving me. Now. Look at me. Ask me. Tell me. Me. Everything. Anything. She delivers a drink and divvies out the change. Her small hands. On me.

I feels a dull pull in me foot and when I looks down at it the floor is further away than it should be. My legs are longer. And then I remembers the pill. Fuck. No. No. It's more than that. I'm open to it. I'm open to the possibility of disappearing. With her. In her. Living. With her. Fixin breakfast and runnin the bath. She sees me there then, remembers me pint and pulls the last quarter from the keg. When the glass is full she brings the head up to touch the mouth of the tap and makes a quick little movement. She carries it over to me, not smilin, just *looking,* with gleaming grey eyes. Right. At. Me.

—You sure you can handle this? You're looking kind of pale. I can get you a water?

I dont have any idea how to respond to that, seems like months now that everybody's been linin up to pour it down me throat whether I wanted it or not. Donna, how she has more fun when I drinks with her. Val with his lines and hot whiskey.

I starts diggin through me pockets for the ten bucks but she's off to the other end of the bar already. I glances at the creamy head of me pint and sees that she's after drawing a little heart in it with the mouth of the tap. That's what she was at. I dont know what it means, me brain is temporarily scrambled with lust and love and the results of that pill. Maybe that I owes her a drink, that I'm to take her up on it, later on, wait till she's gettin off. And then we'll all get off. No. No. I dont wanna think about this one like that. I'll do this right. Have something real.

I turns to have a look at the crowd. The motion of turnin, with me elbows tucked into me chest because of the crowd, and the old weakness in me foot, puts me right off balance for a second and I stumbles forward. The top part of me pint, the froth, me favourite part, the heart, her heart, slops into this big fella's hood. He dont feel it soak into his back though and I takes the opportunity to get clear of him before he does feel it.

There's someone up on stage now, tellin everybody to gather round while the judges decides who's got the best costume. Four of 'em. The Toilet Man, Hugh Hefner (minus his love bunnies), Death, of course, and Strawberry Shortcake. They're to be judged based on audience response, the loudest applause. Hugh Hefner takes a step forward and bows. There's a half-hearted reaction from the crowd, a courtesy. Strawberry Shortcake receives about the same, except for a patch of young ones in the far corner, who're obviously her friends, that're goin nuts. Too obvious. Toilet Man is next. He gets the biggest applause so far. Then Death steps forward, bows, and the place goes up. I dont get it. It's likely the third or fourth Death or Grim Reaper I've seen tonight, but the crowd is goin mental. They starts chantin:

—Death Death Death Death Death Death . . .

Death's arms raised high in the air, victorious. The host hands Death a dozen Dominion Ale and a gift certificate for a free lunch at . . . the Ship! How considerate. The crowd starts to recede. As Death is steppin down from the stage he removes his hood, and it's Monica for fuck sakes. I was wonderin what she was up to with her face painted earlier. Pretty slick. Cause you'd never stop to think of it that way. You just automatically assume Death to be male, like God is.

The crowd starts to shift towards the exits. I'm after gettin way too fuckin hot now and tries to shove me way to the back door. Feels heavy all of a sudden. That little teddy bear doin backflips in me gut. Might get sick yet. She did say I looked pale. The crowd is even thicker where it's tryna clear out and at its worst towards the back, so I makes a go for the bathroom instead. Men's bathroom got a lineup. Fuck sakes, am I trapped in the Ship with no place to vomit when I needs to? What if there was some kinda crisis? I pushes me way into the women's and barely gets the stall door open in time before it all comes up outta me guts. Pina colada. Never fuckin fails. Girlie drinks are for the morning, when you needs the added vitamin C and sugar, no good to go mixing it around with the beer. I had a half case sure before I left the house this evening. Some black-clad yuppie missus at the sink screws up her face in disgust at me in the mirror. I tries to tell her to fuck off but all I can get out is the *f* part.

Cant catch me breath, a chunk of pineapple lodged in me throat. I tries to wash it down with me pint but cant take in more than a mouthful, barely get a drop past me teeth before I'm heavin again. I shoulda opted for water shouldnt I? The pineapple stays where it's to. Must be the tablet, the little blue teddy bear, reachin back up and chokin me with his furry little evil blue paw. I'm really startin to choke to death here. I turns around to see if the yuppie at the sink is still there to help me, but she's gone. There's me in the mirror with me face turnin blue, same colour as the pill that's chokin me. Pineapple, yes. But the pill is what got it lodged there. The little blue teddy bear dippin his paw into the sick mix in me guts, finds the perfect size hunk of pineapple and jams it into me windpipe. Drugs kill. I rams me back off the bathroom stall in an archaic attempt to dislodge it, some idiotic trick I learned on the playground growin up that's since been fanatically dispelled as a valid lifesaving method by that fuckin Heimlich crowd. All this flashes through me head as I beats me back off the door. That pain, that sinkin dark weakness in the stomach, the limits of me vision blackening from the edges inward, pinpoints of light before me, all that's left. And a lightness, a dangerous weightlessness. Then panic. Not me own, but the presence of someone else's fear. A thump in the midsection and then *air*, the precious, life-affirming, piss-ridden, fishy air of the women's toilets at the Ship, rushes to me head, me knees. And I'm back. Like it never happened. Well no. The moment bein so close and all that the panic takes a few seconds to rear its head. Where it never got the chance to in the first place, now it all hits me the once. I turns to see who helped me out. Monica, beautiful deathly Monica. Saved me. She's got tears runnin down her cheeks, streakin black rivers over the bright white death mask. She musta gotten a fright, the poor thing. *Real* death, right there. I opens me arms and collapses into the spongy bust of her robe, buries me face in her firm chest and breathes deep the smell of the musty, smoky fabric. She pushes me away and holds me by the shoulders at arm's length.

—Clayton? Clayton are you h'alright? I 'ave to tell you something.

A faint whiff of cheap house wine on her breath. I stumbles forward again and she latches her arms around me waist to hold me steady. Heart poundin, me chest hot and tight. She pushes me back against the wall and I can feel me stomach revolt again, me head too heavy for me neck muscles to hold.

—Clayton fuckin snap h'out of it! It's Val. Someone told 'im . . .

Me knees gives out and I'm heavier than I've ever known meself to be. I starts to slide down the wall to the floor, Monica's voice a muddy echo.

—Clayton did you 'ear me? Val says 'e's gonna kill you . . .

She tries to pull me to me feet, I latches me hands around her hips and me head falls forward till I'm face and eyes into the stuffy midsection of her death robe. Behind me there's the door, someone tryna shove their way in. Me heel jammed against the bottom of the door. I muffles deep into the heat of Monica's crotch:

—Val? Fuck would he wanna kill me for?

—Can you please stand up?

Monica's head falls back against the wall, her two hands restin on me shoulders, and she lets out a big deathly sigh. Then the door busts in. There's a quick flash of a black wig and the telltale trace of Donna's mall-bought perfume. She goes:

—You bastard!

The colossal, leaden slab of antique cedar that makes up the door of the women's washroom at the Ship hits me square in the forehead. Hard. Harder than I was ready for. I mean, I can ram me head off a wall or the floor or the pavement all night, as long as I'm the one doin the rammin. Dont bother me in the least then, but catch me off guard like that and I'm just as fucked as the next fella. Down I goes. Not out though. Never out. The blow actually brings me around a bit. I slumps against the wall in the corner and slides down to the floor, maybe more outta melodrama than the result of the impact. It just feels like the way it should happen. Monica brings her hands to her face, but not quick enough. Donna gets the first one in, a clever, vicious jab to the bridge of Monica's nose. Hit first and hit fuckin hard I s'pose, no matter whose side you're on. No blood, thank fuck. Monica screams all the same, a throaty full-speed-ahead death howl. I tries to pull meself to me feet but Donna intercepts me attempt with the heel of her sharp black Morticia kickers. She catches me in the chest and I can feel the hard wood heel rippin into the flesh. She puts all her weight on me then and shoves me to the floor. Part of me is lovin it. The other part wishes she was a fella, so's I could have a crack at her. Cant stand the cocky mask of power and control she's suddenly become. I wants Monica to strike her down. She should be able to. But that's the way women are: you expects they can hold their own in a scrap just because they talks rough and got the hard look, maybe the wide shoulders, but more often than not the little scrawny ones are just as savage. Sure enough though, when Madame Death catches her balance she manages to get her hands in under Donna's wig and latched into her real hair. She yanks Donna forward and what's Donna do if not bite down on Monica's chest. Donna's growlin through clenched teeth:

—Stay the fuck away from him. Hear me? Stay away. He's mine!

I scrambles out between their legs and crawls to the other side of the bathroom. There's me pint, on the sink where I left it when I was chokin. I pulls meself to me feet and has a glance in the mirror, the two ladies, Morticia and Death, with their hands around each other's throats. There's a lump on me head, a white streak of makeup smeared across me neck. I pulls up me shirt to have a look at me chest, a bright hickey-red scrape about four inches long. Madame Death hisses in Morticia's face:

—I was savin 'is goddamn life! I dont h'even *like* 'im.

I slips outta the bathroom and while the door is swingin closed behind me I sees the rage in Donna's eyes blaze to full again as she launches another series of jabs at Monica. I knows I should stay and do something, but I cant.

The club is after clearin out nearly altogether. I turns to this one skinny little queen who's grindin his hips off the centre beam of the club. Someone's after paintin an underwater scene onto the beam and this little queen is lickin at a mermaid's crude, one-dimensional tits. Fuck.

I glances at the clock on the wall. It's past three o'clock already. Where did the fuckin night go? I staggers over to bar and there's the manager behind it, puttin dishes into the dishwasher. He sees me comin.

—Last call is gone. Bar's closed.

But I didnt want booze. I wanted . . . I want . . . *her*. I dont even know her name.

—Where's the girl gone?

—What girl?

—The bartender? Is she still here?

—Gone. Might catch her if you hurries out though.

And I knows he's just sayin it so's I'll leave the bar, but I dont give a fuck. I hop-walks to the front door with me pint tucked into the crook of me arm. Just as I'm reachin the door I hears Donna screechin after me to wait, come back. I turns on her:

—Take one step more you crazy fucker and I'll flatten you. I should too.

She thinks I means it. Maybe I do? No. But there's no need of what she just went and done. She puts her hands over her face and starts sobbin. Her wig drops to the floor. Her knees buckles and she flops into a chair. She coulda left Monica for dead in the bathroom. Doubt it very much though. Donna looks like she got the worst of it actually, a scratch on her cheek and a glisten of blood on her bottom lip. My heart goes out to her for a second, and Monica. Fuckin mental night that has nothing to do with me no more.

I darts out through the front door, looks down towards Water Street. Nothing. I takes the steps up to Duckworth. And there she is, waitin against the building with a bag of beer. I tries not to limp as I'm walkin towards her. Feels like I've come a long, long ways, a lifetime, to see her and she's been waitin here forever, waitin for me. She smiles in this dangerous, sulky little-girl way. I reaches her just as her cab pulls up to the sidewalk. She takes a step back when I comes under the streetlight. I tries to touch her face but she pulls it away and takes me by the wrist. I leans in to kiss her. She looks up and down the street like she's seein if anyone is lookin, but I couldnt give a fuck if the whole goddamn world was watchin us on a wide-screen TV. I wants her worse than I've ever wanted anything in me whole miserable life. The cabbie blows the horn. She gives me a sizin-up. I'm terrified in that moment, when she's lookin me up and down like that, that she'll see the ugliness, that dark shit. I wears it on me fuckin sleeve most of the time, but I dont want her to see it now. I wants her to see someone who wants her like I do.

I leans in to kiss her again. She pulls away from me. She opens the door and holds it open for me.

—I guess you're coming with me then?

So fuckin saucy like that. I climbs inside and she slides in beside me. Before she shuts the door I hears Donna shout me name. We both looks back through the rear windshield to see her runnin up the sidewalk towards the cab in her black stocking feet. This new one beside me, she goes:

—Is that your name then? Clayton?

—Yes. What's . . . what's yours?

—Isadora. You can call me Izzy though.

Holy sweet fuck. What a name. Imagine shoutin that name from the bottom of the stairs. And like fuck I'll call her fuckin *Izzy*. Isadora? How can I squander a name like that? Fuck, that's like something outta some fantasy book, the name of some goddess or princess or something. I tells her this, that her name is gorgeous. She smiles shy, says how she's named after some dancer from New York. I'm just watchin her lips move. Then she says how *my* name is nice too. And the way she says it makes me believe that maybe it *is* a nice name. Growin up I always found it to be a lippy and sharp name, right common too, cause where there's more than one Clayton on the Shore. I says thanks. And I says *her* name, kinda under me breath, cause I cant help it. And with that she finally leans in to kiss me. And it's one of those kisses too, the ones that fit. Like Donna's lips were always so tight and thin and just, well didnt suit mine. And some women's lips are nice and full and you thinks they'll make a great kiss but they turns out to be right soft, like there's no meat to 'em atall. But this one, Isadora, her lips, that's where she carries her heart, her soul, that's where all the sex is. Her lips have been waitin for mine for all time. She slides her tongue into me mouth. Here's something *real* now. A beginning. Not the quick, go-nowhere kinda downtown stolen-moment tongue that means we'll never work, we're just here now cause we're lonesome and intrigued and it's just too late to start lookin elsewhere. But *this* tongue, Isadora's tongue, flicks and probes and teases and dances and says: *Let's begin again.* And that's what she makes me want, a clean slate, a new look, a new life altogether. I slides me hand up under her top and she catches me by the wrist, pulls it away. She laughs and goes:

—Okay mister. Slow down.

And yes, that's perfect. That's exactly right. That's precisely what I needs to do. Slow down. Take it easy. Relax. Live for a while. Slow down. With her. Isadora.

There's a nice, warm glow in me belly now. That little blue teddy bear is finally after givin over, curlin up and snugglin in for the night.

As we're roundin the turn onto Prescott I has a last glance out the back window to see the shrinkin form of a now blond Morticia, still runnin to catch the cab. I pats the new knife in the leather case on me belt.

I s'pose I should feel bad.

16. My Heart Beats Kelly's

Well if I havent got the flu yet, I'll have it soon enough. The states I gets meself in. Not fit. And here's me, s'pose to be calmin down. There's Water Street. Only I cant figure out the angle, not quite familiar with this standpoint. Froze solid I am. Cant feel me feet atall. Maybe I'm dead. Maybe I died in me sleep. Cant move, there's about a ten-foot drop to the parking lot beneath me. Maybe this is Hell, clingin to a ledge with nowhere to go but down. Forever. A graffiti message on the far wall in the parking lot beneath me:

My heart beats Kelly with blood as red as the envy of every other man.

Wonder how he got up so high? Had to've used a ladder. Some fuckin obsessed, spurned psychopath I'd say. Or maybe just some guy in love. Or some dyke. Dykes can love too, apparently.

There's the steps leading down from the Ship. Flash. Some dainty, intellectual university type in a long black coat poking her wrinkled finger into me chest, askin me about her purse. Yeah, maybe my survival tactics *are* a bit different. I couldnt even talk. Me grandfather's blanket slung over the back of a chair. I hauled it around me shoulders when I was leaving. I have it now. Prob'ly what saved me. Heavy, down-filled army blanket. I swiped it outta Val's the night he gave me the boot. Fuck, was that last night?

• • •

Me and Val and Izzy, sittin around the kitchen doin lines. He had shitloads, maybe an ounce. He just got a royalty cheque the other day. I heard him on the phone with his landlord. He was months behind on the rent.

We started the evening off alright. Red wine though, goes right to me head every time. And just the smell of it goes to Isadora's. Toss in a few lines of blow, for power, with the Stones on in the background, sure you knows there's gonna be a racket.

Val was well under way by the time we showed up. Him and Iz knows each other from that movie back in September and he went on and on with her about it, these snide little inside jokes that had her scarlet-faced and half shy. And I'll admit, it kinda got to me. Cant have nothing new around these parts. Val was gettin on a bit too familiar with her for my taste. I almost asked her last week if anything had gone on between them before *I* hooked up with her, but I didnt really wanna hear it. I wouldnta been able to do nothing about it. I knows she'd only all too willingly have told me the truth. She's into that truth business. Lucky me. Last fella she was with fucked her around so much she made a pact with herself that everything was gonna be straight up from there on in, that *life is too short and hearts are too fragile to be burdened down with deceit and lies.* Nice and poetic of her I s'pose, but there went me strategy altogether.

Val whipped out his guitar of course, soon as she got talkin about *me*. He couldnt take that. Had to command the spotlight somehow, in the best way he knows how. Started singin some new sappy folk-type song he's been writin, obviously a direct response to his estrangement from Massie. But he was singin it straight at Isadora see, that's what pissed me off. He never looked at me. And it wasnt one of those situations where he'd go: *Hey, I got this new song I'm working on, tell me what you think.* But more like: *Hey Izzy, I was thinking about* you *today and I wrote this song for* you. Repulsive it was. She was tryna smile, tryna be polite about it while he let his eyes roam all over her tits and neck. Lecherous. When he stopped I said:

—Hope you're not plannin on recording that.

But I said it with a grin, a bit of fun, just to break the tension. He didnt take it that way though, he didnt want to. He swung the guitar across the table and pushed it into me arms. He knows I dont play.

—Let's see what young Clayton's got then. The great hope for the Reid clan.

He winked at Isadora. I wanted so fuckin bad to be able to play at that moment, just let fly with some song, even one of Val's old songs, do it better than he ever did it. Or something absolutely mind-blowing and profound that I'd tucked away in me head somewhere. Just for that one moment in time. I mean, I coulda *sang* anything atall, just when there's a guitar there, I'm useless. And for all Iz knew, I was well able to play. So she just sat there waitin, expecting some sorta battle-of-the-family-songsters shit. I picked at some stupid little riff I've known since I was in high school and then just had to put the guitar down. Val picked it up again and shoved it back in me hands.

—I cant . . .

—Sure you can. What's to it? A monkey could do it.

—I dont know nothing.

—Thought you had a band?

—Not no more.

—Well play the one about how you fucked Monica at the General's Inn that time.

Fuck, I figured he knew. I knew what Monica was tryna tell me that night in the women's toilet at the Ship. I just didnt think he'd give a fuck. How could he let it get to him? Sure he didnt even know her then, and she's gone from him now anyhow. What difference does it make?

—What difference does that make?

—None whatsoever, only it goes to show what a little devious prick you are.

He took a big slug straight out of the bottle of red wine then. Izzy just sittin there, pullin at her nose, wondering what the fuck was goin on. I never warned her about this side of Val. I always forgets. Wine dribbled down his chin while he scraped a big line of coke towards himself with his SOCAN membership card.

—Come on now *Randy*.

He didnt like that. He jumped up from the table, hauled off and belted me across the jaw. I wasnt expecting it, so of course me chair went out from under me and I went down in a heap in the corner, struck me head off the radiator. Gave the whole scene that much more drama, made the punch seem way more effective than it actually was. Then he was standin over me and Izzy was tryna hold his arms behind his back. I could tell he was *lettin* her hold him back though.

—I'm not your fucking father! Get that through your thick skull!

I coulda jumped up and had a go at him. His punch was so feeble, no real threat behind it atall. I coulda pounded the shit out of him, knocked him all around the kitchen. But I didnt want to. That's always the way with me for some odd reason. Always with the rackets when I'm fucked right up and never when I'm sober. When I'm sober I'd be delighted to have a dust-up with anyone atall, especially the famous Valentine Reid. Something always stops me when I'm drunk though. And that barely makes sense, I know, cause it's s'pose to be the other way around.

I kicked the chair away and stood up. I wish I coulda laughed at him, laughed it off and made him feel like the puny old fart that he is. But of course me eyes were full by the time I had me jacket on.

—Oh he's gonna cry now is he? For fuck sakes.

I grabbed Iz by the arm and pulled her out to the head of the stairs. She had a last glance back at the mound of coke on the table. Val was already back in his seat choppin up another monstrous line. I shoulda dove at it, stuck me whole face down into it like Pacino in *Scarface* and sucked and inhaled till me heart exploded. Fine way to end the evening. I grabbed me grandfather's blanket then, it was hangin on the rail of the stairs. Val digs it out for his worst hangovers, so technically it's always lyin around somewhere. He'd have me head if he knew I had it now.

That was last night, hey? Jesus.

Of course Izzy had to go turn on me then. That's the way with this town, it's like a domino effect, they all turns on you the one time, pounce when you're down, go straight for the weak spot. Next thing you finds yourself a lump of frozen snot dangling over a ledge in a snowbank behind the Ship.

. . .

I tries to pull meself up but the rear end of me pants is froze into the snow. I rocks meself back and forth with a sound that reminds me of Isadora, *my* Kelly, peelin the wax strips off her legs. One final tug and I busts free of it, but then of course me foot slips over the rim of the wall and the rest of me starts to slip along with it. I digs me fingers into the snow to stop meself from goin any further. I wonder how I got out here. How I never rolled over in me sleep. Funny how you can muster up the survival skills, know exactly where to set your feet down, even when you're technically unconscious. But why in the fuck would I come out here? I leans out as far as I can, to see down to the concrete beneath me. Ten, twelve feet down. A slight slant to the wall, barely there, maybe even accidental, an oversight in the design. But it looks to me that if I gets meself positioned proper, I could slide down it, instead of dealing with a straight drop. There's a snowdrift, three or four feet deep, tight to the wall at the bottom. If I lands in that? Maybe. Gotta be careful of me bad foot though. Meaning I needs to be twice as mindful of the good one. I tosses me grandfather's blanket down onto a bare patch of pavement in the parking lot. It lands with a dead flump, right on the mark. I moves both me legs over the edge so that I'm in a sitting position, digs me hands into the snow to give meself some good shovin power, leverage. Wouldnt wanna drag me spine along the edge of the concrete. All bad enough.

On three. One, two . . . three. Down. Fuck, not quite so much of a slant to the wall as I figured, but me heels stays flush to it on the way down. Me belt hooks in some concrete nipple pokin outta the wall before I hits the snowbank. I'd been tryna keep me bad foot tucked in a bit, so that the good one might hit the ground first. But when me belt catches, even though it dont slow me down none, I loses me concentration and lands in the snowbank with all me weight on the bad foot. An intense jolt, like an electrical shock, from me heel to me hipbone. Me hands automatically clasp onto the bad leg and I falls forward, face first into the soft, loose snow. I'd forced all the air outta me lungs on the way down and now sucks in a half lungful of snow. Choke and smother, the pain in me foot, a burnin in me hip like it's been asleep and now wants desperately to come back to the wakin world. Someone's gigglin. I wipes the smouldering mess of snow outta my eyes and tries to see where the giggles are comin from. There, just outside the rail of the parking lot, Crazy Clara, well bundled up and shovin an empty shopping cart along the sidewalk, the wheels rendered inoperable, welded useless by the toxic roadside muck. She's not even lookin at me, but seems to be tryin hard not to laugh at some private thought. Poor old girl. Fucked up on medication I'd say. I wish *I* was. I pulls meself to me feet and bats the snow off me arms and legs, shakes it outta me hair. There's a bit of pain in me foot, but no worse than it's ever been. I picks up Grandfather's blanket and wraps it around meself like a cloak, walks off towards the Hatchet with me head held high.

Hope I wasnt in the Hatchet last night though. God knows what I got up to.

Dont look to be anyone around. There's a snowdrift up against the door. No idea what time it is. I ducks into the smaller alley near the shoe shop. The fire escape I had to climb to get away from Donna that time. I wont be climbing it this day though. She was waitin for me here, the day she found out about me and Izzy, that we were serious. I was just after leavin the Ship where Iz was doin a day shift. I was cracked. Donna'd been in all afternoon tormenting Iz with her lies about me, tellin her I was dysfunctional in the sack, that I was fucked up, that I'd only leave her when someone better came along. I dont know but Izzy liked all the scandal, for a bit. She said she just smiled and nodded at Donna and kept pourin up the drinks. But then, after Donna saw she wasnt makin no headway, and Iz told her to go fuck herself in that gentle, innocent little-girl's way she likes to make use of, Donna flew in over the bar and got hold of Izzy's collar and ripped it a bit. Iz hadda get some fellas to toss Donna out then. Donna hovered outside the front door, kickin and moanin and threatening to kill Iz soon as she set foot outside. Broad daylight. Izzy called me then.

—Get down here and control your retarded bitch ex!

—Who?

—Donna.

I hadnt left Isadora's bed for a week. Not that I was sick or nothing, mind. We'd just tucked ourselves away, hid from the world, closed the curtains and rented movies and drank beer in bed and fucked and talked and got to know each other, decided there was definitely something there worth lookin into. It's a wicked feeling, when you knows something real is in the works, when you starts to crave the taste of each other.

Big buzz at the Ship when I got there. Donna was after stirrin the place up. Everybody had a gawk at me. Robert Dawe was there, with his ponytail. He was back-on to me when I approached the bar, talkin to Iz, of course. She smiled at me over his shoulder and I distinctly heard him say:

—He's a little prick.

I slid up next to him.

—Who's a prick?

He turned away with his drink and took it down to a table, never even glanced in my direction. I'll have that old bastard one of these days. Isadora saw me starin at him and dismissed the situation with a wave of her hand. She leaned over the bar and let me kiss her. She didnt seem so upset as she was on the phone. She had a beer. I looked around for Donna.

—Where's she to?

—She left about ten minutes ago. She was outside pacing for a while.

—I'll take care of it.

—Yes. Please.

I knew Donna'd be down to the Hatchet. So long as Monica wasnt workin. I was passin by the alley near the shoe shop when I felt a hand clasp around the sleeve of me jacket. I hauled back with me left, thinkin it was some fucked-up rummy. It was her though. Her eyes all puffed up and red. No makeup on, her hair all greasy. Like as soon as she felt rejected she let herself go altogether. Funny that is, how they plays it right up, the *poor me* side of it. You'd think it'd be the other way around, that she'd get herself a new haircut and cake on the face paint and some new perfume or something. But no, because she cant take the real truth, that I just dont want her anymore, she gawks into the mirror and convinces herself that she's been rejected for cosmetic, ornamental reasons. So she can set me up, in her mind, to appear more shallow than I really am. What a load of shit.

—Clayton why? Why?

—Donna you cant bring this kinda shit into my life.

—What about my life? I'm entitled to an explanation. Is this about the dinner? I didnt leave it out on purpose, I was just—

—How many times have I told you Donna? How many? We were never a couple. We were never together.

—How can you say that?

—Look . . .

—Just tell me something, anything . . .

She dropped her head and sobbed, tried to fall into me arms. I caught her by the shoulders and pushed her upright, leant her against the wall of the alley. I couldnt feel. Couldnt.

—Donna, it's simple as this and nothing more: I wears silver and you wears gold.

—What?

—You heard me.

—But what does that mean?

—I dont really know. It means we're from different worlds.

That grim vacancy in her eyes, desolate, and above all desperate to make *me* feel anything atall, anger or paranoia, she didnt care. Did it faze old Clayton? No.

—I've heard a thing or two about this Isadora one you know. Dont get your fucking hopes up. She gets around.

—You knows nothing about her. Dont even go up there no more, drivin her cracked while she's tryna work. And dont show your face at Val's either. That's still my home. I knows you've been up there all week bawlin your eyes out.

—Clayton please . . . Do you love her?

—Donna fuck off and leave me alone.

—I cant go anywhere now!

I left her then. Shriekin her lungs out in the alley. I knows I was harsh but what was I supposed to do? She'll hafta find some way through it on her own. Cant very well turn to the one who's turned you away in the hopes they'll get you through the pain. It dont work like that. It's a strange position to be in though, knowin that I could sweep all her misery away with the most minuscule display of tenderness. All she wanted was the one seed of hope. All I had to do was say *maybe* or *we'll see what happens* or let on that I was feelin confused. But that'd only prolong her torture. I've been there. When I was seventeen I fell to my knees and wrapped my arms around Krista Bradley's legs and howled and begged until she said yes, that maybe we'd work it out. That was worse on me in the long run, of course. I got a letter from her about a week later, tellin me not to come around her apartment no more, wishin me all the best. I thumbed back out to Town and pounded on her door only to be greeted by some big dumb ape she was after hookin up with in the university. What a fuckin row that was, her there screechin in the porch while he dangled me out over the doorstep looking to her for permission to toss me onto the street. And all I really wanted was to have her back long enough so's *I* could be the one to reject *her*. Sick bunch aint we? Humans.

· · ·

I pulls Grandfather's blanket tighter around meself and trudges through the slop towards the other end of Water Street. It's bitter cold and the snow's pickin up. I wish I was the type to wear a goddamn warm hat. Too cool I am. The paddy wagon slows to a crawl as it passes me. They're watchin how I'm walkin, thinkin it's a drunken stagger instead of a limp. Fuckers. No witnesses this hour in the morning. They're dyin for a bit of action. I drops me head down and soldiers on. There's a drink out there somewhere, but more important is where the fuck I'm gonna drink it to. Gotta get warm. Fagan's Pub might be open. That's s'pose to be an early house. I've never been there so I dont know if they'll let me in. Passing by the Rose and Thistle I peeks in through the window. An old fella moppin up the floor. I taps on the glass. *Please*. He looks up and shakes his head, points at the clock in the corner. Jesus Christ it's only half past eight. If Fagan's dont let me in I'm fucked. Two more hours before the Hatchet opens sure. A fuckin seven-minute walk and I could be curled up with Isadora, cozy warm underneath her big down-filled sleeper. Fuck. Dont think I have the energy to talk me way in over her doorstep though. That's the worst thing I could do anyhow, show up weak and cold. She'd eat me alive. She's a hard ticket. This aint the first time she's after heavin me out, and fuck sure it's only been five or six weeks. First time was over a handful of change I swiped from her bedside table. She went lookin for it and I stupidly said I never saw it. I dont know why, just that she seemed to need it so badly all of a sudden. Five or six dollars. I used it towards a pack of smokes. Finally I says *Yes girl, I used it*.

—Oh God, Clayton you're not a thief are you?

—No.

—Well the lie turns the act into a theft.

139

She asked me to leave.

—What the fuck are ya on about girl?

—I just dont know if this is going to work out.

—What? It's only a bit of change.

—No it's not. It's more than that. I think . . . maybe your survival tactics are just too different from mine.

Whatever the fuck she meant by that. Prob'ly just another dig at me for not havin steady work. The high horse she gets on just cause she does a few shifts at the Ship and the scattered theatre thing. I took off then and waited a day or so till she called for me up to Val's and asked me back down. That's all you gotta do is wait 'em out. They'll eventually come around, they always do.

I walked out on her a couple of times too. We were just after havin a romp and after she caught her breath she has the gall to go say, in that distant little-girl's way she got, like we're just youngsters playin house, *I think maybe you're . . . two parts boy and . . . one part man.* We were after havin a conversation earlier about Robert Dawe and I was foolish enough to let her know that I felt a bit threatened by the fact that he's got money and his own thing on the go and that he's fifty years old and shit like that. Givin her the opportunity to reassure me, make me feel more at ease with her. And she just nodded and heard me out, never gave me fuck-all slack like she was s'pose to. Then we goes and has sex and I makes sure she gets off, like always, cause there's no fuckin way I'm stoppin till she does, and she rolls over and says *that* shit to me. *I think maybe you're two parts boy.* Like she'd been thinkin all along about the conversation and decided to withhold her response till we had a bit of sex. How the fuck was I s'pose to take it? That I had a youngster's cock? That I didnt know how to take her like a real man? Jesus Christ. I wasnt long jumpin into me jeans and headin off downtown. She hunted me down a couple of hours later. She was drunk and so was I and we had a big shoutin match out in the street in front of the Gropevine of all places, so's all her friends and the rest of town could watch. She flagged down a cab and we both jumped in, stopped off at

Needs and picked up a case of beer. Neither rhyme nor fuckin reason to us atall.

And then last night, last fuckin night, after we got back from Val's and she's boilin the kettle for hot brandy, she asks me what I'm gonna do. And I says:

—Fuck it, we'll be alright girl . . .

—Well I know *I'll* be alright, but what about you?

—What the fuck is that s'pose to mean?

—Well you cant live here.

—I never asked to.

—Well where will you go?

—I got places.

—Where?

—Do I hafta go right now?

—I think so.

—Where's this comin from girl?

—Just, I dont know. I dont want to be used. I'd rather if you had your own place or something. You dont even have a job . . .

And I took off again. She tried to hold me back but I pushed her away, the two of us chock full of coke and red wine.

And then . . . and then rootin through a purse at the Ship. I thinks on this just as Fagan's Pub is comin into sight. I'd forgotten all about money. I digs me hands into me jeans and finds a crumple of tens and fives and twenties. Seventy-five bucks, all told. Holy fuck. That'll come back on me, I knows full well. Some missus is pretty pissed off this morning. Somebody's mother. Somebody's wife. I mighta stuffed her purse into the back of the toilet at the Ship. I aint sure. It's all so muddy. I searches the rest of me for any sign of who the woman mighta been, maybe a credit card. I knows I'd be stunned enough to pocket a credit card. But no, there's nothing else. Just this little chunk of cash. Jesus, I s'pose I could get a hotel room somewhere outta this. Twenty-four hours lazing around in a clean bed watchin TV and wackin off, takin baths, not a soul to bother me. Maybe go out into the city and pick up some young one and bring her back to the room. Or give Miss Isadora a call and get *her* over to the hotel for the night. Fuck 'er till she's on the brink and then give 'er the boot, the old heave-ho. That'll fuckin show 'er. No. No mean stuff. Besides, unless I wanders into a hotel in the next five seconds I knows I'll never hang on to the price of a room. Seventy-five bucks wont last me the morning. I'm gonna hafta eat at some point too.

Dusty black curtain in the front window of Fagan's. I cant see in. There's music though. AM radio. I walks up the steps and pounds on the bulky steel door. An old woman's face appears behind the little curtain. She looks me up and down. I'd meant to hide the blanket but with the cold and the headache I completely forgot, so you can imagine what she sees. She shakes her head and lets the curtain fall back in place. I gets outta the blanket and drapes it over me arm and straightens out me coat. That's the best thing about suit-coats like this, you can manage to look ragged and rough and respectable all at the same time. I pulls the wad of crumpled bills outta me pocket and bangs on the door again. The old woman comes back. I holds up the money. She looks up and down the street again, then back at me. Finally she pulls the latch and the door creaks open.

—No bullshit now.

—No miss.

That's what comes to mind, to call her *miss,* because she reminds me of a teacher I had in primary school who crucified me for bein left-handed. Red, sweaty, heavy face and distant blue eyes, shirt tucked into her skirt so's her tits dont fall out.

The heat hits me and I feels sick, my body threatening convulsions, my skin tinglin all over. I puts me hand against the wall to steady meself while me blood warms up. If I falls down now I'll never get a drink. A bare bulb burnin in the centre of the room and it takes a few seconds for me eyes to adjust to the dark. A group of five old men sittin around a woodstove in the corner. Dented and stained aluminum pot on the stove and one of 'em stands above it with a blackened ladle and gives the contents a stir. Smells like cabbage, salt beef too. Me stomach rumbles. I stands as close to the stove as I can get without upsetting their little circle. One old fella with a thick pink scar runnin the length of his face, from his forehead to his chin, glances up and gives me a ghoulish grin and a nod that says either *Welcome to Heaven* or *Welcome to Hell,* I cant decide. It is a bit of an inferno in here. They're all clutchin mugs of some sort, chipped teacups and full-sized cups with broken handles and logos like *HitsFM* and *Kit Kat* and *Venture Car Rentals.* When was the last time one of 'em rented a car I wonder? Ever in their lives? When was the last time *I* had a Kit Kat? A simple thing like that.

They all seems to be drinkin the same thing, a thick bloodish drink that smells suspiciously like port, only all the cups are steaming hot. One of 'em starts to nod off a bit and the fella closest to him reaches out to steady his drink for him. I flexes me hands over the stove to try and get a bit of feeling back in 'em. The wood crackin and poppin deep within the hungry heat of the stove. The radio says it's Sunday morning, welcome back to *Jigs and Reels.* Sunday fuckin morning. Figure it all out again tomorrow. Let meself fall today. I was so close, right ready to pack it all in when I met Isadora. Well on me way too. And how I had it figured that she'd keep me afloat, that she'd finally be the one to keep me head above water for good. And now she's drove me to this, this place, with her flippancy, her shape-shiftin and her fucked-up double standards.

I feels me eyelids gettin heavy and I'm assailed by a deep, almost painful yawn that pops me eardrums and sets me back on me heels a bit. The old fella stirrin the pot takes a coughing fit and sprays a bit of phlegm onto the stovetop. It sizzles, a little ball of it dancing back and forth on the damper. In me haze I makes a mental note not to have any Jiggs' dinner today.

—Are you buyin something today or are you just gonna soak up my heat?

This is the old missus who let me in. She's scrubbin at the bar with a wire brush. I looks around at the circle of rummies and sees how they're nursin their drinks like it's their last.

—I'll have what they're havin. A round for the house!

The circle perks right up when I says that and one of 'em tips his frayed old salt-n-pepper cap at me. I notices underneath his rough canvas coat that he's wearing a faded green necktie and what once was likely a decent white dress shirt. His Sunday best.

—Eleven dollars please.

This is the old one again, as she nudges her way through our little circle to get to the stove. She lays a mid-sized cast-iron pot next to the dinner pot, takes the stopper off a dark glass bottle with no label and tips a couple of ounces of murky liquid into the pot. Smells like, I dont know, cough syrup or something. The colour of the bottle, like poppers. When was the last time I had a good romp on the poppers? I tried to get Iz on 'em one night and she flew right off the head, said if I couldnt be "intimate" without the use of drugs then there was something wrong with me, with the whole situation. Fuck though, just a bit of extra fun. I just wanted to see what she'd be like with her guard down.

The old one goes back to the bar and returns to us with a full bottle of Kelly's port. Kelly's. My heart. Beats. Kelly's. She twists the cap off and pours the whole bottle into the pot on top of the mystery medicine. I hands her a ten and a five, tells her to keep the change. None of the lads knows what to make of the tip. They nods and mutters and pulls their chairs a little closer to mine. The old missus hands me a small yellow mug with *CN* written on it. It's hefty and thick, well insulated, a slight stain in the bottom but not chipped anywhere. A good mug. All the men eyes it greedily. I was told in Dublin that to give someone a chipped mug was an insult, that you were wishin them ill fortune. The old one must wish me well.

A song comes on the radio then, an old Newfoundland song I vaguely recognizes from years ago. The old fella in his Sunday best starts tappin his feet and tries to sing along in a raspy, nasal voice:

> *Ye lads and lassies of Newfoundland come listen to my tale,*
> *While I relate the hardships of attending St. John's jail . . .*

He takes a deep breath and throws his head back for the next line and the rest of the circle starts tappin along, but before the next line comes the old bag behind the bar switches the radio off.

—Now boys, you know I cant abide singing at this hour.

And that's that. All heads drop back to the sticky floor and what spark had come to the eyes of the man in his Sunday best winks out obediently.

A thick, sweet steam risin from the pot of port on the stove. I nods towards it.

—That ready yet?

They all drains what's left in their mugs as the one with the scar runnin down his face fishes a thick leather glove from the wood box. He grabs hold of the pot handle and fills up each cup according to whose is closest. I'm well out of 'is reach and I'll be fucked if I dont get a full cup out of it so I stands and holds me mug out. He skips right over it and goes on to his buddy's cup. I feels a rage bubble up in me, but I s'pose they got their system. Finally he pours what's left into mine, a thick sludge at the bottom of the pot that sorta slides into me cup with a muted plop. I takes out me knife and gives the drink a stir before tastin it. Hot. So sweet that a pain shoots back through me teeth like I was chewin on something metal, like a fork. It has a sort of numbing effect, leaves a thick coating from the roof of me mouth to the back of me throat, not bad like cocaine. I can feel the heat of it sinkin down to me stomach, settling there and altering the very chemical makeup of whatever's left over in me gut since last night. Me head starts to swoon a little and a dull, hazy film settles over me eyes, makin the room seem a little darker and warmer than it already is. I can feel it creepin through the muscles in me legs, a hot lava oozin its way into the weak spot in me foot, warmin it, soothin the cold throb that's not let up in years and years. My heart beats Kelly's. Me insides are aglow with a strange new peace. I glances across at the old fella in his Sunday best and he suddenly seems like an old friend, a comrade from another life, from a warmer, simpler time. He smiles and winks at me.

145

—That's the best drop you got, young feller. The gold.

They saved the bottom for me.

I dont know how much times passes while we're sippin at our drinks. No one speaks. The old one turns the radio back on and I feels like singin too. But it takes all that's in me to ask for a cigarette from the man with the scar runnin from his forehead to his chin. I realizes then how huge a leap it was for the man in his Sunday best to have lifted his head up to sing when he did. It musta taken every last ounce of energy and I dont blame him in the least for retreating from the song so easily when he was told to stop.

• • •

I'm dimly aware of a thump at the door. It feels more like someone else's heart beatin. A murmuring, hushed voice behind me. "Let Me Fish Off Cape St. Mary's" lulling our mute circle further into a dreamlike state of tenderness and tranquility. A hand on me shoulder.

—Fuck, Clayton. Is that you?

I nods me head without turnin to inspect the owner of the voice.

Yes, it's me. I think.

I'm bein scooped, hoisted outta me little nest. Me chair falls to the floor with a distant clatter. A furrowed and gnarly set of fingers reaches out to pluck me empty mug away. I clings tight to me grandfather's blanket. Some devil is dragging me away from the perfect heat of the woodstove, spinnin me around towards the front door. The hand on me back, gently guiding me down the steps to Water Street. It's cold out here. I needs to get back to where I was, to the peace and warmth of . . . I cant quite remember where it was that I've been taken from. The passenger-side door of a shiny black pickup is opened before me. I'm nudged inside. The heater is on, full blast. I've been in worse states than this. Of course I have. I'm Clayton. Clayton Reid. I am.

• • •

I comes awake when my head clunks off the passenger side window outside a Tim Hortons drive-through. Mike Quinn hands me a coffee. Black, steamin hot. The first sip brings me head right back around, almost. A box of doughnuts on the seat between us. Mike stuffin his face. I picks out a chocolate one and devours it in one go. Neither one of us speaks, just sits there in the parking lot and eats the dozen assorted doughnuts till we're almost too sick to talk. Mike takes a swallow of his coffee and lets out a huge belch.

—What ahhh . . . brought you to Fagan's this morning Mike?

—Just about to ask you the same thing. I was collecting the rent. I ahhh . . . owns the building.

—Figured.

—Fuck are you at drinking that codeine, that'll kill ya.

—Is that what that was?

—Where you staying these days Clayton?

—N-nowhere now.

—Keith moved out. Gone off to Halifax again. His apartment is free.

—Dont got no money.

—His shift is open too. If you'd like to try your hand at bartending. Might as well, you're spending all your time there as it is.

I manages to say *When do I start?* Then I'm hangin out the door, heavin a putrid mixture of coffee and chunky, sugary doughnut grease and codeine and Kelly's wine and last night's cokey red wine onto the pavement. The Sunday morning cars snakin their way up to the window of the drive-through, tryin not to notice what it is I'm up to. Go fuck yourselves. Mike snorts and says *Not for a few days yet.*

• • •

He hands me a set of keys outside the door of Keith's ex-apartment. I climbs the wobbly iron steps. There's a condom hangin from the rail. I brushes it aside with the sleeve of me coat. Mike is telling me something about the rent comin straight outta me pay. Six bucks an hour, keep all me own tips. No drinkin behind the bar. I nods as I'm workin the door open. I have a faint appreciation for the fact that Mike Quinn has saved me from . . . something. I turns to say thanks as I'm steppin in through the front door of the apartment, but he's already gone.

I locks the door behind me and follows the stairs up to the main floor. Near the top step, right before I makes it to the landing, me foot goes right through the floorboard, me leg vanishes to the knee and a nail or sliver of wood gouges into me shin. I can barely feel it.

Keith's got most of the walls covered with hideous murals of demons and slain angels and I believe what must be a crude rendering of Iron Maiden's Eddy, eatin a naked woman who looks like she's rather enjoying it. Not a bad job really. A bit dark, but liveable.

I looks around for me table, searches the two bedrooms and even the bathroom. I looks out on the back roof, but it's nowhere to be seen. In its place is a rusty and shaky old pale green chrome one. Val's history lesson. Fuck him now.

The lights are workin fine. I forgot to ask Mike about that, if it's all inclusive. There's this wicked painting just left flat on the floor of the kitchen. I leans it against the wall and has a good look at it. This big hand clutchin a live crow. It's kinda loud, but it's nice and dark too. I like it. It says something to me.

I turns the heat on bust and drags me grandfather's blanket into one of the bedrooms. The first room is practically empty, but the other one, the bigger one, has a huge queen-size mattress in the corner. I strips the sheets off and fires 'em into the corner. Like fuck I'm sleepin in a year's worth of Keith's piss and sweat and jerk. An ancient portable heater propped up in the corner. I plugs it into the wall and it crackles to life. I wraps meself good and snug in me grandfather's blanket and flops down on the mattress. Clock radio flashin on the floor beside the bed. I clicks it on and tunes in *Jigs and Reels*. I dont bother to set the time. I wouldnt know where to start.

Bartending hey? Me own bed. Me own fuckin bed.

Now Isadora.

Now.

17. And to All a Good Night

Christmas Eve. Val is demonstrating how to turn a perfectly appealing line of blow into a jagged assortment of malicious-lookin flakes of crack. Fuckin waste, if you asks me. He holds a candle beneath a soot-black spoon that contains some sinful mixture of baking soda and coke and tap water. Cigarette burnin away in the ashtray and Val's already after warnin me not to touch it, not to disturb it, to just let it burn. No mention of the last time we were together, no apology for smackin me in the chops in front of Isadora. No mention of Monica neither.

I worked the day shift at the Hatchet and Val called down around three to invite me up for an evening drink. And even though every fuckin pore on me body wanted to scream *Go fuck yourself you cunty-balled old bastard,* I said *Yes* straight away and then cursed meself for havin come across so eager for his company. But the truth is that I was almost fuckin elated to hear from him. I am. Christmas Eve. Family. I even thought about callin up the Shore and wishin old Randy a good one too. Fuck that though.

Prescott Street was wicked icy on the way up to Val's. The sidewalk was worse. The wind was bitter, enough to rip the skin off your face. Hail peltin off me cheeks. I spotted Crazy Clara across the street tryna make her own way up the hill. She had half a dozen grocery bags from the Korean shop on Water Street. She wasnt makin very good time, feelin out every step like she expected it to be her last, the

149

bags bumpin clumsy off her knees. Her hat blew off and when she spun around to see where it went, a couple of cans burst out through the bottom of one of her bags and started rollin back down the hill. She moaned into the wind. I darted across the street then and after a little scuffle with the ice and the wind and me bad foot, I had the cans and her hat scooped up, and a knot tied in the bottom of the busted bag. She didnt know what to make of me. Like she'd never seen me before in her life, even though most of the time she calls me by name. She had a look in 'er eyes I'd never seen her with before, like an old dog that's come to expect a kick before a kind word. I had a hard time talkin 'er into takin me arm, lettin me help 'er up the hill. I made me voice as soft, as calm as I could, like the way I would when I was young and tryna trick a dog into comin near enough so's I could give it a good boot. When I was young. When I was *that*. Finally she let herself lean on me, old Clara. We edged our way up the greasy sidewalk and I told her me name maybe a dozen times. She kept muttering about her landlord, about what a lovely man he is, how he fixes everything when it's broke and never charges her a cent in rent. Poor old girl, I asked her if she got any family and she said *No, not now I dont. Not no more.* Every now and then she'd lose her footing and grip me arm so tight I thought we were both goin down. When we finally made it to her doorstep she started diggin through her change purse for something to offer me. I told her to put her money away and not be so foolish. She wouldnt hear tell of it though and finally I let her press two shiny quarters into me palm.

—There you go, my love. There.

I made sure she got her door opened alright, wished her a good Christmas and then turned back down the hill towards Val's.

. . .

Val, more steady than I've seen him in a long long time, removes the burnin cigarette from the ashtray and taps more than an inch of what he calls "virgin ash" into a brownish glass pipe he'd selected from his collection in the bottom kitchen drawer. He asks me for a knife and I'm delighted to whip out my silver Bristol pocket knife. It's fuckin razor sharp and I'm kinda hopin he'll ask me about it. Sounds foolish and maybe a little juvenile I s'pose, but any way into a conversation with Val where he's not the ultimate authority, I'll take it. But no. He's so intent on scrapin the flakes from the spoon onto the ash in the pipe that he barely notices. I says a quick and quiet prayer that he nicks himself on the blade.

Val hands me the pipe and a fuckin pink Bic lighter that somehow doesnt suit the event at all. I found a Zippo down behind the mattress in the apartment, musta been yon hippie Keith owned it. I draws it from out me inside pocket and lays the pink lighter aside. Val barks:

—No, no. Dont use that. The flame's too heavy. And you'll spoil the taste.

I picks up the pink Bic, lights it, and holds the flame to the mouth of the pipe.

—Steady now. Steady.

I watches the white flakes liquefy and melt down through the thick grey-white ash. The dry, angry fumes of smoke pounds me chest like someone's after stuffin a wire brush down me throat. Me windpipe almost seals shut, me lungs ablaze. But I wills meself not to cough in front of Val. I fills me lungs to capacity instead, then closes me eyes and lets me head tumble over the backrest of the chair. The heat floodin through me body, washin away all the sore spots. I feels Val take the pipe from me hand, hears the click of the flint wheel from the lighter. I holds me breath, a tingle in me knees, an itch, a flutter in me nostrils I'm refusin to scratch.

Warm jellied heaven seepin into the marrow of my bones.

The thump, thump thumpin, poundin, hammering roar of me heart.

Fuck, I've just done crack.

• • •

On me way down Military Road towards Isadora's I suddenly realizes I've gotten her nothing for Christmas. The only person I got anything at all for is Brent. He's s'pose to show up sometime over the holiday. I stashed two cases of beer in the room he'll be takin in the apartment. Other than that I havent even bought a fuckin card for anyone. I made sixty bucks in tips today at the bar. That's unheard-of for a day shift, but I s'pose Christmas Eve could be exceptional. Derelict regulars with nowhere else to go and no one to buy presents for, tippin me extra in order to alleviate their guilt and loneliness. Yeah, quite the festive and desperate day and didnt I exploit it to the max with me brightest of moods and me most dashing and seasonal grin? Fuck.

I'd been meanin to dart across the street to the little Korean store after me shift to pick Iz up a set of salad dishes she pointed out to me a couple of weeks back, but I s'pose maybe I was so nervous and distracted at the prospect of seeing Val again that all else slipped me mind. And now I'm on me way to her house with nothing. Christmas Eve. She'll never let me hear the end of this one. Over the last two weeks she's been worse than any youngster you can imagine in her excitement over Christmas and presents and shit, countin down the days and droppin hints about what she's plannin to get me, tellin me what I wasnt allowed to buy her and askin me advice on what to get for people I dont even know. I mean she's cute about it all, and it's kinda rubbin off on me, her enthusiasm, but what do I know about Christmas? All it ever is for me is a socially acceptable excuse to get plastered and stay that way for a week. But I'm gonna take it easy this year. I got a job anyhow. And tomorrow I'm gonna go meet Iz's mom in St. Philip's for Christmas dinner. Maybe even go to fuckin mass. And tonight is s'pose to be a quiet night at Iz's for a movie, some wine, and of course we're to swap our presents. It's all just a fuckin test, I knows that. And I'm more than a little ill prepared aint I? No present, an hour late already and fried on crack. I should just say fuck it and hit the town for the night, resurface sometime in the New Year.

I ducks into the Needs shop on the corner of Military and Bannerman instead.

The fuckin fluorescent lights are so bright and gross I'm fuckin near blinded when I walks in through the door. Painful it is, like some bastard is pressin the pads of his thumbs onto the backsides of me eyes. I staggers sideways and reaches out for a shelf of chips to steady meself, but I cant get no contact with nothing solid and I feels me arm slip right through the stack of chips and I knows before I tries that me bad foot wont hold me up. And down I fuckin goes. Me head bounces off the dirty brown slush that's collected near the front doormat and then I just lays there, right still, with me eyes closed, feelin kinda stupid about the commotion I just caused. I knows everyone's watchin me. Customers and staff rushes to help me up and I starts in laughin, not really at what state I'm in right now but at the flickering memory of this wild drunken night I spent in Dublin last year, first pub I walked into when I landed, somewhere on the North End, cant remember. Some man, 'bout thirty odd, with a heavy northern accent. He was knocked down by a bouncer after saying something nasty to the barmaid cause where she wouldnt serve him. He was mid-sentence, demanding one final pint when the bouncer grabbed him and started shovin him towards the exit. The northern fella started pushin back, of course, and somewhere in the scuffle he lost his footing and fell beneath the snooker table in the middle of the room. The bouncer barkin at him to get up. The man said he couldnt.

—What de ye mean ye cant move?

—Cant feel the legs man, cant feel the legs.

Every customer in the bar was hoverin around the scene, meself included. The bouncer started to get nervous then, nudged the man's leg with the toe of his boot. Nothing. He kicked it harder. The man's leg didnt budge. Someone at the bar said:

—Christ lads, someone better call for the Guards.

The man beneath the snooker table muttered something about a lawyer. I started shakin too, nervous about what I was seein. The bouncer put his two chunky hands on his shaved head and started pacin back and forth around the room sayin:

—Fuck no. C'mon. Fuck no. C'mon . . .

And then the big belly laugh from under the snooker table and the bouncer cracked, havin learned nothing, grabs the poor maniac by the collar of his coat and drags him out to the exit. The northern fella kept laughin even when he was tossed out onto his back on the piss-stained street.

And that's kinda like the laugh that's comin outta me now too, this sorta involuntary aggressive laugh that I knows is just drippin with contempt and maybe embarrassment. This scruffy young pup in a shit-brown Needs jersey and oversized matted Santa hat is tryna lift me up. I screams:

—Ahhhh . . . fuck man, watch the foot, watch the foot.

He lets go of me then and I slips back into the slush for a second. Little fucker. I grabs hold of the banana stand and pulls meself up. I cant meet his eyes or utter a word of thanks or apology. Not that he deserves either one. I cant say a word cause I dont know, I'm afraid I'll burst out with what madness and chaos that's been lurkin in the outskirts of me brain since I sucked back that pipe-load of crack at Val's. I holds me head up and hobbles into the heart of the store, road slush drippin off the side of me face.

I wonder where that fella might be tonight, the northern fella. Christmas Eve. What might he be up to right this very moment? Assuming he's alive. Is he alright? Or out there somewhere face down in a pool of his own vomit? Or worse, someone else's vomit.

I gets thinkin about this as I'm scoutin the aisles for something suitable to get for Izzy for Christmas, how lives and personalities and long-ago happenings just have their way of carrying on in the minds of other people. Memory. Consciousness. I had this friend in high school, his name was John. He drowned. He jumped off the narrow bridge along the main road in Cape Broyle and struck a rock, knocked himself out. I can see him now, clearly, for the first time since he died. Funny that. In a sense he's not really dead then is he?

He's alive and well in my head right now, no more removed from the world than Isadora or Val or Mike Quinn. No more dead than Petey Thorne or that Clyde Whelan cunt.

Me hand finds its way onto a small box of strangely ahhh . . . elegant goldfish dishes that seem a little outta place here amongst the Newfoundland scenery pictures and 4x4 racers and holiday cookbooks. There's four dishes in the box, they look like blown glass and one of them is almost the precise shade of brown as Val's crack pipe. I'll take that as a sign. I tucks the box under me arm and sallies on over to the counter. Nobody better not say a fuckin word to me or even look at me sideways either. The dishes costs fifteen-fifty altogether. I gives the clerk a ten and a five and the two shiny quarters Clara gave me back in me other life.

• • •

Outside on the steps of the shop I stops for a second and breathes deep the night. The big maples in Bannerman Park, elaborately strung with a mix of blue and red lights. Soft snow just startin to fall and I can hear the tail end of Springsteen's "Merry Christmas Baby" from a house a few doors up the street. I fills me lungs and leans back against the wall of the shop and tries me best to soak up what wholesomeness there is in the air tonight. Christmas Eve. I always tries to appreciate this night actually, that dense calm in the air you can almost cut with a knife. The night when everyone, everywhere, the world over are entitled to let the reality of their lives slide to the wayside for a few short hours. Makes me feel sharp and grounded and almost lighthearted. I tucks the dishes into me coat and hums me way down Bannerman to Isadora's doorstep.

• • •

Standin at the desk in Iz's bedroom with me back to her as I'm wrappin her present. She's skippin and bouncin and dancin around the room behind me. Fuck, she's gorgeous. I'd eat her right here on the floor right now. She's drunk, no doubt about that, but for now she's kinda teetering in that grey zone between girlish silliness and complete annihilation of the senses. But I can kinda tell how she's fightin to hang on, tryna maintain control, that she's at odds with herself about something or other. She's quieter than usual. I'm watchin her in the mirror while she keeps peekin down the hallway towards the main room, out where the tree and all that shit must be. Seems to me like she got someone out there.

She tries on an old leather cowboy hat from her closet. Maybe she's just excited about opening her present. Maybe she's tryin not to be pissed off that I'm over an hour late. Maybe she knows I'm outta me own head. Maybe she knows the smell of crack and she's tryna find some way to confront me on it. Naw. I knows her well enough by now to know that she couldnt possibly hold in any fuckin knowledge or opinion that might give her the upper hand.

—Something wrong Iz?

—What? Oh no. No. Just . . .

She peeks down the hallway again, then skips back across the room to me. God she's fuckin dandy. I'd devour her right here and now. Suck all night I would. But I knows better than to try anything till "the mood is right," till we're "connected." Jesus, never so complicated a piece of tail has there been for me. She puts her hand on me jaw and pulls me face to hers so we're absolutely eye to eye for the first time since I arrived.

—Just that I love you Clayton. And it's Christmas . . .

She kisses me then, soft on the lips with no tongue, no force behind it. Tender, like the way you'd kiss a child almost. I still got hard though, almost instantaneous. Dont take much for me where she's concerned, the smell of her, the sound of her voice sometimes.

When I finishes wrappin her present she hands me a glass of red wine. She takes me by the hand then and leads me through to the front room where guess fuckin who is perched on the arm of the couch, quietly tunin an electric guitar? Robert Dawe. In all his ponytailed splendour. Merry fuckin Christmas. I feels me stomach knot and drop at the same time, like I'm on a swing set or free-fallin on an elevator. A smallish amplifier on the floor at Dawe's feet. He's fiddlin with the guitar cord, tryna make the connection with the amp. He dont bother to turn around and say hello or nothing. He's obviously loaded. Great. I needs to sit down now. How could she fuckin do this? Christmas Eve. Toddler fuckin Dawe. This is some kinda outrage. See what I was sayin about it all bein a big test? I turns around to walk back down the hall but Izzy grabs me by the arm and pulls me in towards the tree. Dawe keeps pluckin away at the guitar. Cant say I'll last too long without havin a few words with him, let alone sit through a private concert on Christmas fuckin Eve. Even if it means walkin out, leavin her to cry on his shoulder. As if she'd give a fuck.

She's in her pyjamas by the way, giddy and girlish as she roots under the tree to retrieve my present. I bends down beside her and whispers:

—What the fuck is goin on here?

She looks up, wide eyed and smilin.

—Nothing sweetheart, I'm getting you your present.

She thrusts it into my hands. It's soft. I tries not to look too disappointed, but I knows fuckin well it's some tacky piece of clothes like a sweater or something that she thinks might somehow "brighten me up a bit," enhance me already well-enhanced personality, her attempt to "tone down" me image. How many times have I gotta tell her that I fuckin feels comfortable just the way I am. Worse than that though, despite all that, whatever it is, I'll still hafta wear it for a while and pretend I likes it. Yeah, she's been doin this, takin me out to these second-hand places like Value Village and makin me try on the most ridiculous shirts and pants. Tight, flashy seventies shit that gets me thinkin she must take me for a bit of a fruit. But if it's not black, or at least grey, then I aint puttin it on.

I glances across the room at Dawe and splits the present open the way you'd crack a pencil in half. Isadora standin on her tiptoes, grinnin big from ear to ear. It's black, whatever it is. I pulls it out and it takes me a minute to figure that it's actually a heavy fleece blanket. Practical enough. I been lookin for something to put up in the window of me bedroom to block the daylight out. This looks about perfect. Isadora takes it and wraps it around her shoulders like a shawl. She does a little twirl.

—So do you like it?

—Yeah, I do. It's perfect. You're not gonna like yours though.

Dawe raises his head in our direction when I says that and I realizes that because neither of us have acknowledged the other yet, that all chance of any feigned Christmas civility has escaped us. Too much time is passed now for it to seem like anything else but weakness to do so. And the first to speak will be the weaker of the two. Well, he'll not get a word outta me the old fucker. Iz drains another glass of red wine, completely oblivious now to the tension in the room.

—And did you see what Robert got me?

She plucks the electric guitar from Dawe's hands and I suddenly understands with horror that both it and the amplifier on the floor beside it are brand new. Dawe bought her a brand-new guitar and amp for Christmas. Well fuck me. An image of me bashing Dawe's head in with the guitar, pluggin the amp in and rammin his bloody head through the mesh speaker. Merry Christmas to all . . .

Dawe cocks his head at me, triumphant once again. But I'm determined not to give the old bastard the scene he's lookin for. I'll make sure that amp never works though. I will make sure of it. Isadora bops around the room with the guitar strapped around her shoulders. I says fuck it and holds me own present out towards her, waits for her to stop and notice it. When she finally sees it she stops her twirl and lets the guitar fall to the floor with a clunk. I has a glance at Dawe. He jumps slightly and then tries to cover up the fact that he's slightly insulted. Fuck him. Iz does this sorta bunny-hop thing across the floor and snatches the present outta me hand. She rips it open with one vicious pull at the wrapping. Her face lights right up, maybe a little too much, in my estimation. The dishes dont seem to have the same . . . peculiarity under the dim lights of the tree as they did under the bright fluorescent ones at Needs. They look not at all elegant, but rather dull and cheap, which I reckon they are anyhow. She slides the dishes out and lets the box drop to the floor. I sees I left the price tag on the box and I boots it under the tree.

—Oh Clayton, sweetie, I just love them, they're beautiful!

She rushes over to show Dawe.

—Look Robert, arent they cute?

Dawe looks the dishes up and down before snorting:

—Fuckin ashtrays.

—No Robert, no. They're for dip. And salsa.

I'd sorta thought they had something more to do with the bathroom, meself. But outta the box they seems too small to be soap dishes and too shallow to be candle holders. Who gives a fuck, so long as she's happy and makes a fuss over them in front of Dawe. She rushes back across the room and throws her arms around me and kisses me full on the lips, tongue and all.

—Thank you sweetheart, thank you.

Dawe stands up with his gloves in his hands. He drains the last of his wine and goes:

—Fuck this then.

Iz whips her head around in perfect anticipation of the first sign of trouble.

—What's wrong Robert? It's Christmas.

—Fuck Christmas.

Dawe starts movin out the hall towards the front door. I bolts out the hall behind him.

—What the fuck's your problem old man?

Dawe veers around on his heels and comes straight at me. Iz jumps in between us, but I manages to get enough of a shove at Dawe's shoulder to throw him off balance and send him staggering backwards amongst the tangle of boots near the doorway. I can feel the power of the crack resurfacing now, feel the madness and the chaos rise up again and I got this sudden overwhelming and rampant hunger for a racket. I'll fuckin destroy him tonight. Showin up at Izzy's some nights, loaded drunk, usually when I aint around too, like he's watchin the house or something. Or maybe she's been callin him over, who the fuck knows. Writing lame-ass poems for her and reciting them outside on her doorstep like he was goddamn Shakespeare. Always and forever tryna fuckin out*man* me somehow. I takes a jab at him and just barely grazes the side of his grey head. He wasnt expecting to be punched at though, no. Fuckin townies. Arts fags. He stumbles backwards again and steps on a slipper or something. A horror dances across his face like he's accidentally stepped on a kitten or like he's fallin off the edge of a cliff. But he composes himself quick enough and as far as I'm concerned that's an open admission that his whole twisted and supposedly eccentric persona is just an act he can turn on and off whenever his sense of self-security calls for it. He is so full of shit. I can only hope that, despite Iz's inability to remember anything past the third glass of wine, she'll somehow remember this one little detail outta the whole evening and come to see Dawe in the same light as I do. He finally manages to open the door and huffs out into the night. Tears are runnin free down Isadora's face now.

Dawe keeps shufflin down Bannerman Street. I shouts all manners of sauce at him but he wont turn around. I scoops up a handful of snow, packs it tight into a ball and lets it fly at him. The snowball explodes against a telephone pole not a foot from Dawe's head. I laughs and turns to go back inside, but just as I does so, Izzy tosses me coat onto the sidewalk and slams the door in me face.

—Go.

—Isadora? For fuck sakes. It's Christmas Eve girl.

She opens the door once more and throws the black fleece blanket at me.

—Iz? C'mon . . .

—Juzz go.

She's abandoned her wine glass and is now standin there drinkin straight outta what looks like a fresh bottle. A new heaviness to her eyes and the swivel style motion of her head tells me that she's left the grey zone altogether and is now officially out of it. That's her way, one minute she's fine and the next she's just not there anymore. I knows there's no sense tryna reason with her.

—He was fuckin askin for it girl!

—Well *I* din ass for it . . .

—Look girl . . .

—GO AWAAYYY!

. . .

I hangs around and boots at her door for a while, till I spies a cop car cruisin past and decides it's time to make a change of plans for the evening. I stumbles down her steps and feels me head go heavy again, something I cant quite grasp. I was thinkin so clearly back at Needs about all this, but I cant seem to no more. How this night should live on, this moment in time. Christmas Eve. Bannerman Street. This night will survive in my head, but not hers. She wont remember a fuckin thing. So I might as well not even have shown up at all. Or not existed in the first place.

The crack is almost worn off completely now, me mouth dry and sour from the wine. I leans into the wind and follows Dawe's footsteps through the fresh-fallen snow. Isadora. Jesus Christ. A child is cryin from inside one of the only houses along the street that has no Christmas lights up. A man's knotted voice is shoutin:

—Shut him up will ya. Shut him up.

I hangs a left when I hits Gower Street and realizes without much surprise that I'm circling back to Val's place. Cold sweat trickling down me spine.

I tries to remember who spoke first, me or Dawe.

18. Spillage

Just pullin up to the scales at the landfill out in Robin Hood Bay and Mike starts back muttering and cursin under his breath. He goes:

—Now, it's a truck goddamn it. Dumpsite A.

—What?

—I dont know. They always send me to B, where the cars go. This is a fuckin truck.

There's a gruesome city garbage truck on the scales ahead of us and the driver seems to be just havin a lark, some chat about the weather with the guy behind the glass. Mike leans on the horn and the driver flips him the finger in the side mirror. Mike grabs the door handle and pops the door of the truck open. I grabs his arm:

—Fuck Mike man, calm down. Fuck it.

He looks at me like he's gonna chomp the head right off me shoulders and squish me brains around in his mouth like Listerine. He slams his door closed. I moves closer to me own door. He's on edge lately. He's on the brink. The other night I was workin the bar when this scruffy fella came in for a drink. Looked like he was off the boats. Mike was sittin in the corner readin through some papers, had his eye on the guy from the moment he walked in. Fella kept to hisself though, never gave me no trouble. And that's all that counts really, that you dont fuck with the bartender. Mike watchin, sendin out the evil eye. Then I slaps on the *White Album* by the Beatles and this scruffy fella starts tappin his boot against the bar, just keepin the beat. Mike charges across the room and gives the fella a fuckin hard, solid tap in back of the head. Buddy gets the big fright, but when he turns to see the look on Mike's face he decides it's likely best not to react. Mike tells him to settle down, no trouble, no hassles in his bar. Buddy just nods and goes back to his drink, Mike watchin the whole time outta the corner of his eye. But then a few songs into the album and buddy starts doin this strange hippie shit with his hands, twirlin his fingers and swishin his wrists like he's on acid. Coulda been too, I heard there's good acid on the go. Anyhow, Mike sees this and makes the second charge across the bar, grabs buddy by the shoulders and pulls him off his stool, drags him like that across the floor and into the porch, then throws him so hard against the door that it pops open and buddy lands out on the sidewalk. And all the while the guy never said a word, never made a peep. Mike standin in the porch, locks the deadbolt on the door. Then the guy starts shoutin for something, only he's not speakin English, more like fuckin German or some such Nazi shit. I sees that his jacket is there on the floor of the bar and it was freezin out that night so I says to Mike:

—His jacket. Right there on the floor Mike.

Mike picks up the jacket and brings it back to the porch. He holds it up in the window and the fella starts noddin and almost smilin. And Mike laughs at him through the glass. This finally sets the fella off and he starts shoutin some more Nazi shit and gives the door a couple of boots, pointin at Mike the whole time. Mike cups his hand around his ear like he cant hear what the guy is sayin, beckons for him to come closer, closer, a little closer. When the guy gets handy enough to the glass Mike hauls off and gives it to him, right in the fuckin mouth. And I'm talkin *through* the window too, and not no regular window either, this is one of them shatter-proof ones with the wire mesh runnin through it like what they got in schools and government buildings. Mike brought his hand back then, all fulla blood, from the fella's face or from the glass I couldnt be sure. Buddy flat on his back on the ground and Mike opens the door and tosses the jacket onto him. Then, get this, sly fucker that he is, Mike reaches around and pushes all the glass back the other way, so that it looks like the window got broke out from the other side. Slick bastard. Calls the cops then, says somebody's after rammin his face through the door of his bar, after knockin himself out. Mike hauls a glove on over his hand and goes back to his paperwork. Ten minutes later the cops are loadin buddy into the back of their car, no questions asked. And like I said, he was a decent enough fella for how long he was in the bar, never gave me no trouble, and that's the main thing. Cops prob'ly kicked the shit out of him too. I never said nothing to Mike about it. I knew better. All I can say is that it's a good thing he's gettin outta the bar business, the sooner the better too.

The garbage truck pulls off and then it's Mike's turn on the scales. The old guy behind the glass in the booth has a glance in the back of the truck and goes:

—Dumpsite A.

And Mike's spirits does a complete one-eighty, big grin stretches across his face, and as he tears past the big green garbage truck he thumps the horns a couple of times and waves up at the driver. I dont think you're supposed to pass people on this road.

I says to Mike:

—So is it true that Silas Lawlor is takin over the bar soon?

—Six weeks time, if all goes according to plan.

—And so are we all out of a job then?

—Not *all*. I advised him to keep you on. And Monica. Dont know if he will or not.

—Right on. Well thanks.

—Well I figured it's in my own interest to make sure you got money coming in, I'll still own the building. And I'll still need rent.

Right, and I thought there for a second that he was doin *me* a favour. Prob'ly a blessing though, come to think on it, if I did get the boot. Isadora's been talkin about me movin in anyhow, and I dont know about this bartending racket. Although I must say I kinda like the power. And if you thinks a bartender got no power, especially on Friday night, think again. I controls everything, depending on what mood I'm in and what music I plays. I can pump up the volume and get the biggest kinda rockin party on the go or turn on some Tom Waits and scrunch me brow and ignore people's orders till everyone wishes they were dead or someplace else. I usually just jacks up the music though, better tips. And I likes bein busy too. Mixin up the weird drinks with shakers and strainers and milk and brandy and cherries and shit. I likes it when I got ten drinks to make and they're all shoutin for more, wads of cash comin in over the bar, when I finds meself in that fuckin zone where I'm just spinnin on me heels and not thinkin about what Izzy's up to or who she's with. I'm unstoppable then, on me own and in fuckin charge. Course then Mike walks into the bar and it all goes to shit on me. Really. I'll be clippin along just fine, in the groove like I said, mixin up some fuckin girlie drink like a brandy Alexander and Mike walks in and I'll drop it or shake it all into me own face. I did that one night, didnt tighten the shaker enough and Mike walks in and I gives the big old shake and the whole works exploded in me face, milk and Baileys drippin from me chin and the whole crowd around the bar in the knots laughin. Mike didnt laugh though. He looks at me and says:

—That's called spillage Clayton. You'll have to write it down next to the tabs or the stock'll come up short tomorrow.

And he walked away then, and I never fucked up the whole night long till he came back and I was walkin across the bar with a tray full of dirty ashtrays and dropped the whole works on the floor in front of him. Broke nearly every one of 'em too. Cheap fuckin things. But yeah, Mike has that effect on me I s'pose. Like what's his face, old Randy.

Once, when I was fifteen and stoned on weed, I climbed a tree in Cape Broyle. All us young crowd useta pass the nights in a scraggly patch of woods behind the ball field, just drinkin and screwin. And one night I climbed the highest tree, a massive, half-dead evergreen in the middle. I'd just had a great big blast and it wasnt fully kicked in yet, so on the way up the tree it was like I was racin the buzz to the top. It was pitch-black but me hands and feet knew exactly where they were goin, every notch and groove, every isolated little pimple in the trunk that could pass for a foothold and had the strength to hold me, was just waitin for me. I went up and up, smooth and fluent, me joints and muscles more than happy to obey. I had no limp then either. I was made for that tree.

No one saw me climb it. I never made a sound. And when I got high up enough I sat there on a good sturdy branch and looked down at the crowd, listened to their conversations, listened for me own name and generally enjoyed the power of spyin on 'em all. I watched the cars pull in down on the road, people lookin for dope or droppin off young ones or sellin beer outta the trunk. I never budged. I felt whole. I coulda jumped and controlled the speed of me descent and landed in the middle of 'em all without a sound. I was cozy in me own body. I sat there and listened and watched, potent and prepared for anything.

Then an all-too-familiar car pulled up, and I felt me heart quicken, a little jolt of anxiety to rattle me calm. And out he fell, Randy, the old man. He opened the car door and actually fell out onto the ground. The crowd below me laughed and pointed:

—Look at buddy, look, cockeyed.

I watched him crawl up the bank towards the crowd. That old grey jacket that still stank like a mixture of fish guts and diesel and sewage, I could smell it from me perch. He burst into the crowd like a man who'd been lost in the woods and was setting eyes on the first human life forms in weeks. He was bleedin, but I couldnt tell where the cut was.

—Who got all the draws then?

The crowd all stepped away from him at once and a couple of young ones squealed. I sat and watched. That was my old man down there.

—Who got all the fuckin draws then?

He could barely hold himself up and was sort of swingin his arm in the general direction of the crowd whenever he spoke.

—Where's my Clayton to?

And I heard someone say *Oh, that's Clayton's father. He's fuckin cracked.*

Someone shouted my name. It died in the trees. I sat perfectly still, directly above 'em all.

—Clayton! Come get your father!

And then Randy, lookin up:

—There he is! Look at him.

And he pointed. And they all turned and looked.

—What the fuck are you doin up there, ya foolish article? Get down b'y.

And I dont know why I listened to him. I coulda just sat and stayed and ignored him, nested in me little bubble of calmness. But I went down, suddenly clumsy and uncertain, me foot testing the dark for a safe place to step, branch ends gougin at me palms, painful, me legs shakin, a fresh stutter in me brain. I hooked me pants in a branch not four feet from the ground. I tried to jump before I realized I was caught, and turned bottom up, me head bouncin off the spongy ground while me leg stayed up in the tree. The crowd laughin. Randy:

—For fuck sakes Clay, are you stunned or something?

The crowd laughin. And Randy, loaded, looking for draws off teenagers, his own son there amongst 'em. I got me leg free from the tree and took off runnin into the woods. He was too drunk to give chase. I heard him yellin after me:

—Something wrong with you b'y. You're off your head, you are. Clayton? Clayton?

The cops picked him up that night. Drunk driving. He had to sell off yet another Monte Carlo. Fucker. I'd love to go back, you know. Go back about fifteen or twenty years and meet him face to face, the way I am now. I'd catch him off guard too. He'd nod at me, recognize me vaguely from somewhere. And as soon as he acknowledged me I'd whip off me belt and say *now, which end do you want? This end or the buckle end? Them's your fuckin options.* Then down with his pants, his hairy white arse, his face pressed into the floor or the couch or the bed or wherever I takes him. And then I'd nail him till he bawled and then nail him for bawlin. And of course I'd use the buckle end, for badness. I s'pose I'd go till he bled, then I'd stop, and then I'd vanish. Call him up later and ask him if it was still stingin. And if he said *yes* I'd say *good* and if he said *no* then I'd do it all over again. Yeah. That's what I'd do. But I know there's no goin back now. Maybe the next time around, if you believes in that sorta shit.

. . .

Mike is flyin by the time we comes to Dumpsite A. The sign said maximum 20 at the entrance. Mike dont give a fuck though. We rips right down to the bottom, the very bottom of this fuckin stinking cesspool of sludge and filth. The truck dont even feel steady no more, the ground squishy and kinda empty beneath the wheels, even though it should be froze solid this time of year. There's hardly any snow on the ground either, whereas back in Town there's mountains of it, piled up seven and eight feet onto the sidewalks. And in the hills surrounding us now there's all kinds of snow too. Aint that some kinda fucked? There's millions of gulls, scroungin and squawkin and pickin at the ground and swoopin at the truck. Mike swerves at one and for a second it seems like the gull gets sucked under the truck but then it pulls up at the last second. Some fuckin stink too, this real thick, sweet, fermented, sour-yogurt kinda smell that makes you wanna hold your breath for the rest of your life, or die on the spot. Mike's gotta spin the truck around to back in alongside the other trucks, the other Men. A guy with a white facemask and hardhat and an orange vest guides us in and lets Mike know when to stop. Mike cuts the engine and we both jumps out, me holdin me breath as long as I can and then takin deep breaths through me mouth when I finally needs to breathe again. Mike dont seem too troubled by it though, he's in his glory. He says:

—Could be worse Clayton, you could be working down here.

And when he says that, the guy who waved us in, the guy with the facemask, he glances over at us. I cant see how he heard Mike over the screech of the gulls and the grinding of the trucks and the backhoes, but he did. He looks over and squints at the two of us and his eyes sort of bug out for a second. And he's fuckin familiar too, yes by Christ. I'd recognize that broken, slumped frame and them despairing, sunken permanently bloodshot eyes anywhere. That's Jim McNaughton, I'm sure of it. He meets me eye for a second and I'm positive it's him. I nods but he sort of shakes his head ever so slightly and starts walkin backwards and around the side of another truck till he's outta sight. Mike, heaving a box full of what looks like baby stuff, clothes and busted toys and blankets and shit, down into the smouldering mess behind us, he nods and says:

—McNaughton. Poor fucker. Thinks no one knows why he stinks like he do.

And holy fuck, that smell, this one in the air, I knew I recognized it. Every fuckin time Jim walks into the Hatchet lately he brings it with him. Mike says:

—I think it's temporary, till his union clears things up for him.

—What's that all about?

—Never mind . . .

And just as he says that I'm reachin into the back of the truck and I cuts me index finger open on a big slice of broken glass. I lets out a yelp and pulls me hand back. There's blood, but not too much, it's not a deep cut atall. But it still feels pretty gross, cuttin it open down here amongst all this toxic shit, down here in the wasteland. Mike lets out a full-bellied roar.

—Ha! Well now, that's fuckin karma for you.

—What's that mean?

—That's a piece of the frame from that picture you tossed out your window.

—I dont know what you're talkin about.

—C'mon Clayton, I'm not stunned.

He's not. I knows that. But neither am I.

169

Sometime after Christmas me and Iz had a racket upstairs in me apartment. Just one of them bullshit rows that pops up outta nowhere. She was talkin about goin sober again. And I was wantin to go downstairs for a drink. Then her eyes locked onto that big painting propped against the wall in the kitchen above the fridge. She laughed at it, said it was the tackiest thing she'd ever laid eyes on. But I kinda kept it around cause I liked it, it was challenging. It had this dandy border of Celtic knots, which is likely why she took a dislike to it right away, where she resents anything Irish, especially the fact that I had such a wicked time over there. The picture itself was this huge snarled white hand squeezin a crow. It was pretty detailed. The crow had this strange look in its eyes, like it had some kinda secret and wasnt the least bit concerned that it could be crushed any second atall. Isadora said the painting was juvenile and started pointin out places where the artist fucked up or didnt mix the colours properly. Of course I couldnt give a shit about that, I was more interested in what was goin on with the hand and the crow. I'd sat around and stared at it lotsa nights before *she* ever laid eyes on it and I got to figuring there was some kinda message to it, how the hand was havin this dilemma about whether or not to crush the crow or let it go free. But the crow didnt seem to care too much, so it was deceptive, which of the two players was in control. I never did get a firm grip on what it was tryna tell me, but I kept it around cause I liked to look at it, simple as that. Isadora kept bitchin about it, criticizing the frame it was in and the background colouring and how it was so pretentious for someone so obviously amateur to use oil when they hadnt the first clue how to use it. She kept snickering at it, laughin at me for likin it. I knew she was only tryna rile me up, but I said fuck it anyhow.

—Want me to get rid of it then girl?

—By all means.

I grabbed the painting and walked through to me bedroom, opened up the window and slung the fuckin thing down onto Water Street. It landed with a deafening smash, right on the bonnet of a brand-spankin-new Dodge Ram 2500 parked in front of the doors at the Hatchet. Fuckin forty-thousand-dollar vehicle, easily. I ran and shut the light off in me bedroom and slid the window back down. Isadora came in and we peeked down onto the street. Me heart was racin. Sure enough, Mike Quinn comes outta the bar and takes the painting off the truck. He brushes the glass off the bonnet and then looks up at me window and points. No way he could see me, but he knew where the fuckin thing came from. He shakes his head and walks back into the bar with the painting. Iz looked at me then and said:

—You're a wild one Clayton Reid.

I laid her down on the bed then and had her, so it wasnt all for nothing I s'pose.

I was half shitbaked to go down to the bar later cause I thought it mighta been Mike's new truck or something, but it turned out to be Silas Lawlor's, thank fuck. Monica was bartending and she said everyone heard the smash, but when Mike came back with the painting he fed Silas some story about how someone musta been drivin by and tossed it out their car window, went on about how people got no value for good art no more. Silas looked the painting over and took a shine to it, asked Mike if he could keep it. Then a minute later he signed the contract to take over the bar. Fuckin moron.

The contract gave Mike sixty days to clear up his ties with the place. There was some kinda hefty down payment involved too, so says that Clyde Whelan cunt, and that Silas had so much time to come up with the rest of the money before the bar landed back in Mike's hands. So it's a win-win situation for Mike, when you think about it.

• • •

Mike still laughin to hisself, tossin a piece of a crib into the inferno behind us. And I says:

—Karma's bullshit. We're all just shat out from somewhere and fendin for ourselves. Dont matter if we're good or bad.

Mike stops then. He stares at me, the bottom end of a Mickey Mouse lamp in his hand, held by the neck, the bulb busted and jagged. He looks me up and down.

—Bullshit hey? Well how now would you explain *your* situation? If you were to take a good look?

—And what's my situation?

—Always fucked up over that young one, what's her name, Isabelle. Always beating your head off the bar or showing up with blood on your face, destroying property and shit like that? How do you suppose *you* wound up like that? The underdog?

—I aint no fuckin underdog.

—It's karma. You crucified that Donna one when she was dying about you. You wouldnt give an inch. All you did was fuck her and drink her booze. Crucified her. And now it's all come back around.

—I aint crucified.

—Well you'd never say by the look of you most nights. I mean, think about what you have. You got brains to burn and you're doing your goddamn best to burn 'em too. You got a roof over your head, a good job that pays the rent, women around, someone told me the other day you were writing stuff. You're young, and at least halfways handsome. So stop for a minute and appreciate it, cause if you dont, I guarantee you it's all gonna blow up in your face someday soon. And *that's* karma.

Preachin at me again the old fucker. Halfways handsome. Fuck's he mean by that? Gone queer now too is he? He reaches into the back of the truck and pulls the rest of the broken picture frame out. As he flings it, Frisbee style, into the pit, he curses hard under his breath and brings his own bloody finger to his mouth. I tries me goddamn best not to smile. He sucks his finger for a bit and then carries on like it didnt happen. He says:

—You do good by people and good things come back at you. Screw people over, start fucking around with people's hearts and heads, and it'll come right back on you. That's the way I see it.

—Well then *you're* fucked.

—What the fuck is that supposed to mean?

—Nothing . . .

—What about your buddy Brent there? Think he did nothing to warrant that knife in the back?

—Well he certainly never *stabbed* no one . . .

—Everything comes back to haunt you Clayton. Everything.

We heaves the rest of the junk outta the back of the truck in silence. From the looks of the stuff we're tossing out, I'm wondering if Mike's after evicting some welfare mom and her youngster, fuckin 'em out on their holes. But that's none of my business, *karma* should take care of that.

. . .

When we're done and headed back across the wasteland towards the entrance, I has a glance around for Jim, but he's nowhere. There's this fuckin huge machine bulldozing piles of garbage towards the cliff. It's got these thick metal wheels with twelve-inch spikes for diggin into the limp ground, for climbin the piles of rubbish and shit. What a rig. If anything ever goes down, like when the apocalypse comes to town, I knows what I'll be driving. Up and down Water Street in that thing, crushin everything and everyone in sight, that'll be me. Naw, bad karma.

I says to Mike:

—So what then, we're here and so long as we're good, then good things'll happen back to us? Simple as that?

—Well no, I wouldnt go that far. The big guy plays a part I suppose. I dont think we're as random as you says, just shat out like that, like a fluke, like just slopped into existence by mistake. I dont really know. But I do think you can make your time here a whole lot easier on yourself Clayton. You gotta be grateful for the good things and stop wallowing in what's wrong. And *that's* karma.

—And what's the big guy, fuckin God, got to do with anything anymore? Look at the state we're in. Just look in the rearview . . .

—Well Clayton, I know it'd be some lonesome and hollow down

here, for me anyway, if I didnt have something like that to cling to. Holy fuck—

Mike veers to his left just in time. The truck narrowly misses this huge gaping hole in the ground in front of us. I'm talkin *gaping* too, like about ten feet wide. Mike puts the truck in park and puts his head down on the steering wheel. I jumps outta the truck. We're not even on the road we came down on the way in, but it's like we were pulled, drawn, sucked across the wasteland here, right to the mouth of this hole. I looks down into it. It's about fifteen feet deep, layers and layers of green garbage bags and juts of scrap metal and flickering glass of all colours. The whole way down to the bottom, no solid ground whatsoever, just a black puddle of sludge down there. I s'pose that's why they calls it a landfill. Cause the land is absolutely full, stuffed.

Mike's still got his head on the wheel when I jumps back in the truck. I gives him a playful tap on the shoulder.

—Now is that karma or God at work Mike? Or fate? Or is it just fucked up? S'pose we hadda go right down in that—

—Well we didnt.

—No but, just, *what if* we had . . .

—Fuck off Clayton. Just fuck off.

And of course that's just what I does. Mike pulls the truck back to the main path and we're off again, flyin. As we're nearin the entrance we meets another garbage truck, Mike doin about sixty clicks in this twenty zone. The garbage truck slows down and swerves a bit to avoid us, honks the huge horn at us. Mike gives 'em the finger. I looks into the passenger seat of the passing garbage truck and there's lanky Jim McNaughton, not lookin at Mike's truck, leaned as far back into his seat as he can get, his eyes to the floor. Yeah, could be worse I s'pose, could be fuckin worse.

19. Shards

A thousand more years before Clayton goes:

—Yes please. A coma. Yes please. That'd suit me just fine.

I got to piss so bad my teeth are dancing in my gums. Could always go in my pants again. Might have to. Cant think in sentences, not full ones, sensible ones. Not what's here in my head. Clayton got a beer, he's been ranting about a table. This apartment is like a tomb, a bottomless black hole. Daylight poking through the blanket that's tacked up where the upper door should be. If I let my mind wander I can convince myself that it's really coming on dark. The floor doesnt look stable. Just a reminder that we can always sink a little further down. The linoleum is warped and sort of heaving, like lookin out over the salt water just before a storm comes on. All is calm on the surface, but you can see the swell underneath and you know some powerful, unstoppable force is just waiting to do its dirty work.

This patch of bog behind our elementary school. We werent allowed playing on it. We called it the bouncy ground. If you stood in one place too long the bog water would soak through your sneakers. When you jumped on it you could hear it sloshing underneath your weight and the bog would rise up all around you. My foot broke through it once and my leg went down, past my knee, before someone grabbed me and pulled me up. The leg of my pants was soaked black. Clayton picked me up once and body-slammed me on it, right in the centre. I didnt know who he was. I landed flat on my back with the wind knocked out of me and I couldnt move. I started to sink. Clayton helped me up. The cold black muck soaked my uniform from the collar of my shirt to the cuffs of my pants. Teacher was watching and we were both sent to the office. The nun had a little box on her desk labelled "consequence cards." We each had to pick one at random and then write a paragraph in response to whatever was on the card. Mine was a question, religious, something about God having shaped us in his own image. I cant remember it exactly. I didnt know what to write. Me and Clayton were left in the office on our own and he was going through the nun's desk. I read my consequence card out to him and asked him what I should write. He slipped something into his pocket and shrugged and said *It's all bullshit anyhow. Think God gives a fuck? Just write a few Hail Marys.* And then *Sorry about your uniform, by the way.* I never did ask him what was on *his* card.

• • •

I'd kill for a drink, but not beer. Water. Another few hours until the bars are open again. I hope I'm asleep by then. Thick, ugly smell off this couch, deep-fried something. Clayton looks to be holding on to something more than a beer. His girlfriend's gone again. Isadora. She's a doll and a half. He needs to clear that up. But she's wild too. I dont know. She showed up last night right after she said she wouldnt. So me and Clay were already after going ahead and dropping some acid. I wasnt really up for it to tell the truth. I came back east to clean myself out more than anything else. But he seems to want to go, go, go every night of the week, and that's just not me anymore. Anyhow, Clayton, thinking he was in the clear for the night, was just after dropping the acid when his girl's all of a sudden standing in the main room, hands on her hips and looking like she'd been listening in on the whole thing, whatever kind of retarded dirt we were getting on with. She smiled at me so gorgeous, but there was no play in it, just pity. I took the hint to give them a bit of privacy. I jumped in the shower. I got lost in the shower. I shaved and I thought I heard Clayton crying, high and childish and loud. Must be how he is with her, unguarded and dramatic.

I found vodka under the sink in the bathroom. I downed it. I dont know why. I had a shave. Made me feel false, like I was trying too hard. I looked at my face in the mirror. I cant be this same old bag of scum. Same old sad waster. I ground my teeth and smoked and stuffed twisted cones of toilet paper up my nose to clean it. Same old ugly beast.

The bathroom here is like a grubby, long-abandoned cocoon. Cant imagine it's launched that many butterflies. Moths maybe. A crack running down the left-hand side of the mirror. I read some-where about that, a bad omen, a constant reminder that your life is not whole. My reflection is split down the middle, the crack running a jagged line between my two eyes. One half of my face deformed and childish.

An explosion of glass in the main room behind me, Isadora shout-ing at Clayton to grow up and get on with it.

Missed a spot shaving. I brought the sticky razor hot and dry across my neck. Blood. The sight of it. First time seeing my own blood since that night in Edmonton. I watched the tiny bead trickle down my neck beneath the collar of my shirt. Nothing like Edmonton.

Isadora skipping back down the stairs. She said goodnight to me, but I never answered. I walked into the main room. Clayton looked fine, never say he was bawling at all. He had a bottle of generic codeine that he wanted me to snort. I showed him some-thing better, the results of my education in western Canada. Drop six or seven tablets in a cup of boiling water, stir and let it settle. The milk that floats to the top, that's almost pure codeine. Let it cool and drink it down. Avoid the sludge at the bottom. Instant. Clayton loves anything instant. I had a tiny sip, at his insistence.

We played Nick Cave. *Murder Ballads.* Dark shit that got us won-dering out loud if we're ever going to kill, if we're capable. We got talking about high school, about mushrooms and a murder that almost happened. I hadnt thought of it in years, how close we can come sometimes. All the fellas from phys-ed class on a canoe trip into the Butter Pots. Overnight. Mushrooms. Seven of us sitting on a grassy hill away from the campsite while the mushrooms were kicking in. The rest of the group, the nerds and suck-holes and jocks, back collecting firewood and setting up tents. The teacher, Mr. Spurrell, a real cocky jerk from Mount Pearl with a weasel's accent, the ultimate authority on everything, sooky and viciously competitive and useless. Screwing around with one of the girls in grade eleven. Punched some young grade-niner during a basketball game the year before, and broke his rib. Got off with it too, no apology. Long, hooked snout on him. Two false teeth, souvenirs from back in the days when he had no power over no one. I know that clown too well. Failed me just for showing up. First time I saw him, back in grade nine, I goes:

—What're ya at b'y?

And he grabs me by the shirt and slams me off the locker, gets right up in my face with his sour coffee breath and says:

—I'm not your *boy*. Dont forget it.

That's the kind of arsehole he was. I was only saying hello.

But we had him in the woods now, a four-hour hike from the highway. We were *born* in the woods. And at some point we decided that he should *die* in the woods. Madness, like only the mushrooms can serve it up. We'd strike him over the head with a paddle, knock him out and hold him under the water.

We got excited. The sky turned a brilliant red and then was gone again. Nothing for miles. A loon. The night coming on. I pictures Spurrell his cold white face floating just beneath the surface, dead eyes wide open, his curly hair swaying back and forth with the current. Nothing to get away with it. No one would tell. A secret to take to the grave. The grave. We turned quiet, paranoid. Someone could be listening, down there in the shadows of the trees. Spurrell could be listening. Night coming on. The loon further off now. We trudged the path back to the campsite in single file. No one spoke. Clicking their jaws and watching the steam rise from their mouths, stretching their knotted backs. I was in the lead. I stopped. We all stopped. The smell of the fire. I looked at Clayton, who wasnt limping back then, and was even more cracked than he is these days. I couldnt remember if we'd decided anything, if any of it was real.

—So, are we gonna do it?

—What?

—Kill him?

—I dont know.

We sat around the fire all night, listening to Spurrell talk his townie crap, no one making any eye contact, the suck-holes doing just that: sucking hole. Some dunce put a can of soup on the fire without puncturing it first. It blew to bits, like a gunshot. Everyone screamed, even Spurrell. He had a long noodle hanging from his nose. He swore oaths we never knew existed. We all laughed together. He laughed with us, not at us. He told us about a fight he had with his father two weeks before he died. Men. Out in the woods. Living life away from the greyness of our lives.

Saved by a noodle. How close we can come.

• • •

Clay freaked out for the first hour last night. Stuck his fingers down his throat as far as it's humanly possible. Spewed chunks and bile and blood and maybe a bit of codeine onto the floor in the bathroom, trying to get the acid back up. No chance. Once it's in, it's in.

A good ten hours now. Well, not all good.

I waited around for him to clean himself up. I tuned up my guitar and played one of his uncle's songs:

> *Too much, too fast, too young, too soon.*
> *Not quite ready to shed this skin,*
> *Still a minor bit confused.*

Seemed to fit. Clayton didnt recognize it. I never let on it wasnt one of my own. I wish. He came out of the bathroom dressed to the nines with his fancy so-called IRA jacket and black pants and them crunchy biker boots shined and polished to a gleam. Bandana around his neck, no fingers in his gloves and his hair slicked back tight to his head like De Niro in *Cape Fear.* So of course then I had to go change cause I looked like I just crawled out of a dumpster, knees gone out of my jeans, paint and mud splattered on the toes of my boots and a big streak of grease on my shirt.

After I got done up we went downstairs to the Closet. Clayton's idea, believe me. That's the bar on the middle floor of the building. My Place, it's really called. I did not want to go there. We could hear all night that there was some kind of bash on the go down there. The Closet is a strange spot. Ten o'clock in the morning and you're liable to hear fellas havin sex down there on the floor or the pool tables. Clayton thinks they must be making porno. Clayton dragged me down there once or twice already. Late-night fuckery. Give some old queer the eye and it's free booze for as long as you can stand it, or stand up. I dont know, passes the time sometimes.

The entrance is down in the alley. A flight of stairs up to the bar. Dark red place. Eyes in the corners. I've never been able to penetrate the place, but could only ever hang at the corner of the bar, keep as close to the exit as possible.

A nasty and messy murder in the Closet years ago. Mike Quinn told us about it, the day I announced my intentions to move upstairs with Clayton, back in January. The manager was found one morning behind the bar with a broken rum bottle stuck in his throat, floating in his own blood. The case is still unsolved, but Mike says everyone pretty much knows who done it. One of those guys that no one's gonna stand up to. Some skeet.

Another time the cops were called in and found the bar empty, except for one young fella who was strapped to the pool table with a broken mop handle shoved up his rear end. And here I am now, living right above the place. No wonder I'm having the nightmares lately.

Me and Clayton made a grand and loud entrance. I had a bit of cash on me, from busking, but I decided to give the old credit card a try. It's maxed out beyond repair, but I was pretty sure they had a manual machine. Clayton filled me in on the manual machines, how they got some sort of insurance policy on the go. You can charge up to seventy-four dollars at a time, and even if the card is maxed, so long as it's not expired, then the bar is covered. And once you get up around seventy-four bucks, you can just start a new bill. When Clayton's working downstairs I'll write him thirty- and forty-dollar tips and he splits it with me. I dont know, it's a scam. I know it's all going to blow up in my face one day. They shouldnt have been so stunned to give me one.

I yanked the card out of my pocket and slapped it on the bar. The greasy bartender barely looked at it, but he seemed happy enough to see me and Clayton. Half a dozen old queens slumped around the bar. You could feel the shift in the atmosphere when we made clear our intentions to hang around.

—Take Visa?

The bartender nodded. His eyes dropped to my crotch. I nudged Clayton and he grabbed me by the chin and planted a sloppy one on my lips. I tried to pull away but he held tight to the back of my head. This is how he gets his kicks. He was so fried he probably didnt know but I was Isadora. I managed to pull away when I felt his tongue flicking off my front teeth. He slammed his hand down on top of my rogue Visa and shouted across the bar:

—Drinks for the house!

Bastard. The bartender flew into action, afraid we'd change our minds before he broke even for the night. They were all drinking beer, all the old queens. That's all any of them ever drinks, as far as I can see. And they wonders why they cant get laid. I ordered two pints of Guinness, Clayton's choice poison. Anything Irish, even his accent. He's been slamming me about mine, how it's gone so flat and grand from my time out west. I dont bother to call him on *his* though.

Clayton was nearly asleep at the bar by the time the pints got to us. I slid the glass into his hand. He looked at it, lifted it to his mouth and drained it. That's not fit, how he does that. Cant have a sociable drink with that fella. No. Every time has to be the last time. As hard as you can go. I flattened mine too, just so we could keep the night balanced. I ordered two more. I never had so much as a taste of the stuff before I started knocking around with Clayton again. It's good. Heavy. Clayton says it's nowhere near what you gets in Ireland though. But neither are the cigarettes or the music or the women or the draws. Sometimes I feels like choking him.

When the greasy bartender turned to the taps I got a glimpse at the sign taped to the mirror behind where he was standing:

Exotic Dancer
Brutus Bentley
Appearing Tonight!

Must have been the commotion we were hearing from upstairs earlier. I looked around the bar, but none of them old queens were exotic dancers. Clayton bravely wandered into the darkness of the room and slumped down at a table with his pint. I asked the bartender:

—Where's this exotic dancer to?

—On break. He'll be back—

But before he could finish, Brutus Bentley himself was standing right there beside me. Mid-thirties, buzzed head, all pumped up with barbed wire tattooed on both biceps and reeking of baby oil. Skin-tight tee-shirt with the words *Not Gay as in "Happy" but Queer as in "Blow Me"* emblazoned across the front. He leant over my shoulder and I got the impression he was smelling me.

—And just who, might I ask, is re-ques-ting me?

Flat, mid-Canada accent. Husky voice. No lisp.

I dug around for a good name but all I came up with was:

—Brent.

—Brent? My, my. How . . . ex-o-tic. And what brings Brrrent to a place like this?

I knows what brings *him* to a place like this. Yes. He's a washed-up callboy. Answered an ad in some tabloid on the mainland and decided a change was just as good as an arrest. Exotic dancer. We'll see. He licks his tongue into the corner of his mouth. I leans in and breathes my thick, smoky Guinness breath in his face.

—I'm just looking for a bit of fun.

He gets a kick out of that and I can tell he's relieved too. He must be pretty sick of being ogled by these old geezers all night. I cant believe this, I came back home to get clear of the scuzz, find a sane woman. This is all Clayton's doing, how no one our age ever sets foot in this place, even though that's what the old queens are out looking for. Here's his analysis:

—They're all just sad fuckin closet cases with child seats in the backs of their cars and the wife thinkin they're off to an AA meeting, while they're really out suckin each other's cocks on their knees in the pissy bathroom stalls. Best place for a free drink when you're strapped for cash.

Brutus Bentley looks me up and down and flashes his healthy, well-kept, disgracefully white teeth.

—Well then, you've cer-tain-ly come to the right place for fun havent you? Be-cause fun is my spec-i-al-i-ty.

I can feel a rage just below the surface, swelling up around the corners of my mouth, an itch in my gums. It's a battle to push it down deeper. That's not me. It's the acid. I flattens my pint and glances over at Clayton. He's smoking a cigarette and staring at the floor. Brutus takes note.

—Is that your boy-friend?

—Maybe. If he plays his cards right.

—Oh my. Such con-fi-dence.

—So are you gonna fucking dance or what?

He feigns shock, but I can tell he's lapping it all up. He looks at the greasy bartender.

183

—The lan-gu-age. Young pups these days. We're go-ing to have to cut him off Ger-ard. Or per-haps he's al-rea-dy cut? What say you Brrrrrent?

Whatever the hell that means. I'm struggling to hang on to my good nature here. I order another pint. Brutus clears his throat in an exaggerated way. I nod at greasy Gerard and he mixes up some ornamental cocktail for Brutus. Brutus raises his glass.

—To Brrrrent. And fun.

He sips his drink and places it gently on the bar. I glances back at Clayton, his head in his hands, staring at the floor like he'll burst into tears any second. That's no good, not for acid. I'll only end up ditching him to save my own trip. Cant do that. I looks back to Buff Brutus.

—What about that dance then?

He puts his arm around my shoulder and gives my back a little rub.

—Well it's kind of lone-ly out there on the dance floor. Per-haps you might like to join me?

All the old queens are listening in on the conversation. I can feel their anticipation, their need. They knows I'm not gay. They must. But they're hoping against hope they're gonna see some action. Brutus stirs his fancy cocktail. I throws another glance at Clayton. Have to liven him up. Bit of fun.

—Alright, let's do it.

I whips off my jacket and marches in behind the bar. Greasy Gerard doesnt know how to react, so he slinks back to the far end of the bar, giving me full swing of the place. I flip through the CDs until I finds the perfect song. The Clash, "The Magnificent Seven." Not my favourite of theirs, mind. If they hadnt recorded *London Calling* I wouldnt even have given them a second spin. But "The Magnificent Seven" is most definitely the song for this moment in time, with Brutus Bentley on the dance floor at the Closet. I slip the disc in the player and crank it. The beat kicks in and I strut out to the dance floor. Brutus follows but I stop him. I have to shout in his ear:

—Lose the shirt!

—What?

—Lose the fuckin shirt!

He does. He flings it back over his head and it lands on Clayton's lap. Clayton looks up from the floor, sees me out on the dance floor with some fella with no shirt on. He roars laughing but I cant hear him over the music. I look at Brutus to lead, but he just stands there, tapping his foot and snapping his fingers and shaking his hips a bit. To hell with that though, I'm here to dance, push this dark and angry acid in a whole new direction. I catch the beat.

Now, I was never one for dancing. Never. School dances, I was one of the ones standing back in the shadows of the gym waiting for a slow song to come on. I could do a slow song, but with the fast ones I could never let myself go, never had the rhythm, always felt too self-conscious and generally stumbled around waiting for the song to be over. But something came over me, out there in the middle of the floor at the Closet with Brutus Bentley. Pretending to be gay. Maybe that was it. Bent Brent. It was like wearing a mask. It wasnt about cheering Clayton up. I got lost. I trapped the bass in my core, held it there, let it gush through my veins, swivelled my hips and pumped my crotch and lifted off the floor accordingly. I got lost. Brutus hooked his arm around my waist and leaned back with his leg fixed in between mine. He kept giving Clayton these aggressive, competitive glances. Clayton roared all the harder. I rocked my shoulders and clapped my hands and the bar clapped along with me. Look out! Here comes the vacuum . . . and there goes the poor old budgie. Love that song. Had a great laugh to tell the truth, even took my own shirt off.

And then the song was over and that girlie "Rock the Casbah" song came on. Someone should have shot Joe Strummer before he had the chance to record that one. I picked up my shirt and walked back to the bar, left Brutus in mid-thrust on the dance floor. Clayton was up now and waiting at the bar with a fresh pint for me. Brutus looked suddenly feeble and awkward out there on his own. I felt kind of bad. Clayton went in behind the bar and shut off the song.

Greasy Gerard stood back and let him have the place. Gerard looked at me like I was a god. Clayton flipped through the CDs and slapped on Guns N' Roses, *Appetite for Destruction*. One of the best rock-and-roll bands that ever walked the face of the planet, hands down. Welcome to the goddamn jungle. That opening riff is a masterpiece, makes you want to eat glass. That put Clayton right back on track, although I'd like to think my little dance routine had something to do with his transformation too. Brutus slithered in between us. He opened his mouth to talk and Clayton pretended to cough, spraying beer in Brutus's face. I didnt really agree with that. Brutus stood there with stout running onto his chest, looking back and forth between the two of us. He knew right there that he'd lost the game.

Axl Rose guiding us through all the broken moments, all the scraps and slivers of gloom just lurking in the backs of our heads. Nothing like a good dose of GN'R to wake up the old devils. Brutus wiped himself off with his shirt and took on this wounded beast-of-the-field stance, as if he'd never been so insulted in his life. But I could tell that he'd let us go a lot further than that, that he was good and used to taking all manners of abuse from lowlier shitheads than us. I didnt have the heart to crucify him though. Clayton dug his finger in Brutus's chest, hard.

—Do yourself a favour Brute, and go back to where you came from, before this night gets out of hand.

Brutus turns to me, his eyes dripping with desperation.

—What's wrong? I thought . . .

—Dont mind us Brutus. We're just arseholes.

—What do you want me . . .

Clayton piped up then:

—Look buddy, we've seen your dance and now we're finished. So excuse us, please, we're tryna have a goddamn conversation here.

Clay finished his pint and ordered another. Brutus watching him and it looked like he was gonna sideswipe him. But there was nothing and no one taking Clayton off guard. He's always watching. And if he's not, well I am. Brutus looked back at me, all misery-eyed and pouting, silently pleading with me to alter my behaviour. Clayton laughed in his face and snapped his fingers and pointed towards the backroom.

—Go.

I felt bad for him. He sulked back behind the bar and tried to mix a drink. Greasy Gerard took the glass from him and poured the drink himself. Before he handed it to Brutus he looked to me to see if I was paying for it. I wanted to buy it for him, but I knew Clayton would never let me live it down. Gerard handed Brutus the drink and then wrote it down in a little notebook near the register. Brutus disappeared into the backroom with his fruity drink and freshly broken spirit.

Clayton ordered two more pints and two shots of whiskey. He'd drink all night on my Visa if I didnt put a stop to it. One of the old geezers nearest us, plaid shirt and Donovan's Industrial cap, gave Clayton a quick, harmless wink. Clayton slammed his cigarette into the ashtray and sparks went flying in the air.

—You fuckin wink at me?

The old plaid queen gripped both hands to his beer and sank deeper into his seat. Christ, he was only saying hello.

Gerard laid the drinks in front of us.

—Guys, please. No one comes here for trouble.

Me and Clayton looked at him, then at each other. Clayton laughed so hard that a chunk of brown phlegm dislodged itself from the back of his throat and landed on the bar in front of us. I couldnt catch my breath or keep my balance. That shrill, maniac, faraway laughter that generally occurs mid-trip, at the peak. But I knew we were nowhere near peaking yet. The Closet was only our first stop. Gerard shuffled back to his place behind the bar and tried not to look at us. We drank.

I needed to piss. Clayton was off, to the point where I couldnt tell if he was crying or not, so I couldnt leave him at the bar on his own. I measured the distance between the bar and the bathroom, how many steps it would take. I clenched my gut and drew my balls into it, tried to reduce the pressure from my bladder. I could feel the head of my cock suddenly wet and cold. It got to the point where I couldnt move. This is how your bladder works on acid after half a dozen pints of stout. Cold sweat on my forehead. It came to the point where I couldnt talk, for fear of breaking my concentration. Couldnt even breathe. Clayton lit a smoke, held the package out to me. I reached for a smoke, and I let go in my pants. Warm piss filled my right boot, puddled onto the floor around me. It felt kind of pleasant.

We stayed on drinking for another while. Brutus resurfaced only once to get a refill, like a dog that's after crapping on the carpet and now's trying to nose back into the room to see if it's been forgiven. Clayton snapped his fingers and pointed to the backroom.

—Go!

He went. "Paradise City." Take me down. Time to move on to the next hellhole.

Booze does nothing but fuel acid. We. Are. Enhanced. Yes Clayton, Shane MacGowan is a god. We. Have. Become. I let go in my pants again. It hardly made a difference the second time around. Clayton looked down and saw the puddle, my fine blue cords stained black and shimmering wet beneath the red lights of the bar. We. Have. Become. Two shots down the hatch. Whiskey, hot in my throat. Clayton opened his hand and dropped his empty pint glass on the floor, never so much as batted an eye to acknowledge it. Gerard rushed out with a broom, nudged past me and slipped in my piss. I tried to catch him before he fell. Legs in the air, his rear end hit the floor with a muted thud I could feel right through my bones. Clayton swiped the credit card from the bar and slipped it in my back pocket. He nodded at me.

I wanna go. I wanna know.

Oh wont you fuckin please take me home.

Bye Axl. Seeya Slash.

• • •

Down the stairs and out to the street. I've taken my pint with me. I take a sip as we're walking onto Water Street. It's suddenly warm and bitter slop. Irish bog water. I sprays some in Clay's face and smashes the half-full glass off the door of the Closet. I'm watching myself do that sort of thing. We round the corner and dip into the Hatchet. I breathe in the stagnant, poisonous air of the bar. My lungs can take more and more with every breath. Clayton lights a smoke and hands it to me. We're both standing in the doorway, looking over the bar like desperadoes from an old western. It's funny. I cant decide if I'm gonna shoot the place up or sidle up next to some whore. Shit. That's harsh. Acid.

Jim McNaughton, right on cue, tips his hat and nods at us before his eyes and heart plummet back into his drink. Neil Young on the box. "Heart of Gold." Clayton's old romp is there, clinging to the bar trying to light a match that just wont give up the flame. No way is she coming back to our shack this night. That's what Clayton is like though. She wiggles her fingers across the bar at us. Clayton shakes his head at her and turns to me.

—I'll be back.

—Fuck you, where you going?

—Find Isadora.

I know there's no arguing with him on that. One-track mind he got.

—Coming back?

—I wont be an hour. Just wants to see who she's with. We'll hook up and hit the Zone for a laugh.

—Fuck you. Dont go telling that to no one.

He's gone then and I has a pang of panic about the whole Brutus Bentley thing. I know bloody well Clay'll tell Isadora right off the bat. Delighted to have something retarded to share with her, anything to bring her back over to his side of the table for the night. He's mental if you ask me. Going on about how he wants to marry her, when they've yet to plug even a full week together. They've fought each other every step of the way so far as I can see. Nice to have somebody though, I guess.

20. If You're Lookin for Drama . . .

On the steps of the Ship like a fuckin retard, gawkin in through the murky old orange glass to see if I cant catch sight of her. I knows she's in there. But I aint lookin for trouble, really, no scene, no dramatics. I reckon I dont know what I'm hopin to see, maybe me eyes wants to see something that me heart doesnt. Who she is, *how* she is when I aint around, how she turns her back on me. Show me something girl, something human: weakness, flaws, disloyalty, dishonesty, fuckin lie to me, humiliate me, dive head first into all them places you swears you'll never go again. Gimme something. I knows she's in there, loaded by now too aint she? Just cant bring herself back after the first one. No goin back. Like this acid. It's in me system now till I sleeps it off. And aint sleep a long way off tonight? With her out here in the city, in some bar without me, entertaining people, talkin, laughin, *showin herself.* Without me. If I cant catch just a glimpse of her, if I cant connect, make amends, or find some reason to justify this guilt, this rage, some discrepancy in how she conducts herself, I knows I'll spend the next twelve hours on me knees, lost and broken and pinin for her with a death wish so heavy on me shoulders I'll never be able to walk upright again. Acid does that shit to me.

I cant make nothing out through this fuck of a window, just shapes and outlines and muted lights. I presses me ear to the cold steel door. The tail end of that Billy Bragg song, from *Mermaid Avenue.* She loves that album. The music dies away and I strains hard to pick out something of her voice through the garble of mumbles and snorts and hoots and cackles from the crowd. That one, that sounds like her laugh. I conjures up her smile, bright, soothin to me head when I brings it into full focus. I tries to match the image of that smile with the laugh I just heard . . . Cant be sure. The moment's gone. And I should get meself gone. Before I goes mad. Or maybe this *is* madness. Maybe there is no goin back from here. Really.

The bartender turns on the Pogues version of "Dirty Old Town" and before the vocals even kicks in I hears Iz scream across the bar:

—Turn that shit off! You know I cant stand that guy!

And within seconds the song gets replaced by one of Val's songs. "Hard to Believe". And Izzy pipes up again with:

—That's good, that's the one . . .

> Greasy Dan is dyin for a taxi
> He feels a little smaller in the rain
> He got a pair of scissors in his old grey coat
> He's goin down to sink 'em in his buddy Shane.

Val's newly "rediscovered" working-class, disillusioned-street-life song. How low we can sink, how desperate we can get once our worlds get shrunk down enough, once the walls close in finally. The radio's been playin this song a fair bit lately, for some reason. I dont know how old it is, or even what album it's on. Val's got lotsa his shit scattered about anyhow. Most of the bar inside starts singin along and I knows full well none of 'em really understands it, that none of 'em have ever or will ever know the pain of homelessness or wandering the streets without love or home or family or hope. That's what the fuckin song is about: bein forgotten, cast out in the cold.

• • •

Forehead still pressed to the door, I grips the handle. Me heart flutters and then sinks a bit. That quiver in me chin, jaw clenched, the

191

grind of me teeth. I glances down at the slushy concrete beneath me boots and it seems to ripple and dip when I clicks me heels against it. Me boots are muddy and streaked with road salt. There's a film of sparkly brown glass dust caked into the leather rim of the soles. That's not good.

I should go now, go back to the acid with Brent and have a good time, drink meself down out of it. Leave her for good. Walk away and suffer it out in some long-drawn-out calm and sober silence. Just find some cozy hole to crawl into and rock meself back and forth till she's outta me system. Walk away. Be the first to drop the bomb. Before *she* guts me.

> Shane is draggin Sissy through a doorway
> He's numb and he can barely feel her pain
> She's sunk another fifty in the VLTs
> Gotta teach the girl a lesson for a change.

I'll just walk in and grab her hand and drag her home and fuckin take her every which way she wont let herself be taken. Wild and free and open and fully fuckin *inside*. See her try and gut me after that. I presses me ear harder to the door. There's talk now. Someone says in a dreary and wintry slurred Canadian accent:

—Is he still alive? What's his name? McGraw? McDougal? I dont know.

And from across the bar again Isadora shouts:

—MacGowan. Shane MacGowan. He's a zombie.

I tried to get her into the Pogues a while back, turned it on in the room when we were makin yet another attempt at decent sex. And didnt she just jump up outta the bed and flick it off:

—What are we in high school? I'm not screwing to the beat of some drunk shit.

—But it's good Iz, there's romance in there, it's poetry girl.

—Poetry? Screaming, howling drunken growls is all anyone can make of it. And you only like it cause it's from over *there* anyway.

I told her then, about the time I saw old Shane with that other band, the Popes, at the Olympia in Dublin. How MacGowan really was a zombie, how it was all true about his demise. And the crowd lovin it all, like they were there to witness a hanging, a crucifixion, a martyring. Heartbreaking, seein him like that. He couldnt find the mic stand, couldnt raise his voice, didnt know where he was. Threw up on stage. It was all so fucked and sad and tragic. And I was tryna relay this to her you know, tryna get her to listen to the songs, the words, instead of the drunk that was singin 'em. She wouldnt bother though, just nodded at me with this distant ghostly smile. I told her about the crusty scars between MacGowan's middle and index fingers, how a technician would come on stage with a fresh-lit cigarette to replace the one in MacGowan's hand. How sometimes old Shane would bring his hand to his mouth to take a draw and there wouldnt even be a cigarette in it, then drop his hand back to his side and the fresh new smoke would just magically appear.

I said:

—It was fuckin soul destroying. If I ever finds meself in that kinda state I hope someone has the good sense to put a bullet in the back of me head.

And she perked up then, finally, and goes:

—Suppose there is a soul Clayton, some part of our essence, our spirit, that carries on through eternity after we're gone. Do you think if *our* souls bumped into each other in like a thousand years from now, just out floating in the void, bumping around . . . do you think *our* souls would recognize each other? Do you think they'd link up, reunite and stay together? Or would one soul just say *Oh pardon me* and carry on?

—I . . . dont know girl. What's that got to do with Shane Mac—

—*I* think, that because there are billions of people in the world right now, which means that in a thousand years there'll be billions more souls out there, that it's irrational to assume you can meet your soulmate in a downtown bar.

—Okay . . .

And she smiled then and took me fingers and sucked 'em into her mouth, guided me wet hand under the sheet and between her legs and said:

—We dont need someone screaming in the background do we? Let's just try and be gentle. And look at me Clayton. Always look at me . . .

> *Sissy was a schemer back in high school*
> *She played a pretty tricky little game*
> *But ever since she "took a spill" and lost that tooth*
> *She's been waiting on the corner in the rain . . .*

• • •

I takes one deep breath, settles me heart, sucks in me gut, gives me eyes a good rub and shakes out the throb in me foot. No trouble now Clayton, no fuss, no commotion.

Head high, with what I hope looks to be a good-natured expression on me face, I barges in through the door, scans the room for Isadora. Twenty-odd bodies in the bar and they all turns to look at me the one time. A few nods, but nothing of the welcoming sort. The Table of Death is there, minus Robert Dawe. That's what they calls the old theatre crowd when they all conglomerates in the corner and drinks themselves into oblivion and bitches about why they aint more famous and why they're so broke and yaks about what big ideas they got and how the world is gonna one day listen up. One of 'em cornered me a few weeks back and went on and on about some novel he was plannin on writin called *The Island,* how there's never been a book like it and how it's the only book by a Newfoundlander that'll ever need to be read by anyone, anywhere in time. That's what he said. And that it was gonna be absolutely brilliant. Just brilliant. I told him to fuck off and go write it then. Arseholes, the lot of 'em. They'll turn on you in a flash if you shows 'em one sign of weakness or praise you to the high heavens if you might be of some use to 'em. I've seen Val at that table from time to time, come to think of it.

194

And now, here's the lady of the hour. Sittin on some cocksucker's knee with her forehead pressed to his. They're both gigglin. See? I aint so fuckin paranoid after all. Fuckface got on these expensive-lookin Buddy Holly glasses and a skin-tight pin-striped fag jacket with flared pants. He's got one hand gripped tight on Izzy's inner thigh. I cant see his other hand. I flexes me arms as hard as I can, to get the blood flowin. Clenchin me hands in and out as forcefully as possible without breakin a bone. To get the blood flowin. I unzips me jacket and marches towards them. No limp. Iz looks up and smiles that smile when she sees me comin. Like nothing atall outta the ordinary is takin place. She says, still smilin, her head rollin loose on her shoulders:

—Hello there you. Do you know Francis? He's directing that movie I was telling you about.

She grabs this Francis wanker by the two cheeks right playful and says:

—What do you think of Clayton here? Dont you think he'd make a great bad guy? Isnt he just so scary?

And she's just drippin with sarcasm of course and maybe *wanting* me to cause the scene that I'll be delighted to cause anyhow. Pokin at me. Mr. Director, cunty-balls almighty, scarcely glances at me and then turns back to Isadora, readjusts his grip on her thigh. You cant imagine how red the rage. You cant fathom how badly I'd just love to take that bottle of beer he's sippin at and jam it down his throat and then knock him to the floor and smash at the outline of the bottle with the heel of me boot and smash crunch stomp and grind the glass into his jugular and watch while he chokes on his own blood and snot and glass dust. Only I prob'ly wouldnt stop kickin and jumpin on his neck once I started, so he wouldnt even have a chance to choke, his head'd just get squat away from his body and then I'd pick that up like a football and fuckin boot it across the bar. I've heard all about this hotshot knob-gobbler with his artsy motion fuckin picture that's makin its way to town. How could I not when the whole fuckin town is talkin about it. Val's been meetin with people about it, readin through the script with fuckers. And Isadora's barely shut up about it for the past three weeks, goin on about how she plans to spend the money she'll make, when she dont even got nothing to do with it yet. Tryna tell me *I* should fuckin well audition too. And me sayin no, that I have no interest in pimpin meself out to some pricks and she goin on then about how I have no concern for the future, for *our* future. And me then, like the fuckin proper tool, I went and said to Val that I wanted in on it, how I wants a part or at least a fuckin audition and he just fuckin smirked at me. He fills me in then, how all the unionized crowd, the *real* actors, gets first go at auditioning. Then when the producers figures they aint gonna find anyone amongst that crowd, they invites the general public in to audition. Just so they can say *well, we tried, we looked,* before importing some wanker from Toronto or some second-rate wash-up from the States to *act* like what they thinks a Newfoundlander acts and sounds like. Make ya fuckin sick. Or they might actually find someone in Newfoundland who suits what they're lookin for and they raises the lucky individual up on a pedestal for a few weeks and then drops 'em like a bag of shit when the shoot wraps. Val's analysis made me sick to my fuckin guts to be honest. And it makes me kinda sad and nervous for Isadora, how she's so fuckin desperate to penetrate that world. Who knows how far she's willin to go to land some role that'll supposedly "make" her. I was fried on hash one day and said to her:

—Look girl, career stuff, that's just how we numbs ourselves. It's a façade that just lets us deny the reality of the shortcomings of our real lives, a life outside of all that, where we're loved and understood, a life where someone looks deep into your eyes and decides that no matter how much recognition you got, or money or talent, or whether or not you're a "name," that there's still *something* there worth lovin and upholding and protecting and keepin close. Look girl, it dont matter a fuck to me if you never sees a penny from that world.

That's what I said to her. Quite the speech, and pretty goddamn insightful if you're askin my opinion. But still, no gettin through to her. She says:

—I just want to touch it. That world. Then decide for myself if it's where I want to be. You go be content working a bar. I'm not.

She got this role a few years back in some sci-fi TV thing in Halifax and "caught the bug," as she likes to put it. It fuckin spoiled her, from what I can gather. They flew her up there and tucked her into a fancy hotel and treated her like glass and paid her a shitload of money and told her she'd be gettin all kinds of work afterwards, that she really had IT. This is what her friend Trish told me anyhow, that's Izzy's best friend I s'pose, another fuckin actress type. The two of 'em had a spat one night and Trish cornered me and started bitchin to me about it all, how Iz had come back from Halifax with her head all bloated and waitin around for the phone to ring. But Isadora told me later how Trish was after goin out for the same job. Trish said Isadora did a few "piddly" interviews in the papers, had her picture taken and even did the weather with that CBC fucker one evening. And then that was it. Nothing. Unless you counts the famous Toddler Dawe stalkin her and writin his shitty songs and poems for her. A few theatre shows, a couple of short films that didnt pay a cent, one line in that same movie Val was in last fall. Half a dozen auditions for bigshot *films* like the one that's comin soon to a mob of starving downtown artists near you. Casting directors from Canada with mobile phones growin out the sides of their pasty faces who comes to Newfoundland and tosses money around and makes promises and stokes egos and offers roles that're not yet even written. All so *smitten* with our quaint little accents and row houses. Buyin up land. Drinkin at the Ship at the end of the day and vaguely recognizing that lovely bartender from *somewhere*. Too full of shit and ignorant to realize she's the same girl who just bared her soul in front of their camera not two hours before.

All this burnin through me head as I hefts across the floor of the Ship. That greasy-money hand on Isadora's thigh. Mine. That little-girl-in-a-candy-shop pout on her face. That's mine too, that's only for me.

197

As I'm nearin the table where she's sat perched on this director fucker's lap, I can feel the crowd swell towards me, feel 'em bracin for trouble, feel the shift in the room. Conversation has ceased at the Table of Death. Val's classic fightin, soul-searchin downtown drinkin anthem punctuating my every step towards Isadora's table.

> Dont let nobody tell you there's a big love
> Our time is but a fleeting little dream
> They'll tell you there's a tunnel and a garden and a gate
> I find it so hard to believe.

Me hand flat on the underside of the little table closest to Isadora and this . . . fuckin . . . haughty little prick. The flex of me acid-fuelled arm. The table lobbed into the air in slow motion, ashtrays and glasses crashin to the floor. The look on that cunt's face. And Isadora still smilin like that, still perched tight and bouncin ever so slightly in his lap, this newest stab at success and recognition. I might kill one of 'em, I dont know. But suddenly there's hands around me midsection, a sweaty forearm tight around me throat and I'm bein dragged back towards the entrance. The bartender, some spoiled young yuppie spawn from Corner Brook I actually useta knock around with, he goes:

—Careful, watch out, guys. No lawsuits.

Isadora bursts up into me face then, hateful and mean and lovin it all cause she gets to take centre stage, her eyes fogged over and bloodshot with drink and sudden rage.

—Who the fuck *are* you? What the fuck are you trying to prove? I have to work here you know. Go make messes at your own scummy bar.

—Oh fuck off girl, I just wanted to see—

—Yeah fuck you! I know what you're looking for, what you came to see. Well here.

She pulls her shirt around 'er neck and digs one of 'er tits out of 'er bra and jiggles it in me face.

—Here. That's all isnt it? Snuggle up to the tit. Right? You and your fuckin—

And then Mr. Director, with his hands around her waist and draggin her away from me. I gives one big surge towards her and there's a roar from the crowd that's got ahold of me and the grip around me throat tightens and I knows I aint goin nowhere but out that fuckin door. The Table of Death all turned back to their drinks and misery. Nothing they havent seen before. And then the door slammin in me face and I'm sprawled on me back on the muddy slushy concrete walkway. Back on me feet then, punchin the heavy steel door till the blood runs free from me knuckles and the scarlet droplets pockin the fresh white snow on the railing.

. . .

Been sat here on the yellow guardrail in the parking lot beneath the Ship for what seems like an hour. *Snuggle up to the tit.* I cleans me hand in the snow, then makes a hard fist just to watch the fresh beads of blood seep and then pool between me fingers. Crazy Clara waddles by and asks me if I'm alright, if I'd like her to call an ambulance. She says:

—You're a Reid you are, yes you are. Val is your father isnt he, yes he is.

—No he's not Clara. He's not me fuckin father.

—Oh he's a wonderful man isnt he yes. Would you like a cigarette?

She holds out a fresh pack of du Maurier and I takes one. She lumbers on up the street then, hummin some old church hymn I vaguely recognizes from me school days. Poor woman. Funny though, cause if some fella with a shitload of money and places to go and people to meet saw *me* slumped here on the guardrail bleedin and shivering he'd likely just cross over to the other side and motor on, pretend like he didnt see me. Cause he prob'ly wouldnt be able to see me anyhow. Someone like Clara though, who lives right down in it, maybe she sees things different. Maybe she sees us all.

I dips me hand into the snow again and up it comes, clean and cold. I stays doin that, not really able to do much else, till I hears someone callin from somewhere behind me:

—Clayton? Is that you?

A heat, a warm presence settles on the guardrail beside me. I breathes a thick female scent of hair and smoky perfume. I wont look at her. I dips me hand again and when I brings it up a voice says:

—Ho-ly. You didnt kill her did you?

I turns to meet the voice, kinda shocked to see that the woman beside me is not Isadora. It's Trish.

—Naw. I just struck the door.

—You alright? Let me see it?

I offers her me busted hand for an inspection.

—It's nothing girl, just me knuckles.

—I heard what happened up there. I wouldnt worry though, the whole bar is wasted. She's a mess. She'll drink her way outta that role tonight.

—Yeah, or fuck her way into it . . .

—Clayton. C'mon now. She's just drunk. And that guy is a total dick. He wouldnt even look at me.

Trish smiles and breathes close on me neck.

—Besides, you know what they say. If you're looking for drama, go get yourself an actress.

—Yeah.

We're quiet then for a while. Trish holds me busted hand between her own and breathes the heat from her lungs onto it. The bleeding's stopped, and I'm kinda disappointed cause I was hoping maybe to lose too much blood and pass out in a snowbank and die. Trish says:

—So what have you got planned for the rest of the night?

—I dont know girl, go home and go to bed I s'pose . . .

She glances over her shoulder towards the steps to the Ship, then turns back and lays her head on me shoulder. She looks up at me, from that angle, with those dark brown eyes, and for a second it's almost like she's really seein me, and likin what she sees. She hooks her arm around mine.

—Want some company?

I turns towards the sound of Isadora's laugh gushin outta the Ship. A crowd surrounding her, dancin her up the steps towards Duckworth Street. They're all singin "Dirty Old Town," even her.

I looks back at Trish.

—Company? Yes. Yes I fuckin do.

21. More Shards

I walk to the far corner of the Hatchet. The smell of urine wafting up from my pants. Never notice in this place though. There's Mike Quinn with a good grip on some silly punk's jacket collar. Mike's leant over the table, chin to chin with the poor guy, talking slow through his teeth and half smiling in that psychotic way he got. I feel bad for the scrawny little guy, where Mike is holding him so awkwardly, with the whole bar conveniently not looking at them. It's embarrassing and sad and I'd trade places with the little imp in a flash. Everybody goes on about how vicious Mike Quinn is, but I figure his nuts are just as soft as mine. I feel my humanity rising up as I pass behind Mike. I fake an awkward tumble onto the table. I let on I'm loaded, grip the end of the table and try to bring it down to the floor with me. The ashtray empties onto my head. Mike lets go of the scrawny guy and grabs me under the arm instead. With one arm he stands me on my feet again. The scrawny shit stands up and moves on through the crowd. Mike sees that it's me and starts to laugh:

—Christ Brent my son, you're worse than the other fella.

Then he starts to lead me backwards, towards the door, and I realize it's going to backfire on me, that he thinks I'm too loaded and wants me gone for the night. I yank my arm away from him and spin around in the direction I came from.

—Who the fuck did that?

I screams it across the bar with as much fierceness as I can muster

202

up. Everyone freezes. Drinks and beer on the way to people's mouths. They suddenly dont know whether to spit or swallow. If the music had stopped at that moment it would've been perfect. All eyes on me.

—Who tripped me?

I zero in on the closest body to me at the bar. Big fella. Soft. Spend enough time in this place and it dont matter how hard you were on the way in. Not me though. I'm just visiting. I step towards him, a cold, sober step. Mike steps back to let me have the floor. Clayton says Mike loves a good racket. A cigarette butt falls from my hair. The big clunker at the bar looks away. I dont know what to do from here, but I gotta follow through now.

—You!

He turns his beady eyes my way.

—Yeah you. Big lummox. You trip me?

He stares blankly at me and shakes his head, his meaty jowls jiggling in time to the spazzy John Cougar song that just came on. A glow around his head that catches the smoke from his cigarette. I can feel the burn in my back. The scar where I was stabbed in Edmonton. The hot, sour breath on the back of my neck before the blade slid in. The pinch. The wet. The blurry outline of the weak little junkie weasel running away under the streetlights and ducking into the park. I would have killed him. *It*. I would have killed *it*. That night. Far, far from home. Collapsed in a pool of blood on a sidewalk in the flattest, deadest city on the planet. That woman with the stroller who crossed the street to avoid me. Then the hospital, the cops with their questions about my criminal record. And then home. East. Halifax with that French girl. Corner Brook with that Corner Brook girl. Trans-Canada to Witless Bay Line. Having to listen to my father all the way up the Shore.

—Back home again are ya b'y? No money, no job. Hope you're not looking to me and your mudder to go supportin ya all winter.

Home. Same old stained mattress. The posters on the wall. On the road to Town the very next morning. Drunk. All the way to this very moment, being a complete arsehole in a bar on Water Street. When all I really want is to play the goddamn guitar, sing a few songs, get my head back together. I never signed up for this, this death-by-association shit. I just wanted a place to lay low. Three or four years ago and I would have gladly destroyed Brutus Bentley with Clayton. I would have taken the whole bar down, and it would have felt fun and natural and justified. But that's not where I am anymore. Not who I am. But that's who he was expecting me to be. There's a whole other world out there with enough shitheads and thieves and boozers and druggies and two-faced con artists and slippery little cretins to stab you in the back. I dont need to be one of them. I can be something else.

My throat is hard and my eyes are wet. I dont know if I'll explode.

Mike Quinn lays his paw on my shoulder and gives it a little squeeze. I'm fully stoned now, I guess. The whole bar looking at me. I force a laugh and it seems like it blows new life and time into the room. Like everybody gets a second go at the night thanks to me. The chatter starts up again and Mike leads me to the bar. He raises his hand at Clyde Whelan and points at my head. Clyde goes over to the taps with a pint glass. I start digging in my pocket for the money, but the big meathead who didnt even trip me shouts across the bar that *he'll* get it. I nod my appreciation at him.

And that's all you have to do to get a free beer around these parts.

I keep to myself for the most part, for a while, and tries not to look mean and dirty. I even catch myself smiling. Soon enough Clayton's old flame comes over to me. Dana, Deena, something slutty . . . Donna. Right. She's a sad-looking case. Her eyes are sunk right in, the skin on her cheeks somehow sagging and pulled tight at the same time. Clay says she's pretty heavy into the coke nowadays. He says she was always skinny as a rake but now she's *really* gone away to nothing. He says she was so bony by the time they broke up that it literally used to hurt to fuck her. I think about this when she's right there in front of me, and I busts out laughing in her face. I knows she's only gonna pump me for info on Clayton. But I might end up pumpin her yet. This night. This night. If she plays her cards right. If he dont hurry up from wherever he's gone to. Jesus. Listen to me. The arsehole I can be. Spending too much time going nowhere, hanging around with that angry fucker.

Me and Donna get a table in the corner nearest the door. I like to be able to watch the street through the blinds, just in case. She buys me a beer special and I tell her a pack of lies about Clayton. Harmless ones though, more to suit my own chances of getting into her pants. If I have to. Dont know if I can do that to Clayton though. I mean I know he wants nothing to do with her, but still. I make Donna coax it all out of me anyway, so she thinks I'm really torn between my interest in her and my loyalty to Clayton. It's sick, but she adores him still. And the more she reminisces about him and praises him up, the more I'm drawn to her, somehow. I hear myself telling her how jealous and possessive he still is about her, how he cant stand to see her talking with other fellas, how he still talks about her all the time and just seems generally confused with his feelings for Isadora. She sucks it all up and starts pouring her heart out about how messed up she used to be, how she had ovarian can-cer when she was twenty, so she can never have children, how she's never mentioned it in years. After a while I realize I'm not really listening to a word. I cant. That's the acid. I can pick up on her tone though and so I know when to nod and say *yes* and *go on girl* and *dont be so foolish girl, you have a gorgeous figure* and reassuring stuff like that that women like to hear. I slip in the odd compliment about her hair and ask her about her perfume and her job. Subtle though, I am. No way am I gonna set her up to turn me down. She wants to know then how come I dont have an accent like Clayton when we're both from the same part of the Shore. I tells her Clayton's accent is just a put-on. Truth is though, it was just that much easier, on the mainland, when I sounded like everybody else.

It's coming on two o'clock now and Clayton still hasnt shown his face. Shag him. The acid is back now and I could screw a hole through my chair. My pants are after drying up but my foot is still sloshing around in my boot. Seems like a week ago I was dancing with Brutus Bentley. I go into the bathroom for a leak. I'm hard as a rock and end up spraying it all over the wall behind the toilet. Hard as a rock. Right then and there I make up my mind to go get her and bring her upstairs. I'm after putting up with enough now, this night. Trying to make sure Clayton keeps his head in order and then he walks out on me.

She's there at the table with her compact open and dabbing some lipstick on when I get back. She snaps it shut and looks up at me and smiles. I take my jacket off the back of the chair and haul it on. She takes the bait.

—You're not leaving already?

—Yeah. I'm just going to go on to bed. Feeling a bit down.

God, how sleazy.

—Down? Why? I'm having a great time.

—Yeah, but, I dont know . . .

—What?

—Nothing girl.

—No say it, come on.

—Well, it's just that, well Clayton's my buddy and, I dont know, I feel shitty sitting here with you all night. He'd have a fit.

She reaches for her coat.

—Brent, you're crazy. We're only talking, having a few drinks.

She stands up and swings her coat on over her arm. I get a whiff of her deodorant. One final hook now, one of Clay's recommended lines:

—Well it's just that, well, my intentions are not quite as pure as you might think they are.

Bang.

Out through the doors, up the alley, up the steps and into my bed. She's got me in her mouth before I even got the bedroom door closed behind me.

Bang, bang, bang.

No sign of Clayton, the gimp. Ditching me on the acid.

She's fucking me just to get to him, I know that much.

But he fucked me.

So fuck him.

• • •

I trot out to the main room for a smoke. I see her coat where she dropped it. I pick it up and search it, an old habit I'm trying to snuff out. In the inside pocket I find a little wrap of tinfoil. I give it a squeeze to see how much is there. Feels like a good-sized gram or so. But I know there's no such thing as a good-sized gram of coke. I know this. That's why I'm here, to wash out my system. Hard for me to be firm and upright about it now though, with the acid ripping through my head like this. I make sure the wrap isnt leaking and then throw it down in the corner behind the table. For later. Her coat is in midair, en route to the couch, when she walks out of the bedroom. She got a blanket wrapped around her, but I'm just standing there, letting it all hang out. Clayton always got the heat on blast. No choice, really, with the top door the way it is.

I sit on the couch and she sits nice and close. I let her snuggle in for a bit, nice warm, sex-sweaty woman in my arms. I'm not one of those guys that turn all icy as soon as the deed is done. There's not much to it, really; just smile and be calm and gentle. A chance to prove you're not a lowlife. I dont get it, how fellas can put on any face under the sun when they're on the hunt for a bit, but once they has their way they cant muster up the good nature to even fake a decent thank you.

—Are you alright about this Brent?

I dont answer. I could pull the Clayton card now I suppose, how I feel so shitty after nailing my buddy's woman. But I dont. Feel shitty. I start workin the night through in my head while she rubs the back of my neck. Nice. That's the spot. She takes the cigarette out of my hand and tucks it in the corner of her own mouth. Saucy. But my

207

head starts to turn, the floor wavering like that, and I'm all of a sudden filled with a burning urge to get out of this place, on my own. Go back out on the beer while the night is still young. I can drink in peace now, without the distraction of having to look for sex. Just drink and let the acid take over until it wears off. Drink my face off until I'm staggering and falling on the floor and vomiting and numb. That's what I want. For tonight. Spend all next week sober. The whole week. See if I cant get Clayton off the beer too. Clean up this hovel, restring my guitar, do some busking, drop by the job centre, finish the mural on the wall, call my mother for her birthday. I'll crack up that credit card too, before I'm arrested. First thing Monday morning, that's what I'll do. Hang on to it for now though, for tonight.

—What's wrong Brent?

—Nothing.

—Something.

—I dont know.

—Well, I have just the thing.

She reaches across the couch for her coat and brings it back to her lap. She digs through her pockets while I watch.

—Close your eyes now.

I squint really tight without closing my eyes. Panic dances across her face. She checks and rechecks her pockets, turns them all inside out. A string of blond hair sticking to the sweat on her forehead. She must be over thirty. I forget how old Clayton said she was. A loud bass beat from downstairs. The Clash. "The Magnificent Seven." Brutus Bentley, revisiting his downfall, trying to figure out where he went wrong. Donna jumps up and the blanket falls to the floor. She's all edges and spine.

It hurt to fuck her.

—It's gone, it's . . . it's fucking gone.

—What's gone?

I'm about to go fetch it, let her know I'm messing around, but then:

—I had coke. Three grams. It's not mine.

Three grams? Holy fuck. Three grams humming in my skull, my throat almost numb already. Go find Clayton and dig into three grams of coke? That's what this night needs alright. I gotta get her gone.

—Check your pants girl.

She darts into the bedroom and comes out with all her stuff. She searches her jeans and then pulls them on to double-check. Her face is red. I light a smoke. She snaps her bra on. I'm scum. She pulls the cushions off the couch and digs her hands through the layers of ash and crumbs and butts and cheesies and pubic hair and crusty jerk-stains that've collected down there since probably before what's-his-face, Keith had the place. I'd fit right in down there. She finds a piece of foil around the same size as the one she's missing and for a second her eyes light up with hope. But it's just that shit from inside a cigarette package. She crumples it and hurls it viciously at the wall. I am subhuman. My heart pounding. She hauls her sweater on inside out and backwards, the flashy white tag scraping the flesh beneath her chin. I almost point it out, but the quicker she's gone from here, the better.

—Did you use any tonight Dana?

—It's Donna, asshole. What do you think?

—Jesus girl, I'm only trying to help. Where to?

She looks at me then, hard, like she knows.

—Where to what?

—Where did you use it girl?

—In the ladies' room.

Like there's a *ladies'* room at the Awl and Hatchet.

—Well girl, I'd get down there and have a look if I was you.

She slips her boots on and puts her arms into her coat, checks the pockets again. She's lost to me now. It's a shitty, empty, broken moment. She's in hell. I could be the hero now, jump up and laugh and let her know it was all a joke, reach down behind the table and *Voila, calm down girl, I was having you on, c'mon lets do a few lines and go back to bed, see how our lives turn out*. But that's just it, if she

209

hadnt told me there was three grams there I probably would have let her off the hook. But I know there's no way I'm doing one or two piddly lines with her and then sittin back while she slips out the door with the rest of it. If I does one line I'm doing it all.

She has a hard time doing up her coat. Her hands are shaking. I'm sleaze. But I want her gone. My eye keeps going back to a Bic pen over on the table. I know the refill is loose in it. That's my straw, waiting. Fuck Clayton now too. She stands above me and I catch her lookin at my cock. For a moment she lets herself out of her new horror.

—Looks like someone's getting their second wind.

I looks down at my cock. It's hard as a rock again. Harder than when it wants sex. It's the bladder thing. It's gonna blow.

The door to Clayton's room swings open and that girl, Isadora's friend, the one with John Hibbs that night a few weeks back when I went mental outside the Ship, she dashes out into the main room. She's drunk looking, her hair all fucked up. Donna turns towards Clayton's door. My bladder lets go and it's the best relief I've ever known. All over the back of Donna's jacket. I pull it away and redirect the stream to the wall behind the couch. Donna jumps and smacks at her jacket like it was on fire. Piss on her hand. Isadora's friend sees me, sitting there on the couch with not a stitch on, hard as a rock, pissing all over the wall.

—This place is fucked up . . .

She laughs and Clayton roars even harder from the bedroom. I drop my head back and laugh too and then make a dart for the bathroom while Donna scurries and curses at me. Her and Isadora's friend are neck-and-neck for the stairs. Neither of them can get down to the front door quick enough. Isadora's friend shouts out to Clayton:

—You didnt see me Clayton, alright?

It's a wonder Donna doesnt lace right into her. I heard tell she likes to fight. But I guess she's more interested in getting her coke back now.

I have to piss in the shower because I'm too hard to hit the toilet. Clayton stands in the open doorway of his room. He's got a condom sagging from his dick, a wild, psychotic haze to his eyes. He looks at me. I'm still hard and dripping, cant turn it off. I grab a towel and press it to my crotch.

I cant believe I just did that to Donna. I cant believe I treated her like that. Stole from her and lied to her and pissed on her, humiliated her in front of Isadora's friend. That's not me. The crunch of glass under the girls' boots as they feel their way down the dark stairway. New friends? Donna shouts:

—You guys can go fuck each other!

Clayton tries to focus on me.

—Was that who I thinks it was?

—Who do you think it was?

—The walls are thin Brent.

—You dont have to tell me, I know.

—Fine then. Gettin dressed?

I haul on a dry pair of pants and socks and my old workboots, toss the wet boots out on the roof with the pissy cords and then I go down and lock the door. I watch Clayton pull his pants on. He dont even bother to haul the safe off his dick. I wouldnt blame him. I dread that feeling too.

We sit at the table and lace into the coke. Clayton doesnt ask where it came from and I dont bother to tell him. I chop at it with my credit card and slide huge lines across the table to him. Enough to stop your heart. But we dont give a fuck. Our hearts stopped hours ago. The night is new again. The coke doesnt do much in terms of a buzz, but it numbs us good. My nose and throat, my whole face. It's the acid stone, that head trip, with a powerful new deadness attached. Invincibility. Someone keeps pounding on the door but we turn the Pogues on bust and devour what's left of a bottle of Lamb's that was in the cupboard. I cant remember, from one minute to the next, what we've been talking about. Him screeching. I never cry. I'd need death for that. He's fucked when it comes to Isadora.

At some point I lifted my head to this new light in the room. Daybreak. Sweet Jesus. Still a pounding at the front door. If it's the cops they'd be in already. Could be someone dead belonging to me, my father out looking to report a death. The building next door on fire. All hands dead. Knock knock knock. Donna back looking for her blow. She got it all sussed out. Death warmed over. Too late now. I'd certainly fuck her good this time though. Dead fuck. Dead and dead. Fuck. Stench of piss. One last line between us. Knock knock knock. Drag our fingertips over the glass tabletop. Every last granule. Coke crumbs. Numb. Dead. *Buried 'neath the sod.* More. Little cuts and scabs on my hands. Yes Clayton, MacGowan is a god. Knock. Knock. Knock. Clayton holds his hand out, asks if it looks swollen, says he struck the wall at the Ship. It's a filthy hand. Knock knock knock knock knock knock knock knock knock knock knock knock knock knock knock knock knock . . .

—FUCK OFF! SHUT THE FUCK UP!

Clayton grabs a cheapish carving knife off the floor and we both march towards the stairs.

So, are we gonna do it?

What?

Kill him?

If it's Donna she'll know. Right away. Where her coke went. A shadow behind the blind. New blue morning. Clayton holds the knife behind his back, slides the latch open. Steps back. Yanks the door wide.

No one there.

Clayton steps out onto the iron stairs and looks up and down the alley. He strains to see around the corner of the old stone steps that lead to Duckworth.

No one.

—Did you hear someone knocking?

—I dont know. I think. Lock the door again.

Clayton cuts his foot on the way back upstairs. He wraps a tee-shirt around it and lets it bleed. He finds half a flat beer in the fridge. God knows who owned it. Daylight. Again. I make my way over to the long red couch with my guitar, haul the blankets up around myself. Clayton looks in his bedroom, the bloody tee-shirt on his foot leaving streaks across the floor. He pulls the big army blanket off his own bed and brings it back to the couch. I make room for him. The couch is long enough for the two of us to lie foot to foot without one being in the other's way. It was here when Clayton got the place. We lie there like that, foot to foot, afraid of our own bed-rooms, more comfortable in the open space of the main room where you can easier see something coming at you. The huge demonic murals, urchins and fiends and devils and sprites on the walls around us. Have to paint them over, or at least fix them up a bit.

Clayton:

—See Brent, this is no good. I just wants something that'll keep me out, so that I'm just floatin and feelin good and numb and drif-tin along in me own world and there's no hangover and I'm never havin to worry about comin down.

Me, years later:

—I believe they call that a coma. Want one?

. . .

There's an angry shard of mirrored glass pulsing with the floor, beneath the kitchen table. Wherever it came from, I dont know. I raise my torso off the couch until I can see my reflection in it. There I am. Part of me.

22. Screech In

I cant 'elp but with the big sigh when I looks round the bar tonight. H'empty, nothing. No one h'out on the go. Sunday night pool tournament cancelled and Mike didnt h'even 'ave the good grace to call a'ead and lemme know. He prolly thinks I woulda called in sick. 'E's right too.

Clayton's girl, h'Isa-snora, she poked her 'ead in round nine, lookin for the man 'isself. I said I never seen 'im all weekend, which is the truth. But she gives me this look like she can see right through the lie. Then she left. Cold, that one. But 'e's better off with 'er I think than that Donna. She shows 'er face in 'ere while I'm workin and she'll get a fucken h'earful.

Val called down h'earlier:

—H'Awl and 'Atchet, 'ello.

—Monica?

I fucken knew it was 'im before I h'even picked up the phone. Wish to Christ Mike'd splurge and get call display 'ooked up. I did this real sweet kinda grand townie h'accent:

—No I'm sorry she's not here right now. Can I take a message?

—Monica, I know it's you, just hear me . . .

And I 'ung up then, h'unplugged the phone too. And I watched the door, for the next hour. H'every shadow passin up the street sent jolts of h'anxiety up my spine. I did not and do not wanna see Valentine Reid tonight. I should cross over to the h'other side for a while, see if I cant find a good woman. Cause good men is just too 'ard to come by. In h'every sense of the phrase.

. . .

Long night a'ead, and nothing to wear youse down like a h'empty bar. The h'only thing to look forward to is locking up h'early. I pours m'self a light beer into a glass of h'ice, then put a straw down in it, so if Mike comes in 'e'll think it's ginger ale.

Shoot some pool now, since the table is free.

Seven in the corner. H'annnnndd . . . no good. Too much spin.

Could clean the filter on the smoke eater? Naw, 'ave to stand on a stool for that.

I walks back be'ind the bar and 'as a good look h'at m'self in the mirror. Three pounds lighter this morning. Know what got said to me 'ere last Thursday night? Mind youse now, the guy was tanked, fresh off George Street and likely spewed the same line at maybe a dozen h'others that very night, but I dont know, it gave me a lift. 'E was cute.

—Mizzuz, lizzan 'ere. I been in ivray bar vrom 'ere to St. Shott's da-nnnite an I 'ave de zay, I juz, I 'ave de zay, yer de zeggziest bar-tenner onna go.

—Well thank you. Would you like a double or a triple?

—Tribble yuh, tribble . . .

I poured 'im a single rum and coke and charged 'im for a tri-ple. They never can tell the difference h'after a certain hour. Funny though, 'e likely cant remember h'even bein *h'in* the 'Atchet, but that line of 'is 'as been playin in my 'ead h'all weekend. Dont take much to throw me h'off course.

. . .

I finally decides to plug the phone back in and the very moment I feel it connect with the jack in the wall, it fucken rings. I h'answers, more from reflex than anything else. Not like I'm concerned for Mike's business h'interests. And of course then I dont h'answer "correctly":

215

—'El-lo?

And 'oo should be on the line?

—Oh I'm sorry, I must have the wrong number. I was calling my bar. This must be someone's private line is it?

—Mike?

—What the fuck is going on down there? I've been trying to get through for over an hour. I cant even find out if my own bar is open?

—Clyde musta turned the ringer h'off today. I just noticed.

—Your shift started three hours ago . . .

—I know, I know. It's been a rough night Mike.

'Is tone changes then, conspiratorial, 'is h'interest shiftin now to money and bar sales. Wrong choice of words. A rough night, in Mike's mind, is when a busy bartender complains of h'actually 'aving to serve a few customers.

—Oh yeah? Few bodies on the go?

I cant lie to 'im. 'E'll be in to do the cash in the morning sure. And I 'avent sold a single drink or a beer.

—No Mike, there 'asnt been a soul in. It's h'empty.

—Well what's so goddamn rough about that?

—Just . . . I dont know, it's dull.

—Well liven the bloody place up some Monica. Put a few candles on the tables. Make it cozy. Turn on the right music. I can hear that angry loud shit you got on. That's not Sunday night music. And smile. I shouldnt have to tell you this stuff anymore. Bartending is more than just serving drinks. You knows better too, dont you?

I knows fuck-h'all as far as youse're concerned Mike. Let's be honest 'ere; I'm just a big set of tits, a good "draw" for your—

—Monica? You know better dont you?

—Yes.

—Very good then. Get to it.

I slams the phone down and 'ave to lay my two 'ands flat on the bar and bite my lip to keep from fucken screamin. Fat bastard pig. I wish the fuck he'd hurry up and give the bar over to that Silas fella. I couldnt care less if we h'all gets laid off either.

I could walk h'away right this second. Leave the door wide h'open to the dogs.

Where does he keep them cheap fucken candles? As I'm crouched h'under the sink diggin through the shoebox the phone rings h'again. I lets it ring a couple of times and then, sweet as pie, I h'answer:

—Awl and Hatchet?

—That's more like it. You still owe me ninety bucks in rent by the way.

And he 'angs up afore I gets the chance to say that 'e still owes *me* a fucken smoke detector in my front 'allway, and that my fire h'escape is not h'even fit to let the cat out on. Pudgy gross flabby slumlord.

· · ·

One by one I lights the candles and places them in the front windows. Two on the stool in the front porch. I flips through the CDs behind the bar, tryna define h'exactly what Mike meant by "Sunday night music." Oh, 'ere's Neil Young. But of course when I h'opens the case the CD h'inside is h'actually *Blondie's Greatest Hits*. Fucken Blondie. And 'ere's the battered back half of Leonard Cohen's *The Future*, with Keith's name and 'is h'old Anderson h'Avenue phone number scrawled 'cross it in faded blue marker. Not a word from that bastard since 'e left for Nova Scotia. How quick I was to latch onto 'im a few years back. I s'pose cause I knew right h'away 'e 'ad anough of 'is h'own devils not to wanna go diggin at mine. We just seemed to want the same thing at the same time: someone to lie down with when the nights were cold and long and dark. No need to get too close, no pressure. Fuck when we's 'orny and be nice friends and let me shut down when I 'ave to. Dont try and break what's h'already busted up anough. It was convenient there for a while. And then of course youse start wanting a little more. 'Ow h'often did 'e play that fucken Cohen h'album, that song? I takes the case and snaps what's left of it and toss it h'in the garbage.

Now, 'ere's about ten Bob Dylan h'albums in a row. H'easiest way to know when Clyde's working: just round the corner h'out around the mall somewhere and youse can 'ear that nasal whine, that senseless rant, that screechin, dyin-gull 'armonica, like nails dragged across a chalkboard. And Clyde wonders why 'e never breaks fifty in tips.

And what's this? A tape of Val. *High Time in '79*. Yeah I'll bet it was an 'igh time too there Dr. Cheese. General Gouda, as Clayton calls 'im. 'Ow fucken stupid was I to let 'im suck me back h'in like that? 'E dropped by the bar 'ere a few weeks h'ago while I was working. 'E looked 'ealthy, put on a few pounds from the last time I'd seen 'im. 'E was h'upright too. And didnt 'e dangle a little bag of blow and h'ask me to drop by when I closed h'up. I said I'd think h'about it, that if I showed up I showed up. Closin time came and I jumped h'into a cab with not a second thought. H'ever a sucker for h'old geezers with drugs. And that'll likely be my downfall, in the h'end. Christ.

I 'ook my nail h'underneath the tape and gives it a good full and satisfying yank. The stream of tape bursts after a few feet and I toss the whole lot into the garbage on top of *The Future*.

I let my 'and roam further h'into the drawer and find h'another CD laid flat on top of the row. Sweet Merciful Jesus. *The Very Best of Valentine Reid*. I'm about to chuck that h'into the garbage too, but then I sees it's signed and dedicated to Mike. I sets it h'aside and then finally decide on a copy of *Rum, Sodomy and the Lash*, by the Pogues, a h'album Clayton usually plays loud on Friday nights. It seems to be a good crowd pleaser. But then, the Friday night 'Atchet crowd is not too 'ard to please, so long as the booze keeps flowin they'll listen to gospel music. Song on 'ere that I likes, "A Pair of Brown Eyes." Clayton played me this album in the 'otel that first night I met 'im, tolt me h'all 'bout the lead singer and his h'antics, most h'impressed with 'ow long it was takin the guy to kill 'isself with booze. Funny, if youse listen carefully anough there's a song to mark h'everything, a soundtrack for all your weakest moments. Fucken Valentine Reid now too.

I crank the volume h'up and position the speakers towards the front door. Deck of cards in the register. I counts 'em out. Fifty-one. The h'ace of spades is missin. Typical. Keith prolly got that tucked into 'is wallet. I stares h'out through the blinds. I h'opens the door in the porch just a crack to let the sound h'onto the street. It's bitter h'outside, freezin rain battering at the window. The tail h'end of one more wasted winter. The sander cruises h'up the street, the blue light flashin 'cross my fore'ead. It slows h'ever so slightly h'as it passes the bar n I finds m'self crouchin back h'into the porch. That could be Jim McNaughton at the wheel. If 'e knows I'm 'ere by m'self 'e'll be in for sure and I dont think I can bullshit my way through whatever boring conversation 'e's bound to h'offer up. Maybe h'if 'e never stank like garbage 'alf the time. Or h'if 'e could get a goddamn sentence out without that stutter. Well now that's not h'all that nice I know. Jim's prolly one of the better ones comes in 'ere, nothing complicated about 'im, just get 'im drunk and be nice to 'im, that's all. But seein the sander gives me the notion to 'ave a real drink. On Jim's tab. A good stiff double Dock and water. Just the thing. Mike'll notice the liquor gone in the morning of course, and if I'm around I'll just say that Jim dropped in for a drink. I'll point to the tabs. Then I'll complain 'bout 'im, 'bout 'ow draining 'e is, whinin 'bout 'is wife, 'ow 'is kids wont talk to 'im. And if Mike cares 'nough to doubt me and h'ask Jim 'bout it the next time 'e's h'in, well Jim wont h'even know h'if 'e was or not any'ow. That medication got 'im wandering in a daze most of the time. Can youse h'imagine puttin a fella like that be'ind the wheel of a big ole sander?

The moment I turns back be'ind the bar I 'ears a crowd of jolly drunks burst into the chorus of some h'Irish drinkin h'anthem. No doubt they've just wandered h'outta h'Erin's Pub or some touristy place h'on George Street. I peeks up the street. Five of them. Business types. Smashed. Staggering through the slush. When their song fizzles I can pick h'up bits of conversation, drunken male wrangling in bland, flat, generic mid-h'American h'accents. The sweet, rummy scent of a cigar on the wind. The prosperous jingle of loose pocket change. Canadian coins though. Monopoly money to them. Disposable. Tips for me. The flash of a gold watch beneath the streetlight. I swings the door wide h'open, h'almost clipping the man in the forefront of the group, a squat, wheezing and balding man in a dated grey suit.

—Evening fellas, comin in for a drink?

I'm h'immediately disgusted with m'self for that girlish voice, but I know at the same time that that's mainly what'll get them h'in 'ere throwing their money round. Fuck it. The bald grey suit, h'older than the others by h'at least twenty years, 'e slips on the sidewalk and catches 'old of the door for balance.

—I dont know young lady. What's on the menu?

With my brightest smile and my nipples gone 'ard as little rocks with the cold, I dredges up that quaint old bouncy stunned touristy h'accent I knows they's dyin to 'ear.

—Whatever tickles yer fancy. Whaddaya 'ave in mind?

And with that they h'all walk in be'ind me, stompin their boots and doffin their pricey wool scarves and leather gloves h'on the table near the h'exit. A tall dark-'aired one of 'bout thirty-five with a two-day scruff that reminds me h'of a *Men's Fitness* cover model, 'e leans in close to the bald grey suit and says:

—Jerry, ask her if she does that thing with the fish.

Behind Jerry another suit snorts loud and slaps 'is leg:

—Get your mind out of the gutter Baker. What a thing to say.

—Fuck off Dawson. I'm talking about a drink.

And h'another, a nerdy type in dark-rimmed thousand-dollar h'eyeglasses goes:

—Yeah, it's called something though. Shriek or Squeal, something like that. There's a poem too. Kenneth and his wife had it done last year.

'Cept for one quiet fella in the back who I cant get a bead on at all, looks to me like the h'aggression factor is pretty low with this lot. H'easy marks for a few dollars 'opefully. Two kindsa Yanks, h'in my h'estimation: the ones that throws their money away like they cant get rid of it quick anough, refusin to h'acknowledge its value, like it's just too 'eavy to be luggin round in their pockets, and the ones that counts out pennies, 'oarding h'every last cent like h'every time they makes a purchase they's potentially bein ripped off. This crowd 'opefully falls h'under the former category. And if they's lookin for a Screech In they'll be payin through their h'eyeballs by the time I'm done with 'em. I'm just about to pipe h'up and tell 'em what they's lookin for when the bald grey suit, Jerry, boosts 'isself h'onto a stool and shouts right proud:

—A Screech In. That'll do us tonight. Can you do that young lady?

I plant my hands firmly on the bar and let my breasts rest softly on the lip of the register. They line h'up h'obediently 'long the bar. Whipped dogs h'already.

—Can *I* do a Screech h'In? Youse 'appened to stumble h'upon the queen tonight Jerry.

Jerry flushes, delighted to be singled h'out by name, by a slender young thing like me no less, h'in front of 'is younger h'associates.

Course I could 'ave, you know, h'at one point during my long and glamorous bartending career, really labelled m'self the Queen of the Screech h'In. I'd say I riddled h'off close on five 'undred in the few years I was workin at Traynor's Quay h'on Duckworth. Some nights I'd do ten or twelve and walk 'ome 'oarse. I begged the manager to let me wait tables, clean toilets, just be a regular bartender, a bouncer h'even. But 'e'd only laugh h'at me and smack my h'ass and tell me I was the best 'e'd 'ad in years, that I was, h'in fact, the Queen. Cant believe I put up with that fat prick long h'as I did. And the tourists, rich, bustin-at-the-seams roly-poly piggies with their h'endless stupidity and h'ignorance, their h'insatiable thirst for 'umiliation. Telling me 'ow cute we all is, Newfoundlanders. H'askin me to say things h'again cause they just loved the h'accent so much, 'ow it was just to die for. Saying stuff like 'ow they wanted to h'adopt one of h'us. And I finally snapped and said to one couple late h'on a Saturday night:

—Yeah, take a run down to B—— and meet the gang. Go scrape my child'ood h'off the bedsheets.

They werent long settling their tab then. No tip for Mon that night.

—H'of course I can do a Screech h'In. So long h'as youse got the paper?

—Paper?

I gives 'im a playful smack on the back of 'is 'and.

—The money Jerry. Silly.

And with that I swear they h'all rises a couple of h'inches in their fine leather shoes and puff out the chests of their 'and-spun suits, diggin for wallets and weighin h'out their change. The very mention h'of money and their cocks just stiffen. See that. Bald Jerry raises a stubby 'and, waves h'off the commotion.

—I'll get this one, fellas. On me. How much sweetheart?

I tilts my 'ead and sets my bottom lip in a playful pout. I reaches h'over the bar and straightens Jerry's tie while I calculates the charge. Jerry goes beet red.

—Let's see b'ys. Five of ya, h'at twenty five bucks an 'ead, that's one twenty-five.

Jerry makes a slight jump like 'e's been grazed in the h'ear with a lead pellet. 'E catches himself fast anough though, h'obviously not wantin to come 'cross h'as a tightwad h'in front of 'is younger, fitter and less laden-down "friends." A layer of sweat beads the bridge of 'is nose all the same. 'E gives 'is wedding band a twirl. 'E seems to be the h'only one wearing one and I kinda feels a bit bad for a moment before Jerry slaps a stack of bills h'on the bar and shakily counts out an 'undred and thirty dollars.

—There you are sweetie, and a little something for yourself as well.

I sweeps the money in and stashes it under the drawer in the register. So I've gotten m'self paid now, no matter 'ow the rest of the night h'unfolds.

Jerry looks round at his company for h'approval but they's h'all

suddenly h'immersed in their h'own language of carbohydrates and
digits and h'exchange rates and stock market nonsense. Jerry seems
so lost. Men's Fitness pauses 'is mumblings about a stewardess in
Boston and slaps Jerry 'eartily 'cross the back.

—Youse're a wild man Jerry . . .

And doesnt that just get Jerry's goat h'altogether. A big, porky
face-splittin grin, delighted that someone's finally said it h'out loud.
'E slips 'is newly flaccid wallet back into 'is shirt pocket. 'E's like
the fat kid 'ose mother's h'after sendin to the playground with a
bag of candy to buy 'is way h'onto the merry-go-round. I gives 'im
h'another little lovetap.

—Is that true Jerry? Youse a wild one?

—You'll find out missy, when you serve up that whiskey.

From "young lady" to "sweet'eart" to "sweetie" to "missy."
Where's this night 'eaded I wonder?

—Actually Jerry, it's not whiskey. Screech is rum. Black rum.

A couple of his comrades snicker and Jerry seems to deflate, beet
red h'again, 'is 'ead down and 'is eyes to the floor. Poor doomed
fucker.

· · ·

Fuck, there's not anough Screech left h'in the bottle on the bar.
I'm sure I can put h'on a decent, believable h'act, but it's gonna
be 'ard to pull h'off a fake, and prolly illegal, Screech h'In without
the main h'ingredient. And a fish or something, cant go without
that. Maybe downstairs. Mike keeps a reserve of liquor downstairs
for busier nights. I searches the cupboards beneath the stock, just
to make sure, before I leaves the bar h'unattended. From be'ind me
comes a thick Texan h'accent, the fat guy who 'asnt spoken yet, 'as
to be. I knew 'e'd be trouble.

—Hwe'll settle foar a hwet tee-shirt contest if yud rather? Yuh
look lahk yud put oan a good show.

I whips round with the near h'empty Screech bottle 'eld by the
neck. The h'entire line pulls back, terrified I'm gonna use it h'on

one of their daily-moisturized faces. I zeroes h'in on the source h'of the voice, jowly and sweaty, 'is paunch belly stretchin 'is shirt buttons to the popping point. A steers-'ead belt buckle. Tie thinner than the h'others, shirt collar longer and sharper. I woulda pegged 'im for a Texan if 'e'd h'opened his mouth or not.

—Well why dont we make it a contest cowboy? I'd say youse could gimme a run for it.

And the crowd laugh, the tension broken. Jerry laughs the loudest, h'unconsciously flauntin 'is relief h'at not bein the butt h'of a joke 'bout male titties.

—She got you there Jackman. Ha!

—Shit woman, Ah was juz yankin yer chain.

Some fucken h'apology. Blubber fuck. I takes the h'opportunity to 'ide the Screech bottle be'ind my back and slip towards the basement door.

—Jerry me old cunt. Will ya watch the bar for me for a sec? Make sure none of these pups take advantage?

Sometimes I knows it's best to tone down me h'accent a bit, some people h'out there dont h'understand plain h'English. Jerry nods with all 'is 'eart, 'appy to be selected as the h'obvious choice to be the man in charge. I makes the dash towards the basement door, and I 'ears Men's Fitness say:

—I'm pretty sure she was supposed to say "me old *cock*."

And then Jerry:

—No, no. That was right. You heard her wrong. That's just the way she talks.

· · ·

At the bottom of the stairs there's a box of liquor. I roots through it. Smirnoff. White Bacardi. White Morgan. Lamb's. Jameson. Fucken Valentine with his h'Irish whiskey. But no Screech, and none of these dark anough to pass for it. In the far corner be'ind the door I finds h'another box labelled h'Imperial Rum. Plastic forty-h'ounce bottle h'inside with the seal not h'even broken. But when I lift it

h'out the bottle's h'only 'alf full. I tips it h'upside down and liquor leaks h'out through the stopper. I digs through the rest h'of
the box and find h'Imperial Rum h'ashtrays and coasters and a few
stray glasses. The loose ends of some promotional drop-h'off. I can
vaguely remember the sales rep droppin off a case at the bar last year.
And Mike sellin it at 'alf the regular price. But there was something
'bout it, this metallic taste. Lead? It was a bad batch, recalled a week
later. But Mike kept it round the bar and managed to peddle it h'off
to the desperate. No sensible drinker would go 'andy to it. It was
h'even a bit of a h'inside joke at the bar for a while, h'offering it to
someone on the 'ouse to get a kick h'outta their reaction:
—'Ere Jim, 'ave a sup of this.
I brings the tip h'of the bottle to my nose and gags a little h'at
the smell. Keith suckered me h'into takin a shot one night, h'evil
little bastard. I spent the 'ole next hour 'eaving up in the women's
toilet. I 'olds the h'Imperial Rum and the Screech bottles together
towards the light. They's pretty much the same colour. Fuck it, if
they wants a Screech h'In they'll get one.
I pours the h'Imperial Rum h'into the Screech bottle, gives it
h'all a shake. Looks good to me. Now, a fish. Or something like it.
I pulls stuff round in the deepfreeze, 'oping maybe Mike got some
salt fish or some fillets. I lifts h'up what looks to be the 'ind quarter
of a moose. Could 'ave the flabby fuckers kiss this, or lick it. But it's
too 'eavy to carry h'upstairs and it stinks like burnt vomit any'ow.
I shuts the deepfreeze and rummages further into the damp tangle
of busted barstools and h'empties, leaky guitar cables and warped
speaker cabinets and kegs and h'out-dated beer promo signs, tryna
find h'anything that might pass for a realistic Newfoundland symbol
or icon or what-h'ever youse wanna call it. Not that them bloated
bastards h'upstairs would know the difference.
And what's this? A pair of rubbers. The h'old fashion kind too,
blue-black with the red soles. I h'upends it and a fine beige dust
flumps h'onto the floor. Some tiny shiftin, a scurry in the dust as a
grey-powdered h'earwig shuffles from beneath the mess. Cant tell

225

if it came from the boot or not and I dont give a shit. Death to all ye that h'enters 'ere. Doom. I brings my 'eel down on the vile little beast without a moment's 'esitation. What was it we useta call them things?

Back h'upstairs I flies h'into h'action with some twisted, 'ybrid version of the h'old spiel rollin off my tongue like I've spent a lifetime re'earsing it. It's just pourin h'outta me, h'easy and slick, h'even slightly removed, h'almost like I'm sick of doin it and now I'm h'only h'experimenting with the tirade in h'order to keep it h'interesting for m'self. Somewhere in the back of my 'ead I knows the words, the "monologue" is not quite h'accurate, far from standard, but it must sound h'official anough to these well-padded h'American h'ears and 'specially where I'm roarin into their faces at full speed. And I know too that they's 'ardly gonna protest because what's h'underneath my voice is as toxic as the contents of the bottle in my 'and.

—Gentlemen, gentlemen (not you Tex), can I 'ave your attention please? Before we begin I need youse h'all to write down your names and mailing h'addresses in this little booklet. And I h'ask youse to do this for me now because I'm dreadfully h'afeard that h'after youse partake of this most sacred of Newfoundland rituals, youse may h'experience a rather confused h'identity and not h'even remember y' h'own names and may be h'overcome with a bizarre, but h'understandable, desire to deny where youse're presently from.

They h'all laughs h'at that and nudge each other, buckin their gullible 'eads at me. And of course Tex pipes up with the h'inevitable question:

—Hwat do yah need our names and addresses foar?

And it just keeps pourin h'outta me:

—Well, my portly friend, once youse 'ave successfully completed the traditional Newfoundland Screech h'In, bestowed h'upon youse will be h'all the benefits and bliss and, sadly, the burdens h'of becoming a H'onorary Newfoundlander. And we will mail you a certificate to prove it. Per'aps one of the most valuable documents you will h'ever possess!

I place a h'empty shot glass in front of h'each of them as they scrawl their precious signatures into my notebook. A h'excited shuffle courses through the line of them, plump Jerry lickin the tip of his pen and bouncin h'ever so slightly on his 'eels, glancin round h'at his buds as h'if to say *'Ere it comes fellas, I told you so. Who's the man?* But as I look deeply into h'each pair of bloodshot, thirsty eyes I 'ave to deduce that there's not a man h'amongst the lot.

When I'm done filling their shot glasses with "Screech," Men's Fitness says:

—Arent you suppose to play a little Newfie music right about now?

I was wondering when *that* word was gonna rear its h'ugly 'ead. But nevertheless, h'even though it's to be fully h'expected h'at a time like this, from the mouths of h'ignorance, as h'usual, I still gets that h'old familiar sinkin in my belly and my 'and grips tight round the neck of the bottle for the second time tonight. H'all these years of bartendin, nervous round h'aggressive, 'orny drunks and I've been surrounded by weapons the 'ole time.

I lays the bottle back down and smiles my brightest once h'again, h'adjust the wiring of my bra.

—Yeah, I can play something like that. Gimme a second.

I turns to the stereo and shuts down the Pogues and pops *The Very Best of Valentine Reid* into the slot. The first track, "Gun Shy," kicks in 'ard before I realizes the choice I've made. Val's youthful vocals fills my head like some long-dead friend come back to convince me to find some quick way to join him in the h'afterlife.

> *A glance through the glass caught you strolling by*
> *Your sights dead ahead as the hardest of hearts stepped aside*
> *For that reckoning glint in your eye . . .*

The h'Americans dont know what to make of it though and Men's Fitness goes:

—What's this crap? This is not Newfie. What about that one, what's it called? "Sonny?" "Sonny's Dream?" Who sings that one?

I spins around on my 'eels, remembering 'ow much I h'always loved "Gun Shy," the strength I useta gather from it when I first 'eard it on that little transistor radio at my bedside in B——. H'only thing got me through 'alf the time, Val's songs. I'm suddenly h'overcome with a wave of remorse or regret or guilt or sympathy for Val. That night I went to meet him after my shift a few weeks back, fuck. 'E was well-on h'already by the time I got there, 'is eyes wide and barren, 'is fingers tucked h'into the waist of his jeans. This thin cloud of crack smoke streaking across the kitchen. And I should 'ave turned back right then and there. Then I saw the 'uge mound of blow on the counter next to 'im and I just went right for it, h'everything h'else went h'out the window, that's h'all I saw. And then 'e grabbed me, tight and rough round the collar of my jacket. Then 'is 'and gropin h'inside my shirt, the h'other on the back of my 'ead, pullin my lips towards 'is. And of course I pushed 'im h'away.

—C'mon Monica girl. It's only me . . .

And my knee, full force between 'is legs like that, the sickening grunt from somewhere deep h'inside that numb 'ead of his. Val, dropping to 'is knees, the tears in 'is eyes. Me flying h'out the front door, my 'eart racin, feelin' like I'd just snorted h'every last line of coke on the h'Avalon.

—"Sonny's Dream" I said. That's Newfie isnt it?

—Look, I 'ave no fucken h'idea buddy. But I'll say this: youse h'asked for Newfoundland music, h'although that's not the word youse used, and I played some. Will I turn it h'off?

A shift in their sad little group then, a confused current goes through 'em, like they's h'unsure of my tone or they's h'uncomfortable with me 'aving a real 'uman reaction when I'm supposed to be their h'unfalteringly good-natured, salt-of-the-h'earth Newfoundland 'ost. They h'all turn towards Men's Fitness and reproves 'im with their h'eyes. 'E drops 'is own h'eyes to the floor in shame, not really h'understandin what 'e's done to warrant such scorn. Plump Jerry seems 'appy that the group 'as come together in a shared distaste h'over someone h'other than 'imself.

> One look at me now, you would not recognize
> This tarnished old relic the lowest of bidders can buy
> I've grown a little gun shy.

Plump Jerry catches the words of that verse and dips his 'ead in consent. I gets back in character h'again and the mood of the room swings back round. I gives Men's Fitness a wink, just to throw 'im h'off a bit more than 'e already is.

—Gentlemen please, if youse'll kindly repeat h'after me: I's-da-b'y-dat-builds-de-boat-and-I's-da-b'y-dat-sails-'er!

They make a snarled h'attempt at it, but I knows I've said it so fast they cant possibly know where to begin. I slows it down some and lets 'em repeat little bits h'at a time, like youngsters h'in school learning a prayer:

—I's the b'y . . .

—I'm the boy . . .

—No, no. Not *boy*. Which one is sayin that? It's b'y. *B'y*, 'ear me? And it's *I's*, not *I'm*. Youse're not listening. *I's the b'y* . . .

—I's the b'y . . .

—That's it! I's the b'y that builds the boat . . .

—I's the boy . . . I'm the . . . I's the b'y that builds the boat . . .

And they carries h'on like that till they can basically get through the 'ole thing, lovin it when I corrects 'em, when I yells and makes 'em feel like the stupid lards they really is. And I knows m'self that's not what the h'actual recitation is supposed to be, but I cant think of a h'alternative, and to be truthful I'm kinda disappointed in m'self. Plump Jerry h'asks me if it's a song.

—No Jerry. No . . .

Once they gets that much h'outta the way they's h'obviously h'eager to move h'onto the shots. But of course I 'ave something h'else in mind before that dont I? I takes the rubber boot and places it beneath the draft tap and fill the boot 'alfway. I sets the 'alf full boot down in front of Men's Fitness. 'E tries to laugh it off but I shoots him a look that should say *if youse dont drink from it I'll pour it down your fucken throat.*

'E lifts the boot in both 'ands and looks down into it.

—I've never heard of this part before.

—It's traditional.

—But I dont drink all of it?

—Much h'as you can.

I start smackin my palm h'off the bar h'in front of 'im and shoutin *down the 'atch, down the 'atch, down the 'atch,* till the rest h'of the group join in. Men's Fitness lifts the boot to 'is lips and a bit of draft sloshes h'over the rim and down h'onto 'is pricey white dress shirt. 'E tips the beer h'into 'is mouth and I give the 'eel of the boot a slight tap, sendin a wave of beer down over 'is neck and chest. 'E chokes on something, slams the boot down on the bar and spits h'into the corner. There's flecks of something, dried mud or dogshit caked into the treads of the sole and some of them 'ave landed on the cuff of 'is coat. The h'others cheer and pat him on the back and make 'im feel like an 'ero. 'E keeps gaggin and pickin h'at something that's h'after catching h'in the back of 'is throat. That's h'all I needed, was for just *one* of 'em to take the plunge, now they'll h'all follow suit. Before Men's Fitness can recuperate, I slides the boot to the next in line, the nerdy guy, and generally there's a repeat of this fiasco right across the board, me coaxin them h'on with my chantin and bangin my fists h'on the bar and then makin sure they h'each gets a good swallow out of it.

Till the fucken boot is h'empty.

Now for the shots.

—Alright gentlemen, if youse will, your glasses 'igh now . . .

They all 'old their glasses h'out, some of 'em still retchin and staggering and pickin at the backs h'of their throats and tryna gag shit up. Tex 'eaves and I jumps back, thinkin he's gonna spew right across the bar. But he 'olds it back. 'E'd never live it down.

—H'up 'igh gentlemen, and repeat h'after me: Long may yer little pricks shrivel.

A slight 'esitation from the group afore they repeats it back to me:

—Long . . . may your . . . little prick swivel . . .

—No *shrivel*. Long may your little pricks *shrivel*.

—LONG MAY YOUR LITTLE PRICKS SHRIVEL!

—Well done gentlemen, drink up.

H'all five h'Americans bang back the shots h'in one go. I h'almost gets sick watchin 'em. H'at first they h'all tries and come h'off like it's not near's strong h'as they were h'expectin, they tries not to twitch or gasp or cough, tries to be the big 'ardy h'American men they fancies themselves to be. It takes a few seconds for their taste buds and guts to react. Retch and 'eave and choke and wheeze and scrrrrramble for breath. Men's Fitness bolts for the front door and buckles h'over in the snowbank h'outside the window.

And I wastes no more time.

—H'alright folks, that's it. Bar is closing. Kindly collect your belongings and be on your way. That's it folks, bar is closing!

I flick the lights on full blast and shuts down the stereo. They's h'all temporarily blinded by the toxic, leaden booze and the bright new silence. I moves around the bar and starts shovin 'em towards the porch. Plump Jerry says:

—Hold on there missy, hold on, let me get my coat . . . .

I grabs an 'andful of 'ats and scarves and coats and gloves and tosses the 'ole pile h'into Jerry's h'arms, spins him round and bullies 'im h'out the door be'ind the h'others. I locks the door h'as soon h'as it shuts. Tex starts poundin on the door, maybe h'only now h'aware that 'e's been 'umiliated and wanting . . . what? From me? What? H'apology?

I picks up the baseball bat that Mike keeps h'in the corner h'of the porch. I whips h'open the door. I 'olds the bat h'up in Tex's face.

—I said the fuck-ing bar h'is closed! Should I call the police?

H'ever spend the night in a Newfoundland jail? Youse'll never be the same h'again.

H'all the bravado falls from Tex's face. The phone starts to ring. Before I slams the door in their faces for good, I shouts:

—Youse the man Jerry. Youse the fucken man!

I pulls h'all the blinds shut. Turn the lights down low h'again. Turn that Pogues song on h'again. I drops *The Very Best of Valentine Reid* h'onto the floor and grind it beneath my foot, then I sets it back h'into the case and slides it h'into the drawer. That phone keeps h'on ringin.

I pours what's left in the Screech bottle h'into the sink and write it down h'as spillage. I gags a little on the fumes. Ring, ring. H'if Mike h'asks me about it I'm sure I'll find *something* to say. I counts out the money Plump Jerry paid up for the Screech h'In. I makes some change in the register and counts out fifty bucks in a h'envelope for Mike. That should 'old the old miser h'off for h'another week.

I've counted thirty rings in my 'ead. If Mike'd h'only bite the bullet and get that message manager. I reaches h'under the counter, h'unplugs the cord from the jack. Now for that double Dock. Three h'ice cubes. Let it sit for a while, bend the temperature, dilute it just so, the way I like it. I writes it down on Jim's tab.

I take a sip and lets the 'ot liquor soak back h'over my tongue till it trickles down the back of my throat. I sets my glass down and goes h'about clearin up the shot glasses, tuck the rubber boot in h'under the sink.

Jesus, rough night Mike. Rough fucken night.

23. The Crunch

An inch of ash on the tip of me smoke. Nearest ashtray is across the bar. Other side of the cash. Trick with this is not to think too heavy about it. Just aim and flick. Be surprised how often you can pull it off too.

Aim.

Flick.

Shit. Dont even come close. Hits the bar, a dull, muted explosion. Right where Mike Quinn just sprayed and washed. He's on the rags this morning and nothing's surer. The ash melts into the gleamin surface of the bar, its healthy silver texture soakin up the Spray Nine.

One vicious swoop of Mike's cloth removes the new blemish, the first for a day that promises too many, I s'pose. He slides the ashtray across the bar to me, a quick, dismissive flick of the wrist like he's tossin a Frisbee to an old mutt. It clinks and tinkles then winds down obnoxiously before settlin a little outta me reach. I places it at the most convenient angle, a little to the right of me smokin hand, so I wont hafta move too much to tap me ash the next time. Got the fuckin life dont I?

Mike twists the stopper off another beer and places it in front of me. What else is new? I been all blocked up lately with the codeine. Brent's little extraction trick is provin a tad habitual. So I'm switched over to Dominion Ale for a while. Me old man's choice poison. Or it *was* once, if I'm to be fair about it. Dominion Ale: like swallowing a pipe cleaner, flushes you right out. Brent drinks it too, when he's not *really* drinkin, so there's always a couple around the apartment. He should be back the weekend. Fucked off to his folks' place for the week, up the Shore. Said everything was gettin "a bit too much," that he needs to clear his head and his lungs out. Cant say I dont blame 'im. Now he says too that he's lookin into applying for the same program I was on last year, the one that took me over to Dublin. That starts up again in the fall. I said I'd help him out, write him a reference or whatnot. But I warned him not to get his hopes too high. And it's not like I'll be around to hold his hand come September. Cause if Izzy dont get 'er shit together soon I'll be gone even quicker than that.

I picks up the bottle of Dominion and takes a drop, waits to see if Mike writes it down. Me tab is gettin up there again. He knows it too. *Brunch* with Isadora in an hour or so. I wouldnt mind pickin up the bill for a change, see how she likes that. But I cant bring meself to ask Mike for me pay. And sure if he takes me tab outta me pay first, sure I'll have nothing till Tuesday night.

That's me shift these days: Friday, Saturday and Tuesday nights. Friday is always good tips. Saturday is usually half-decent, but it wasnt last night. The shits. Tuesday is the pool tournament crowd, usually good for at least fifty bucks in tips and tokens.

I takes another slug. The bottle seems to have more weight than it should. Could be the hour. Or Mike's presence. Maybe a combination of the two.

I got no time for an ex-drinker, at least not when I'm wantin a straightener. Their drinkin tales are always that much more outstanding, more twisted, fascinating, life threatening. Superior. So much more advanced and insane than what yours are now. Because they've grown. They've faced that part of themselves that each and every one of us is capable of facing. Yeah. They've met the demon head-on and conquered. Because why drink, if not to keep the devils down deep, keep the monsters *under* the bed, rather than in the goddamn bed staring you straight in the face?

Well maybe some of us does it cause we fuckin likes it.

Maybe it's a simple matter of thirst and taste.

—Nine fifteen Sunday morning, Clayton. You're late.

I finds meself grinnin, hatin meself for it, always embarrassed that Mike is not gonna get the laugh he so craves. As if it was his job to comment. It's all goin into his pocket sure. And from there into the machines across the street at the Hayloft. Dont see *me* makin digs at customers when I'm behind the bar. Nope. Keep your mouth shut, smile, blast the drinkin tunes, remember names and, most important, remember drinks. That's where the tips are. Nothing a customer enjoys more than the status of not havin to order. Walk in, look dark, nod at the bartender, and your favourite drink magically appears on the bar. Bang. No questions, no comments, no critique of your social habits.

The phone rings. The old-fashioned bell rips through the stale air like a fire alarm from me school days. Christ, that was low, now that I thinks on it: little youngsters sittin quietly in their harmless, trivial little bubbles when some cunty-balled bitch of a nun gets it in 'er head to blast a wave of panic into the room. *Good heavens, nothing going on, nobody's fucked me proper since the forties, why dont I frighten the shit out of three hundred youngsters?*

Mike lets the phone ring three times before pickin it up, just enough to murder any goodwill towards the world that might still be lingering in the corners of me brain. On this fine, first-rate lovely downtown morning.

I knows it's Isadora. She always tracks me down, right when I'm on the cusp of gettin up to something I shouldnt be at. I s'pose I aint that hard to find though. I dont stray far. I reaches me hand out for the phone when I hears Mike say hello. Then he goes:

—No . . . NO! Look, I said dont fucking call here any more. Got it?

Slams the phone down. I raises me eyebrows in mock curiosity. But if it wasnt Izzy then I dont really give a fuck. I dont wanna hear from no one else. Ever again.

Mike takes the bait, shakes his head in disgust:

—Jehovah's Witness . . .

This could be good. An opportunity to break the ice, get on his good side. Get me pay and go back to bed for an hour. Get me head in shape before I meets the missus. Get, get, get. I says:

—I had a couple of them Jehovah's fuckers come to me place on Mullock one time. Two young fellas. Barely twenty years old. Paid their own way from California to go spread the word!

Mike stuffs a filthy towel into a pint glass and grunts.

—Sick.

—Sick? Dont be talkin. I was so fuckin hungover right? I wasnt thinkin when I opened up the door. *Ah know Jesus Chrahst exists in mah life. Ah see Him in the smahle ohn a little girl's face when she's jumping rope in the street. Ah see Him . . .* I dont know, shit like that. I cracked open a beer and sparked up an old roach that was there on the counter. The b'ys just looked at each other, packed up their briefcase and walked out, like I was askin 'em to share a needle or something. Sick fuckers.

Mike dips his hand into the register and removes the twenties. Starts countin.

—I dont know Clayton. Maybe you shoulda heard 'em out. Mighta done you some good. Might not be hanging off the bars so much.

Cocksucker. Ex-drinkers like Mike are *worse* than them Jehovah's Witness crowd. For havin seen the light. Always a brighter light too. Cause that's the thing with alcoholics. It's that bottomless fuckin luminosity they all wants to share, enhance our days with. When we all knows the darkness is never that far from the surface and that the ones who've had to go and get *off* the booze are just the exception anyhow. Couldnt fuckin handle it, if the truth be known. But they walks around with this self-righteousness they gets from the notion that some big step has been taken, that something profound and shadowy has been owned up to. Shakin their heads and smirkin at everyone else's good time. Always hangin around with someplace

236

better to go. A wink when they're passin out the door that seems to shout *You too will have to own up someday.*

Well, I am. Ownin up. Right here and now. Quarter past nine? That's fuck-all. Ole Randy'd have a two-four in 'im by this time. One time. Never say either, not by lookin at 'im. Smell it off 'im, sure. But he'd walk a straighter line with that much in 'im than I could now. And I'm only on me second. Or is it me third? What odds? I'm ownin up. To the fact that it's me own choice what way I wants to go about me own life. I can give it up if I wants to. I can drink meself into the fuckin ground if I wants. No one's business but me own. I'm doin alright, I'll be fine. Just bidin me time, is all.

I saw Randy last week. The Old Man. All straightened out now. Crispy blue Levi's. Clean-shaven. Tough and shiny leather boots that sounded pretty good on the sidewalk. 'Bout time he fixed his fuckin tooth too. He was comin outta that specialty shop up on the west end of Water Street, the one that sells all the dark breads and sweaty, sour cheeses. Isadora shops there every now and then.

I was comin outta the liquor store when I saw him, lobbin me way up towards George Street. There's a bar on the corner that I likes sometimes. Christian's it's called. I almost made it too. Before Randy intercepted me. Him and his whore. Fuck, that sounds bitter. She's not so bad I s'pose. I hardly knows her anyhow. Anne-Marie. They met in AA, 'bout a year after me mother's accident. She moved into the house up the Shore shortly after I moved out. But Randy was on and off with her for years while I was growin up, so she was always around. We just never had much to say to each other. She's been good for him, if I'm to be fair.

They were holdin hands, comin outta that shop, like two fuckin freaks. She had a see-through bag with bread and some kinda dip or spread and a sack of that free-trade coffee, that dark shit that's hardly fit to drink. Movin up in the world I s'pose is she? Randy had a half-dozen beer tucked under his arm. Surprise, surprise.

He looked happy enough to see me though. Quite the shock for us both. I hadnt laid eyes on him in nearly two years. He tracked down me number when I was in Dublin, left me a message, but I never called him back. Message went something like:

—Hi. Just sayin hi. Thinkin about ya, hopin you're alright, not bein too hard on yourself.

Too hard on yourself. Like I was out there in the world beatin meself up over . . . what? *I* aint the one who spent years puttin holes in walls and gettin laughed outta the clubs up the Shore and tossed outta the neighbours' houses on Christmas and smashin up cars and losin me licence every other month. *I'm* the one who cleaned up all the blood and vomit and lugged him into bed and put him on his side so's he wouldnt choke.

Years.

Yeah, he looked happy enough to see me. And some sick part of me wanted to stay and chat. I couldnt look at her though. He stuck out his hand. His eyes all lit up. Smilin. Happy families reunite.

—Clayton! Jesus, Mary and Joseph! How are ya?

I took his hand and shook it. A good, firm grip he got. He looked me up and down. I was after tossin on a pair of old wind-pants and steel-toe workboots. Old wool sweater I found in the apartment. It was freezin and I was snifflin like some druggie. Bit of a flu comin on. I knows I looked the state. Not like I had nothing to dress up for though.

I felt her lookin at me, back at Randy, waitin to be acknowledged. Randy finally took the hint off her.

—Clayton, you remembers my ahhh . . . you knows Anne-Marie, sure. Anne-Marie, my son.

My son. How convenient. Yes I fuckin knows Anne-Marie. Think I'm stunned? You're only with her fifteen years. That's what rises up in me, that's the way I wants to be talkin to him, but I dont. I just nods at Anne-Marie. She was a big drinker too. From Kilbride. I cant believe she's after stickin with him this long. I hope he got his skin out of it though, seein me there on the street in the state I was in. I hope he got a pity fuck out of 'er. I always hopes that for people. Because I hope people always hopes it for me.

I dont know where he went wrong girl. I did the best I could.

My son.

Randy Reid, who useta stash his beer in the grass up behind the house so's they'd be nice and warm and he could better taste the booze off 'em.

—How's your foot there Clayton?

—How's your liver Randy?

He went right red then and I felt bad. I nodded towards the half-case under his arm, just so's he'd understand that I was over our past, that I wasnt makin a dig about his obvious failures as a father.

He held the half-case out to me.

—This stuff? Non-alcoholic. Four years now Clay. Five years, if you lets me off with a little slip-up. I picks up a scatter case of this when I'm feeling the crunch. Piss-water really, nothing only a torment.

The crunch.

—How's ahhh, how's your uncle Val? I seen him there on the box last week. Seemed healthy enough . . .

—You mean your brother? He's fine. Listen ahhh . . . I gotta meet someone. Nice seein you both. Anne-Marie.

I put me head down and shoved past as quick as I could.

—When are you gonna come up for a visit b'y? I seen your buddy down to the shop the other day. Brent is it? Your room is still there. Bed made and all.

My room.

—I gotta get now Randy. I'll give you a call.

I walked on up the street in as straight a line as I could. I could feel their eyes on me. I tried not to limp. He shouted after me:

—Need any money?

I didnt answer, kept walkin, fresh bottle of Jameson tucked under me arm.

. . .

Half past nine hey? Or half nine, as the Dubliners would say. Brunch with Lady Isadora. One hour. I'll be well on me way by then if I dont slow down. She was in to the bar last night with some crowd from that short film she's workin on. Robert Dawe was there, with that fuckin greasy ponytail. He kept puttin his hand on her belly, tellin her to breathe. He was just doin it to get to me. And she was lettin him, knowin full well it was drivin me mental. What am I some kinda fuckin joke? I finally lost it, asked him if he wanted his face bust open. She left then, gathered up her coat, grabbed Dawe by the hand, tipped her drink over on the bar and took off. Dawe grinnin from ear to ear, hopin everyone could see that she'd picked *him* over me. I was fuckin livid. The Hatchet was full and I couldnt chase after her. Mike'd have me head. Think she'd have a bit more sense, or compassion, where she tends bar herself. Nothing worse. That was around ten o'clock and I wasnt expecting to hear from her again, but then she called down when I was lockin up the bar around four, right sweet and gentle in that little girl's voice. She asked me to come up and I almost did. I almost did. I shoulda. Just went up and lay with her. Have a normal morning. Sometimes she likes to go drive out around Scavenger Drive and pick around in the big-box stores. Nice to get up that way, get out into the city. Pick up some nice hot tea and go cruisin. I asked her about Dawe and she laughed. Couldnt remember nothing, only that she came home alone and woke up alone and was wondering why I wasnt there with her. But I'd said no, that I was too tired. And I was. The bar was nuts all night and the thought of her fuckin off somewhere with that slimy shithead wore me down even more. So I said no, that I'd hook up with her for lunch. And *she* said brunch, just to get that extra little dollop of control, so's she wouldnt feel like I was the one deciding. But it felt good, turnin her down like that. She didnt deserve her own way. I cashed in me beer tokens and went upstairs and blasted Steve Earle for an hour and turned up the heat and drank a few beer and passed out on the couch.

Woke up too early this morning though, that's what happened. Eight o'clock and I was just lyin there, wide awake, starin at the ceiling and smokin. Needed to piss something wicked. The bucket by the couch was full. So I hadda get up. I started cleanin up but then I heard Mike's truck down on the street. So I went down, thinkin I'd have the balls to ask him for me wages.

And here I am.

And I'm lookin around for me balls but they're eluding me right about now.

Jesus, quarter to ten. The door opens behind me. I hope it's her. No. Jim McNaughton. He's shakin something awful. That fuckin smell too. He shifts his eyes around nervous, like he's never been in the Hatchet in his life. When in fact he practically lives here. He wasnt in last night though. But Friday night he drank the whole town under the table. He came in at six o'clock, right when I was takin over the bar, and stayed on till four, to the moment I turned off the last light. He drank *fourteen* pints of Smithwick's before switchin over to the London Dock. Seven double Docks. I knows because he was on tab and I was keepin count. That's what he does every night he's in: when the beer gets too heavy he turns to the liquor. And he stood there too, at the bar, all night. Left once or twice to go for a piss. Never opened his mouth to no one. Only time he perked up was when Monica came in looking for *her* wages. But she never even stayed for a drink so he sunk right back down again. He'd flatten one pint and then sip the next; flatten one, sip the next. Around two o'clock he switched to the Dock. A layer of sweat on his forehead, but that was about it. When I was closin down he got me to call a cab and actually walked out and got in it on his own. The human body can take some fuckin punishment, especially when you're tryna kill it, like Jim is.

Mike doesnt look at Jim, so consumed he is with his precious tally sheet. Jim clears his throat and nods at me. Mike still doesnt look up.

—Ahhh . . . b'ys. N-nice day ahhh . . . Mike, I ahhh . . . I must have left me j-jacket the other night. Did it turn up?

Mike looks at me. I shrugs. Mike *still* dont look at Jim.

—What's it look like?

—Ahhh . . . brown, d-dark brown. My ahhh . . . pills . . . my prescription is in it.

That must be how he does it, how the booze dont seem to have no effect on him, the pills. A menacing smile finds its way into the corners of Mike's mouth.

—Just looking at your tab here Jim.

—Yes, yeah. I ahhh . . . I'll be paying that on ahhh . . . on Wednesday.

Jim useta drive the snowplough, but sometime before Christmas he went and got hisself busted for bein fucked up on the job. Thinks no one knows about it, how he tore someone's front step off with the plough and just kept on goin. Someone put in a complaint and Jim was radioed back to the base. He was out of it, loaded. They were wantin to fire him, but he went through his union, claimin that his condition was just the same as any other handicap, that he should be kept on so long as he's seekin treatment, that's it's a sickness and all. I s'pose he got a point, or at least an argument. The majority of his "treatment" seems to take place at the Hatchet, mind. And of course the union got the last laugh when they relocated him down into the bowels of Robin Hood Bay.

His wife called down a few times the other night. I kept sayin he wasnt there. Third time she called down she goes:

—I know he's there. What are you protecting a pisshead like him for? Think he'd do the same for you?

And I thought about that for a second before handin the phone across the bar to Jim. He said hello, realized it was her, and ever so gently placed it back in its cradle. That's where he switched over to the London Dock, come to think on it.

• • •

Mike digs around in the lost-and-found cupboard beneath the stereo shelf. He pulls out the jacket. The rattle of Jim's prescription. A sheepish smile spreads across Jim's face.

—That's it! Right on.

Mike Quinn looks at Jim for the first time. He returns Jim's smile, but it doesnt spread to his eyes. His eyes stay as always: carnivorous, hunting.

—Nice fuckin coat McNaughton, good to know the City is treating some of us alright.

Mike flips it over his shoulders and forces his two arms in. Jim starts shiftin on his feet, tryin his best to play along. Mike tries to zip the jacket but it's a tight fit over his big belly. He forces it. Jim winces, expecting the stitching to let go. Mike spins around and has a look at himself in the mirror. When he raises his arms to fix the collar, the cuffs slide up to his elbows.

—What do you think Clayton?

I reckon you're a niggardly, bloated tightwad there Mike.

—Custom fit there Mike, custom fit.

Mike searches me face for signs of sarcasm. I'm too slick for that. He turns to Jim.

—Pricey garment McNaughton. Tell you what, you settles up your tab and I'll see to it that you get it back.

—But, but, but . . . My ahhh, my p-p-pills . . .

Mike squeezes his hand into the left hip pocket of Jim's coat. He digs. There's not enough room in the pocket for him to close his hand around the pill bottle so he rolls it out with the tip of his fingers. He holds the bottle up to the light and squints to read the fine print.

—James C. McNaughton. Take two tablets three times daily as needed for stress. McNaughton, you're not stressed are you?

Jim scuffs his toe on a trampled glob of dried gum on the floor. He stares down at the glob and nods slowly like a child who's been sent to the principal's office and asked whether or not his behaviour is ever gonna change. He reaches for his cigarettes, his hands shakin so bad he can barely hang on to the smoke. I reaches out with me lighter, just to save him the hassle. He sucks deep on the smoke. Mike opens the bottle and taps two pills into his palm. Holds them out to Jim.

—Well here b'y. Go for it, look. You shoulda said something.

Jim takes the pills. He looks around for something to wash 'em down with. His eyes settles on my beer. I slides it over to him, but Mike intercepts.

—No no. Here, look Jim. Have one on me.

He takes down a shot glass and fills it to the brim with London Dock. Jim looks at the shot. Looks at me. A fresh bead of sweat trickles down his forehead, runs down the bridge of his nose and hangs there on the tip.

Mike's eyes. Always on the hunt.

—Go on Jim.

—I cant . . . ahhh . . . not supposed to ahhh . . . just trying to . . .

—Very well then.

Mike snatches up the shot and walks over to the sink with it. Jim lunges at the bar.

—Wait now. Wait now. Here. Here let me . . .

Mike hands Jim the shot. Jim pours it down his throat. Hundred-proof. Strongest liquor in the bar. He dont even flinch.

—Thanks Mike, thanks. Appreciate it . . .

—No problemo, Jim buddy. Any time. So listen now, you knows where the coat is. And if you're feeling sssss*stressed* later on, you know you can come back. Alright? And when you clear up that tab, she's all yours. Alright?

—Alright. Thanks Mike. Thanks. Y-y-you're a good man. G-good man.

Jim waves and nods, waves and nods, buckin his head like a horse tryna clear his sinuses, as he stumbles clumsily backwards through the front door.

Mike wrestles his way outta Jim's jacket and hangs it on the knob of the cupboard near the phone. He hunches over his money then, starts recounting the twenties.

—One two three four—one. One two three four—two. Two three four—three. Your tab's getting up there Clayton. Rent shifts are coming up too.

—I know b'y. I know.

—I s'pose you want your pay though? Do you?

—I was hoping . . .

—So when are you on again?

—Tuesday night.

He counts out three twenties on the bar in front of me.

Just like that.

—Stay in tonight now Clayton. Watch a movie with the missus or something.

Yes master.

The phone rings. Mike's arm shoots out for it like a snake on one of them nature shows that finally makes its move on some senseless, unsuspecting mouse.

He grunts his hello and hands it to me.

Isadora. Wondering where I'm at, says I'm late. I says it's early yet for brunch. She says no, she said *breakfast* and that she's already after orderin for me. It rises up in me to argue, but I knows it's no sense. Besides, I'm starved.

I gathers up me smokes and flattens the last of me beer. A slight cramp in me gut, things loosening up down there.

—Well thanks Mike. I gotta get now. Meetin Iz for breakfast.

—Is that Rob Dawe's little one you're sneaking around with now?

I laughs for him then. Uproarious. Because that's what he needs.

His big stuffed jigglin belly.

I straightens me pants cuff down over me boots and tucks in me shirt. Feelin a bit tipsy, as they says. Prob'ly have a bit of a slur to me words by the time I meets Isadora. Dont know how ole Randy pulled it off for so long.

A nice cuppa tea now. Wonder what she ordered? Better not be none of that whole grain vegetarian slop she's into. Bacon and eggs and sausages and fried tomato and fuckin white toast is what I wants. Nice Irish fry-up.

Mike sighs and pops open Jim's pills. Taps two into the palm of his hand. Tosses 'em in his mouth, ducks his head under the tap and takes a long drink. He stands up again, hauls a hairy forearm across his face.

He holds out the bottle to me.

—Want a couple?

I holds out me open palm. Mike taps half a dozen pills into it.

—Say when.

Six more.

—When.

He looks into the bottle and shakes it around to see how many are left.

—Poor old Jim. Have to leave him something I suppose.

24. Maybe You Shouldnt Speak Right Now

Dont even fuckin ask me about this audition I went to. Me and
Isadora were down at the Ship and some horn-rimmed little yuppie
mainland casting director fuck came up to us and gave me her card.
Said she liked the look of me. And I s'pose I'll admit, I liked the
sound of that. She knew Iz, where she'd been in to audition earlier
that day. Iz said hi, and missus gave her this real put-on, lofty smile
while she walked away. Iz started chewin her nails and warned me
not to get me hopes up.

The bar was all abuzz. *Everybody* was apparently guaranteed to
get a role.

—Eighty speaking roles.

That's all you could hear, and how there wasnt even eighty actors
livin in Town. One frosted-blond fruitcake was prancin around the
bar signin his name on matchbooks and cigarette packages, tellin
people it'd be worth something someday. Word was out that he was
up for the lead role. The casting missus cracked up laughin at everything he said and did. Sickening. I wanted to bust his face open, but
Isadora wasnt payin no mind to 'im, so I let it go.

Isadora said her own audition went over the best kind, but that
she didnt really care if she got the part or not. I could tell she didnt
mean it though, that she was prob'ly only buildin up her defence for
the possibility of rejection.

She wouldnt have a drink. Three days she was off it. I even went up and got her one and laid it on the table in front of her, chilled glass and all. She shoved it aside and sat there at the table, watchin me guzzle away. Wasnt near as much fun drinkin with her then.

We had a racket.

She leaned across the table and said, right low so's I could barely hear her, that she didnt know if she could stick it out with me if I wasnt prepared to admit that my own drinking was "a hindrance to the relationship." *Relationship*. What a fuckin dirty, underhanded word. But I s'pose that's what I went lookin for. I shouted back that I could quit if I wanted to. She turned right red and looked around the bar and laughed, so I poured me beer on the floor. We squared off for a bit, arms crossed, not talkin. That casting director came back to the table then. She gave me a bit of a script and I tucked it into me pocket without lookin at it. Word went around the bar like a fuckin woods fire. People nodded at me and someone I knew vaguely from a poster on a pole bought me a pint. I flattened it in two tips of the glass.

On the walk back to Isadora's, she said she couldnt see how we'd last if she was tryin to make such a "drastic move" with her life while I stood around with me belly full of beer and gawked at her. She said what she needed most right then and there was support. I said:

—Look girl, I'm bloody well supporting you. But dont try and tell me there's something wrong with havin a fuckin beer.

—Every day?

—What's wrong with it? In Dublin sure . . .

—When will you get it into your head that you're not in Dublin, you're not in the IRA, you're not fucking Irish!

I ignored that.

—Look girl, I aint sayin I wants to be loaded all the time, but just to have the scattered beer.

—But how's that being supportive? I'm struggling with, with, with the absence of the only escape I've ever had, while you completely indulge in anything you can get your hands on.

—Escape? What're you talkin about?

—I'm talking about me and you Clayton. If you stay on drinking, even one or two a day, while I'm tryin to go sober . . .

—It's not fair for you to ask me to do that Iz. You cant be serious?

—It's just, you're completely unreliable when you drink. I *need* support Clayton.

—Listen to yourself, it's only been three days. Wouldnt know but you're *never* gonna have another drop. You'll be plastered by the weekend!

We were passing by Donna's old place and I felt like jumpin in through her bedroom window and shovin the poppers under her nose and fuckin the hole off her for hours. Sometimes, I just dont know, especially when me and Iz are in the sack, I just dont know what I was thinkin to leave such a first-rate fuckfest behind like I did. Donna was some nice and slutty. And what more do we need, really, but someone who wants to get fucked every which way, any time atall, and then go out drinkin? Everything's gotta be so fuckin precious with Isadora. All this kissing and gentleness till *she's* good and ready. Never anything up against the wall. Now, I aint sayin I have anything against eye contact or intimate moments or any of that shit. But I do think that, sometimes, fucking should be just for the sake of fucking. It shouldnt always hafta be this grand romantic occasion that's meant to take your *relationship* to another level. Fuck that, that's a drain. I'd rather wack off.

That's another fuckin thing. Know what she said to me a while back? She told me that she dont masturbate. Her exact words *I dont masturbate*. Not *I never masturbate* or *I dont like to* or even *I've never tried*, but *I dont*. And she was right fuckin flippant about it too, her tone, like she'd been enlightened some time ago and decided that masturbation was not for her but was a sort of low-minded vice better left explored by people like me. People like me. But then she tells me that I should feel free to do it in front of her. Sick or what? And I tried it, like the fool, I did. And if she had to be atall interested in lookin at me hand or me cock while I done it, then I prob'ly wouldnta minded. But no, she wanted to look into me eyes, count the wrinkles

249

in me forehead and have me breathe right on her. She said it was something that should make me feel close to her, but it made me feel more gross than anything else and I couldnt come, couldnt *get* there, like I was too distracted with what me face might give away or what she might decide I'd exposed of meself in that tight little moment right before I got off. And then it'd all be over, and what then? I can barely look at *meself* sure when I does it on me own.

I dont masturbate. That's what she said. How can she expect *me* to feel comfortable doin something that she's so opposed to herself? And, I mean, she must've done it once or twice, in front of *someone*. I found meself picturing her doin it for the ones who came before me and it was almost crippling, the feeling in me guts, this nauseating heat in the pit of me stomach. Makes me feel kinda short-changed, cheated, like she's only deciding not to offer that side of herself to *me*. Like I'm flawed or something. Maybe I'm just not hairy enough or not defined enough or maybe I'm thirty years too young. Who the fuck knows? *Two parts boy.*

Sometimes when we're doin the dishes or the laundry or something I'll have a little grab at her, put me hand between her legs and hold it there till she pushes it away. It's more aggressive than affectionate, I'll admit, but it's either that or none atall. I dont mean her no harm. She says I'm just lookin for a reaction out of 'er, but really I'm just tryna be spontaneous. That's the way sex should fuckin well be, on hot folded sheets in the laundry room. I tries to tell her that we got no spontaneity in our lives. She says there's no sex because I'm aggressive and angry all the time. I says I'm angry because there's no sex. And why cant sex be fuckin angry anyhow? Why's it always gotta be this delicate matter of the heart, this organized event? Why cant sex be fuckin angry? Pisses me off.

• • •

She busted into tears then, out in front of Donna's old place, after I said that about her likely bein plastered by the weekend. She crumbled, put her head down and fell onto me shoulder. I just held her for a while and let her wail away. I thought I seen the curtain in Donna's bedroom flick aside.

—Come on girl. I didnt mean that, you knows . . .

—It's not that, it's . . . I'm just so sick to fucking death of this place, this town, my life. I'm sick of p-putting myself out there for people like that.

—Who? What are you talkin about?

—That fucking bitch, producers, the camera, shitty self-obsessive directors who just ooze fucking mediocrity and wouldnt know the real thing if it—

—Isadora, sweetheart, you're the real thing.

—You think?

—Of course you are. Fuck that crowd. You knows better than to depend on a situation like that. You says it yourself sure, how it's all just hit and miss.

—Exactly. That's it. And I dont mean any offence to you but, it's like, I've spent years now spilling my guts out on stages and pulling my hair out waiting to see if some dickhead director thinks I'm fucking good enough and really thinking I was getting somewhere and then right after my audition that bitch comes up and offers *you* an audition. And you're not even an actor. It's too random. It's like as soon as you stop and take a breath you're right back on the bottom rung again. Headshots and resumes and reels. It's all shit. And you're right too, I probably will be drunk by the weekend . . .

She fuckin howled. I didnt know what to tell her. She had a point. It's all shit. But still, I was kinda excited about goin in for an audition, especially after bein invited. Good fuckin money. Iz made six hundred bucks a day on that thing in Halifax.

On the walk home I let her lean on me the whole way. I started spendin the potential money in me head. I could quit the Hatchet, get outta that hellhole apartment. Maybe even get meself a motorcycle and clear right the fuck outta town the proper way. Take a fuckin trip back to Dublin, that's what I'd do. Live in a hotel right off the Liffy for a couple of weeks and write shit. Take her too.

By the time we got to her door I was keen to start learnin me lines. I was plannin to go back to the apartment but she wanted me to come in.

—I just dont want to be alone right now.

—Alright girl.

We had a hot bath together and I got hard and pressed it into her back to let her know it was there, but she ignored it. We were beet red from the bath. She had the bed all made and the room was right fresh and cool and clean. I started to rub her shoulders and then I slid me hand down between her legs but she just clenched her thighs together and rolled over.

—Cant we be close without that Clayton?

That's her fuckin thing, right, that she "cant go there" with me if we're not feeling close or if I've been too distant or if we've been in a racket. She dont believe in a makeup romp. But I tries to explain to 'er that that's what fuckin well *gets* people close, that's how we gets back to each other when we're lost—by screwin each other's brains out.

She was solid asleep within five minutes. I was cracked. Walk 'er home, let her bawl on me shoulder, take a bath, fuckin massage her back and there's still no goddamn payoff. I went out to the kitchen and made some tea. I picked through the fridge but she had fuck-all fit to eat there, only vegetables and yogurt and fuckin meatless wieners. What the fuck is the good of a meatless wiener? You wouldnt pay me enough to eat one. Fuckin soymilk. Jesus. Veggie this and veggie that. She's not after eatin so much as a morsel of real meat since she was a teenager. Can you imagine? She's got a good excuse though. When she was nine or ten she was drivin with her mother over on the west coast somewhere and there was this big load of cars stopped along the highway, watchin a moose grazin on the side of the road, everybody out takin pictures. Then some fuckin bigshot gets out of 'is pickup with his shotgun, walks right up to the moose and shoots it in the fuckin chest. The old moose musta got some fright, took off down over the bank and jumped into the bog, swam a little ways across a gully and tried to pull itself up on the other side. It couldnt get out though, and just lay there diggin its hooves into the peat moss and bawlin, blood stainin the water. And buddy just walks down to it and puts the gun to its head and fires it off, right between the two fuckin eyes. Little Isadora opened her door and threw up her guts on the ground. The law's changed now though, you gotta be at least a kilometre from the road to fire a shot. I do believe. Iz then started drillin her mother, lookin for some kinda sense as to why the fella shot the moose down like that, and so her mother told her that he was gonna eat it. Iz put two and two together, found out where hamburger comes from and Mary Brown's snack packs. But her mother wouldnt let her be a vegetarian for a long time, just cause it was too much trouble. And it *is* too, nothing but fuckin trouble. Isadora asks me to cook up something for supper and I havent got the first clue where to start. Gimme a few potatoes though and some onions and a bit of garlic and some fresh-bottled moose, toss it all on the pan, fuck, some feed. She dont know what she's missin.

Even the fruit crisper is all fucked up. Neither apple or orange or fuckin banana, just them goddamn mangoes and these little star-shaped things that always ends up goin bad, and fuckin massive pink grapefruit that'd almost stop your heart they're so bitter. I took out one of them mangoes and hacked it open with me pocket knife. I never did figure out how to peel the fuckin things cause you never know where that goddamn pit is gonna be hidin. Izzy's got this neat little way of doin it, this criss-cross pattern with the blade and then she turns it inside out and there's all these little chunks ready to be eaten right off the peel. I cant get me head around it. I likes cuttin into 'em though, I likes the way they bursts open, all that bright orange meat inside.

I sits down at the table with the mango and me tea and pulls that bit of script outta me pocket. Two pages. The first page is a contact sheet, tellin me where to go for the audition and what time. The second page is the scene:

(MALE, 25-30, Ambulance Attendant #1.)
Scene 86A EXT. Highway Intersection, Night

Nathan is on a gurney. Two ambulance attendants wheel him towards the back of the ambulance. Nathan raises his hand and attempts to speak.

Ambulance Attendant #1—Maybe you shouldnt speak right now.

Nathan's eyes close as he's loaded onto the back of the ambulance.

One fuckin line. One fuckin line. Maybe you shouldnt speak. Right now. *Maybe,* youshouldntspeakrightnow. Shut your fuckin face buddy, I cracks ya one. Maybe you should watch your fuckin mouth there, cunty-balls. I wouldnt try it if I were you buddy, hafta be careful over your last words you know. You cant talk to a fuckin Ambulance Man like that! SHUT YOUR STUPID BATTERED UGLY MANGLED MESS OF A MOUTH.

Maybe you shouldnt speak right now.

Still, I does the line over and over till I got it down. I manages to find a sturdy, professional tone and then tosses a little humanity into the mix. I'm the right age and the right gender. I s'pose I got just as good a shot as the next fella. I hauls on me jacket to go home and Isadora calls out to me from the bedroom.

—That you Clay?

I pokes me head in through the bedroom door.

—Maybe you shouldnt speak right now.

She rolls over and goes back to sleep.

25. The Audition Tip Checklist

Up to the Ship the next morning, couple of Mike's Hard Lemonade. Me audition wasnt till eleven. It wasnt so much that I was nervous, just anxious to pass the time. I was startin to like the Ship in the mornings, not as dark and closed in as the Hatchet, there's more floor space and tables and you can have eggs and bacon and toast and there's not as many hardcore drinkers. So I'm less inclined to let meself get carried away. I called Iz from the pay phone and had a little chat. She wasnt too pleased with me for leavin her on her own the night before, but she let it go cause she was after gettin a call-back from that casting director first thing in the morning. Delighted with herself, her hopes sky-high all over again. She told me not to tell no one. She said she'd meant to give me this thing called *The Audition Tip Checklist* that highlighted all the dos and donts. I had to laugh at that though. I mean, it was only the one fuckin line.

—Call me as soon as you finish your audition. Okay?

—Okay.

—Or better yet, why dont you just come over?

—I could do that, yeah.

—Well, I'll be waiting.

• • •

Bit of a crowd outside the entrance to the LSPU Hall. Everybody got scripts. Philip Lahey and that Clyde Whelan cunt are here, they got scripts. They nods at me. I gets a smoke off this blond missus named Charlene who's been hangin around the Hatchet again lately. She talks through her nose. I hear she's balls-deep into the crack and even started hookin. Social Services took her little girl or something. She's here to audition too. Keith storms outta the Hall and bangs the heavy steel door behind him. Thought he'd skipped town again, but maybe not. Or maybe he's already gone and back again? He crumples up his script and fires it on the ground, sorta shoulders me outta the way when he goes past. I lets it go, but I makes up me mind to call him on it some night in the not-so-distant future.

A crisp band poster tacked to the balcony. The Cold Shoulder, ONE NIGHT ONLY!! The Green Room on George Street. A blurry picture of the band. It turns me stomach and I wants to rip it down but I figure that'd look too petty, even though no one could know my connection with them. I dont mean to, but I makes a mental note of the date.

I finishes me smoke and goes inside cause I cant concentrate with everybody yakkin. There's another crowd inside. One fella got a full fuckin ambulance outfit on and I curses meself cause I got this dandy old RNC shirt down in me closet that I coulda worn, if I'da thought on it. Some fellas must be about forty odd years old and I has glance at one of their scripts and it's the same role I'm supposed to get. Dont make no sense. Then there's one young fella who looks to be about fourteen. Not too many women around. Trish is here, Isadora's girlfriend. She smiles at me. Havent laid eyes on her since that night I ahhh . . . that night I done the acid with Brent. Trish. Yeah. Her and Iz went to school together and what roles one dont get the other always seems to. I reckon there's a bit of a rivalry there. Some fuckin rivalry though if Isadora finds out about . . . Ahh fuck sure, you gotta be allowed to mess shit up a bit when you're first startin off with someone. What good would it do at this point to lay all that on Iz? We're gone *way* beyond that stage now.

First time I met Trish was this night when I was workin at the Hatchet and Isadora was workin up at the Ship. Busy night for me, but slow for Iz. Brent was playin pool at the Hatchet, half in the bag. He was just after movin into the apartment that week and so no one even knew who he was. The phone rings and it's Iz and she's bawlin. Some fella up at the Ship named John Hibbs was givin her shit. He's some kinda theatre director who gives acting classes too, so he thinks his shit dont stink. He was there with Trish and there was no one else in the bar. I didnt *know* him, only that he was a snide and loud-mouthed blowhard a couple of times at the Hatchet and he owed Mike Quinn a huge bar tab. I spied him a couple of times too, hangin around the edges of the Table of Death at the Ship. Anyhow, he was after sayin everything to Izzy, called her a little bitch and a fuckin cocktease, just cause she wouldnt let him have happy hour prices. He banged his fist on the bar and screamed at her that he'd been comin to the Ship for twenty-five years and that he'd seen dozens and dozens of little princesses just like her behind that very bar and that he was after spendin enough money in there over the years that he was entitled to happy hour prices. She wouldnt give in to 'im though, God love 'er. But she was some upset that she hadda take that kinda shit when all she wanted to be doin was actin and paintin. I was fuckin vicious. I asked her what she wanted me to do but she wouldnt let me go up. I couldnt anyhow, cause the Hatchet was hoppin and if I left me post Mike woulda had me head. So I called Brent over from the pool table and described that scrawny fuckin Hibbs prick to him and told him what was after goin on at the Ship with Isadora. Brent'd only met Iz a few days before. He'd wandered into the Ship and she was there loaded and they got talkin and he asked her if she knew me, and of course she did. She figured out who he was then, where I was after tellin 'er about him movin in with me, and she turned on him and tossed her full beer in his face, accused him of bein up at the Ship spyin on her for me. Brent didnt give a fuck, hardly the first beer he's after havin slopped in his face. She came down to the apartment a couple of hours later and went into his bedroom and jumped on him and forced him to accept her apology. What's she like atall? And I reckon he *did* forgive her too cause he wasnt long marchin up to the Ship when I told him what was goin on with that Hibbs cocksucker. Or maybe he was just bored, I dont know.

I got three versions of the story later that night, from Isadora and Trish and Brent, but basically they were all the same, just that everybody had their own details to offer up.

Brent met John Hibbs and Trish when they were on their way outta the Ship. He gave Hibbs a shove.

—Are you John Hibbs?

Hibbs was flustered, to say the least. None of them old downtown theatre arts fuckers ever gets called on anything. They thinks they're above it all. But they're not.

—Y-yes, of course. And who might you be?

—You stole my fuckin b'yfriend!

Brent grabbed Hibbs by the jacket and pushed him up against the door.

—I-I'm sorry, I have no idea—

—Dont lie to me, fucker. You stole my fuckin b'yfriend!

Hibbs got all embarrassed then, with Trish standin there. He was prob'ly hopin to take her home and fuck 'er, as is the way with amateur acting teachers. He tried to shove past, but Brent slammed him against the wall again. Isadora poked her head out through the door when she heard the racket, but she had the good sense not to say Brent's name out loud. She didnt wanna be associated with what was goin on I s'pose. Slick enough aint she?

—But, but I'm not even gay.

—No b'y. Look at yourself sure.

—Who's your boyfriend?

—You fuckin well knows who he is, you fucked him! And look here . . .

Brent bashed the bottom of his beer bottle off the wall of the building and held the jagged end up to John Hibbs's face.

—. . . if you ever come near him again, and I means *ever*, I'll cut your fuckin cock off. How's that sound?

—Please, I—

—Shut your fuckin face!

Brent smashed the rest of the bottle at Hibbs's feet and took off up over the steps towards Duckworth. I thought that was pretty smooth, takin off in the other direction like that. Hibbs and Trish went back inside and Isadora said later that he was so shook up he couldnt even talk. He called a cab while Iz locked up the bar and then he had the two of the girls wait on the street with him till the cab showed up.

Brent came back to the Hatchet, all outta breath and laughin his head off. Ten minutes later Isadora and Trish walked in. Trish got pretty freaked out when she saw Brent, so we had to explain the whole thing to her. She was good buddies with Hibbs and didnt find it near as funny as the rest of us. But in the end she warmed up. I mean, Hibbs only got what was comin to him, tormenting my fuckin missus like that. He's lucky it wasnt *me* wavin a broken bottle in his face.

• • •

Trish smooths out her top and starts to say something to me, but before she can get it out, that casting director woman comes and shouts out her name. Pomeroy, that's right. I knew she had a real townie name. That casting director missus looks at me and smiles and says:

—Hello Clayton.

I takes it as a good sign, that she remembered me name. Trish jumps up and follows her down the corridor. All hands are sittin around mumblin their lines, so I wanders into the art gallery where I can be alone. I still got the lemonade with me and I'm startin to feel a bit flushed in the face, bit of a heartburn. Strong stuff. I glances at me script and says me line out loud a few times.

I wanders around the gallery and looks at all the different paintings. I coulda painted half of 'em meself. Couple of nice ones there though. One huge oil one called *Sneaking Around* that shows two pickup trucks in the dark meetin each other in some remote, wooded area. I likes that one. Reminds me of home. There's another one called *Anti-Christ* that I'm after readin about in the paper earlier in the week. Some Catholic priest issued a statement about the depraved nature of the arts. It stirred up quite a bit of shit too, and I can see why. The painting shows an altar boy on his knees and a pair of some man's black pants and shoes pressed dangerously close to him. You cant see the boy's head, but it's obviously level with the man's crotch. There's a set of rosary beads dangling from the man's pocket and a big stained-glass window with a crucifixion scene in the background. Pretty obvious, what's goin on there. If I had the money I'd buy it for Isadora. She's always goin on about how she's got no religion no more, how she useta feel "watched over" but that now, when she goes to say a prayer or whatever, that she dont feel no "presence" anymore. I argues with her that it's all propaganda anyhow, all that Catholic shit. It's all one big guilt trip, and that's prob'ly all she's feeling. And if she came clean with herself she'd prob'ly be relieved to admit she didnt really believe any of it in the first fuckin place. There's nothing and no one watchin over us. There's no fuckin God. If there was, you think he'd be lettin priests get away with all the shit they been gettin away with for so long? I dont fuckin think so, unless he's some kinda perverted fuckhead himself, which would make a whole lot more sense, when you takes a good hard look at the world.

Trish walks out the door to the upstairs theatre with a big grin on her face. She hooks her finger into the breast pocket of me shirt and gives it a little tug when she's passin by. It kinda takes me off balance a bit, where me foot is fucked, but I manages not to tumble.

—Break a leg Clayton!

—Yeah, I'd be good and fucked then wouldnt I?

—Oh my God. Sorry. I forgot.

—Ahhh, it's nothing girl. Just tryna be funny.

—Where's Izzy?

I thinks about that then, before I answers, I dont know why. *Maybe you shouldnt speak right now.* I loves Isadora and everything, I mean, I fuckin adores her, and I have no more intentions of fuckin her around, cause she's been fucked around enough in her days, but it's like I cant turn off that part of meself that wants to be on the hunt, like I have this need to keep me options open, just in case the shit hits the fan. Trish's big old jugs. Forbidden fruit.

—I have no fuckin clue.

—Oh? Are you still together?

—Yeah. I s'pose.

—Well, I'll see you then.

She sorta blows me a kiss and twirls around and disappears. I feels like shit and starts to panic and I wants to run after her and set her straight on me and Iz's situation, that we're fine and in love and un-fuckin-stoppable, that I'd never dream of hurtin her like that. Again. That it'd all been a big messy fuck-up in the first place. That night. And I mean, what if Trish was just settin me up, to see what I'd say? Never know with these artsy types. What if Isadora put her up to it? What if she already knows everything? Fuck.

The door busts open and that casting director missus sees me standin in the gallery.

—OK Clayton. You can come up now, if you're ready.

I tosses me script into the garbage as I'm walkin up the steps behind her. She got on a little short skirt and I can see the thick blue veins on the backs of her legs. She prob'ly thinks I'm tryna get a gawk at 'er hole or something, which I kinda am.

—I'm Yolanda by the way.

I offers her me hand but she dont turn around, goes into the theatre without noticing. I gotta sign me name and leave me phone number and make note of the time. I leaves the number to the Hatchet and squeezes a little note into the margin that I mightnt be there but to leave a message. I turns around and Yolanda takes a Polaroid picture of me that leaves a big blue blotch in front of me eyes.

—You can stand in the centre there please Clayton.

She walks away, flappin the Polaroid in her hand behind her. I walks into the centre of the stage. It's all I can do to cover up me limp. There's a camera on a stand off to the side and a guy fiddlin with it. I nods at him but he dont nod back. The front row, where the audience usually sits, has about seven or eight people. Some're talkin to each other and one's talkin into a cell phone, takin notes. Yolanda presents me:

—This is Clayton Reeves, he'll be reading for the role of—

—Reid.

—Excuse me?

—It's Clayton Reid, not Reeves. You got me mixed up with Superman.

Nobody laughs. I feels like a stick of shit. Cold room. Yolanda clears her throat.

—Clayton will be reading for Ambulance Guy Number One. Clayton, this is Francis Crane, our director.

Francis fuckin Crane hey? Well fuck me. This is the guy who had Iz bouncin in his lap that night I walked into the Ship on acid. This is that same crowd who were gathered around him gigglin after his every word. Isadora's comin bread and butter, if she gets the part she's lookin for. And how far will she go to get it I wonder? How much lap dancing did she do on camera to get that call-back? Fuck me anyhow. Here I am. And I can tell neither one of 'em even remembers me. Fuck the lot of 'em.

I takes a step ahead and sticks out me hand and Crane just looks at it and nods at me. I feels like a much bigger stick of shit, one that's startin to stink bad.

—Slate please.

—What?

—Slate.

—I'm sorry, I dont . . .

Yolanda comes to me rescue.

—Just look into the camera and say your name and the role you're reading for.

I looks straight into the camera and does what she told me to do.

—And begin when you're ready please.

I looks at Mr. Director, Francis Crane. He's scribblin something into his notebook. He leans over to the girl sittin next to him and whispers something and she giggles. I clears me throat. Yolanda:

—Just begin when you're ready Clayton.

I keeps starin at Crane. I'm fully prepared to stand here all day. Finally he looks up, sees that I'm waitin on him to be quiet, sits up right straight in his seat with his two hands flat on his legs and gives me a big exaggerated nod.

—Maybe you shouldnt talk right now.

As soon as I got the line out Crane starts whispering to the girl again. She's tryin not to laugh out loud and her face is gettin red. Yolanda smiles at me.

—Could you try it with a little more urgency maybe? And it's "speak." Maybe you shouldnt *speak* right now.

—What? That's . . . well what did I say?

—You said "talk."

One fuckin line and I fucks it up, first go. Off to a grand start anyways.

Urgency, urgency.

—Maybe you shouldnt *speak* right now.

—OK, now, how about bringing it down a little, like perhaps the person you're talking to could be a good friend that you care about?

I pictures poor old Nathan from the script, gettin wheeled away to the hospital with his face all bust up, after gettin struck down or shot or whatever. I imagines Isadora and then Val in the same situation. I thinks about me mother, all them years ago, her body broken in bits after rollin her truck twenty times just past the Ferryland graveyard. A lump comes to me throat. I takes a deep breath, lets the line bounce around in me head. I opens me mouth. The girl next to Francis Crane suddenly busts out laughin, then catches herself and walks outta the room as fast as she can. What the fuck is goin on here? Crane stands up and looks right at me.

—My apologies Christopher, please continue.

—It's fuckin Clayton, alright? I aint Christopher fuckin Reeves.

He sits down then and looks around at his entourage and smirks. A nervous ripple goes through the row of bodies, everybody readjusting themselves in their seats and wipin their eyeglasses or reachin into the black leather bags at their feet. No one lets Crane meet their eye and I realizes that maybe nobody else in the room actually likes him. Yolanda dont miss a beat:

—OK Clayton, whenever you're ready?

I looks straight at Francis fuckin Crane.

—Maybe *you* shouldnt speak right now.

Yolanda:

—And once more please? Maybe this time with a little more presence, and not so surly?

Surly? I'll give ya fuckin surly. Buncha spoiled fuckin herbal-tea-swillin moneyed mutts. Holy sweet fuck. One goddamn line. Presence? I looked right into the camera for the last one.

—Maybe, you shouldnt *speak* right now.

Crane stands up and starts clappin his hands. I cant tell if he's mockin me or not. The girl who'd been laughin comes back in with a cup of tea on a saucer and gives it to him.

—So tell me then, have you done much acting?

—Well I bartends. *That* takes a lot of bullshit.

—Yes, well, I see, but never any paid acting work?

He slurps at his tea and sort of waves his other hand in a circle to make me answer faster.

—No.

—I see. Well then, sir. Thank you very much.

Yolanda interrupts him.

—We've been having some people read for another role today too Clayton. Just a dry read, right off the page. Should we hear him read that one Frank?

Crane looks at my boots and then lets his eyes climb up my body till he's taken in every inch of me. Fuckin creepy.

—No, no. Thank you Yolanda, I think we've seen all we need to
see. Is there anything you'd like to add Clayton?

*I can add the print of me fist to the back of your throat, subtract a
few of them pearly-white store-bought teeth. Spindly, cunty-balled, soul-
less wanker.*

—No.

—Very well. Thank you for your time. We will be in touch.

I turns to go then, not the way I came up, but instead towards the
EXIT that leads out to the wheelchair ramp, just to show the bastards
that I knows me way around, that I'm on me own turf and coulda
slain the works of 'em if I wanted to. Yolanda wont look up from
some little beepy gadget she's playin with. Then someone says:

—How did you hurt your foot, by the way?

—Stompin some fuckin arsehole's head in.

I dont know why I said it, it just came out.

$\cdots$

I walks out into the blinding sun and lights up a smoke. The sour
stench of thawing dogshit on the wind. First true sign of spring in
Newfoundland.

I realizes then that I still got the Mike's Hard Lemonade in me
hand. The whole time. Trish is sittin down on the bandstand above
the steps that lead down to Duckworth. Waitin for me. There's a
Cold Shoulder poster on the ground near her foot, another one
stapled to the beam near her head. Fuck.

She jumps up when she sees me comin.

—How did it go?

—Oh, pretty good. Not much to it.

She links her arm around mine and we walks down over the
steps.

—Will we go for a drink then? Celebrate?

Isadora, home detoxing, sweatin her demons out and dyin to be
havin a drink, not wantin to be alone and worried about God and
money. I so wants to just shuffle on up the road and go flop down

beside her and bury me face in her and maybe even have a good bawl for meself. I wonder would *that* be close enough for her, me bawlin in her arms.

But I'm more in the mood for a drink. I'll have a couple and then grab a cab to Iz's and crash. I starts to cross the road towards the Ship, but Trish pulls me back onto the sidewalk. I reaches out to balance meself and accidentally sets me hand on her big sturdy left breast. I feels the nipple, hard under the padding in her bra. She giggles.

—No. Let's not do the Ship Clay. Let's go somewhere new. I'm sick of all those seedy bars.

I just nods and sorta leans me weight against her and fills me lungs with the smell of her hair as we walks up the street.

I'm pretty fuckin sick of them seedy bars too.

26. Colder Shoulder

This raw, burnin lump of agony in me throat I just cant swallow
through. Thick layer of scum across me tongue, the roof of me
mouth. Me sinuses dry as a nun's cunt. Water, I can hear it drippin
somewhere. I needs it. Me left eye is a throbbin nuisance that *will
not* open for me and I cant seem to straighten out me arm to reach
it. I'm lyin on me back, alive still, on a concrete floor. There's a thin
blue vinyl mattress beside me, a ragged grey blanket draped across
me boot. Something scuttles in the shadows behind the stainless-
steel toilet. Two beady yellow eyes blinkin, watchin, waitin. The
stench of piss, vomit, chicken grease, cigarettes, sweat, stale booze
farts and maybe even dried-up jerk. Maybe blood. Me boots are
too loose. The ceiling is a good fifteen feet away, circular, the concrete streaked with rust from the iron support beams. A steady dollop of cloudy condensation collects in the middle of the ceiling. A
drop hits the floor right next to me and I realizes me hair is fuckin
drenched. There's a body in the far corner, huddled beneath the
same kinda grey blanket I got, but with no mattress beneath. I'll
never stop shivering, never be warm again.

That dream, my mother, the day I kicked and screamed to go
with her to the shop in Ferryland, the day she never came back from.
Same dream again. Hard rain. I woulda been standin in the front
seat of the rig. No seatbelts then. I'da never made it, woulda been
tossed through the windshield. In the dream I'm tryna distract her

somehow, tryna draw her away from lookin for her keys, delay her somehow by even a few seconds. I can never see her face, just an outline, a suggestion, a feeling. I yanks on her arm and clings to her legs but she dont seem to know I'm there. And in the dream I already knows, I knows what I aint supposed to know: that if she leaves now she's never comin back. But if I cant communicate that to her, if I cant change her mind or slow down her departure somehow, then I needs to be there with her, I needs to *go out* with her. So she wont be alone when she breathes her last breath. My little boy's whine as I'm clingin to her ankle *I need to go now too! I cant stay here! I'll get lost* . . . The words flutter in midair before me and drifts like feathers to the floor. The last word, *lost*, rests on her shoulder for a second before she slips out the front door, her keys jangling in her coat pocket. I reaches out for the word with my soft, chubby little hand. It disappears before I can reach it.

· · ·

Where in the fuck am I? How did this . . . fuck. Isadora.

Shit.

—How long do you think you'll be?

—I dont know girl, couple of hours.

—Well what's a couple? Two? Four?

—A couple, like two, maybe not even that long.

—I'm just . . . I've got this awful feeling.

—I'm only goin out to a club girl.

—But you hate those guys, you cant stand any of them.

—No I do not. I said we dont get on too well, that's all.

—Well why would you want to go watch them play?

—I dont know, I'm curious.

—Can you please call me if you're going to be late?

—I can.

—Promise?

—Of course.

—And dont drink?

—Well now Iz . . .

—Clayton please? Dont get drunk?

—I wont.

—Promise.

—Look girl . . .

—Clayton, we can have a good life you know . . .

—Yeah.

That's the sorta stuff that's come about since she's been after me to move in with her. Like she cant take it that I dont say yes right away, and then suddenly she wants to know me every move, callin down to the bar twenty times a night when I'm on a shift. But I been kinda likin it too, this turnabout, how anxious she is for a definite answer. Sex comes a lot easier, that's one thing, and no minor thing either. It's like as soon as she has any doubts about where I'm standin and how I'm feelin, she drags me into the sack to try and get me back on track. Nothing wrong there. Only as soon as we're done she gets talkin about us livin together and when I dont give in there's the big old racket. Anyhow, no matter what answer I coulda given 'er, I knows it'd change everything. No more limbo sex, that's for sure.

And I'll hand it to 'er, she's after gettin through the past few weeks without a drop of booze, not even a beer. But then of course I'm after findin meself stuck on the couch with her more often than not watchin a movie while the party rages on downtown. We're after rentin a bunch of the *Rocky* movies now, and bawlin in the end of every one, even number three, the one with Hulk Hogan and Mr. T, and we all knows what a piece of shit that one is.

• • •

The Cold Shoulder was playin at the Green Room.

Keith, back from somewhere again, sold me six hits of acid in the alleyway beside the Hatchet. I ate one on the spot and pocketed the rest to sell. He was goin mad askin about Monica. No one's laid eyes on her since she quit the bar, or since Silas gave her the boot, however you wants to look at it. Since the night she caused a fuckin riot and robbed the place blind, god love 'er. Things is changin fast around the Hatchet, no doubt. Buncha little delicate queens infesting the place since Mike took off. I drank a pint inside with Charlene, sold her a hit. Smell of sweat off her. Gave Brent a hit. He put it in his pocket and then ran out to the street to catch the Number 4 bus, bound for the top of Kenmount Road to some party I had no fuckin interest in goin to. And I left then, knowin full well, in me gut, that I'd be ten times better off amongst the Hatchet crowd. But amblin west on Water Street towards the Green Room I just built up me anger towards me old band and the Shore crowd, and then filed it away in me head for when I might need to use it. I'd shook off most of me limp by the time I was standin in the lineup to the Green Room.

There were faces from the Shore, girls from high school I couldnt remember the names of but pretended I did, and smiled like I was happy to see 'em. I noticed too that me accent came out a bit stronger when one of 'em mentioned she'd heard I was away in Ireland. I cant help that sometimes. Someone else asked if I was in university, one of those what-are-you-at-with-your-life kinda questions, and I reckon I went on a bit too much about my screenplay then. Cause I'm just so fulla shit.

Paid the cover charge then, and tried not to resent it too much. I was determined to have an open mind and to try and look as supportive as possible. The bar was blocked. I tried not to resent that either. Me boots polished to a shine, the red and green lights from the stage reflecting off me toes. Made me too self-conscious and I scuffed 'em beneath the footrest of the bar. I tried to think good things about the Shore, but all the old feelings came bubblin to the surface. How close I came back then to just tossin meself over the cliff.

I had to yawn then, had this crushing urge to lie down across the plush leather benches that lined the walls of the dance floor. But I couldnt do that, only make me look petty and resentful. Me lips started to pulsate and I hadda take deep breaths while I ordered me beer. I couldnt bring meself to order a pint. People would only think I was braggin about bein in Ireland. Yeah, that's the Shore for ya, circling vultures, waitin to rip you apart at the first sign of weakness. I minds I was lookin around the bar, hopin to fuck I'd see some familiar face from me present life, Jane and Philip maybe, or even that Clyde Whelan cunt.

I had a minor spat with Stevie Hayden then, an old face from high school. He useta be the big star fuckin hockey player. I always hated him. Afraid of him too I was, if only cause he ran in packs of jocks all the time. He was too slick to ever wander down my road on his own. All the women he wanted. Parents had money, so he was always with the wicked new sneakers, his own car. On his way to the NHL of course. Or at least he *was*, back then. But I'm delighted to see he's gone soggy, picked up a big old gut and an extra couple of chins since high school. Everything comes out in the wash, as ole Randy always said.

Stevie comes up to me, all buddy-buddy and says:

—Well look of himself. How's she cuttin there Reid. Long time no see.

And before I can answer he starts on about the oilrigs and his Ford F250 and the strippers him and his circle-jerk rec-hockey buddies just left behind at the Cotton Club. He pulls a Polaroid from his back pocket and sticks it up in me face. The picture is of him with his flabby head stuck between the silicone-packed tits of some tanned and muscular late-twenties blonde. The very type he always expected to end up with. I knows he's looking for the appropriately *manly* reaction outta me too. I goes:

—Can I keep this?

—For what?

—I needs something to wack off over.

He snatches the Polaroid away and slips it back in his pocket. I cant help but throw me head back and roar laughin when he says that the woman in the picture is after inviting him to come and collect her after her shift is up.

—What's so funny about that Reid?

—The fact that, if it's true, that you believe she's serious. And if it's not true, that you'd make it up to impress me, thinkin that I'd give a fuck.

—Same old fuckin asshole Reid.

—Go fuck yourself ya fuckin brain-dead, sexist fuckin homo.

And then a bouncer was standin between us askin what the matter was. Stevie noddin, not takin his eyes off me as his freckled dog-faced girlfriend pulled him into the crowd.

—Watch yourself Reid, your time is comin.

And at that moment, not because I'm afraid of Stevie Hayden, but because of the acid, I gets this sudden wave of terror and nausea and paranoia. Lookin around the rest of the bar I realizes this is likely the worst possible place in the world for me to be right now. I tries to make a cut for the door but there's some sort of scuffle with a couple of bouncers and some young one from Renews I cant quite place. I holds back for a bit. Then the band starts. The ceiling sinks a little lower. Me barstool is too short and I feels like a child against the bar cause I cant rest me arms over it properly. Someone shouts me name and I feels a finger poke me rib cage but I wont respond, wont even turn me head. There's a girl over there I went out with years ago. She caught me at a party in Cape Broyle, in the laundry room with her first cousin. I runs me hand through me hair and it feels really, really greasy. Me scalp is so itchy and me eyes feels tight at the corners and puffy and likely sunken black with shadow. I havent shaved in two weeks now. Isadora made some comment about this man with a beard we saw in a bookstore. I cant exactly remember what she said, but I stopped shaving that very day. Me face feels dirty and sweaty.

The band is loud as fuck. Too loud. Perfect. I wants to turn around and watch 'em but I dont wanna make eye contact with anyone in the crowd. I gotta get meself outta here, but I cant move. Enemies, old grudges, rumours and lies, ignorance. They're just waitin, watchin. Vultures. I catches me reflection in the smoked mirror behind the bar and realizes I must be just radiating weakness and vulnerability. I'm just fuckin askin for it. Fuck this. Before I went to Dublin I read this statistic about how the most dangerous time to walk the streets of any major city was Sunday morning. The streets are deserted, the pubs and shops are not opened, and the only ones roamin the streets are the ones with nowhere else to go. Strung out, hungover and more often than not, after a weekend spent flyin and sinkin and drownin in their particular drug of choice, left with nothing to show and fuck-all left to lose. Predators then, lashin out at anyone showin the slightest sign of weakness, bullyin for cigarettes and money and blood. And me, I lands in Dublin on a Saturday night and didnt I find meself wandering down O'Connell Street first thing Sunday morning with a fuckin disposable camera, me eyes to the rooftops, searchin for the famous bullet holes. Next thing I knows I'm struck hard on the shoulder and knocked to the ground. I looks up to see this scruffy fella with scabs and sores sprinkled from his neck to his scalp. The cuff of his green army jacket was burnt and his hand was wrapped in a filthy old red bandana. He crouched over me and raised his arm like he was gonna backhand me.

—Fook ya loogin ad?

I broke eye contact, got to me feet and started walkin back the other way. He kept pushin me shoulder from behind and I kept stumblin forward with the force. But I wouldnt say nothing to him, or turn around, or fall down. I'd heard the stories of needles as the weapon of choice. I quickened me pace as best I could without breakin into a run. A good old Irish copper then, fuckin Garda Síochána, rounded the corner of the GPO and when I finally turned around the scabby fella was vanished. But I learned me lesson didnt I? Walk the streets like you're fuckin born there. Take on the look of the place, let 'em all know that you're just as fuckin cracked and ready to rumble as they wants you to think *they* are.

• • •

I tears me eyes away from the reflection in the bar mirror, spins around on me barstool to face the crowd. I clenches me jaw and cracks me knuckles and flexes me arms hard, to get the blood flowin. I takes out another hit of acid and swallows it down. Two brothers from Fermeuse, fuckin ugly square-faced freckled pricks. I'll fight the two of 'em the one time if they so much as glances over.

I orders a pint then, and relaxes a bit and listens to the band. My old band. Cant make out the lyrics. They got a new singer of course, but his voice is too high-pitched. They're heavier too, sorta bordering a death-metal sound that I dont care much atall for. I watches Corey, me old friend, on guitar. There's fuck-all reality to whoever he's tryna be up there. But then, Corey was always more consumed with the *idea* of bein in a band, come to think of it. The music is secondary to the image of it all. Anyhow, Corey's more into the folk music than metal, he wouldnt be caught dead in a pair of cowboy boots or leather fuckin pants in the real world. But he's not a real songwriter anyhow, so he'd never have a go at a song that you could actually make out the lyrics to. He'd rather hide behind a wall of sound. It's all so transparent I cant help but feel relieved. I wanders over to the booth where they got their CD on sale. There's a display copy open and I removes the insert to have a look at the credits and the acknowledgments. Me own name is nowhere in sight, of course. But what the fuck do I care? I digs into me pockets for the price of the CD, and I'm just about to hand me money over to the girl at the booth when me ears tunes into the song bein played on stage. By my old band. That riff. That's mine. I drops the CD and whips around to face the stage. I catches Corey's eye but he dont acknowledge that he even recognizes me. The heat rushes to me upper chest and me face. I marches across the open dance floor to the stage. Stevie Hayden tries to get up in me face but I shoves him so hard he topples over a barstool and falls to the floor with his beer slopped all down his neck and the front of his jacket. This counterfeit singer they got, this faggot, he's got his eyes closed and so doesnt see me approach. I'm only barely aware of a cold hand on me shoulder as I grabs the mic stand and screams into the mic for the whole bar to hear:

—This song is fuckin stolen! Do you hear me? Fuckin imposters.

The music stops and I feels the distinct, muted thump of a fist against me cheekbone, just below me eye. Me ears ringin from the blow, but as I'm fallin backwards I manages to sling the mic stand as hard as I can at the face of Corey's precious Marshall amp. There's the screech of feedback and groans from the crowd and then me jacket is rippin at the seams as I'm dragged by the shoulders across the beer-soaked floor through the crowd.

Me stomach heaves as I'm tossed onto the front steps of the Green Room. I holds me hand over me mouth to keep from spewin. *We can have a good life.* Retch. Spew. Hot beer squirts through me fingers and splashes back onto me chin and cheeks and dribbles down me neck inside me shirt. Someone pushes me from behind. Another wet, slimy heave. The sickening smell of another drunken downtown night: hot-dog grease and sauerkraut, sickly expensive student cologne, pizza, latex, car exhaust, gutter sludge. From the open window on the top floor of the Green Room I hears Corey's voice through the mic:

—Clayton Reid everybody, hometown boy! Give a big hand, c'mon, big hand.

• • •

I managed to stagger and crawl as far as the courthouse steps before the cops finally picked me up. I was kickin and screamin while they held me down to cuff me. I could see the Hatchet from where they picked me up and I kept pleadin with 'em:

—Just let me go home. I lives right fuckin there man . . .

And both cops laughin at me:

—I wouldnt doubt that for a second pal.

And because we were already on the steps of the lockup they didnt even need to put me in the back of the car. I lashed out with me elbow and caught one of 'em in the chest, next thing me eye is swollen shut and I'm screamin for Isadora, howlin for me phone call, shivering on the concrete floor, kickin the old drunk in the corner of the cell, warnin him not to get any strange ideas during the night. The cell door opens and I'm grabbed from behind, me arm twisted behind me back to the breaking point. I settles down then. They takes the laces from me boots so's I cant use 'em to hang meself or choke me roommate. I'm shoutin, me voice cracked and dry:

—It's my fuckin song! My song . . .

And then me mother, standin in the doorway with her keys jangling and there's the screech of tires and Randy with his face in his hands and a bottle of rum cradled between his knees and Anne-Marie rubbin his shoulders and all that chocolate and pity and dollar bills like the whole town came to pay me for a job well done. My pudgy little hands reachin out to take the money, not knowing what it's for.

And the cell door slidin open.

—Reid. Up. You're free to go.

Free? Me? Free to do what? Go where? Isadora?

I staggers down the long hallway towards the front desk where an outstretched hand dangles an oversized Ziploc bag with me laces and necklace and me silver Claddagh ring. There's a couple of twenties too and me heart lifts a bit cause I knows exactly what I'm gonna do with them now dont I? Yes.

I hafta sorta slide along the wall for support and the guard at the desk whistles when he sees me. A voice from deep inside the room behind the desk says:

—Look out lads, look out. Here comes our famous singer. Here's our rock star.

—Is he anything to what's his face, Valentine Reid?

—Dont know, ask him.

The guard looks at me for verification. I slowly shakes me head.

. . .

Church bells boomin out across the empty streets. A greasy brown paper bag dances down the sidewalk and lands on me boot. There's a Cold Shoulder poster on every goddamn pole and I has a brief laugh at one that has the word *fags* scrawled across it in thick black marker. Then I remembers writin it there meself a few nights ago and it dont seem so funny no more.

I stops at the pay phone outside Erin's Pub and dials Isadora. I holds the quarter in the slot and waits for her to pick up.

—Hello?

Her voice is choked and heavy, her sinuses plugged, like she's been up all night cryin.

—Hello? Clayton is that you? Please . . .

The digital clock on the phone reads 7:17. I pulls the twenties from me pocket and looks 'em over. Me stomach rumbles, but breakfast is the furthest thing from me mind.

—Hello? Clayton?

Only one place open at this hour.

—Answer me!

I lays the phone back down on the cradle and turns west towards Fagan's Pub.

27. Big and Ugly Enough

Me forehead went numb a few miles back, but I can still feel the drops peltin off it like BB shots, like the wars we had in the woods around the cliffs back home on the Shore. This is real fuckin rain, from the heavens, if you believes in shit like that, if you believes that the apocalypse, when it comes, is gonna be a personal event. Rain like you've never seen it. The kinda rain that swamped beneath me mother's pickup that day, liftin her off the road and into the arms of that quick death. Rain like the way Randy stared at me across the supper table in the years to come. Rain like the fat boozy tears that streamed down his face in the mornings after he'd lost a job or a car or left another piece of his soul in some bottle somewhere. Rain like the way she never even said goodbye.

It bombards me like hail, raw, vicious pinpricks on me neck and eyelids and wrists. The sting of the raindrops like a handful of beach sand whipped into me face. Me pants are plastered to me legs, so tight I can hardly walk, the threading around me crotch is diggin into me nuts, a steady stream runnin down the back of me pants, fillin me boots like Brent the time he pissed hisself that night at the Closet. Fuck me, if I could have that night back right now. The night I slept with Trish. The first night. I wouldnt do that this time around. If I had me time back, I wouldnt. Isadora drunk and saucy at the Ship, sittin on that Crane fucker's knee. Bouncin like that, like she'd never with me. Impenetrable, no way to hurt her without actually smackin her one. I shoulda seen it all comin right then and there. I did. I saw all this comin. Me, fried outta me skull. And Trish, Trish on the guardrail beside me, skin tight with liquor on her breath. She never looked better. The best way to hurt Isadora, best way to get at her, I thought: heave into 'er best friend. Keep it to meself till the time comes to use it against 'er. And didnt that fuckin well blow up in me face?

It's so fuckin black out here on the Trans-Canada. So many miles from nowhere. There's not even the hint of a light in any direction. I could be anywhere. I dont know how many hours have passed, cant think how far I've come since I left Isadora's little squat in Port Rexton. It was a three-hour drive out from Town. Me grandfather once told me he useta fuckin *walk* to Town from the Shore. That's a little more than an hour's drive. Walkin, took him three days to get there, three days back. Him and his horse. Assuming the horse mighta slowed him down a bit, I'd say it'll take me . . . eight days to get back to the apartment, back to me bed. But I could very well be headed in the wrong direction now. Or maybe there is no wrong direction from here.

I might be dead before this night is over.

Wouldnt that be a fuckin laugh.

I tried to scream a few miles ago, threw me head back and went to let wail. But I nearly drowned, me mouth full up as soon as I opened it, drops splatterin up me nose and down me throat and chokin me. It's all I can do to just keep me head down and feel for the side of the road with me gimp fuckin leg.

Too many big trucks on the go now and I gotta get way in off the road when they passes cause, sure, they wont even stop for a moose, they'll just barrel on through a big old bull and pick the legs and grizzle outta the rack at the next gas station. Fine way to get meself back to Town, all mangled into some trucker's moose rack.

Thought I saw an overpass up ahead a while ago and I tried to run for a bit. Shelter. But when I got to where I thought it was, it just wasnt there. Some hole in the fabric of the world. And I woulda gladly disappeared into it. How could she ever live with herself after that, knowing that she turned me away at her door and then I just vanished into thin air? There'd be the odd report from fucked-up, drug-addled truckers about a dark figure that mighta been a rock or a big dog or a moose. Or an apparition. I'd like that.

• • •

I'd been playin it all straight. I knows the fuckin rules, the only ones that'll get you through—dont call, no matter how much it's killin you, no matter if you're curled into the foetal position holdin a shard of mirrored glass to your own throat. Dont fuckin call. Dont talk to her friends. Just *dont*. And if by chance you bumps into one of 'em, put on your brightest smile and say how you've never felt better, say how much lighter you feels now, now that it's all said and done. How you never loved her in the first place. And always, *always* look your best, dress your best and smell good and hide your eyes whenever you can. Do your crumbling behind closed doors. It's only heartache. It's only pain. It cant fuckin kill you and you'll be stronger in the morning for havin looked it in the eye.

So I'm goin along like that, gettin through the days, healin up and movin on and reprogramming meself to just not want her anymore, when all of a sudden she strolled into the apartment, back from the boonies for a night, no Crane in sight, and found me on the couch and sat right close. She put her hand on me leg and shook her head at the mess. She asked to do her pee. She went into the bathroom and then came out without even mentioning the toilet. I shoulda showed her to the bench out on the back roof.

It was comin on dark and she wanted me to go have a look at this house she was plannin to buy from the money she was makin on that stupid fuckin movie. That's what the Port Rexton thing is about, she's been stayin with another bunch from the movie in this apartment while they does rehearsals and shoots a load of outdoor stuff. I saw the fella who's doin Ambulance Attendant #1. He's forty-something, easy. Ugly bastard too. Woulda been so fuckin nice hey, for me and her to get outta town like that and live together for a few weeks and work on a movie and make money and shit. But no, soon as she gets the call for the part, she's gone. I calls her up then, that first weekend she was gone, and she tells me she's not so sure about us. Nothing new about that, but there was something else. I asked her if she was with someone and she says yes, just like that, cause where she just gotta be so fuckin disgustingly honest all the time.

—Who? Who the fuck is it? Dawe?

Someone told me they saw her and Dawe out there somewhere in a café havin dinner. Soon as he heard I wasnt out there with her, he hops in his car and tracks her down and tries to buy her back all over again. He'll get his.

—Clayton . . .

—Who the fuck is it Missus? I hafta live in this town too you know.

—He's not from here.

—Who? Do I know him?

She was quiet then, and I fuckin well knew.

—That Crane faggot aint it? Mr. Director.

—Clayton . . .

—Fuckin tell me!

—Yes . . .

—Did you fuck him?

—. . .

—Iz? Did you sleep with him?

—Well, he was inside me for a little while . . .

—Is that right? Well I suppose we're even then arent we?

And I hung up then and got shit-faced. Put the final touches on the apartment. Saw Silas Lawlor down on the street from me window and drilled a glass at his head. Fuckin old queer. *Inside me. He was inside me.* Just for a little while though, Clayton. I finished him off with my mouth. And what's he? All man? *Two* parts man and only one part boy? I'll fuckin slay 'im.

She came back then, after her big fuckfest weekend, gave me the keys to her apartment before she left again, asked me to look after her plants and shit, make sure the place looked occupied while she was away. She was all happy and giddy about movin on and concerned about how I'd get on. Bein right gentle and fuckin motherly with me. She went off to the grocery store to buy some specialty veggie shit that's not available out in Port fuckin Rexton. While she was gone I wacked off into her shampoo, this real expensive shit she buys downtown, eighty bucks a bottle. I wasnt even horny or nothing, just twisted meself and smacked at and when I was hard enough I hauled at it till I blew a load onto the rim of the bottle. Scraped it in from around the edges with a joker from an old deck of cards. I turned the bottle up and down till I was pretty sure it was mixed in. And I didnt do it to be gross either, even though it sounds a bit sick, I did it for . . . I dont know . . . it was a spiritual thing, if you believes that sorta shit. First thing she did then when she got back was to wash her hair in the sink and I stood there and handed her the bottle when she reached out for it. And then a horn was blowin. I looked out the window and there was Cunty-balls Crane sittin in the passenger seat with the big black sunglasses on, talkin into his little silver girlie phone. I was right ready to go out into the driveway and haul him outta the car and pound the livin shit out of 'im, drag his face up and down across the asphalt till his cheekbones showed, but of course Isadora told me not to make a fuss. And I listened to 'er. If I had me time back now I'd be in fuckin jail. That Yolanda bitch came to the door then to get her and the first thing she mentions is how lustrous and shiny Iz's hair is. I shoulda shouted *yeah, that's my doin. She just scrubbed my semen into her scalp. You want some?* But I let that go too and tried to find it funny. Yolanda never even spoke to me, never even looked at me. I grabbed Isadora's arm when she was finally leavin.

—Iz, please . . .

—Clayton. I cant. I'll call you. Dont get lost. Be strong.

I didnt drop to me knees.

—Isadora . . .

—Look, lets just see where we are in a month's time Clayton, when this is all over with.

—But, just, please. Are we finished?

—I dont know Clayton. I think so. I'll call. Dont you call me though.

And then she was gone. And I poured Javex into all her plants. They turned a pale yellow and shrivelled and died within an hour. I felt even worse, cause really what did the plants do?

• • •

Another big old tractor-trailer now. I tries to get as close as I can to the shoulder of the road and starts wavin at him. He pulls his horn and blows on past. How can another human being leave one of their own out in the middle of nowhere on a night like this?

• • •

When I'd finally found the place where she was stayin in Port Rexton, she wouldnt even come out on the step to talk, just told me to go home. She said she knew I'd show up sooner or later, that it was typical. I wouldnt beg her though, stayed on me feet too I did. I heard someone from inside. I reckon it was that cocky Crane fucker, shoutin to see who was at the door. I tried to push past but gave up when I saw the look in her eyes. I didnt wanna cause the big scene for her, I wanted to talk. It was just startin to rain then and she opened the door wide enough to toss an oilskin coat into me hands.

—Here, you'll need this.

—Iz, you cant just . . .

—Look Clayton, you're big and ugly enough to look after yourself.

—What? How can you—

—You know I dont mean it like that. It's a figure of speech.

283

Me legs were like rubber. She shut the door. I never knocked, never kicked nothing, never said another word, just walked on down the gravel driveway hopin and prayin she'd come runnin after me. Whatever good prayer ever did anybody, that's another fuckin story. I never looked back. It was pitch-black and pissin down rain by the time I made it out here to the TCH.

She's blamin it all on that night I got locked up, see. Says how she just crumbled and gave up, how she died a thousand deaths, waited up all night, thinkin I walked out on her. I tried to explain over and over that the fuckin cops wouldnt even let me use the phone. If they'd let me make that phone call none of this woulda happened.

• • •

She was supposed to be gone with the movie till the end of August, but she'd come back to Town see, no warning. The night she found me on the couch. And I was stunned enough to go with her. Me there livin in the scuzziest hole on the ground floor of the city, escorting her to her soon-to-be new house on Monkstown Road. The roses in full bloom in the little garden by the front step. Dandy big two-storey house, the floors so fuckin solid and even, every room empty, and I could see her eyes lightin up in every room we went to while she pictured what to put here and which one would be her bedroom and where the bookshelves were gonna go and how to best situate the kitchen table for maximum lighting and *flow*. She's all about fuckin flow since she quit drinkin. And all the while, roamin through the big empty house, I was expected to be so enthusiastic for her, the life *she* could have, fixin up the back garden and maybe get a dog, for protection. Cause you cant fuckin well depend on someone who's only two parts boy to protect you, no.

We wandered around and checked the taps and the windows and flushed the toilet and turned on the shower. A wobbly wooden swing out in the backyard and we sat on that and I didnt even smoke even though she told me to go ahead. She leant her head on me shoulder and I put me arm around her and she said:

284

—Do you think it's too late to start again Clayton?

And the next minute we were diggin blankets out of an old chest and flingin 'em across the floor of the room that she picked to be her bedroom and she had her skirt hiked up and I stayed steady till she was shoutin out the only words I ever really wants to hear from her again:

—Oh God, Oh God, I'm coming. Clayton I'm coming . . .

And I kept steady, waitin for me own turn like I'm suppose to and what do she do but start in fuckin bawlin. And the house so empty then that her wails just bounced and echoed off the walls and into the dusty corners so fuckin loud. And then she was sayin:

—I cant. I cant.

—Well you just fuckin did girl, c'mon.

But she pushed me out of 'er then and wanted to talk, of course. Talk, talk fuckin talk. She got on again about me goin sober and havin a life and how I aint supposed to grab her in the middle of the night, wherever that came from. It was all pourin out of 'er. I latches on to that then, about me grabbin her. I says how that's one of the best ways to have sex, just fuckin half awake and shit, but she's somehow after convincing herself that I does it in the hopes that she wont notice, like I'm tryna rape her for fuck sakes. And she thinks I'm expecting her to lie there and take it without makin a fuss, when in actual fact I'm scarcely awake when I does it, just gone hard in me sleep and attracted to her. And she says well whatever the case it feels creepy to her, kinda implying that I'm some kinda pervert.

But at least we were talkin like we were gettin back together or something, makin moves towards fixin things, so I settled down and reassured her that that kinda shit wont happen no more if she feels so strongly about it. Jesus.

She dropped me off down on Water Street then. She didnt think it was a good idea to spend the night together so soon. She wanted to be alone. She was goin back out to Port Rexton the next day. But we were back, she was back, she came back to me, far as I was concerned. I walked up to the Ship and got shit-faced. Had a good time too, felt better than I had in months.

Next day I calls out and she's fine, tellin me all kinds of gossip about who's screwin who on the set and how she despises Cuntyballs all of a sudden, Crane. How hard it is to work with him after . . . well after she fucked him, but she never said it like that. I tried to lend a sympathetic ear but in truth I could barely contain me rage. We were back though, that's all that mattered to me. I tried to clean up the apartment a bit and even went out and bought a new plant for her. Next day I calls her and everything is gone right to hell all over again and she's askin me what I meant when I told her we were "even" after she first told me she fucked Crane. I knew it was too soon to lay that card when I did. I told her it was nothing, that I was only tryna get her paranoid, just reachin out for something I could hold over her head. But she knew. She fuckin knew. That Trish slut got a little walk-on role in the movie and they had their little chat and Trish spilt the beans. But of course *they* were fine with each other, bosom fuckin buddies all over again, and *I* was the prick. I tried to deny it first and only made meself look like more of a fucker. And I says to her, I says:

—Look girl, we were always at each other's throats back then. How was I s'pose to know we'd be all fucked-up in love and after lastin as long as we did?

I tried to explain to her that I was laced on acid the night Trish dragged me off. I reminded Iz how she fuckin snubbed me in favour of lap-dancing her way into a fuckin movie for Christ sakes. And I couldnt have known I'd be *this* much in love with her months later sure. But no, she wasnt hearin none of it and finally slammed the phone down on me in mid-sentence.

Me then, off to the Ship. Tried to get shit-faced all over again. I had a good look around at everybody havin their dinners and behaving so sensible and I realized I was the only one in the bar drinkin. And I knew I had to get her, had to find her out there and bring her back around. I just wanted to talk, needed to make the trip, collect meself, fess up and convince her I could clean me slate. I knew she was out there and everybody knew by now that I fucked around on her and that she was sober and everybody'd be tellin her to move past it and forget about me, that I'm a draining little bastard and she's destined for so much more, shit like that. That's always the way. I tried callin but she wouldnt hear from me. Keith walked into the bar then and sidled up next to me, even bought me a drink. We got chattin and I told him what was up, how I was tryna conduct meself in the face of it all, how I'd been holdin firm to the rules but she'd come along and fucked me all up again. Keith never said much, only nodded here and there, but when I was finished he goes:

—Just go fuckin get her man, right now. Walk every step of the way if you have to. Women loves that kinda shit.

So I hit the road. I wasnt lookin to be melodramatic or nothing, I didnt ask for the rain. But I couldnt have planned a better death, now that I thinks on it.

· · ·

Another truck roars past and the force of the water off the wheels knocks me back on me hole, gravel and muck runnin down me face. I props meself onto me knees and just stays there for a while. The traffic picks up for a bit but I just lets 'em all go cause I knows they cant see me and if they did they'd only think I was cracked and wouldnt want me in their car soakin the seats and plannin their murders anyhow. I tries to think through the rain, tries to think about the rest of the world, real people out there havin hard times, gettin drove outta their homes and losin their families. Prob'ly someone right here in Newfoundland might die on the TCH tonight on their way home from a wedding. People on their way to funerals or on their way to jail, fellas locked up down in the Pen by Quidi Vidi and the whole world after givin up on 'em. But no matter how hard I thinks on all that stuff, I still cant take meself off the side of the highway. It still feels like it's only raining on *me*, that everyone else on the planet is bone-dry and cozied up to someone they loves. *Well, he was inside me.* I wants so much to just throw meself into the ditch and pound at the rocks with me fists and scream and then maybe run like mad into the woods and never come back. I tries to cry but it wont come, feels fake, even though it's only me here to witness it. I realizes then that I'm on me knees and that's the last place in the world I wants to be caught dead and the last position I intended to be in tonight. I stands to me feet and takes a deep, snotty breath. I unzips the oilskin coat she gave me and slings it back into the alders down aways from the road. I starts staggering towards what I hopes is Town. Cause I can fuckin make it. Right away I trips on a piece of board from an old road sign and I splats face first into the mud. I lies there for a bit and squeezes big handfuls of gravel in me fingers and rubs it off me face till I knows it must be cuttin through. I gets up again. Walk. Dont limp. Walk. Three parts man. Head high. And I starts to sense something, like a presence lookin down on the whole pathetic scene, but not like watchin over me or anything like that, more like makin sure I gets what I deserves. I throws me head back and arches me back and screams up into the sky:

—FUCK YOU. C'MON! DO AWAY WITH ME THEN! WHAT ARE YOU WAITIN ON? FUCK YOOOOOOOUUUUU!!!!

I throws me hands into the air and spins around like that with the rain beatin down on me and me voice not travelling two feet past me mouth but instead gettin swallowed up in the relentless downpour that seems to fuckin . . . fuckin . . . encapsulate my entire existence. Not that I wants to be melodramatic, like I said. A car whizzes past and I just gets off the road in time. I'm walkin backwards now and me heel catches in a swell of gravel and I'm down again, on me back in water and road sludge up to me neck, laughin and pointin at the sky, at whoever or whatever is up there deciding what becomes of me.

—FUCK YOU! FUCK YOU!

I can see meself so clearly, last fall, the end of the summer, fancy free on me own two feet, unencumbered by want or guilt or heartache. Sober. Clean. Powerful. Indestructible. New in town and not needin nothing. Armed and fuckin dangerous. Un-fuckin-touchable.

—FUCK YOU! FUCK FUCK FUCK YOOOOOOOUUU!!!!!!!

And then there's a slender red glow in the mud on the pavement beside me and the laboured hum of an engine and a car door creakin open and a cautious voice sayin:

—You alright buddy?

I props meself up on me elbows and a chunk of pavement gives way and slithers into the mudslide leading down into the black woods to my left.

—Yes b'y, I'm the best kind.

—Well . . . you wanna run? You'll catch your death.

And I likes that expression. Long time since I heard it. Catch your death. Maybe that's what's up there, lookin down, mockin me, knowin that sooner or later I'll hafta own up, fess up. Come clean. *He was inside me.* Maybe if she'd just said *yes, I fucked him* or *yes, we had sex* or *we fooled around for a bit.* I dont know. I knows she tried to say it as clean as she could, cause that's her way since she quit the booze.

He was inside me.

There's just something so final about it.

Because it's somewhere I've never been, somewhere I just couldnt get.

28. Picture Perfect

Christ, I feels like cuttin loose t'night. Tell ya that much for nothing. Been rentin this room 'bove the massage parlour h'on Duckworth. I can see the street from my bedroom window, watch the men that comes and goes, 'oo they is on the way in—nervous and forcibly casual—and 'oo they is on the way out—boosted some'ow, lighter. I'm sometimes tempted to take shots of one or two of 'em. City councillors, businessmen, sailors and 'ockey players and h'otherwise 'orny young bucks lookin for a h'easy time. But I never do, cause the h'urge to do so dont really come from a h'onest place. And I knows that once I 'olds the developed shots in my 'ands I wont discover h'anything *new* about h'any of these men that I cant h'already tell with my h'own two eyes. They's all 'ungry for something way beyond sex.

My room 'as a bed and a closet, a h'ugly white dresser. The bed was h'already 'ere, but the sheets is brand new. The blankets I got second 'and at St. Michael's Salvage on Bond Street. The h'only thing in the room I 'ave h'any fondness for is the table I got h'off Val this past fall. Jesus, Clayton ranted h'on 'bout that table for weeks. I could never bring m'self to give it back though.

There's a deadbolt h'on my door that I'm glad's there, but I dont know, sorta makes me feel like a target when I locks it. If that makes h'any sense. Some nights I leaves the door wide h'open and listens to the girls gigglin and cursin and squealin downstairs.

290

I finds it comforting some'ow. My bathroom I shares with a ahhh
. . . "voluptuous" I guess, youse wouldnt call 'er fat, older woman
named Debra. She's the manager h'of the parlour and seems to
believe 'ole'eartedly that h'all her girls h'adores her. She h'asked
me twice now if I'm h'in'erested in "punching a few shifts." H'of
course I've declined. Bartending was anough of a dead-h'end road
for me. Next thing sure I'd be sellin m'self, and not even givin a
fuck. And then word'd get back to B—— some'ow. Perfect. Feed
right h'into their 'ands.

My mother called h'again shortly before I quit the bar. Said she
was comin h'into Town, said she missed me, wanted to know 'ow she
could make things h'up to me. Says Dad's h'on 'is last leg now, not
likely to make it to the h'end of the summer, that 'e's been h'askin
for me still. I 'ung up on her. I thought if I spoke I'd lose it right
there at the bar. I said it back then, nine years h'ago, n I still means it
now: I'm *never* goin back, lestwise it's in a pine fucken box.

There's a girl works downstairs named Candy. She's 'bout nineteen. She saw me with the camera one day and whispered to me 'ow
she'd like to be a model. She got the most piercing, 'ypnotic blue
h'eyes. I said I'd take a few shots of 'er near the window in the 'allway, h'even though she'll never be a model with them 'ips. Besides
that though, I was disappointed with the finished pictures. Just boring. Cause if youse can h'already see it with y' h'own h'eyes then it's
just a waste of film to take the picture.

Candy *loved* the shots though, h'offered to pay me for 'em but
I just gave 'em to 'er. Cause really, what good is they to me? She
never stops bitchin 'bout 'ow cheap Debra is, or braggin 'bout 'er
thirty-year-old boyfriend 'oo works on the h'oilrigs and dont mind
for a second what she does for a living. She says this *h'every* time I
sees 'er. And h'every time I 'aves to force m'self not to grab 'er by
'er pudgy cheeks and h'ask 'er do she really and truly think she's
livin, do she really believe she's h'alive. Once, I swear, she 'ad a big
shot of jizz h'on 'er shoulder and I didnt 'ave the 'eart to tell 'er it
was there. Any'ow, I wonder if *I'm* h'even alive m'self sometimes.

Most days I sleeps in till three in the h'afternoon. I should say fuck it and just *go* to work downstairs with the girls, we's h'all on the same clock h'anyways.

I'm just waitin now. Nothing new about that 'ey?

Waitin to be either welcomed or denied. I've h'applied to three schools for the fall: Corner Brook, Stephenville and 'Alifax. And I dont give a fuck which one takes me, so long's they takes me the fuck h'outta this town for a while. And I think I got a good chance with h'all three schools.

My portfolio was made h'up of three black-and-whites. There's one with Clayton sleepin h'at the table h'in the Ship with his girl-friend. She's fucked h'off again I 'ear. In the picture they's h'each passed h'out with their 'eads leanin 'gainst h'each h'other. There's a picture h'of Mike Quinn countin h'out money be'ind the bar at the 'Atchet, and the h'other one's Jim McNaughton standin in the street h'outside the Rose and Thistle with an 'alf pint of Guinness in one 'and and 'is car keys in the h'other. I called all three shots *There's Always Suicide*, one of Clayton's favourite "toasts" h'after 'e got a few drinks in. Whereas most people raises their glasses to good 'ealth or to h'absent friends, I've watched Clayton dozens of times raise 'is glass and shout 'cross the bar:

—Well, we can always kill ourselves. There's always suicide.

An' of course none of my "subjects" h'even knew their picture was bein taken, or've h'ever seen the developed shot. Maybe I'll send 'em in the mail once I gets in school.

• • •

I wont bartend, h'ever again. My final shift at the 'Atchet was packed tight with the screamin little queens that Silas Lawlor 'ad gathered h'up for 'is grand *re*-h'opening. Rumours goin round any'ow that 'e was plannin to fire all Mike's staff soon's 'e took h'over, so there was no way some chubby little pedophile fag was goin firing *me*. 'E'd come in be'ind the bar too, playin the bigshot and fucken up my h'orders, givin out free drinks on *my* watch. So I broke the golden rule for the first time h'ever and got plastered be'ind the bar. Fuck that old fruit. I slopped milk and stout and ginger h'ale down be'ind the register and h'all h'over the h'inside of the counter, knowin full well I wasnt comin back, makin sure Silas 'ad a fine mess to clean h'up in the morning. See 'ow 'e likes 'is new business when 'e's scrubbin piss h'off the men's wall in the bathroom. Although 'e prolly *would* like that, or 'e'd 'ave one of his new little nancy-boys do it for 'im.

Clayton and Brent came in and I fed 'em free doubles and triples h'all night. Clayton smashin 'is h'empty glasses on the floor and spittin booze cross the bar and then bawlin 'is h'eyes out and then catchin 'isself bawlin and laughin 'bout it till 'e bawled h'again. What a fucken mess 'e's gotten h'into h'over that woman. Brent with 'is 'ead down, drained and surly and wantin to be somewhere h'else, prolly 'fraid to leave Clayton h'on 'is h'own, for fear 'e'd make h'off with 'isself. That's h'all Clayton talks 'bout anymore, ways to die, ways to h'end it h'all. Nobody pays 'im h'any mind though. I slipped 'em a full bottle of Jack Daniel's when they were leavin. Then I let Sissy Maher and Clyde snort lines right h'off the bar in front of Silas. 'E screamed h'at us to take it h'elsewhere but we h'all laughed in 'is face. I guess I was turnin 'is grand *re*-h'opening into my h'own farewell party. The pool balls were robbed from the table and a wall mirror shattered to the floor in the women's toilets. Silas started to panic, 'is "new" bar slowly gettin destroyed h'all round 'im. I was good and drunk by then, I didnt give a sweet shit. Mercy. Someone threw a beer bottle and it smashed h'on the wall h'above Silas's 'ead and I just turned the music h'up louder. AC/DC. "Back in Black." Mike stuck 'is 'ead in through the doors h'at one point, grinned h'at the chaos and left again. Silas screamed h'over the blare of the music for me to *do something*. I shrugged and laughed and slammed back another shot of tequila. Fuck right h'off youse stout little queer. 'E tolt me to get h'out from be'ind the bar then:

—Go, get. You're fired.

293

I laughed, mercy I laughed. Joined the party on the h'other side of the bar. I watched Silas try and take my place. Some chance. The party swelled and raged. 'E turned h'off the music and the place went h'up. The h'actual bar shook and seemed to shift a little. The terror on Silas's face, h'almost felt bad for 'im, I did. H'almost. Them little queens were long gone by then, the 'Atchet full h'up with Mike Quinn's faithful regulars 'oo h'obviously resented Silas's presence and would never, h'ever, show 'im the respect they showed Mike. And then there were them faces what were so long barred, mosta the time h'unjustly, h'on one of Mike's whims, that returned to the bar with a vengeance h'after 'earing of Mike's departure, determined to take h'out on the bar what they'd been too 'fraid to take out on Mike. Silas knew 'e didnt 'ave the power to turn none of *they* away. I started bangin my palm flat h'on the bar and led the chant for music, the Stones, Tom Petty, Guns N' Roses, Neil Young, Blue Rodeo! Mercy, 'ow bad was I. Silas near tears. 'E tried to get the stereo workin again but didnt know which button to push. The gall of 'im then, 'e looked to me to 'elp 'im. I just winked. 'E pressed the tuner button and white noise blasted h'out the speakers at fucken h'ear-splittin volume. Some woman screamed and ran from the bar clutchin the collar of 'er blouse, like she got 'erself molested. Some big bruiser I'd never seen before bit the top of 'is beer bottle and blood spilled h'onto the bar. Sissy Maher shouted for a screwdriver and Silas 'ad no idea 'ow to make one, the stupid lout. 'E didnt know where the juice was kept or h'even 'ow to ring a drink in. A cigarette butt h'exploded h'off 'is fore'ead and the 'ole bar laughed. Mercy. A chair 'it the far wall then and knocked a painting to the floor. I was workin the bar the night that painting landed on Silas's truck. It was New Year's, the night 'e signed the contracts with Mike. Silas, the fucken tool, took the battered painting to a frame shop on Long's Hill to 'ave it restored, this gross picture of a big 'uman 'and crushin a live crow. I 'eard 'im goin on 'bout it a while back, 'ow it was some symbol of 'is "coming reign" at the 'Atchet. Fucken h'arse'ole. Then h'on 'is first night as manager, there's 'is precious painting shattered down in the corner. I'd say h'at that point 'e felt more like the crow than the 'and what was crushin it.

A fight broke h'out then, h'in the corner. I didnt recognize h'either of the guys goin at it. Silas threatened to call the cops and h'as 'e was reachin for the phone 'e finally noticed that the cash register was wide h'open. 'E lifted h'up the drawer to see h'if there was some kinda trick to it. I watched 'im rootin round for the money what shoulda been there. 'E'd left a thousand-dollar float at six o'clock. But the register was h'empty now, save for a few nickels and dimes. 'E 'adnt bothered to check it afore 'e "fired" me. And too much time'd passed h'in the chaos to be h'able to definitely say it was *me* what took it. And this was past twelve, so 'e could 'ave no h'idea 'ow much was supposed to be there. I felt the wad under my left boob and 'oped there was h'at least twenty-five 'undred. I slipped into the crowd then, watchin h'as 'e h'opened cupboards and lifted papers and grabbed 'is 'ead in panic.

I went h'upstairs and laced right h'into that Jack Daniel's with Clayton and Brent.

· · ·

Jim McNaughton shuffles to the front door h'of the parlour on the street below. I aims my camera and snaps a shot h'of 'im with 'is 'and on the door 'andle, 'is h'eyes focused h'on the street towards the h'oncomin traffic. I dont know for the life h'of me why I did that. I should feel 'orrible, but I dont. Jim's been spendin near on two h'ours a week with the girls downstairs. The wife is h'after leavin 'im for good, so Charlene tolt me a couple of weeks back. Charlene's been workin a few shifts at the Piccadilly cross the street and I runs h'into 'er h'every now and then at Kane's shop h'on the corner. She tolt me the cops were at the 'Atchet and the Ship h'askin for me. She wanted to know h'if I'd ripped h'off Silas Lawlor. I laughed so 'ard the tears rolled down my face. Charlene's pretty much the h'only contact I've 'ad with h'anyone from the 'Atchet in weeks. I saw Clayton h'outside Fred's Records one morning and walked right past 'im, never h'even spoke. 'E was fucken h'out of it, 'oldin h'onto a mailbox like 'is life depended h'on it, and I could smell the sweat h'off 'im when I passed by. Saw Keith too, once or twice. H'even though I've been pretty lonesome the past few weeks, I couldnt bring m'self to let 'im know where I was stayin. Cant let h'anyone know. Besides, Keith stank a bit too.

I locks the deadbolt h'on my door, pulls the table h'away from the wall so's I can h'open the drawer. I takes out the film bottles and h'envelopes of pictures and h'all the small, no-good knick-knacks and lays 'em h'on the table top. I reaches my 'and way back h'into the drawer and flicks the switch that releases the false bottom. I slides h'out the thin slice of h'oak and lays that on the table too. I loves this drawer, it makes the table. I pulls h'out my h'envelope and removes two twenties from the stack h'of bills h'inside. Then I puts h'everything back in place, pushes the table back h'into the wall to hide h'even the presence of the drawer. You'd really 'ave to know what youse're lookin for to rip me h'off.

In my 'ead I does a quick figure of 'ow much should be left. Nineteen 'undred and sixty? From what started h'out bein twenty-four h'eighty. There's no way h'anyone can prove it. No way. I can talk to the cops right now with the wad of it dangling h'out my pocket. Nothing no one can do. Lestwise Silas wants to set a few of 'is little teenie-boys h'after me to rough me h'up a bit. But sure, I'd only welcome that. Silas Lawlor. I'm supposed to feel bad 'bout rippin that h'off? Not likely. This is my way h'out. And if 'e's got h'any real business sense, or h'any balls, 'e wont h'even feel this by the h'end of the month, 'e'll be alright. H'if not sure Mike'll just take the bar back. I mean, Silas must 'ave money to be h'able to take h'over the bar in the first place. I'm not gonna lose no sleep h'over it, tell youse that much for nothing.

The plan's to 'ave h'at least, *h'at least* fifteen 'undred left come September, just anough to get me h'outta town and set m'self h'up h'in Corner Brook or Stephenville or 'Alifax, I dont care. Picture that, me in my new spot, some nerdy boyfriend, maybe h'even a dog.

Clean break from the h'eyes glarin, waitin, the whispers h'echoing be'ind my back:

—She's that one from B——. She charged 'er father that time. She's fucked up.

Yeah, too much coke again, I knows. Too many pills showin h'up in the tip jar by the time Silas took h'over any'ow. I was months ready to leave that scene. My mother callin the bar for fuck sakes. And youse know what, I've been clean h'ever since, except for the h'odd toke with Candy h'on the stairway. But no coke, no h'effys, no laxatives h'even, come to think on it. Fuck, I needed h'outta there so bad. And now looka me, walkin round Quidi Vidi Lake in the h'evenings, chattin with the rowers, tossin bread to the ducks. I wrote a bunch of letters to Mom and took 'em all down to the mouth of the river and tore 'em h'up and watched 'em get sucked down h'under the bridge h'on the way to the Gut. I'm clean, skinnier than I've h'ever been.

But tonight, I dont know, feels like cuttin loose a bit. Maybe I'll 'ave a drink, blow a few dollars, celebrate. Cooped h'up 'ere long 'nough, 'avent I? Yes. I 'eard tell mosta the h'old regulars from the 'Atchet is 'angin h'out at the Georgetown Pub these days. Afore I h'even fully decides to go h'out I realizes I've got my makeup 'alf done. Christ, I 'avent worn lipstick in a month. I does my h'eyes and then dabs a bit of foundation h'over the little scar on my chin that I got when some little guy in B—— tossed a rock at me shortly afore I left:

—My dad says youse're a slut!

. . .

Fully dark h'out by the time I'm h'on my way h'up Duckworth to Kane's. I 'avent been smoking h'over the past few weeks h'either, but I knows soon's I takes a drink I'll be bummin h'all night, so might as well buy a pack now and save m'self the bother.

Jim McNaughton comes h'into the shop be'ind me.

—J-Jesus Monica! Llll-look at yourself! H-how are ya?

—Oh good Jim, pretty good. What about y'self?

His face drops, like some 'uge, h'evil beast just settled on 'is shoulders. Christ, why did I h'even bother h'askin?

—Well girl, you know now, I wont be back with the City the fall . . .

—Oh really? That's too bad.

—Yeah, the wife is g-gone too, you knew that though I s'pose?

—Nope. I 'ad no clue Jim.

—Yeah well, that's how it goes. The young ones though, my girls, they wont even . . .

I h'asks Mrs. Kane be'ind the counter for a pack of Player's Light. Jim bulls past me with a h'outstretched twenty in 'is 'and, h'almost knocks me back h'into the chip rack. 'E h'orders 'is h'own brand too.

—I-I'll take care of that M-M-Monica.

What's it Clayton h'always says? Never turn down a free dinner? What's the rest?

—No Jim, that's fine. I can—

—No now, n-no. My treat.

I pluck the smokes h'out of 'is 'and, then leaves the shop and h'of course 'e's right be'ind me. I gives 'im a little wave of my fingers and starts to walk up Wood Street.

—Where're ya off to girl?

I dont want to be rude, dont want to 'ave to tell 'im to fuck h'off, 'e'll likely collapse.

—Nowhere, just, you know, h'out for a walk. Tryna do some thinkin.

'E reaches into the breast pocket of 'is flannel shirt and pulls h'out a fat joint. 'E looks h'up and down the street to make sure 'e's bein discreet anough.

—Wanna come for a draw?

There's a deep brown h'oil stain runnin down the side of the joint. Looks like good gear. A slight breeze pushes the smell h'under my nose and I h'almost salivates. Think 'e'd just *give* me the fucken draw and leave me alone with it.

Jim h'unlocks the passenger door to 'is Jeep and lets it fall h'open. 'E seems relaxed and calm as 'e makes 'is way round to the driver's side. Fresh h'outta the massage parlour too, come to think on it. Prolly well spent. The h'engine roars to life and 'e gives the 'orn a little toot. It's h'only Jim for fuck sakes, from the bar. Go and get stoned and then 'it the Georgetown for a few white Russians and a game of pool.

It's shockin really, 'ow clean his Jeep is on the inside. Mercy.

* * *

Jim takes the Jeep h'up Signal Hill Road. I guess we's headed for the castle. There'll be cars h'up there, parked, people h'up to the same thing, lookin for anough privacy to get comfortably h'outta their 'eads. Jim 'asnt h'uttered a word since we left. There's no radio, just a big 'ole in the dash where the radio *should* be, coloured wires stickin out. I's about to mention that to 'im when 'e suddenly 'angs an 'ard right down the gravel road to Dead Man's Pond. I reaches for the door handle. Jim looks cross h'at me and speaks for the first time:

—Too m-m-many c-cops on the Hill. These days anyhow. No one ever comes out here.

The last of 'is words h'echo round in my 'ead as 'e shuts the h'engine down and pulls the joint from 'is shirt pocket. There're the lights to a few 'ouses a good ways down through the woods below us. From the time we left Kane's a fog 'as settled h'over the 'arbour. No panoramic view tonight. My 'and firm on the door 'andle, ready to pull.

When Jim lights a match I'm kinda surprised to see 'ow blood-shot and sunken 'is h'eyes is. 'Ow come I never noticed it before? Prolly cause I never looked 'im in the h'eye till now. He takes a big draw h'on the joint and passes it to me, but my lust for a different 'eadspace is h'after leavin me now. I shakes my 'ead.

—Go on girl look. N-nice and m-m-mellow stuff this is.

'E 'olds the joint there like that and reaches h'under 'is seat with the h'other 'and. 'E comes back h'up with a flask of Smirnoff.

'E takes a slug, h'offers it to me. I've got my shoulder pressed to the door, my 'and grippin the 'andle.

—What's wrong with ya girl? Thought you wanted . . .

—I changed my mind Jim. I—I need to go now.

His laugh at that, lecherous, a laugh you'd never believe 'im capable h'of. 'E takes h'another slug from the bottle and taps the h'ash from the joint h'onto the floor.

—Need to go. Th-that's what they all says. N-need to go.

'E pounds h'on the steering wheel with 'is fist and I feels m'self lift h'off the seat for a second. My brain tells my 'and to pull on the 'andle, yank it, wrench the door open. But my 'and is not listening. It's gone weak and shaky.

—Jim . . .

—Know my wife?

—Jim?

—Know what I'd like to do to her?

That sickness in 'is h'eyes, the red, raw vacancy. Same sick greed my "father" brought h'into my room for h'almost ten fucken years. Staggering 'ome from darts or men's 'ockey and h'after a while not h'even bothering to check in h'on Mom first, to let 'er know 'e was 'ome, just 'ead straight for my room. My mother, not two feet from me h'on the h'other side h'of the wall, floatin in a Valium stupor. Or did she know? Did she h'always know?

Shhhhh, shhhhh, sweetheart, it's h'only me.

That 'and h'over my mouth, h'engine grease and tobacco. That 'ot, sour breath in my nostrils while 'e pummeled 'is load 'ome. 'Ow it was h'always *my* fault, 'ow I *h'asked* for it. Nine times, not h'includin the countless pawings and nipple tweaks and fingerings and maulings h'on car rides, movie theatres and h'anywhere h'else 'e got me to 'isself for more than five minutes.

I can see 'is face now, clearly, for the first time since that day in court. Sobbin 'is black little 'eart out, 'umiliated by the h'ordeal of bein dragged to court for *allegedly* screwin 'is h'own daughter.

When h'anyone could fucken h'easily see 'ow screwed h'up in the 'ead young Monica was. *Lookit the fucken scars h'on 'er h'arms sure. The black lipstick and black hair and black black black h'outfits. She's h'off 'er 'ead sure.*

Nine scars on my wrists. Shallow ones, h'attention wounds they's called. The 'ole fucken town on 'is side, all 'is 'ockey buddies in court, some h'even cryin along with 'im. And didnt 'e *forgive* me then, right h'in fronta h'everyone, like the saint that 'e was. And my h'own mother, shakin 'er 'ead and 'olding *his* 'and. The fucken 'owls and sobs h'out of 'er when 'e was found not guilty.

And now that same sick, bottomless, sallow h'indifference in Jim McNaughton's sagging, bloodshot h'eyes.

—Kn-know what I'd like to do to her? See her k-killed dead.

I pulls the 'andle and the car door falls h'open. I h'almost rolls h'onto the ground h'outside the Jeep. Jim's claw h'on my leg.

—Monica?

'E's h'after parkin the Jeep near a steep slope and I loses my footing, slides down h'over the loose gravel h'on my knees. I digs a slice of slate rock h'under the flesh of my knee but I can 'ardly feel it.

—For fuck sakes Monica . . .

'E comes round the passenger side and I picks h'up a rock 'bout the size h'of my fist. I 'olds it h'over my 'ead and takes h'aim. Will I kill 'im?

—Stay the fuck clear from me you sick bastard. I'll split your face h'open!

He staggers backwards and leans h'against his Jeep and giggles.

—Jesus girl, it's only me . . .

I lets fly with the rock. Jim ducks and the passenger window shatters.

—Jesus Christ woman! Are you off your head?

I turns and darts down through the woods towards the distant glow of a porch light.

—Monica?

Branches lashin at my h'eyes. There's the lump in my throat, the 'eat, the pressure and I wish I could cry, I wish I could just h'explode. But I knows I cant. There's a limp, a pain shootin from my knee to my 'ip, my h'ankle weakening with h'every stride. The porch lights not gettin no closer, the woods deepening, darkening. I wonder how Clayton really did get 'is limp.

I dont see the drop till it's too late to stop m'self. The h'earth gives way beneath me, the tumble of loose rock and sod and sun-baked topsoil. Total darkness, just the sensation of falling forward. I reaches out blind for something to catch 'old of to lessen the h'impact of my comin fall.

There's a deafening crack when my 'ead 'its. But I'm not too bad. I'm perfectly still. My leg seems like it shouldnt be h'able to go that way though. My 'eart is beatin. Feels like someone is sittin h'on my back, this weight h'on my spine. But there's no pain. Something warm trickles down my neck h'inside my shirt and I 'ear my mother's voice:

—Yay! Good girl . . .

I'm h'in the bathtub. She pours a bowl of water h'over my 'ead to wash the shampoo from my 'air. So warm. Calm. Safe. The plug for the tub 'as a chain with a yellow duck attached, bobbin in front of me, the h'eyes of the duck worn away.

The image fades, I reaches for it, tries to 'old it for a while. Cant keep it.

My body is burnin, itchy. I should 'ave brought my sweater.

—M-M-Monica?

Where's that voice comin from? Monica?

A h'engine starts. Familiar. Wheels crunchin h'on gravel.

No one ever comes out here.

Moonlight. I'm in a clearing. Something 'bout fog.

I tries not to blink, it feels too 'eavy and it's too 'ard to get my h'eyes back h'open, too 'ard too focus. Something moving next to my 'ead, nuzzling into a rotted h'old condom. Scorpion thing. H'earwig. Something? Devil's coach horse! Right. The type of creature what

Satan would deploy to drag 'is wagon 'ome h'after a long night of soul searching. Poor little guy, just wants to settle down and nest. I tries to breathe some 'ot h'air next to 'im. Breathin is 'ard. 'E raises 'is little pincers in warning. 'Ow very h'arrogant, 'ow ridiculous. I feels like laughin, but my face dont move and I 'ears no sound, like that part of my brain that would 'ave liked to laugh shut down years h'ago.

The rock cold and wet next to my cheek and I suddenly sees m'self, a powerful and lucid h'image of m'self, of what I must look like from h'above, from the sky h'overlookin the 'arbour—a woman down, fallen, broken in the woods.

What a perfect picture that would make.

...old
...een
...day
...ew,
...ult-

Avalon Post   Mon aug 2

Early this morning three teenagers discovered the body of a woman near Dead Man's Pond, near Signal Hill Road in St. John's. The woman's remains were found to be in the early stages of decomposition. Sources reveal that the Dead Man's Pond area has been steadily gaining popularity amongst prostitutes and their customers in recent months. The woman's identity will not be released until all next of kin have been notified. Police have not ruled out foul play.

Two loo...
sexually
girl. Re
accepte
after...
bu...

A 63-yea...
...hile

...hy a

29. Shitting on Your Own Doorstep

Monica. Dead. Prostituting herself up near Dead Man's Pond. Imagine. Just think about it for a second. Her body starting to rot. Sweet Jesus. I barely knew her. The night she slipped me and Clayton the JD. Was that the last time I saw her? I try to remember the last thing I heard her say. Her last words. In my presence anyhow. I'm hoping it'll come to me, and that it'll be something worthwhile, maybe even insightful or . . . I dont know, sacred. But that's never the way. Imagine though, lying up there in the woods rotting away while we're all out knocking around town pouring beer down our throats.

The bar is full, but no one seems to be paying too much mind to the news. It's just another Saturday in the city. I feel like jumping up on my barstool and demanding a moment of silence. I'd need a few more drinks for that though, and then it'd only come out wrong. Jim McNaughton seems to be the only one either bit upset over the whole thing. He's been over in the corner bawling his face off for the past half hour, chain smoking and drinking the straight Dock. I should smack him one, cause I can see right through it. That's the way some people are, they latches onto other people's tragedies and misfortunes so they can have a good bawl over their own fucked-up situation. Maybe.

The cops were talking to Mike Quinn. He went up and cleared out this room Monica was renting above some whorehouse. Imagine. He's apparently gonna pay for her funeral too. She's already after being shipped home to B——, getting buried right next to her father I heard. They says he took a stroke or something when he got the news. Imagine. And prostituting? I mean, we all knew she was hard up for money, to go robbing the bar last month, but hooking? Must be the crack. Poor girl.

Clayton hasnt shown his face yet. I'm pretty sure he slept with Monica last year sometime. He said he did. He was cruel with her too, that night she quit the Hatchet and came upstairs. He was loaded, liquored up and saucy. She *gave* us the bottle we were drinking out of. And she was just wanting . . . I dont know.

Silas Lawlor is nowhere to be seen, bastard. Fired her so's he could surround himself with all his little queenie-boys. He'll get his. I met Keith on his way out when I was coming in. I think him and Monica had a thing on the go for a while there. He was head to toe in black leather, had a bottle of Jim Beam his hand and his eyes were red and puffy, his nose swollen up. I havent seen him take a drink since I moved to Town. He's supposed to be after giving it all up. He stopped when he saw me, I guess maybe because we knew each other years ago. Sometimes I feels so far away from home, from who I am and who I was, even though I'm only an hour's drive away from the Shore. But we gets lost out here in the world. I knew he needed something from me. I stuck out my hand.

—Keith. Sorry. Sorry you lost your friend.

—Thanks Brent.

And he walked away then, kicked a beer bottle into the street and it shattered off a parked car. I could tell that he was going off somewhere and getting fucked right up, that he'd probably end up in the lockup or back in the mental. Isnt it funny that he said "thanks"? Thanks for what? My sorrow? Thanks for shaking my hand. *Thank you for being sorry.*

· · ·

I couldnt finish my beer at the bar. So sick to death of beer. I tossed some change into the tip jar and went to go find Clayton, although I wasnt much in the mood for him either. I wont be around the apartment much longer. Gotta straighten myself up now. I'm gonna have to tell him, eventually, my news. He'll be cracked. But Christ, we cant live like this forever can we? Look what happened to Monica.

I turn the corner into the alley and Clayton is there sitting on a pedal bike. That Charlene missus, I think she's into the hard stuff, she's whispering something in his ear and then gives him a little peck on the cheek and stumbles past me without saying hello. What a fucking hum of sweat and, and . . . something else off her. Jesus, I suppose he's not screwing her? God knows what he'll catch off her. He's back-on to me. I could just walk away without letting him know I'm here. I should. He revs up the handle grip on the bike like it was a motorcycle, makes the sound and everything. The bike looks like a good one too. I've seen it left in the alley before, propped against the murals, never a lock on it. I can tell by the way his head rolls around, how loose his neck is, that he's hammered. If he mentions Isadora I'll hit him, I will. *She's not coming back Clayton, she's gone, it's not the end of the world, but hurry up and kill yourself if that's what you need to do.*

I mean, I got a nice little young one now that I've been knocking around with over the past few weeks, but I'll be good and goddamned if I let her get under my skin enough to make me want to *die.* Besides, I'll be heading off in a few months anyhow, so I cant let it get too out of hand. Clayton's gonna be vicious when I tell him.

—Hey Clayton.

He lets his head fall back in the direction of my voice and then turns away again.

—Fuckin . . . look who it is. We'll hafta slaughter a cow, or something. Slaughter something . . .

—Hear about Monica?

—Yeah. Well. That's it.

307

That's it. I suppose he's right. But still, I feel like smashing his nose in, the way he dismisses it. All the nights upstairs with his big speeches about how fragile life is and how short our time is and the tears in his eyes when he's getting on about how in a hundred years none of us are gonna be around and there'll be no one to remember who we really are or were. And now Monica, his drinking buddy, his friend, his co-worker who he apparently slept with one time—and he cant face up to it. He wont. It's not in him. He cant see past his own line of vision, like nothing exists outside his own head.

—Whose bike Clay?

—Wanna buy it?

—Who owns it?

—I fuckin owns it. I'm the one on it sure. Right?

I suppose he has a point there too.

—Wanna go up the road for a coffee or something?

I knew it was a stupid thing to ask before it was even out of my mouth. Stupid thing to ask Clayton anyhow. But I cant face the apartment, because I dont want to get in a situation with him where he can break down, and I dont want to go to a bar. I'm sick of it. All of it. Clayton looks at me like I've got something growing out the side of my head, then he busts out laughing, his roars echoing up through the alley and bouncing back and forth between the two buildings. He says the word "coffee," over and over again, like I just told him the punchline to the funniest joke on the planet and he's trying to get it right for when he wants to pass it along to someone else. He falls off the bike and lets it drop to the ground.

—Jesus, Clayton. That's someone's bike you know.

And I feels like such a shit again, cause the last time we were on the go was the night we ran across the tops of all the parked cars on Bond Street, stopping sometimes and jumping big dents into the roofs. And I did the most damage too, where he's got the bad foot. I even kicked out a window and took a bunch of CDs out of the last car and set off an alarm. Tossed the CDs like Frisbees down over the rooftops of Victoria Street. Now here I am giving out to him about knocking over a pedal bike? He stands it upright, still giddy over the coffee thing and says:

—Wanna see something?

—What?

—Wait right here.

He hooks the bike up under his arm and staggers around the corner up over the iron steps to the apartment. I stand there, looking around to make sure no one is handy. A couple of minutes pass by and then he comes out onto the back roof of the apartment with the front wheel of the bike rested on the edge. He shouts down at me:

—Heads up!

Before I can think to talk him out of it he sends the bike flying off the roof down into the mouth of the alley. That's a good fifty- or sixty-foot drop, easy. Earlier in the summer we used to climb the fire escape with our beer and sit up on the top roof, the very top, and drink and smoke. I brought the guitar up a few times too. Finish our beer and drill the empties way down onto Water Street and listen for people cursing or tires screeching. Wonder we never killed nobody. Wonder we werent locked up. I threw a floor-model TV off our back roof one time too, trying to impress a young one. How retarded was I getting on at all? I cant believe I went along with it all for as long as I did. But I suppose we all have to make these kinds of stopovers. And then there was the night we were going to try and make the jump over to the *other* rooftop. From up there it looks possible, but now that I get a good look from the ground I can see that we would have been killed. Or *I* would have been killed, I should say. I remember being so determined to make the jump, Clayton tormenting me, leaning out over the side saying how easy it was and that if he had two good legs he'd do it no sweat.

I watch the bike make its slow-motion plummet to the concrete below. The handlebars hook in the iron railing of our front steps and it does a little flip before landing hard on the back wheel, which explodes, the rim a sudden twisted and snarled mess and the brake cables snapping like bits of rotten string. Rotten. Monica. Rotting. I peek out around the corner towards the Hatchet, but no one seems to have heard anything. I look up at the window of the Closet but there's no one about. Boot it now, up over the steps into the apartment before anyone sees me. Lock the doors behind me and wait it out. I know bloody well there's going to be a sing-out over this.

Clayton's already hauled a blanket around himself and curled up on the big red couch, the only thing left in the whole place that seems to have been spared his childish, destructive rampages since Isadora left. He even busted my stereo in half. I kick a bottle across the room. He snaps out of his haze and pokes his head up.

—Hey . . . look who it is . . . slaughter . . .

And then he's out again. I go through to my room and pack a few things, then I lie down on the sweaty mattress and make a mental list of all the things I'll have to do over the next few weeks. Passport, that's the biggest thing. And I'll need to put a few bucks away. I was thinking I might need to get stuff put in storage, but when I take stock of what I got, I'm sure I'll pretty much be able to carry everything with me.

The rent is behind and, technically, I still live here. Maybe I'll clear it up myself, a little consolation gift for Clayton, cause God only knows he'll need it. I lay there, thinking about how to break all it to him, and after a while the sound of his drunken snores lull me off to sleep too.

About an hour later there's a pounding on the front door. I get up and go out onto the back roof to see who it is. That's what we usually do, so we can look down to see who it is. The disgusting odour of sour piss and shit from the other side of the roof is almost nauseating. After the toilet got busted a while back, me and Clayton set up a bit of a bench where we could sit with our arses over the edge and crap down into the small gap between ours and the next building. We'd be shot, we'd make the news, if the health department ever found out.

The pounding on the door gets louder and I almost shout at whoever it is to hold their G.D. horses, I'm on my way. But that'd only defeat the purpose of coming out here. I have this kind of vague hope that it might be Isadora, come back to change Clayton's life back to the way it was, rid me of this impossible obligation I feel towards him. As if his life was so dreamy when they were together. I lean out over the roof as far as I can without showing my face. It's not Isadora. It's an RNC officer. He's got a motorcycle helmet on. I creep back into the apartment and wait until the pounding stops. Clayton in his deep, drunken stupor. Four o'clock in the afternoon and this is the state he's in, bringing the cops around. All he had to do was say yes and come on for a coffee.

I pack some more, jam what junk I dont want or need into a heavy-duty garbage bag. I glance out my window onto the street below. There's a small crowd gathered out front of the Hatchet, Clyde Whelan and Petey Thorne and Charlene and I do believe that Reynolds fella, the guy who puts up all the posters. Maybe it was his bike. The cop is there, writing stuff down in a notebook and shaking his head. All of a sudden the whole crowd look up at the apartment. I step back out of the window and then Clayton is there behind me, asking about the bags I'm packing.

—The cops were here Clayton.

—What for?

I can see his mind racing, wondering what it is he might have done over the past few weeks to bring the cops around.

—You think it's about Val?

—Val who?

—Reid b'y, me uncle.

—What's wrong with him sure?

—Nothing, just . . . you never know.

—Sure he's up for some big award. You didnt know? It was in the *Post* today. Lifetime Achievement.

—Yes now?

—Yup.

—Well what did they say, the cops?

—I wasnt talkin to 'em. I'd say it's about the bike though, for sure.

311

—What bike?

—Fuck off Clayton, dont try and tell me you dont remember what you just did.

—What? Fuck you. I was asleep.

I has to tell him then and he just stands there nodding at me, waiting for me to crack up. When he realizes I'm serious he says:

—Fuck, that was other-fellas bike, the guy who goes around cleaning up garbage. What's his name?

—Not Chad Reynolds? Fuck Clayton b'y.

—Well I dont know. Why didnt you stop me?

—There're gonna blame us you know.

—If we admits to it.

—Clayton, *I* dont have to admit to nothing cause it was you done it!

And he looks at me then, with that sly smirk that tells me that yes, no matter what happens he'll never own up to it and we're in it together unless I go and rat him out. Fucker. I might as well go along with him.

—Well we better make an appearance downstairs then, less suspicious than hiding out up here.

—Good enough.

* * *

Downstairs they fly aboard of us like we're after killing someone. You can tell Clyde Whelan was talking about it to this old bag at the bar. He nods over at us with this satisfied sneer on his face, like he's delighted to see that we're finally going to get what we deserves. But there's no *we* this time, no. I'm not taking the shit for this one. Clayton's on his own. Petey Thorne is over in the corner talking to Chad Reynolds, who's got his head down with a cup of that vile Hatchet coffee in front of himself. Petey comes over to us soon as we're in through the door.

—The boys! Just the ones we were looking for. You know how much that bike cost?

—What bike?

—Oh yeah, what bike. Twelve hundred bucks. That's his livelihood you know.

—What the fuck are you trying to say there Thorne?

Clayton ignores the situation and saunters over to the bar. He orders two pints but the little queen behind the bar shakes his head and I hears Clayton saying:

—What the fuck is this then?

—Silas says not to serve you in the daytime.

—What? Fuck you little slut. And fuck Silas. I useta practically run this fuckin place. Will I come around that bar and help meself?

I go over and grab Clayton by the sleeve. He spins around, ready to have it out with me. He dont give a fuck if everybody hates him, so long as he's not cut off from the bar.

—Clayton, just let it go.

But then Clyde Whelan has to get in on it.

—Who's gonna pay to get that wheel fixed now? You? You fellas have been getting away with too much shit around here for too long.

And he pokes a finger into *my* chest, thinking I'm gonna take it. I grabs the finger and twists it around to the breaking point until he manages to pull it away. Clayton laughing at the bar. I cant believe I came down to be around the whole Monica thing, pay some respect, and here I am wrapped up in another of Clayton's bullshit larks.

—I aint paying for shit. Tell Reynolds he shouldnt be so stunned to leave it lying around like he does.

—How do you know anything about where it was left?

—Look Whelan, take your face outta mine or I'll bust it in half, how's that?

Clayton then, gets it into his head to march over to Chad.

—Reynolds. Hey? Look at me.

Chad Reynolds looks up from his coffee. You can tell he's heartbroken over the bike but at the same time enjoying the attention he's getting from having it destroyed.

Clayton leans down close to his face.

—Look at me, look into me eyes for fuck sakes.

Reynolds stares hard into Clayton's eyes.

—I never touched your bike, I knows nothing about it. Think I'm foolish enough to shit on me own doorstep like that?

That's one of Clayton's big proverbs he took back from Dublin with him, how he used to drink with some old fella who wouldnt meet in the bar across the street from where he worked cause it wouldnt look too good to his co-workers. *Never shit on your own doorstep Brent.* And of course he's been doing nothing else for the past year or more. Literally.

Reynolds keeps looking deep into Clayton's bloodshot eyes. After what seems like five minutes he nods and says:

—I believe you Clayton.

And then he glances over at me but I cant even look in his direction. Clyde Whelan then, grabs Clayton by the shirt and starts shaking him back and forth. Clayton's shirt rips at the neck and his necklace busts, pieces of it flying all across the floor. Clayton tries to get his hands around Whelan's throat but he's being shaken so hard that he cant even keep his footing. Clyde gives him a dart into the eye. And sure Clayton's eye is hardly even settled down yet from the night he spent in the lockup a while back. Clayton starts shouting in Clyde's face:

—C'mon then fucker. C'mon welfare boy. Fuckin pissy welfare bastard. You and me!

Even though I'd like to see him take a bit of a nailing for the bike business, I have to jump in between them. I push Whelan into the bar, the reek of cat's piss off him enough to gag me. He sees how sober I am and breaks his grip from Clayton's shirt. Clayton laughing again and Chad Reynolds is over talking to Clyde and Petey, reassuring them that he's pretty sure we had nothing to do with it. *We.* And honest to God, I dont know what comes over me, but I shout over at Reynolds:

—How much to replace a wheel?

—One fifty.

—Fuck. How about we do a little benefit show?

—What do you mean?

—Here at the bar tonight. Pass the hat sorta thing? I'll play. Petey can play.

And I know it makes me look even more like the culprit than Clayton, but the way Reynolds's face lights up at the notion of a show in his honour, Christ, it's already a done deal.

I leave Clayton at the bar. He's back haggling with the queenie-boy for just the one pint, one beer. I jump a bus uptown to Sarah's, that's my new girl, and has a bite to eat with her and her mother and then I practise a few songs until it's time to go downtown again for the show.

There's a lot more old faces around. McNaughton is there again, still bawling in the corner. People are quiet. There's a picture of Monica on the wall behind the bar. Chad Reynolds is there and everyone is buying him drinks that he dont seem to be drinking. Clayton comes in and helps me set up. He gives a little speech from the mic about the atrocious destruction of Reynolds's bike, about how the bike was Reynolds's livelihood, where he works for the LSPU Hall and for certain bands, putting up posters all over town, and that we'll be having a collection. He does the first few songs, Fred Eaglesmith and Hank Williams songs that we used to sing upstairs. Not a bad voice on him, except he dont really know how to use the mic very well. He's been more and more taken with the idea of getting a band on the go ever since the night he saw his old band play at the Green Room. The night he lost Isadora, as he tends to put it. He's been at me to start a band with him, but I cant really see myself going there with him. I'm more into doing it on my own, really. And besides, I'll be skipping the country soon enough.

I play for about an hour and I even throw in a couple of origi-nals. Then Petey gets up for a few. By the end of the night there's a big basket of bills and change and me and Clayton take it into the bathroom to count it out. Three hundred and twenty-six bucks. Jesus. Maybe people are feeling that much more generous because of Monica. We count out a hundred and fifty bucks and I hand it over to Reynolds.

—Right on the money there Chad, hope you find out who done it, all the same.

He's delighted with it.

—God, thanks. Listen I'm . . . I'm sorry for the trouble earlier, I feel so bad. Here.

He takes a twenty out of the wad and hands it to me.

—No Jesus, no. You need that more than I do.

—No really, take it. Buy yourself and Clayton a few drinks.

I reluctantly take the money, even though I got close to two hundred in my pocket from what we skimmed off the top. I grab Clayton and pull him away from the bar.

—C'mon Clay, let's hit the town.

He's out the door before me and people are patting him on the back for doing the right thing and pulling the benefit together, even though it was *me* who played for over an hour. He just shrugs it all off. I gather up my guitar and has a last look around the bar, with full intentions of never setting foot inside it again. Monica's gorgeous blue eyes staring back at me from the picture behind the bar. She doesnt look like herself, like there's something the camera caught that you wouldnt normally see in a person, some neediness. Imagine. Monica. Selling her body to pay the rent. I stand there staring at her picture for as long as I can stand it, and then it hits me, the last thing she said that night, the last time I saw her, as she slipped down our stairs with her belly full of Jack Daniel's:

—Alright guys, that's it for me. I'm finished with this place.

I let the phrase bounce around in my head a few times and then Clayton is shouting to me from the street, telling me to hurry up. We'll lace into the money now and terrorize some young bartender for a couple of hours before getting tossed out, drunk and broke and on the hunt for cigarettes more than likely. One last jag and then I'll wipe my hands clean of the whole scene. Hopefully.

That's it for me. I'm finished with this place.

30. Lifetime, Achieved

Dear <u>Mr. Valentine Reid</u>,

On behalf of the Arts and Cultural Industry Association of
Newfoundland and Labrador, I am pleased to inform you that
you have been nominated for this year's Lifetime Achievement
Award. The directive of this award is intended to honour
outstanding contributions to our provincial artistic community
by an artist or artists who have been producing professional-
quality work in the fields of music, theatre, film, literary and
visual arts over a non-specified period of time.

This year the award boasts a cash value of five thousand
dollars.

Please forward us your CV and biographical information as
soon as possible. Also, the committee would be ever so grateful
if you were to consider performing a five-minute set on the
night of the ceremonies.

Congratulations! We look forward to hearing from you.

Respectfully,
George C. Waters
Arts and Administrations Director, ACIA

A lifetime, already? And something has been achieved, apparently.

Massie. That used to be good.

The train sets at Christmas. That drafty old house on Military Road. Every cat in the city bawling to get in. Massie with her hand-made bowls set out along the step.

Massie and Rachel, Clayton's mom, they were thick as thieves. Jesus. A whole lifetime ago.

Five grand? Lifetime Achievement. So what now? That's it? I've achieved my life? I can hang it all up now, sit back and relax and live off my lifetime achievement money?

Bi-o-graphical in-for-mation? Let's see: Valentine Reid is a singer/songwriter who had to scrounge up five dollars this morning for milk and toilet paper. Because he still wipes his own arse, of course, and drinks milk. Because it does a body good, and eases the ulcers brought on by years of self-abuse. He is a crack-addled, binge-drinking, calcium-deficient father of possibly seven or eight children scattered across this vast and beautiful land that he so loves to call home.

Five lousy grand. I should call them up, who is it, George C. Waters, I should call old George up now and tell him to shove it so far up his hole. Hey George! Why dont you get onto the boys in Vancouver and get me my royalties back?

Just take it Reid. Smile and say thanks.

Take it? Take it. That's all I've been doing for the past thirty years, and what's to show for it? Bend over and take it like a true blue Newfoundlander. Society of catamites, that's all we are. Take a long hard suck on my knob. How's that sound Newfound-fuckin-land? How's that sound Vancouver? *The Very Best of Valentine Reid.* They havent heard a peep outta me since the eighties sure. And why would they want to, I suppose? Should be called *The Most Profitable Songs We Ever Swindled Out of Valentine Reid.* Valentine Reid. Lame. Where's that fucking pipe? I'm not hungry. I dont eat. I wanted to be here. I like where I am. That fuckin Brooks fella. Flavour of the week. It's all his fault anyhow. Dropped everyone with under ten thousand in sales so they could finance that muppet's world fucking tour. And I had that UK distributor lined up and ready to go. Then bang, you're off the list. Like I never was. And where's Brooks to now? Living off the fucking royalties, face down in a mountain of coke and pussy.

Reid, it's gone. We're moving forward now.

Yeah? Where to? What for? *The Very Best of Valentine Reid* is digitally remastered now sure, meaning that they drowned the heart out of it for the radio. Where to? *The Very Best of Valentine Reid* happened almost fifteen years ago for fuck sakes.

Take it, be gracious, you need it. Massie needs it.

It's a goddamn embarrassment! Lifetime Achievement. It means no one is expecting anything else out of me, ever again.

Stop the whining and get your head out of your hole. What about Massie?

What about her? Where's she at when I need her? She's a woman. Going on about my "condition" when she's the one got me tangled up in it all in the first place. And now she's "outgrown" it has she? Now she's reformed. Personal power, woman, that's all it takes. There's nothing and no one can get their claws into Valentine Reid. You found that out, didnt you girl? Personal power. I can walk away from anything or anyone at any time.

She just wants to help.

She wants a cut! She wants to still be close enough when the time comes so that she'll have some say over this legacy of shit I leaves behind. That's all any of 'em wants. Their own little slice of fame. Clayton with his eye on the old Gibson. I'll smash it in bits, I'll take it to the grave.

The grave?

It's a ways off yet. I'll still be kicking when *they're* all said and done. I'll still be banging 'em out. It never goes away. No such thing as writer's block, no such thing as drying up or washing out. There's only laziness and mediocrity and weakness.

You've just fallen off course a little then?

Maybe. Or maybe this gear is the shits. Maybe Walter needs a good dart in the chops next time I see him. Maybe I need to hit the town and stir up some real shit, celebrate.

Or just take it easy and get healthy, write for a while. Clean up and go underground. Look good for the ceremonies? Dark circles under your eyes Val, the nosebleeds, you couldnt move the couch last week, come on. It's more a matter of—

What? Life and fuckin death? Bullshit. It's a stopover, just a little numbness dropping by for a while. I'll know when to pull out, I always did. Personal power.

None of that makes any sense Reid. You're stalling, for what?

For . . . I . . . I've achieved *something* else havent I? I've managed to stay alive havent I? That achievement enough? Let alone that I've stayed on top. Need a tissue now. Need a fucking . . .

Intervention.

Fuck that. Who'd come? Walter? He'd give me the proper intervention. Where's that number?

Reid, Val, please. Something simple. Tea. Hot bath. Process it. The best news you've gotten in a long time. Be good to yourself.

I cant, I cant. I need . . .

You need to let yourself fall down. You're not Clayton's age, you'll never see those days again. You have to let yourself get old, be an old man, be gentle to yourself.

It's a slap in the face, Lifetime Achievement. Dangling five grand in my face so I can get up in front of the whole province to let them know that I've given it everything I had and now I'm finished.

And are you?

I made a stab at it. Made all the right moves. Stayed straight when I needed to be, played the game with the big boys, sang my guts out in every seedy bar from Trepassey to Port Alberni. Galway, London, Leeds. Paid my band, paid every last stagehand till I wasnt left with the price of a pack of smokes. Did everything by the book, signed it all over. Just to have it all swept out from underneath me by that fuckin dogan-faced Brooks.

So that's it then? That all you got?

No by fuck.

So it's just five grand then, that someone wants to hand to you. And you're playing that night anyway? Beats the pay at the Ship doesnt it?

Yeah.

Well then?

31. Nose Dive

Brent busts into me sweaty room with the grand big announcement that Jim is after shootin himself, that he spent the weekend boozin and bawlin in some club in Torbay, drove his Jeep late, late Sunday night *through* gates at Robin Hood Bay, polished off a dozen beer way down in the bottom of the dump with the gulls and the rats, then blew his fuckin head to bits with a twelve-gauge.

There was no note.

The gun was registered to his father.

A picture of his wife in 'er wedding dress lay on the seat beside Jim's body.

Jim McNaughton. Dead. That fuckin conniving bastard.

And yeah, although the gloom and commotion of a real live suicide weighs kinda heavy on me conscience, how someone you knows, even someone like Jim, is capable of such darkness, can face themselves to that degree, I dont know, I'm still kinda fuckin jealous. Cause he got there first. Like back in school when someone'd show up with a cast on their arm or leg, I'd get right fuckin cracked about it, everybody makin the big fuss over 'em. I wanted a broken bone too. Because that's what got you *in*, for a while.

But at the same time, and Godspeed poor old Jim, not sayin nothing there, but I'm kinda pissed a bit too. Cause now what's the fuckin good of doin it meself? Two suicides right in a row, right close together like that. Fuck that. Mine wont have nowhere near the shock value now, it'll be all diluted cause where they'll all have just gotten through Jim's suicide. *Not another one.*

Jim, old fucker. Couldnt he have waited awhile? Let me get around to me own fuckin thing? Who's gonna bother to analyze *my* situation now, *my* predicament? They'll already have dug so deep into Jim's story that they wont even have the energy to put into mine for fuck sakes. Mine wont have near the impact it shoulda had, not now. Not after this. Cause they'll all have so recently come to the conclusion that there's no real answers, that you cant turn back the clock, that there's no one to be held accountable. I wanted all that, goddamn it. It's all a part of the package, that they'd be replayin shit in their heads and wishin they had some time back.

And now too, with the whole Monica thing, sure my demise'll only get swept up in it all and put to rest as a sign of the fuckin times or something. The Summer of Death. Depersonalized, if that's a word. Reduced to yet another contaminant on the already foul history of the Hatchet. Monica's body found in the woods near Dead Man's Pond, Jim's soggy brains and bits of skull splattered all over the inside of his rusty old Jeep. My nosedive. *Another one? So tragic* . . .

And the world moves ever forward.

Sure no one hardly mentions Monica no more. Even me, I pushes her face out of me mind whenever I catches it there. It's only human. Christ, the night she slipped me the bottle of Jack Daniel's, the lost fuckin anxious *need* in her eyes when she showed up after her shift. And didnt I lash out at that? Wearin her weakness on her sleeve like that, reflecting everything back on me, everything *I* didnt want to feel. I cut her down then, drove her away with nothing more than a glance. How she smiled when she was haulin her coat back on, her head high, the click of her heels down the long dark stairway. The way Brent looked at me when she was finally gone. Monica.

· · ·

I've been comin awake lately with this feeling, this vague sense of . . . anticipation. The prospect of escape maybe. From me bedroom, if nothing else. Sticky, damp shithole full of dust and spores, mice. But I'm only really able to get ahold of this feeling when I'm just wakin up, or comin to, more like it. Cant really grasp it on a conscious level, as I'd like to. But it's kinda like, I dont know, like the way you feels when you buys something different at the porn shop, maybe. Like some kinky magazine with women fucking horses or she-males. And just say you got the magazine tucked away on yourself somewhere, and you knows it's looked upon by society in general as a filthy thing, perverted and near criminal, but you cant help but feelin this excitement about gettin home with it, that your thirst can soon be quenched, maybe. Or that escape is just around the corner. Well I've been wakin up lately with that kinda feeling hovering in the air, all the hurt and misery gone for that little moment while I'm comin back to the world. Like some twisted, sinister gardener crept into the twisted, dried-out jungle of me brain overnight and watered down me grief a little.

And left a little seed of hope behind.

Maybe I've been hopeful.

And now of course, with Jim's inconsiderately timed suicide to contend with, I got no fuckin hope at all. Fucker.

I've been milkin this image of meself climbin the fire escape up to the roof. I has me last smoke. Then I does the big nosedive, right smack down onto the hustle of mid-afternoon Water Street. I'm pretty sure too that if I makes the jump right and proper, maybe tie me hands somehow, that the building is high enough so that I'd be good and dead when I hit the street. I'd need to land on me head of course. Face first. Right there in front of the door of the Hatchet. Me blood stainin the sidewalk for years to come. Cause that's the only way to go: preposterous and public and historic and horrifying and fuckin depraved. The big fuckin melodramatic war cry.

I dont know sure, how to fuckin express it no more, the black panicked globs of misery sloshin through my head all the time. How do you really and absolutely convey that? Especially when people dont even *want* to understand. Cause they dont wanna have their *own* shortcomings brought into the light. Cause what if my slop and shit matches up with theirs? Well then sooner or later it means they'll hafta look it all in the face. And what if they cant take it, cant deal with it? Well then, they'll be tossin themselves right off the roof behind me.

And I mean, I aint no self-pitying hard-done-by young savage, sulkin and screamin for no good reason. Or at least I aint *just* that. But that's what they likes to reduce you to isnt it? That's the easiest, most comprehensive and accessible approach.

But hey, they all loved it first, loved me. When Isadora first fucked off and they all saw me with me head down on the bar, there were all kinds of sympathetic shoulders to bawl on. Lotsa free drinks too. Not two months later then and you can tell they're all right weary of me, cause I'm just such a fuckin drain I s'pose. Just cause I aint afraid to show me human side and have a good bawl every now and then and I likes to beat shit up. It's good though, to get it all out that way. I mean I'm only after smashin a few glasses. That's half the problem with this crowd from Town, they cant take it. They thinks violence and aggression comes from the TV, they wont believe it's happening right in front of their faces. Like they thinks too that they can say whatever they like to you and you'll just find some way to take it, that you wont *really* smack 'em in the face.

Anyhow, that's how I finally got the boot at the Hatchet. I was up here in me bedroom, hangin out the window with a beer glass and I slung it empty down at Water Street. It smashed right at fuckin Silas Lawlor's feet and a shard of glass nicked his cheek. It was some fuckin funny. Silas looked up then and saw me laughin. And that was "the last straw" of course. And I shouted back:

—That's fuckin original aint it.

He was supposed to have fired me anyhow, when he first took over. But he kept me on cause Mike recommended it. And Monica too, he kept her on for a while. Till she fucked off with the float. And didnt I try me fuckin best to get the heave anyhow? I was rob- bin beer and little bits of cash and then arguing right loud in Silas's face when he asked me about it the next day. I'd come into the bar on me off night and pick rackets with the new little daisy-queenie boytoys Silas had lurkin about. I did it all, pissed in the sink in the women's toilets, smashed a load of ashtrays one night, stogged up the toilet with the eight ball. Generally for a while there I was just goin around bein a little prick lookin to get me face smashed in.

Cause that's always what it comes back to aint it? If you cant get through to 'em either other way, like lettin yourself be vulnerable and sad, then you might as well turn on 'em, push 'em to the point where they'll at the very least do ya the favour of smashin your face in for ya. And that's all I'm lookin for I s'pose, someone to bash me teeth out, if ya wants to stop and analyze it. Either fuckin shut the fuck up and stop lookin at me, or fuckin well kill me.

It's fuckin hard you know, to get someone to have a go at ya. But I s'pose once you've crossed over to where I have, once you've announced to the world that you couldnt really give a fuck if you lives or dies, that no pain, no punch in the face or knife in the guts or bottle the throat or transport truck in the nuts can possibly compare to the heartsickness you're feelin right now, then even big hefty longwinded pricks like that Clyde Whelan cunt are more of a mind to keep their distance. And I mean I *knows* it's just weakness, that it's scrawny and stupid of me not to just pick meself up outta the rubble and get on with it, but they all thinks it's me gone cracked, that I've no fear left in me. That I'm fuckin insane. And I reckon you can capitalize on that if you knows where to draw the line.

Couple of weeks back, the night after I got back from *her* place in Port Rexton, the night of the big downpour that almost saw me dead, the night I finally did fuckin die, I walked into the Hatchet to see that Toddler Dawe hunched over the bar with his chin stuck out and that fuckin underbite, showin off his disgusting jagged row of rotten bottom teeth. Smackin his hand on the bar for the music to be turned up louder, louder. Screamin nonsensical senile gibberish at a group of women in the corner.

Philip and that greasy Jane Neary and Charlene what's-her-face and that Clyde Whelan cunt at the other end of the bar shakin their soggy heads and gigglin at Dawe's latest drinkin fit. Pisses me off, how that old prick is still allowed to get away with carrying on like that, how he's allowed to be this obnoxious fuckface just because he put out a couple of crappy records. I dont get why he's considered fuckin "eccentric" when I'm just dismissed as some kinda punk drunk. And how fuckin dare they say we're *anything* alike. For one thing, I have a fuckin conscience, dont I? And how fuckin dare any one of 'em think for a second that *she* actually gives a black fuck about the likes of Toddler Dawe. That just because she wont have nothing to do with me no more, then he's all of a sudden back in the running, that he's just as significant a contender for her fuckin affections? That she cant decide between the two of us? Go fuck yourselves.

When I walked into the bar that night and saw him there droolin and mumblin like that, I dont know, I wanted to kill him. I did. Cant remember ever despising another human so much. I hated him like the way I fuckin hates meself sometimes, like I hates *her*, for not havin the guts or the heart to see this thing out, for terminating shit before we even got a chance to see where it might go. And I mean, she fuckin exploited him, that's all. Used up his money and free drinks and coke in return for her company. Just served his sick, twisted need to obsess. So he could keep on writin his stupid middling so-called poetry. Because, like it or not, as Val says, even if St. John's could tell the difference between mediocrity and greatness, they wouldnt *want* you to be great, wouldnt want you to stand out. They'd want you to be mediocre. *If* they could tell the difference.

Dawe's just lucky he knows how to exploit the town's lack of common sense.

How fuckin retarded, how fuckin absurd that anyone could think for a second that me and Toddler Dawe were rivals for *her* bed.

I pushed in next to him at the bar.

—I hear you took her out to dinner.

He wouldnt look at me, but he knew what I was talkin about. He stopped his rantin and slobbering though. It's all a fuckin act with him. Maybe that's why no one pays him no mind, cause maybe they can all see right through it, who knows. I leant right next to him and whispered so no one else could hear:

—She thinks you're a pathetic old man you know. She pities you. And in case you're interested, I slept with her last night. And when we were finished, I fell asleep *inside* her.

Of course she never even let me in the fuckin house, but Dawe couldnt know that. Got 'im though, I thought his face was gonna explode, the veins on his fuckin forehead like big old nightcrawlers squirmin just under his skin. He grabbed me then, just like I wanted him to, right in front of everyone and for no reason that anyone could tell. He grabbed me by the collar and shook me and tried to lift me off the floor even. I was surprised, didnt think he had the strength in them piddly soft townie arms. And I came back at him of course, just defending meself as far as anyone shoulda been concerned. I booted him in the shin and latched me hand onto his throat and started squeezin. C'mon, gimme death if you can divvy it out. Give it to me you old second-rate prick. I tried to get ahold of his ponytail but it was too slippery, too fuckin slimy. Dawe gruntin and wheezin, tryna breathe, tryna cut off the circulation to *my* brain at the same time. And the bar, that fuckin comatose, apathetic little bar, came right to life then, all hands in a frenzy. Next thing though, that Clyde Whelan cunt and Silas Lawlor got *me* by the arms, draggin *me* out into the porch. Shoved *me* onto the street. Told me to go home and sober up. And me, more sober than I'd been in weeks, hadnt had a drink all evening. And havin to go in to me shift then the next day and pretend I felt bad for doin what everyone must, on some level, wanna see done to Toddler fuckin Dawe. I never apologized though. No fuckin way. I looked Silas straight in the eye, me head high and me two feet planted firm on the floor. I was just waitin to see if he'd fire me. Cause then I woulda went off in *his* face too.

Then a few nights later I tossed the glass out me window and got the official boot. I was sittin on the big red couch afterwards, fuckin fried on that liquid codeine shit, body-stoned, on me own. And I dont know, maybe I had one of them breakthroughs or something. Just a little bit though. Just sittin there thinkin about why in the name of fuck I'd let her get to me that much that I'd go sabotage me job, me only source of income, get on like that in the place where I works. And I started thinkin that maybe I could slow all this down if I wanted to, decelerate things. But then I lost it, the moment, it got all fuddled up again, me head. Anyhow, it's me own business, all this. Cant deny me own nature for the sake of appearances. If I wants to lash out and stir shit up I fuckin well will. No crime in speakin me mind from time to time is there?

Brent said to me a few weeks back, big philosopher that he is, that it's like I just dont *want* nothing good in me life. That I dont want nothing to be thankful for. That I wont be satisfied till I'm flattened out on me back on the very bottom. But I just thinks, you know, that the top count for much if you havent punched a shift or two on bottom? And besides, I've been way up there too, havent I? I've been on top. Yes. And I knows what it's like when someone kicks that ladder out from underneath you. So what's the point of bein up there, tryna keep your balance amongst all them vultures who just wants to see you plummet anyhow? When you're on the bottom you got nowhere else to fall.

●●●

Mike Quinn came by, few nights back. Lookin for the rent. Jesus, I s'pose it's six or eight weeks in the red now. But the apartment is just fuckin destroyed. And I dont mean destroyed, like if I took out a mop and a broom and had a go at the place it'd be in shipshape in a few hours. I means it's fuckin destroyed. Like I'd need to hire a bulldozer just for starters. So I certainly didnt want Mike to see it did I? I mean, he's usually pretty good about rent and shit with me, I wasnt afraid of hagglin with him. I coulda just said how I've been partying too hard and that I'll cut down and get me shit together. Offer him some definite date when I'd have a chunk of cash for him. He'd appreciate that kinda talk. I just didnt want him to see the apartment. The murals that were here since Keith had the place, me and Brent went mad here one week and did 'em all over with the darkest kinda shit, covered every conceivable inch of the walls, even the ceilings in some sections. Demons and creatures gettin their limbs tore off and sharp cutthroat angles on everything, all black and brown and blood red. And there's holes fuckin everywhere and I dont know where half of 'em came from. Furniture smashed to bits and piled up, snarled in the corners. Gouges in the floors. And the toilet, fuck, that's smashed this months now. But I dont think I done it. I got a bench set up out on the roof and just lets go down in the alley between the two buildings. If Mike ever went out on the roof and had a whiff and glanced down, fuck, he'd lose it, he'd kill me. There'd be no written eviction notice or nothing like that, he'd just heave me right out over the roof onto the concrete. Save me the trouble of doin it meself though.

And it's not really that I'm *afraid* of him or nothing like that, like I could manage his presence if he was just cracked and tryna kill me. But knowing Mike he'd milk it a bit. He'd be so disappointed and betrayed. And I just dont have the energy to take on them kinds of situations these days, them kinds of emotions I s'pose. Anger and violence, yes. But the other stuff, no, too intense. Mike's been good to me over the past year, I knows that. And me beatin up this place got nothing at all to do with him. Maybe it's just my reaction against this whole fuckin scene. The ahhh . . . physical manifestation of my fuckin disgust for all this downtown artsy, theatrical, fuckin filmic and musical slop. It's Monica's dead corpse rotting in the woods near Signal Hill. My own self-loathing, hunger, failure. Yeah, I'm aware of all that. That when I looks around the main room it screams *I hate this life, please just kill me now.* I just dont see no other way of expressing meself. But how can I explain that to Mike Quinn? Besides, I reckon I'll be long fuckin gone before anyone other than Brent has a chance to survey the damage in here.

330

When Mike came knockin the other day, I stood at the top of the stairs wrapped up in me grandfather's old army blanket, shivering. I watched Mike's shadow peekin through the crease in the slab of plywood that covers where the window useta be. Brent put that up, first time I laid eyes on him in a week. He came in to collect something out of 'is room and then banged that bit of board up over the window. He left then, with his bag, never even asked how the window thing happened. Never even said goodbye. He got himself tucked away now with some young one from up Kenmount Road, after slackin right off the booze too. Fucker.

I went cracked the morning I found the window broke out. I went down to the Closet and fuckin crucified a few old geezer queers. I got pretty good interrogation skills too, especially when I does me Irish thing. I asked if they'd seen anyone suspicious, if there was anyone lookin for me, any strange noises. I let it all out, all the fuckin turmoil and shit that I'd pent up since *she* fucked off, I fired all that across the bar at them poor old miserable girlie-men. I let 'em all know I'd fuckin *kneecap* someone if I found out they were lyin. Of course no one ever *sees* anything on the east end of Water Street. No. Unless they're paid to. Smashin glass, screamin in the middle of the night, a gunshot, a car bomb, a fuckin nuclear disaster wouldnt scarcely rouse the curiosity of them sad, paranoid and self-obsessed loner types you'll find clung late night to the bar at the Closet.

I moved me investigation downstairs to the Hatchet.

Petey Thorne was there. I flew into him. He'd crossed me mind as soon as I saw the broken window. His face popped into mine like some gloating, bloated, sneering imp, laughin down at me from the front steps of my apartment while I hove up in the alley. I was dead fuckin sure he was at least *there* when the window got smashed. And didnt he run his fuckin mouth off good and loud during the Million Dollar Pedal Bike Fiasco?

He was leanin over the pool table, this tight white tee-shirt that seemed to add about thirty pounds to his swollen belly. He was preppin the cue ball for the final shot at the eight. He was playin himself by the looks of it. Straight shot in the corner pocket, easy does it. He didnt know I came up behind him. Just as he had the shot lined up I fuckin nailed the butt of his stick, drove the cue ball straight into the wall near the toilets. A few heads turned. Petey turned around all shocked, then went so far as to fuckin *smile* when he saw it was me. And I goes:

—What the fuck do *you* got to smile about ya chunky fuckin imposter?

—Imposter, what's that supposed to mean?

—You, up there every night with that crap guitar manglin every decent song Neil Young ever wrote. Go get some fuckin lessons b'y.

That's what you gotta do see, if you wants to get 'em on the go: attack where the ego is most fragile. All Petey got is that open-mic gig. Only thing that keeps 'im goin I'd say, all the pats on the back from this endless stream of drunken slobbering barflies who're not really even complimenting *him* but rather his selection of no-fail crowd-pleasin drinkin anthems. And plus I'm after hearin 'im go on a bit much about that fuckin guitar too, how his father gave it to him and it makes him feel closer to him when he plays it. That stupid kinda stage talk that he thinks offers some substance to his show, when in fact if he didnt open his fuckin mouth at all he'd be ten times more interesting up there.

He looked at me then, when I said that, and I knew he just wanted to bash my head in with that pool stick. He was dyin to.

—Get outta my face Clayton. You're drunk . . .

—Or what? You'll use that stick on me? Come on then look, give it your best crack.

I tilted meself towards the floor and scooped me hair forward, exposing the back of me neck to Petey. That's gotta be one of the most detrimental spots to take a crack with the heavy end of a pool stick. That spongy spot where your skull stops and your neck begins. C'mon and fuckin do it, fuckin kill me you big bastard.

I braced meself, for show, knowin full well he wouldnt do it. And of course he didnt. See what I'm sayin? If they thinks you're afraid of it they'll take full advantage, but it confuses 'em when you asks for it. I stood up straight again.

—You bashed in me fuckin window didnt ya.

He laughed.

—You're cracked Reid. I was there. You smashed it yourself. What do you think happened to your forehead?

And I touched me head then, this lump of swollen jelly. I glanced in the far mirror. Pale blue with little scratches around it. I hadnt thought much of it when I got up that morning, cause where I usually has a go bangin me head off something when I'm on the beer these days anyhow, the floor or the pavement or some greasy bathroom stall.

Petey went back to his pool game then, and I saw that he re-arranged the cue ball a little closer to the eight than it was before I fucked up his shot. Everybody in the bar tryin not to look at me. I shambled on back to the front door, me foot suddenly ablaze and throbbin worse than it had in weeks. I went home and slept for almost twenty-four hours.

• • •

So Jim is dead hey? Brent, the death messenger, harbinger of sorrow. I mean, I should feel sorrow or something. At least I knows I'm s'posed to. Cant move. I'm like some stiff meself here. This grimy mattress. I looks at me cigarettes and lighter on the busted old chair next to me head. I'd fuckin kill for one of them right about now. Imagine takin one outta the package, settin it in me mouth and ligh-tin it. Imagine the energy that takes. Maybe if I hollers out to Brent he'll come and light it for me. How will I say it? The sound of my voice, bouncin around the big empty room. Imagine talkin. A whole different kinda energy. I manages to slip a hand down between me legs and give the head of me lad a little squeeze. It's colder than the rest of me, take a lot of fuckin work to get the blood runnin to it. I could cry I s'pose. If I tried hard enough.

Not a fuckin cent to me name, last I checked.

This is fuckin hopeless.

Brent out there in the main room crunchin through the glass, kickin shit out of 'is way. He's quieter than usual. Maybe it's to do with Jim? Or maybe it's the state of the apartment. I can safely say it's at its worst. But what the fuck is it to him? He barely fuckin lives here no more.

. . .

Someone's callin me name and there's a pinch, an angry screamin itch on me hand and the smell of burnt hair. I wants to reach out with the other hand and scratch the itch. I'm thinkin about it. Thinkin.

—Clayton? Clayton. You're gonna burn the place to the ground.

I forces me eyes open. Brent. He's got two cigarettes lit. He bends over towards me and pulls a burnt-out butt from between me fingers. It's kinda stuck there and he's gotta give it a little twist to free it. He puts one of the full cigarettes in its place. I cant imagine smokin it. Cant imagine movin, talkin, breathin. And there's some folks out there on their way to dinner, or breakfast maybe. Church. Payin bills at the bank. Readin newspapers. Rentin movies. Eatin toast. Flyin somewhere. Runnin somewhere. Tyin ties and huntin for lint brushes. Brushin teeth and shavin and pickin kids up at daycare. Gift wrappin some sorta fuckin . . . gift. Throwin a party with plates and glasses and big bowls of dip and crackers and punch. Tryna light the stove. Feedin the cat. Washin dishes. Fixin a radio. Settin up a tent. Fuck, imagine the energy all *that* must take up. Other lives, whole, or at least movin forward.

Brent starin out me bedroom window onto Water Street. I wonder if he sees the same dead-end street I do when I looks down there. Some people sees different shit differently, I know. He stays there like that and dont say a word, just lookin down. Fine with me too cause I knows I cant squeeze a sentence out. Anyhow, if I gets talkin I'll get thinkin, and fuck that.

He clears his throat. Here it comes now, some tirade about the state of the place, something he heard I said or done some night in some bar, something about *her* or something some Ship leech said about me. Cops lookin for me, Mike Quinn lookin for me, the fuckin mob, the IRA. Maybe I robbed someone or murdered someone or shit in someone's living room? Out with it, c'mon. Gimme the worst of it now.

—Speak Brent, for fuck sakes.

—What? Oh. Just thinkin maybe we could go out for a drink . . .

And with that, I'm up, me two feet on the floor and pullin me laces tight and I splashes a bit of water on me face in the kitchen and hauls an old face cloth across me teeth to get the scum from off me gums. Cause there's no way in hell I'm goin in that bathroom and brushin, with fuckin toothpaste, lookin at meself in what's left of that mirror. Brent says:

—If you want to get a shower I'll wait.

Like we can just wash it all away like that, hey? Scrub it clean. Fuckin shower? You could slap a fuckin brand-new suit on me today and cut me hair and shave me and flush out me liver and *bleach* me teeth and shoot me eyes fulla Visine and gimme a dab of some kinda pricey cologne and I knows I'd still feel like a proper scumbag, sleeveen, cunty-balled fuckwad. And besides, imagine what might pop into me head in there, in the shower, while I'm scrubbin two weeks' worth of grime and bar sludge off meself? What if me conscience kicked in full force? What if *her* face flashed in front of me? What if I got hard or something, thinkin about her in there? I might lose me fuckin mind. No thanks, I'll pass on that shower business.

• • •

The Hatchet looks to be fuckin packed. Petey Thorne playin some Dylan tune, the one about Billy the Kid. I always liked that tune, and to be honest, Petey's not doin such a bad job. The bar looks to be full up of all the old faces that were around last winter, during my heyday as Bartender in Chief. Jim's heaviest drinkin days, come to think of it. A sombre reunion. Not two steps in through the door and Mike Quinn is standin in front of us. Rent. Just wont go away will it. I racks me brain to tap into me old stockpile of landlord/tenant excuses but I draws a blank. Mike steps towards me, I takes a step back. I starts to open me mouth and Mike holds his hand up before I can speak. He dont wanna hear a goddamn word outta my mouth. He takes another half step at me and I've nowhere else to go, me back right to the porch wall as it is. Maybe this is it then, maybe this is the end I had comin all along. C'mon then you big bastard slumlord fuck . . .

Brent's suddenly holdin a wad of twenties out and wavin 'em under Mike's nose. I reckon it's more of a shock to me than it is to Mike even.

—Oh, here's the rent by the way Mike. Sorry, it's late again.

Mike snatches the money outta Brent's hand and stuffs it in his pocket without even countin it. He's still lookin at me:

—And what about your half?

Brent, to the rescue again:

—His half is there too.

Mike digs his hand back into his pocket and gives the money a little squeeze, like he can tell by the density of the wad how much is there, if it's off by even a bill. He wont count it in front of us. But if it turns up short he'll fuckin well come lookin wont he, and who are we to argue then? And if it's over? What then? He'll take it off next month will he? I fuckin doubt it.

Mike turns and takes a step back into the bar. It's kinda like he's disappointed that he got the rent outta us, like he was dyin for a good dust-up and now he's been deprived. Fucker. But at least it's a fuckin load off my mind for another while. We starts to push into the bar behind him and then he whips around again:

—What happened to the fucking front window up there?

And at that moment Petey Thorne breaks into "Wild Horses" and I'm brought right back to the night of me birthday last fall when Donna tried to get me out dancin. I nods towards him:

—Petey busted it out with a bottle the other night. Says he's not gonna pay for it either.

Mike turns, all nonchalant, in Petey's direction.

—Did he now? We'll fuckin see about that then, wont we boys?

I laughs louder than I wanted to. Brent looks down at the floor. Mike stands there, stone faced, flickin the wheel of a Bic lighter on and off inside the pocket of his coat. I already knows what's comin:

—You're gonna have to clear out by the end of the month. Consider this your official notice.

And I'm almost relieved to hear it. At least . . . at least something's gonna shift, change. Who knows, maybe I'll move right onto the street. Or maybe they'll be scrapin me off it soon enough anyhow. Who knows. Maybe I'll just hit the Trans-Canada and fuckin vanish. Wash up in some small hickish town in Northern Ontario. Fuck it.

Brent just stands there noddin like the news got nothing at all to do with him.

Mike turns and walks into the bar without another word.

Brent walks back onto the street.

He's almost up to the courthouse steps before I catches up to him.

Me foot is like murder.

—Hold up Brent. Thought we were havin a drink?

Brent turns and looks at me like I'm some kinda apparition from his distant past, someone he hasnt laid eyes on in years and woulda been content to have gone the rest of his life without ever bumpin into again. He looks me up and down.

—Clayton, I think that's the exact rigout you were wearing back in January when I first moved in.

I looks down at meself and it's true. The cuffs of me jacket are tattered and stringy, the shoulders are busted at the seams. Stains on me shirt, this assorted mix of Guinness and blood and ash and sweat and grease. S'pose I havent shaved in a while now, two months maybe. But me boots, you cant knock the boots. I can see meself in 'em for fuck sakes. Clears me head out, polishing 'em like that.

—Where to?

—Naw Clay, I think I'll pass on that drink.

—What are we gonna do for a spot? End of the month is what? Two weeks?

—I was planning on talking to you about . . .

—What? About what?

I kinda got a vague idea what he's gonna say. I takes a steps closer to him.

—What the fuck are ya sayin Brent?

He lays a hand flat on me chest and pushes me back a bit.

—Fuck man, you really need a shower.

—Plannin on talkin to me about what?

—I got the job.

—What job?

—Same one you had last year. The Dublin program.

Now, I dont know what it feels like when the inside of your head fuckin collapses, but I'd say this is pretty close.

—Well Clay you knew I applied . . .

—Yes but I didnt think . . .

—Didnt think I'd actually get it?

—No . . . well . . .

I'm tryna be big here, I am. Tryin. I knows it's a great and fuckin fantastic move for Brent, my old friend Brent, to make at this point in his life. Best bone anyone in Brent's situation can expect to be tossed. Just remembering me own life, right before I got that same job. Year and a half ago now. Done me interview from the pay phone in the old detox centre. The fuckin *high* of comin back to St. John's after bein away so long. Brand-new man, fulla stories, everybody wantin to get next to me. The future laid out right there in front of me. And I wants all that same thing for Brent, I do. I wanna be happy for him, celebrate it with him, or at least help him feel good about it. And I knows, I fuckin knows he's even got the good grace right now not to appear too excited about it in front of me. I'm tryna be big here, I am:

—Well, what about our fuckin band then?

I fuckin hates the sound of me own voice, the fuckin desolation.

—C'mon Clay. Look at yourself.

—What? Sure you cant be leavin for another couple of months? Where are we gonna stay till you goes?

—And you're welcome by the way for the rent . . .

—I was gonna say th—

—I'm thinking I'll stay with ahhh . . . Sarah for a while, clear my head out before I leave.

Sarah? Must be the new little fuck toy he's latched onto uptown. Slick bastard. He digs into his pocket and comes out with a crumpled twenty-dollar bill. He holds it out to me.

—You want that? I've been saving. Busking in by the mall. No competition in there.

A fuckin mobile phone starts beepin from somewhere inside his coat. Well sweet adorable fuck. What next? Brent's face flushes while he digs it out. He looks into the bright blue screen of the phone and then shuts the power off.

—Sarah's . . . she's ahhh . . . wanted to be able to get in touch with me. I cant stand the goddamn thing.

I looks at the twenty. He's still holdin it out to me like that. I dont know. Is it all just one big long sloppy string of betrayals and payoffs?

I takes the twenty.

Brent just nods and sorta half smiles, awkward like, then turns and walks on up Water Street. I knows I aint meant to follow. I shouts after him:

—Congratulations.

But it comes out wrong, sarcastic like, and self-pitying. Which I'm not, never. Brent dont bother to turn around or respond. And who the fuck could blame 'im?

I heads back towards the Hatchet, the crumpled twenty tight in me fist. I stops outside the door of the bar, lights a smoke and glances up at the eaves of the building. Long fuckin drop there, from the roof to the ground. Right down onto the concrete.

I kicks me heel hard against the sidewalk.

I feels a little lighter now, I dont know, maybe even hopeful.

32. Swan Song

What took you so long you buncha dogan-faced bastards, that's
what I'm wondering. Fella needs to be near onto his deathbed
before they recognize . . .

*Easy now Val. It's not in your hands just yet. Cameras too, careful
where you put your fingers. Remember the Junos.*

I'll show em all the finger if this night goes on much longer.
These chairs . . . not much breathing space is there . . .

*Hey. Here it comes. This is it. Put on the grace face. Grateful.
Gracious.*

—Ladies and gentlemen, it gives me great pleasure to present
our final award this evening. The ACIA presents the Lifetime
Achievement Award to those individuals or organizations who have
made. . .

Yeah, yeah, mythic status achieved, priceless contributions, music
being that worldwide language shit. Get on with it George.

Grace Val. Graciousness. Be patient.

Thirty fuckin years. Lucky it's not posthumous. They're lucky I
even showed up, way I'm feelin tonight.

Calm now. Ten more minutes, tops. One song. Then home.

Oh look at the Toddler himself over there, stroking his statue like
no one is watching. Dont glance over this way Dawe. Dont smile
over at me like we're in the same league or something. No friends in
this . . . just gimme, just . . .

Val?

Fuckin . . . just cant catch my . . . alright, there it goes . . .

It's alright to be nervous Reid, humbled.

Nervous? I've played every fuckin dive on the map, dined with royalty, played for my own father for Christ sakes. Sang for my *father.* Take more than this lot to make me break a sweat.

Heart is pounding though, just relax. Breathe. Nothing to it.

Nothing to it is right. Thirty years tryna put it . . . tryna lay it out for the world . . . to pick through and dismiss . . . dodging the landlord . . . bar tabs . . .

— . . . but by no means does the Lifetime Achievement imply that this man has reached the end of his career, but to say that he is an artist truly at the peak of his powers.

That's fuckin right, that's exactly . . . peak of my powers. Slay the lot of 'em next time . . . next . . .

Val?

It's all dead ahead hey Massie girl, lifetime . . .

Val?

—Ladies and gentlemen, please give a warm welcome to our very own Valentine Reid . . .

See? Hear that? Yeah that's it, stand up and fuckin . . . you buncha . . .

Val? Are we . . .

—Look, that's him.

—Give him room. Give him room.

—Is that him?

—Somebody call an ambulance. . . .

33. Bury the Hatchet

There's supposed to be a psychiatrist comin in to see me sometime this morning. I hope it's a woman. Women doctors gets right in there with you, emotionally, and you usually gets a good bawl out of it. Plus a woman is more likely to prescribe something to take the edge off, when a man just figures it's in your best interest to tough it out. Fuck that. I toughed it out and look where it fuckin got me.

They fitted a new cast on me arm this morning. I've been tryna move the tips of me fingers. Starin at 'em, tryna will 'em into doin what they're supposed to do. No go. Me whole hand is useless. They had to do some serious stitchin, had to sew the ligaments back together and fit a little plastic tube in me vein that's supposed to dissolve within a few days. It's not painin all that much, but I been tryna look miserable and uncomfortable so's they'll gimme something, anything for the boredom, for the non-stop pangs of useless rage and embarrassment and anxiety. No go with that either.

—We found nine different types of drugs in your system Mr. Reid. What you need is a few days' rest. And perhaps you need to rethink your lifestyle.

Yeah, perhaps.

At least they gives me something in the evenings to help me sleep, knocks me right out. Fuckin doctors. Go do a little sensitivity training will ya? I done a week in hospital when I first moved to Town. I was around nineteen. I was after gettin these pills for

343

me foot and I brought the bottle to a party up on Gosling Street, where one half of the band use to live. Washed 'em all down with a flask of Screech. Wasted. I knows that dont sound so smart now, considering me present circumstances, but that's how we hafta get by sometimes. When I woke up the morning after that party I was in the racks of pain, like I was after swallowing some kinda angry, inflatable creature with poisonous claws that just kept gettin bigger and bigger, gougin at me insides, tryna pop me ribs out. And it felt like I had to shit too, those same kinda cramps, only exaggerated a hundred times. I couldnt walk, could barely stand up. I called an ambulance and they brought me to St. Clare's. I waited on a stretcher for about three years, dyin with the pain, beggin for a drink of water, which the nurses wouldnt give me, till finally this young fella had the good sense to hook me up to an IV and blast me veins full of Demerol and Gravol. That's some wicked little cocktail. He gave me a glass of ice cubes too, God love 'im. Sent me home then, blitzed and not carin what was wrong with me in the first place. Woke up the next morning even worse. Called the ambulance again. This time they brought me to the Health Science. Doctor looked me over, saw the pain I was in and sent me home in a cab with a prescription for Atasol-fuckin-30, even after I told him it was pills and booze that fucked me up in the *first* place. Take two every four to six hours as required for pain. Well, they were useless for that kinda pain. I lay on the bed all night, tossin and turnin and tryna get comfortable. I'd come around long enough to take four or five pills, then drift off into a stupor again. Next morning the pills were all gone and me face and hands were swole up like balloons. But me face was hard as a rock and numbish, like when you're stung by a wasp. I didnt recognize meself in the mirror. I was hideous lookin, like I'd put on seventy-five pounds in me sleep. No strength in me limbs either. Called the ambulance again, and when the doctors saw me this time, they got a room ready for me. They knew they were after fuckin up, see. They hooked me up to an IV then and fed me that wicked little Demerol cocktail every four hours for a week. I was in heaven. Dont ever send me home, please. Then one morning I woke up and there's some doctor with a bunch of med students gathered around me bed. The curtain drawn. Little clipboards and lab coats. This doctor, who I'd never laid eyes on before, pokin at me guts and tellin me to breathe and askin if I feels pain here or there. They were all takin notes, 'cept a couple of 'em kept whispering and makin faces behind the doctor's back like they were in fuckin high school. He tests me reactions with a little rubber hammer, then tells me I'm free to go. He says:

—Lay off the Jockey Club son, you'll be fine.

And they all giggled and walked on to the next bed. I was barely awake.

Sensitivity? Fuck.

• • •

All hands are after bein in to see me this past few days. Philip and Jane. Philip never said much and I could tell that Jane was after draggin him in to see me. Fuck him anyhow. Jane got all worked up though, about what an arsehole I was to go fuckin with me life like that, to go scarin everybody. Yeah, some fright they all got I'm sure. Who coulda seen it comin? I nodded at her. She gave me a slip of paper with Donna's Fort McMurray address and phone number, said she'd be delighted to hear from me, that she's worried sick about me. Jane says Donna is three months pregnant, shacked up with her ex again. I tried to react with a bit of enthusiasm but all that came out was a deep, raspy, malicious laugh. As soon as they left I balled the paper up and tossed it in the garbage. Donna.

That Clyde Whelan cunt was in with some foolish new missus hangin off his arm. She looked kinda Cuban and had this real spaced-out way about her. Right horny lookin too. She must be some fuckin horny to be clingin to Clyde the way she was.

Ahh fuck, I'm tryna be nice with people. It's hard.

Brent hasnt shown his face yet, or Val. I aint expecting Val. I s'pose he's out livin it up now anyhow, with his fuckin Lifetime

Achievement money. Five grand or something like that. Think he'd throw a chunk of it my way.

Mike Quinn was here yesterday evening. Brought a basket of fruit with him and I laced into this huge five-point apple, stuffed as much of it into me mouth as could fit. I almost choked on it, juice runnin down me clean-shaved chin. Funny, what a few days off the booze can do for your appetite. The nurse told me that I had all kinds of vitamin deficiencies, so maybe it was just me system reacting to something it needed, something in the apple that I wasnt use to havin. I hadnt been eatin hardly atall towards the end, not even the burgers and subs from the Korean store across the street from the apartment. Fuck. The apartment.

I figured he was there to slaughter me. But he was half decent. He never tried talkin down to me about what I'd done with meself either. He more or less got on like he was just droppin in on me for a visit, like we were out at the bar or something. Speakin of which, he was right delighted to let me in on his latest streak of good fortune: that poor unfortunate Silas couldnt make his payments, that he'd never quite recovered after losin all that cash the first night he took over, and so the Hatchet had, as of the first of September, gone back into Mike's name. I never let on that I'd already heard the whole story from Clyde. Mike, twenty-five thousand bucks ahead, due to Silas's non-refundable down payment, and a full summer's vacation out of it besides. He was some fuckin pleased with himself. I was kinda happy for him too. Or maybe I was just happy to see Silas get what he had comin, for bein such a greasy old closet whoremaster. Mike said the first thing he done on Monday morning was fire all them little queens that Silas had hired on. An awkward moment then. Maybe Mike thought I was expecting to be asked back on the job. Or maybe he felt obligated to offer me the job. I dont know. All I do know, now, is that there's no fuckin way I'm ever goin back to work at the Hatchet. I dont care if he begs me. Dont know what I'll do for money, but I'm never setting foot in through them doors again. Not even for a social one.

Mike leaned against the far wall with his big hands tucked behind his back, sizin up the sterile little room. Something on his fuckin mind, no doubt about that. I was just waitin for it, for the bomb.

—When are you getting out?

—Dont know. I gotta talk to a few doctors first. Psychiatrist. But dont mention that.

—No, no. Jesus no. Well I suppose there's no rush getting your stuff out of the apartment then.

—No rush, no.

He took a step towards the bed with his two hands outstretched like he was clutchin at an invisible head, tryin not to crush it, the way you do when someone's goin down on you. His hair was all sweaty and stuck to his forehead. He stopped himself from comin too close, like he didnt trust what he might do if he got within arm's reach of me. He stepped back again.

—Listen Clayton, ahh . . . I had a look at the place. It's . . . well it's like a fuckin war zone. The toilet is broke in half. There's a mound of ahhh . . . How . . . how do you expect me to deal with the likes of that?

I knew it. I fuckin well *knew* he was only here to power-trip about the apartment and the rent and all that shit. I just shrugged at him. I mean come on and kill me if you needs to Mike b'y. Easy enough target, hooked up to an IV in a fuckin hospital bed.

—I'll figure something out Mike . . .

—What happened up there?

—Partying, shaggin around . . .

—Some fuckin party. I should, I should fuckin . . . Well, when they let you out you can drop by and do some cleaning up then.

—Very well.

But I knew as I was saying it that I was never setting foot in that apartment ever, ever again.

Mike zipped up his coat, a brown leather jacket that was way too tight around his gut. He picked up the basket of fruit that he'd brought in with him.

—Want anything else out of this? I got another visit to make.

Well how fuckin miserable is that? I picked out another apple.

—Anybody I knows?

—Who? Oh. Yeah, I dont know. You know the old girl Clara? She's always on the go downtown?

—Yeah. Is she . . .

—She's fine. Had a mild stroke the other night, couple of days after you came in.

—She a relative or something?

—Yes. No. Not really. She stays . . . she's a tenant.

He left me then. It was goin on eight o'clock and I knew there'd be no more visitors. I almost wished he'd stayed a little longer.

. . .

Dr. Susan Miller. Closing in on fifty. Wicked shape though. Decent tan. I'd say she got a tidy little house around the bay somewhere. Wonder if she's still married. It's a safe bet to say she *was*, one time. That's all a part of the dream. Livin high on the hog and lowering yourself to dealin with the sickness and accidents brought on by the vices of the lower classes. Scoot off to "the bay house" every chance you gets. Fill it with *real* art. Go fuck yourself missus. Think I'm gonna just spill me guts out to you, just like that, so's you can sit around the table next week at some dinner party with your member of parliament and turn me into some anonymous statistic?

—So tell me Clayton, how did this happen?

Six months' worth of self-abuse and a lifetime worth of self-loathing busts outta me in one loud primal howl, right from the very bottom of me guts. Tears almost squirtin outta me eyes onto the bedsheets around me, like the way a cartoon character cries. And I am a bit of a cartoon, aint I? This is all like some big joke. People starvin to death and bein shot down in their homes and buried in mass graves and little girls out there whose stepfathers are fuckin 'em on a regular basis, people with little children dyin of cancer. Monica rottin in the woods. Jim splattered across the wind-

348

shield of his Jeep. Fuck. I should be grateful for what I got. I'd like to be, just cant see that far ahead yet.

How did this happen? Well girl, see it all started back in grade one with the nuns. *No. Come on Reid. Get fuckin real.*

She hands me a wad of tissue and I dabs at me eyes with it. I'd like to blow me nose but I cant in front of her. My nose-blowing is usually a messy affair, something no other human should hafta look at.

—Would you like to maybe sit over by the window in the sunlight? That might help your mood a little.

I shakes me head. I havent budged from this bed, only to piss and shit in the bathroom, since I checked in. Monday morning, when I came in, that dandy little nurse who I havent seen since, she told me to just think of it as a little break from me life, a little vacation. And that's exactly what I'm gonna do, lie here in this bed and sleep when I'm tired and eat what food they puts in front of me and read their junky, crappy magazines and medical journals. That's my idea of a vacation.

Dr. Miller takes out her clipboard and scans it with a thick silver pen. There's something engraved on the pen but I cant make it out.

—So it says here Clayton that the wound is self-inflicted?

Where's the blood coming from?

Everywhere. It's everywhere.

Which fuckin wound would that be now missus? Aside from the obvious one, I s'pose. I stares at me hand again and tries to flex it.

—It'll go back to normal Clayton. You'll probably need some physio, but it *will* mend.

It better fuckin mend. It's not easy wackin off with the other hand. There's a lot more work involved. I had a go at it last night. Me door was open and I could see one of the nurses leant against the desk in the hallway, her pale pink uniform stretched right tight around her backside so's I could see the outline of her big ole drawers. Me mouth was right pasty and I couldnt build up no saliva for lube, so I dragged me IV into the bathroom and lathered a bit of soap on meself. Time I got back in the bed I was after losing me hard-on and by the time I got it *back up* the cheap-ass soap was after dryin right out again. The bed was right squeaky too, so I had to find the right position to be able to get the proper rhythm up without makin too much racket. The nurse musta known, she musta heard me. She wasnt six feet away. I s'pose they're use to that sorta thing though. It was so dry and I went at it so viciously, I wound up burnin meself, like a friction burn. That fuckin stings. There's the start of a little scab on it now today. I minds this one time with Isadora, and I was after burnin meself in the same way, wackin off. She put her hand down me pants and I winced from the pain. Of course she wanted to see what was the matter then, and I hadda show it to her cause there's no saying no to Lady Isadora. I told her I jammed it in me zipper. I wasnt thinkin though, cause it was the second time I used that excuse with her in as many weeks. She just looked at it, right close up like she was thinkin about painting a picture of it or something, and smiled and cocked her eyebrows at bit. I knows she knew. She fuckin knew. *I dont masturbate.* Why couldnt she just have come out and said, you know, it's alright Clayton, you're allowed to have a bit of fun with yourself, everybody does. Maybe we coulda moved on to some other level together. But no, always with the disappointment, the dismissal, the hint that I wasnt yet a man. *Two parts boy.*

Isadora. If I looks back over me days you know, I can honestly say that when I was at me most fucked up it's always been over a woman. You'd think we'd learn? You'd assume the heart could remember all that pain and turmoil. You'd think I shoulda been able to just turn it off this summer, turn off that need, that want. Stop wanting Her. But the head and the heart dont always communicate so well I s'pose. They aint the best of friends. Because if there's one thing I knows in me head it's that that feeling, that sinkin bottomless dreadful misery that comes from gettin rejected, it cant kill you. You might feel like you're gonna die, but you wont die. Unless you tries to do the job on yourself, like I did.

How did this happen? See Dr. Miller, Susan, me woman took off and I cracked up. Simple as that. I was absolutely number one, this here noggin was in shipshape before that though. Number fuckin one. That what you wants to hear?

—Clayton?

—What?

—Would you like me to come back later?

—Okay. That might be better.

• • •

How did this happen?

On Monday morning I climbed the fire escape to the roof. I drank five beer. I threw a bottle. It smashed on the steps that lead to Duckworth. I didnt find any pleasure in it. That's a sign of depression, they says, not bein able to enjoy the little things that one time woulda gotten you right off. Brent wasnt around. Maybe that was it. Not the same when you're on your own. It was over a week since I'd seen him last, strollin up Water Street with his hand on his new mobile phone, waitin to turn a corner so's he could whip it out and dial the missus. What's he like? I heard him on the radio then, a couple of days later. He was with two or three more who'd gotten selected to go overseas. Missus asked him what had gotten him interested in the program and he said he couldnt right-fully say, that he's always been interested in Ireland and saw it as a great opportunity to "expand his horizons," wherever he picked up that kinda faggy talk. Never even mentioned me name. I tried to feel good for him though, at least he's gonna be straightened away for a while.

I lay on the edge of the roof and stared down onto Water Street. No one was about. Seven thirty. Too early. Monday morning. Everyone so reluctant to move into the week. The smell of the comin fall. Pigeons. Gulls. The bronze sparkle of beer-bottle glass in the gutters. The sun blazed down on the back of my neck. The travel agency a few doors up. Mockin me. St. John's to Heathrow for sweet fuck-all. If I had a thousand dollars I'd disappear. Vanish. And Crazy Clara, yes, that's right, tyin her laces on the steps of the Korean store across the street, havin a heated debate with herself about something I couldnt quite make out, but something she was obviously pissed off about. Sweat runnin down her face in buckets. No surprise that she had herself a stroke. Poor old girl. I wanted to shout out to her, but I couldnt. Maybe I was afraid she wouldnt recognize me. Or that she would.

One of me buddies in Dublin, he had an apartment around Christ Church with a rooftop just like mine. There was lawn chairs and stools and a stereo and even a tabletop hockey game set up. It was wicked and no one ever fell off or wanted to jump or threw anything down into the street. Why couldnt I have thought of all that? What a spot for a summer bash. Hook up a band and blast it down into the streets, put up a rail of some sort, sleeping bags.

I gawked down at the street, thought shit over. How low I'd let meself sink. Sour smell off me skin. I stood up and balanced meself on the edge. I wasnt even feelin the five beer I drank. I looked down, down, down into the face of a possible death. A possible ending. The end of this whole mess. The way it all turned out. His gruesome finale. The closing moment. Swoop. Nosedive. Splat. No pain. All over in a matter of seconds. Or maybe so *much* pain, maybe a wheelchair, drinkin food through a straw and havin someone look after me for the rest of me life, cleanin me hole when I shits meself. Locked inside me own private hell for the next fifty years, or however long it took for me to die naturally. Die a natural death.

Wander into the world instead.

Get out on that highway and stick your thumb out and just *go*. Wherever.

I couldnt do it, couldnt make the jump.

I went back downstairs and curled up on the couch.

. . .

I'm in a hospital bed. There's a nurse. She pulls open the blinds and the sun bursts across me face. She sets breakfast on the stand beside me bed. I gotta piss. She says:

—There's someone here to see you Clayton.

Me heart almost explodes in me chest. It's *her*. It's her. It's gotta be.

No.

A woman walks in. She's maybe in her mid-forties, long black woollen coat and silky scarf. Sunglasses. Black leather handbag.

—Hello Clayton.

—Hello.

—Dont tell me you dont know me?

I dont have a sweet clue who she is.

—It's Massie for God sakes. How are you?

Massie? Aunt Massie? Holy fuck. She's after sheddin some fuckin weight, about a hundred pounds. It must be what, three years since I saw her last? She looks rested and relaxed. I s'pose she would be though, now that she's clear of Val. They were shacked up for fifteen odd years. *Odd* years too, I'd say.

—Massie, sorry. I'm barely awake girl.

—It's okay Clayton. Weight Watchers. I quite like my new anonymity. So, how are you, other than completely fucking mental like the rest of your tribe? What are you after doing to yourself?

—I'm . . . I'm . . . How did you know I was here?

—I came in with Val.

—Where is he? Send him in.

—You mean you havent heard? God b'y, you've been living in the dark.

She had no idea how true that statement really was.

—He collapsed at the arts awards. It was on TV. He fell down in a heap. I drove right across the Island. He's downstairs now, checked into the new detox unit.

—Holy fuck.

—It's a step. Imagine, two crazy, strung-out Reids in the one hospital. Is it big enough I wonder?

—I fuckin wonder. Listen, who won what other awards?

—What?

—The music awards, who won the other ones?

—Ahhh, Rob Dawe won for Best Independent Album.

—Fuck no . . .

—Yup. And, oh, your old friends, that crowd of hooligans you used to play with? You didnt know that? They won Best New Rock Group or Entertainers or something.

—Fuck no . . .

—Yeah. And what's his name, the guitar player . . .

—Corey.

—Yeah, he thanked you, said something, I cant remember now.

Fuckin right they thanked me, the bastards. I betcha Toddler fuckin Dawe never did though, old prick.

Massie stayed for about half an hour. We laughed and bullshitted about different times. She reminded me of who I use to be, when I first moved in to St. John's and started hangin out at her and Val's. How fuckin cracked and unbreakable I was just a few years ago. She obviously had a different idea of me than I ever allowed meself to see. But when she left I felt it, I did, I felt like I was unbreakable, or maybe that I wasnt meant to be broken just yet. It was a good visit.

The famous Valentine Reid, detoxing downstairs. Who woulda fuckin thunk it?

I lay in bed and let me mind wander back over the months and years, tried to remember who I was, tried to feel the way I useta feel, when nothing in this world could stop me, how I useta think I needed nothing, just the clothes on me back. I never looked ahead and I sure as fuck never looked back. But I reckon that changed somewhere along the way, without me noticing it. Like I got dead fuckin tired and kept goin anyhow. What must it be like to have a place to feel easy, where you can relax and not hafta put up any fronts? Just *be*.

Home. Randy. My old man. Who's been tryna make it up to me for years, tryna better himself, when all I could do was spit back in his face. The time he punched one of me high school teachers in the face. Fuck, I was some delighted with 'im after that. I was after messin up one of the classrooms upstairs during lunchtime, when I wasnt supposed to be up there. Teacher asked me about it, fuckin Mr. Spurrell. I told 'im I wasnt nowhere near upstairs during lunch. He didnt believe me. Got me down in this empty classroom and picked me up by the throat. Said if I ever lied to 'im again he'd wrap me nuts up around me chin. I dont know how word of it got back to Randy, but when he came down to the school that evening he just let fuckin drift, flattened Spurrell right there on the lobby floor. Fuckin wicked. He was dead sober too, Randy was.

Lyin there in the hospital bed thinkin about the old man like that when he called. I dont remember askin to have the phone hooked up.

—Are ya gonna live or what?

—I s'pose b'y. So they tells me.

—Sure you'll hafta come to a Meeting with me sometime. When you're ready of course.

—I just might.

—Your room is here still you know. You can lay low for a bit, make a comeback.

—Thanks Dad.

—What?

—I said thanks.

—Yes well . . . well I'll be out now tomorrow or the next day, to see you. You heard about Val I s'pose?

—Yup.

—Very well then. You hang in there. You mind if I brings the missus, ahhh Anne-Marie, with me when I comes in?

—Not at all.

There's the distant glow of the gathering morning, shadows stirrin in the corner of the room. A song, one of Val's. "Hard to Believe." But it's slowed right down. The sound seems to come from everywhere, from nowhere. Shadows dancin.

Everybody tells me there's a light out there, even the blind can see.
I borrowed a needle and popped out my eyes
I find it so hard to believe . . .

I lays me head back on the pillow and tries to absorb the song, tries to find something in there to take me through the horror, through the terror, the dread, the stench of death. I'm fully aware of the shadows, these dancers waltzin back and forth, shufflin across the pale yellow floor. This song was never a waltz. Visiting hours have not yet begun.

Dont let nobody tell you there's a big love
Our time is but a fleeting little dream
They'll tell you there's a tunnel and a garden and a gate
I find it so hard, I'm tryin real hard to believe . . .

The dark and damp smell of old meat and topsoil wafting across me bed each time the dancers pass. The taller shadow turns with an empty bar glass outstretched towards me. Jim McNaughton's distinctive stutter clouds the room:

—H-how about a r-rrrefill there Clayton? And, and b-buy one for yourself.

A deep, cavernous moan drowns in me throat. I tries to pull the blankets over me head, but the other dancer pins the bottoms of 'em tight to the railing. It's Monica, this second shadow. Her face pale and loose, a nest of crawly bugs high on her left cheekbone. She smiles wide, one of her front teeth snapped clean off.

—Come on Clay. First two rules of rock-and-roll. Remember?

· · ·

Evening again. And she's there. She. *Her.* Right there at the foot of me bed. Is she? I cant trust me mind to believe it. But I'm tryin real hard. Her hair is cut short. I like it. My arm stretches out to her, reachin, tryna pull her to me, command the space that lingers so heavy between us. Impossible distance. She takes a step towards the bed and stops. She sees the cast. She fades out. I struggles to keep me eyes open, but I cant. Whatever this shit is they've given me, a little something to help me sleep. Something to help me die, the coma I've been craving.

· · ·

I can smell her smell. Feel her in the bed beside me. We're a good fit. I remembers learnin about the continents in school, how they're all like little pieces of a puzzle, how they all came from the one big piece, long, long ago. The teacher cut Europe and North America out of an old map and fit them together, almost perfect. We fits together like that, me and her. A few new grooves, erosions and scars, some pieces even missing altogether, forged outta distance and separation—but still a decent fit. You could look at us and say yes, they definitely *used* to be one.

She'd be Europe I s'pose, for obvious reasons.

· · ·

Dark now. Again. The nurse pops her head in to say that visiting hours are over. The woman in the corner, scribblin into a notebook, she nods to indicate that she'll be stayin. The nurse winks at the woman in the corner. I dont know if that's good or bad, or if I'm even awake. Or alive.

· · ·

With my breakfast there's a form to fill out, says Father James Molloy will be visiting patients in the afternoon and would I appreciate a visit? I checks the box to say yes, bring 'im on.

357

· · ·

Brent calls, says he cant make it down to see me, not today. Not today. I dont care.

· · ·

Dr. Susan Miller wants me to move downstairs to the psychiatric ward on Monday morning. Just for observation. I'll be allowed out for a smoke, no more nicotine patch, no more crazy, fucked-up dreams. But I kinda like the messy dreams, come to think of it.

How did this happen?

First time I was caught drinkin, home in the house, I was just thirteen. I barely had a half-case in me. I wasnt drunk when I went to bed, but after an hour I woke up and walked into Randy's room and pissed all over his bed. He was vicious, but what could he say? He had to smack me awake. I s'pose I was sleepwalkin. And I done it a thousand times since then too. Go to bed sober, but then it's like what tiny drop of booze is in me system leaks into the wrong part of me brain when I lies down and I wakes up demented an hour later, screamin me head off and tryna walk through walls. One night the winter sure I pissed in Brent's guitar case. He didnt like that.

But that musta been what happened, how I wound up here. I musta been sleepwalkin. I musta been *demented*. I left the roof and went downstairs to the couch. Next thing I knows I'm crossin Water Street towards the sounds of shouts and laughter. It's startin to rain. I lurches down to the waterfront. There's a bunch kickin a soccer ball back and forth. They're foreigners, off the boats, dont speak English. There's vodka, ice cold. They're happy to see me. I'm tryna explain meself, tryna make sense, tryna connect, tryna say, say, say that I feels like tossin meself into the harbour. I pretends to jump. I mimes it. I slips and one of 'em catches me. A cheer goes up. One guy says, over and over:

—Clay-ton, you craaa-zy, you craaa-zy.

They're laughin. At me. I cant make 'em understand, cant connect. I slugs back the vodka. It rains harder. Me hand latches onto

358

the knife on me belt. I pulls it out and the smiles fall away. The circle spreads out. Her face reflected in the blade, murky and blurred, not lookin at me. I presses the knife, hard against the back of me wrist. The skin pops open, like one of her mangoes, the layers of flesh and muscle and ligament, the white flash of bone underneath, clear as day for a second, before the blood comes.

It pours outta me like water, surges down the tips of me fingers and splashes into the puddles beneath me feet.

I tries to take it back, get the moment back, squint me eyes and clench me gut and beg the heavens, beg God, the devil, anyone, to give me just the last five seconds from *my own* history to do over again. Five measly seconds. Me hand flops over, useless. I cant understand why it wont work. I holds me arm above me head to hinder the flow. The crack of thunder across the harbour. Blood streamin down me face, drenchin me shirt. The smell of me own blood. I spins back in the direction of the Hatchet, the apartment, the mattress. Curl up there and wait. I falls onto the road. Blood in me eyes. A river of blood, gushin towards a sewage grate. My blood. It swirls round and around till the drain can hold no more. It floods over and washes back down across the waterfront. The screechin of car tires. Blood. It swamps to the edge of the moorings, pickin up bits of kelp and chip bags and feathers and cigarette butts with it, sweepin up everything in its path. My blood. Teeming down over the side of the wharf. The freshly stained St. John's harbour. The deathly, rusty red glow on the cliffs outside the Narrows. The rain peltin down on me face.

—Good God! Are you alright buddy?

—No I'm not. Not at all.

—Where's the blood coming from?

—Everywhere. It's everywhere.

• • •

It is her. Is it? She's been downstairs, brought up coffee. She's bought me a new toothbrush, a package of socks, a book called *Living Sober*.

She's brought pictures, shots of that house on Monkstown Road, the backyard with its stone walkway and the garden in full bloom. There's a picture of a small, bright room lined with dark hardwood. There's a table in the middle of the room, wooden with a blackened butter-knife scar near the centre. Cant be. Iz says she bought it at St. Michael's Salvage on Bond Street. There's a sheet of paper laid in the centre of the table. There's words on the sheet. It says *This can be your office!*

She flips through the pictures and says things like:

—I was thinking we could take a run down to that new antique shop in Petty Harbour and see if we can get a deal on some pressback chairs. Wouldnt *that* be nice?

I nods yes. I shakes me head no, whenever it's appropriate. There's a sense that some disaster has been narrowly averted, just to make way for an even greater, better quality, more superior, more devastating one.

—Try to move your fingers Clayton.

I give it everything that's in me, like me life depends on it. The ring finger gives a little twitch and her face lights right up.

—Yeaaaayyy, for you.

She slips her hand down under the sheets.

—And how about this? Still workin fine I hope?

There's a twitch down there too. I nods me head yes.

Father James Molloy walks in, an old fella, pushin seventy for sure. Full battle regalia. He stops when he sees Isadora in the bed with me.

—Oh. Pardon me, pardon me. I was told you were on your own.

Thick, grand, refined Irish accent that sets me mind reelin, brings on this tidal wave of utter uselessness. Me eyes are fillin up.

—Are y'alright son?

Isadora smilin, ever so soft, so girlish beside me. Beside me. Now.

—It's okay Father.

—I can always come again? I'm here for most of the day.

—That'd be nice, Father.

—Okay, so. I'll stop in again on my way back around.

He pauses and looks back into the room before he heads off.

—Dont worry my son. God has a plan for you. Good day young lady.

—Good day.

. . .

She presses her mouth to mine. Her lips are dry and tight. She flicks her tongue into me mouth, but it feels foreign and I cant tell if she's doin it because it feels right to her or if that's just the way she thinks she should kiss me. I'm afraid to close me eyes. She pulls away, takes me good hand to her mouth and sucks me fingers into it. I makes a shaky attempt to withdraw, but she's got a firm grip on me wrist. She guides me saliva-soaked hand down under the sheets, under the elastic of her panties, into her. *Her.*

—Do you think God has a plan for you Clayton Reid?

The flattened tangle of her pubic hair. That devious little bump. Slippery. Her heat. *Her.* Here. Now. In my hand.

—God? Fuck. I dont know, girl. I dont know . . .

Acknowledgements

Much gratitude and thanks to my tireless agents, Shaun Bradley and Don Sedgwick, at TLA; my editor Iris Tupholme, for her invaluable wisdom and unfaltering belief in my writing; and to Noelle Zitzer and all the dedicated staff at HarperCollins who made this book possible.

Thanks to all who've come out to my shows and gotten behind my work in recent years. I would not be here without your support.

Thanks to the Newfoundland and Labrador Arts Council, the City of St. John's, Resource Centre for the Arts, Rattling Books, the March Hare Committee, the CBC, Newfound Films, Pope, Insight, 2M and Kickham East Productions.

If I thanked you in my first book, then thanks again. That's not including those of you whose names didnt really belong there in the first place. You know who you are.

If this book had a soundtrack it would be Blair Harvey's latest album *GutterBeGutted*. Hunt it down and buy it—it kicks ass.

Now, throughout the construction of *Right Away Monday* there were people who gave me the keys to their homes, fed me, booked plane tickets and hotels, hired me, let me know it was alright to bawl my face off, talked me down from the ledge, opened their hearts and just generally loved me and accepted me at times when I really didnt deserve it.

Thanks to the lovely and beautifully talented Jenny Rockett. And to Mary-Lynn Bernard, Sarah Blenkhorn, Erin Breen, Lois Brown, Mark Callanan, Steve Cochrane, Alicia Loving Cortez, Hugh Dillon, Kim Farewell, Risa Bramon-Garcia, René Garcia, Debbie Hanlon, Jonny Harris, Connie Hynes, Lily Hynes, Lois Hynes, Mary Hynes, Michael Hynes, Andy Jones, Robert Joy, Nicole Kane, Susan Kent, Ruth Lawrence, Mary Lewis, Tony Nappo, Adriana Maggs, Shaun Majumdar, John Peddle and family, Helen Peters, Dave Picco, Elizabeth Pugh, Justin Simms, Sheila Sullivan, Alana Steele, Monique Tobin, Sir Charles Tomlinson, Todd Wall, Mary Walsh, Des Walsh, Sherry White, Dyane Gjesdal. And above all, thanks to my son, Percy, for bringing me into the world.

About the author

About the book

Read on

Ideas,
interviews
& features

Author Biography

Joel Thomas Hynes

JOEL THOMAS HYNES comes from a small town called Calvert along the Southern Shore of Newfoundland's Avalon Peninsula. Hemmed in by spruce and rock, a collapsed fishery, a disgraced church—the usual fixings. Nothing much to do for fun but drink and fight and chase girls and fight and smash windows and run from the cops and get stoned and bust into the school after hours and put cigarettes out on each other and steal cars and get caught by the cops and go to court and blame it all on everybody else and start a band.

Time enough to move to the capital city and hunker down in a scuzzy basement apartment with no windows and a nice, quiet family living above who are likely traumatized to this day. Writing away the nights— naive, angst-ridden rants and lyrics and twisted poetry just a few bloodstains short of a prolonged suicide note. Checking in with a psychotic probation officer every Friday morning. Sleeping pills. Beer. Tattoos. Port wine because Jack Kerouac says so. Black, black coffee and Drum tobacco. Girlfriend leaves and Hynes gives chase, manages to make a nasty situation ten times worse.

Back downstairs, alone with the cat. Gets a poem published! Bob Dylan. Roddy Doyle. Irvine Welsh. No heroin in St. John's. University. "Mature" student. English classes— T. S. Eliot, Philip Larkin, Steinbeck, Layton, Plath, Heaney—the usual fixings. Drinking hot brandy from a coffee cup in the back of the classroom and trying to figure a way under the professor's skirt. Failing, failing. Friends falling by the wayside.

Downtown! A bar called the Spur. The last of the bona fide drinking holes. Gone now, never coming back. Drinking some more. Nick Cave. Springsteen. Dodging the landlord. Caught stealing a Snickers bar at Wal-Mart. Three days in jail. Serving one-third of his sentence and then trying to walk the straight and narrow. Writing a play. Still failing out of school. Detox. Rehab.

Answers an ad in the paper for a job in Dublin. Gets the job, miraculously. Sent to Dublin for six months to "explore career options." Wanders the country looking for work with the IRA. Makes an arse of it all. Solidifies his alcoholism.

Back to St. John's with a haircut and new clothes. Back to the Spur. Things is all changed around. There's an air of excess. The new millennium breeds panic. Get it in you as quick as ever you can. "Why dont you try bartending, Hynes? You're here every night anyhow." Becomes overnight sensation as the angriest bartender in St. John's. Rakes in the cash and beer tokens. Weed and wraps of blow in his tip jar. Meets a new girl, loses his mind. Detox, auditioning, writing, no more band. Has another go at his play. Spiralling, stumbling, staggering the streets. Hits the pavement at seven in the morning, comes to in the back of an ambulance with a tourni-quet on his arm. Lots of blood. Two weeks on a short, short leash. Goes back out into the world and doesnt drink anymore for a long, long time. Head starts to clear up a little.

Goes back to that play. It keeps getting big-ger and bigger until he finally has to admit it's a book. Finds himself on camera now and again. Tries whole-grain bread for the first time. Eats an avocado. Spends time in ▶

> **Becomes overnight sensa-tion as the angriest bartender in St. John's.**

Author Biography (*continued*)

the bush in Northern Ontario, treeplanting, while his girlfriend's belly is swelling with a baby boy. Comes home and hunkers down to be a dad.

Beautiful child born in the fall of that year, changes everything. Finally gets that play produced, called *The Devil You Dont Know*. Co-written with S. White, starring Hynes and White together. The play is a smash hit, by St. John's standards. *Down to the Dirt*, the unpublished novel the play is adapted from, wins the Percy Janes First Novel Award. Killick Press publishes the book a year later. Everything changes again. Another year later, HarperCollins reissues the novel in Canada. French and Serbian translations follow. A U.S. edition. *Down to the Dirt* is nominated for the International IMPAC Dublin Literary Award. Hynes wants that hundred thousand Euros. He wants to go back to Dublin a published author and a happy, sober dad. He doesnt make the shortlist.

Gets a good job performing and writing on a CBC television show called *Hatching, Matching and Dispatching*. Works on another play. Starts writing another novel. Chelsea Hotel in New York, typically. Cant find no heroin there either. *Down to the Dirt* becomes a movie script. Hynes finds new accommodations in St. John's, by himself, but shares his son, of course. Writing, writing. Book, play. Buys a vintage motorcycle. Finds an old abandoned house around the bay and starts fixing it up. Heads off to Los Angeles and wanders Venice Beach. Cant find no heroin there either.

> ❝ Spends time in the bush in Northern Ontario, tree-planting, while his girlfriend's belly is swelling with a baby boy. ❞

Back to St. John's. Launches audio book in Brooklyn. Gives worst reading of his life in Boston. Almost dies from mystery virus. Virus renders him deaf for a couple of weeks. While deaf, he cuts up hot peppers and rubs his eyes afterwards. Goes blind. Crawling around on the floor and shouting to his son to come help him get to the sink. Son thinks it's hilarious that Dad is both deaf and blind. Later that night Hynes takes a shower and gets the hot pepper on his balls too. It burns. Sometimes it surprises him that he's smart enough to write books.

Finally goes back to Ireland with a whole gang of Newfoundland writers and musicians. Tours the southeast. Lands in Dublin like a madman and completely discredits himself all over again. Same old Hynes, worse now that he's got a book out.

Second novel comes out in May 2007. Called *Right Away Monday*. New play, *Say Nothing Saw Wood*, hits the stage a week later. About the murder of an old woman by a seventeen-year-old boy. Based on a true story. Sold-out run in St. John's. Hynes begins to turn it into a novel. *Down to the Dirt*, the movie, is shot in the summer of 2007. Hynes plays the lead. Wicked, intense, very challenging. Back and forth between St. John's and Toronto. Waiting, waiting for something big to fall from the sky.

Writer-in-residence at the Drake Hotel in Toronto for a while. No one lines up to get his autograph. Goes out to auditions and pitches TV ideas. A few bites. Grows weary of the concept of a ladder, realizes that you're only as good as the last time you worked. That you have to keep on going for the rest of your natural life. That you might stop to catch your breath but you cant actually stop to breathe. ▶

“ **Sometimes it surprises him that he's smart enough to write books.** ”

5

Author Biography (*continued*)

Nothing falls from the sky. It seems there's no commercial appeal in killing a poisoned cat or beating off into a bottle of shampoo. Most people want to talk about the weather. We are all alone.

Starts in on another novel. Teaches creative writing to the inmates at Her Majesty's Penitentiary in St. John's. Starts working on a screenplay. Applies for grants. Tries to be a good dad. Tries to take it all a day at a time. Sits down to write an extended bio in the third person, as if someone who knows him really well wrote it, and not him.

In Conversation with
Joel Thomas Hynes

Can you tell us about your formative years and how they shaped your creative imagination? Was reading and writing a big part of your world growing up?

I was very much an outsider as a child. I wanted to be involved in dangerous activities, and I was up for more imaginative adventures than, say, getting a ball game underway. I liked setting things on fire and going places I wasn't supposed to go. I didn't have much time for competitive sports, even though I was marginally involved in softball and hockey for years. I'd say the only sport I put any real value in was, and is, cross-country running, and that's a very solitary, masochistic activity, which suits me fine. But where I come from, hockey players are hailed as community heroes, no matter if they happen to be illiterate, bullying narcissists. And if you don't excel at sports, then you're pretty much useless. I think that's the way with a lot of Canadian towns. There certainly wasn't any room for creative thought or artistic expression. And, of course, when you're really young, you don't have any way of knowing that you're an artist or a writer. So you just think you're useless or fucked up somehow. There's something wrong with you if you don't care about the Stanley Cup. So with me being a rather rambunctious individual, I just found ways to rebel and satisfy my interests.

My father was a voracious reader and I always strove for his approval, so from a young age, I found a lot of comfort in books. ▶

> ❝ As a child, I wanted to be involved in dangerous activities. ❞

It never really occurred to me that I could write until I was in my early teens. I discovered The Doors, typically, and thought I was Jim Morrison for a while. And through The Doors I got on to Bob Dylan and Jack Kerouac, and then Steinbeck and Hemingway and all those crazies.

My mother is a closet-case songwriter and spent her entire life playing the piano. My uncle is the renowned songwriter Ron Hynes, and so I felt I was close to creativity somehow. Ron would put out an album every couple of years, and he'd be all over the TV and the papers. He was quite famous on the Southern Shore, and I remember finding some sort of indirect inspiration from all that, a feeling that it was possible.

So I started writing poetry. Flat out. Three or four full poems a day. Perfect rhyme schemes. Teenage stuff. Then I moved on to journal writing, and fictionalizing my journals. I started a band and we played the bars. We were all hungry and young and naive, and we had fun. I was reading all the while.

I guess I've been writing since I was a child—stories and essays and poetry and lyrics—and I've always identified with books and writers. So I am a writer, and always was, long before I was ever published.

Writing offers me control. I always feel like I am moving forward when I write.

Many of your characters, but particularly Keith Kavanagh and Clayton Reid, have a propensity toward self-obliteration. Yet they don't seem to take death too seriously;

> ❝ I always feel like I am moving forward when I write. ❞

rather, they get a thrill out of courting self-destructiveness. In fact, one of Clayton's favourite toasts is "There's always suicide." Can you talk a little about that?

I've never taken death too seriously. I have an egotism that lets me believe I'm immune to it, or that my own death will be timely and poetic. Or that it can't happen to me. Or that I'm not one of the ones who actually will contract lung cancer from smoking. Or that AIDS is something that happens to someone else. Or that I can become involved with certain drugs and can pull out whenever I like, no trouble. That I am different. It's stupid, I know, and maybe it's a sort of defence mechanism. Maybe it just means I'm a bit of a nutbar. But I have a suspicion that a lot of people think that way. The truth is, I've had a few close calls and lived to tell the tale, and I feel like I've been spared for a good reason, like if I didn't check out that night ten years ago with all those downers packed into my system, I won't kick it on my way to the grocery store tomorrow either. And that attitude helps me run red lights and give lip to big guys downtown.

But seriously, once when I was seventeen, I was kicked out of a club on the Southern Shore because I was practically legless. I walked a small ways down the road toward home and collapsed in the woods in the snow. That night it rained a little and then warmed up for a while before it got really cold again. When I woke up the next morning, my hair was frozen into the ice—I had really long hair back then—and I had to yank hard to get out of it. I didn't die, and ▶

> ❝ I have an egotism that lets me believe I'm immune to death, or that my own death will be timely and poetic. ❞

In Conversation with Hynes (*continued*)

I always think I defied physical reality by living. And something else in me believes I was being watched over and kept here for a reason.

What are you working on now?

These days I'm working on a number of different projects, some personal and some commissioned. I'm writing a screenplay, a new stageplay, and I'm developing a new novel. I also teach creative writing at Her Majesty's Penitentiary in St. John's, where I'm helping the inmates create an anthology of their work. I've always got a lot of things going at one given time, even though half the time I feel like I've got nothing going on at all.

The novel I'm working on is called *Say Nothing Saw Wood*. It's based on the true story of a murder that happened in my hometown in 1971. A teenager killed an old woman after she woke up to find him robbing her home. She had known him all his life and looked out for him from the time he was a small child. The story is basically an exploration of a life gone horribly wrong, how one split-second decision can change the course of so many lives. It's a look at how we are remembered, how we would like to be perceived and received by the world, and whether or not we can ever truly rise above the stigma of the worst thing we've ever done.

> " I've always got a lot of things going at one given time, even though half the time I feel like I've got nothing going on at all. "

Joel Thomas Hynes on Writing

By the time I finished writing my first novel, I'd pretty much taught myself how to write a novel. So I was ready to try it for real. That sounds kind of self-deprecating, but it's actually not so far from the truth. Who can teach you to write a novel? I dont think anyone can. The only way to learn is by sitting down and having a go at it and letting yourself get it wrong, opening yourself up to criticism and advice, submitting your work to publishers and journals, swallowing the rejection letters, elbowing your way onto the reading circuit, crying and chain smoking your hair out. That's what I did. But I suppose it does help to be a little prepared as well. It'd be kinda hard to write a novel if you hadnt ever read one. You gotta read a lot of books, read the way other writers tell their stories. I tend to latch on to particular writers and then hunt down everything they've written and look for the commonalities that bridge their work. I will read until they disappoint me, and then I'll start on someone new.

Books have always carried me through. Reading is the one thing I do always, no matter what state my life is in. Whereas writing, on the other hand, comes only when I'm completely backed into a corner. Because when I'm not writing, then it's the last goddamn thing I want to do. I know I *should* be writing, but I just dont want to. But the longer I'm away from it, the more unravelled it seems my life becomes. I get restless and dark and I push people away. I take to ▶

« When I'm not writing, then it's the last goddamn thing I want to do. »

the bed. I might take a drinking fit. I drive faster on the highway. I might start writing poems. I have even started jogging. And then comes the moment when I realize what an absolute arse I've been for the past weeks or months, and I own up to what I am and what I need to be doing, make up my mind to start in writing on a certain date … and the cloud lifts.

I've often thought about this restlessness, about what makes people write or paint or sing or take pictures. I guess, at its most obvious, it's the need to capture how you see the world, the need to convey an opinion, the need to express what is in your head and your heart—where you come from, what you feel. But where does the need originate? It comes from a crisis of communication. I think those with the creative bent are considerably more alienated individuals than more conventionally minded folks. It's the artist's twisted attempt to socialize. Writing is a way of announcing that we feel alone and that we dont *want* to feel alone anymore.

For me, when I write, I want to recreate how things went down. I want to reinvent what happened in my own terms. I want to alter the memories of those who might have brushed against me when I was not at my best. Put words in a character's mouth that wouldnt necessarily come out in real life. Renegotiate the conditions of my history. And I like to toss a bit of fiction in there as well.

I started writing *Right Away Monday* before *Down to the Dirt* was published. The latter was signed with a publisher already, so I had no idea what to do with myself. All I knew

> ❝ Writing is a way of announcing that we feel alone and that we dont want to feel alone anymore. ❞

was that I wanted to keep exploring roughly the same themes and types of characters as I had brushed against with my first book. I guess that's always what the next book is—the attempt to get it right the next time around. That's the constant state of dissatisfaction that all writers and artists endure. But imagine being satisfied. What a horribly flaccid idea. People come up to me and say how they loved this or that piece I wrote and how I must be delighted with it, and all I can think is how much I'd love to go back and rewrite it.

A big part of publishing your work is also learning to let it go, coming to terms with the fact that it no longer belongs to you but to the reader. That it's going to be interpreted and misinterpreted or praised or shit on, and there's nothing you can do or say because it no longer has anything to do with you. I remember seeing copies of my books on the shelves and freaking out because—for whatever personal reason or mood I was in—at that moment I didnt want anyone to read them. I wanted them back. It's hard sometimes for me to be proud of work that is often perceived as being over-the-top angry or dark or destructive. Couple this with the notion that my work is largely autobiographical and it gets me feeling a little raw and naked.

But it's difficult when complete strangers believe that you are one and the same as the characters you write about. We all know how dull and boring and uninspired real life is. Sure, there's lots of sex and lots of ways to entertain yourself of a Friday night, and of course there are the ones you love, and there's motorcycling and trouting and birthday parties and opening nights and travel and strange lands with stranger customs, ▶

> **I remember seeing copies of my books on the shelves and freaking out because at that moment I didnt want anyone to read them.**

but there's fuck all to *believe* in anymore.
Our beliefs are fuelled primarily through
propaganda. We are told to recycle, compost,
boycott, strike back, to not stand for it. We
are told to subscribe, conned into believing
we can make a difference when we know in
our hearts that something else is more accurately true: that there is no God, there is no
country, there is no one, big forever love, no
soulmate, there are no miracles, no ghosts, no
second coming, no one ever *really* wins the
lottery, no one really gets their own TV show,
there are no coincidences, you will never
get that apology, your lover can never truly
come back, nothing will ever really change
out there, not for the better, not according to
your own terms. Smoking in public is gone
and it's *never* coming back.

A Lifetime in a Heartbeat

Last week he was playing with Lego blocks on the floor. He built a stairway, lifted it up to show me. I said:

— Oh, good job. Is that the stairway to Heaven?

He took on that broody look he's salvaged from my side of the bloodline and said:

— No, it's the stairway to Hell.

And I said:

— Good, very good.

I found it funny for a moment and went back to my book. I glanced at the clock to see if it was getting close to his bedtime. I stood in his doorway around midnight to listen to him breathing, and it echoed through my head, what he'd said. I was numbed for a moment, standing there. How in a few small years his world had been tainted to such a degree that he now understands the opposite of Heaven to be Hell and that one place is much easier to access than the other.

Trucks and action heroes and all things "boy." I choose to believe he came to these on his own. Ask him what he wants to be when he grows up—he says he wants a punk rock band. Ask him his favourite band and he'll tell you it's The Stones or The Clash. Then he'll glance at me out of the corner of his eye to check if he's gotten it right. It started as a party trick of sorts, something precocious he could pass on to those leaning in to hear what he'd say next. But it's just his way of getting the nod from me. It's already begun, this corruption I cant help but contribute to, pushing him down the paths I wish I'd taken. How the parent lives vicariously through the child. He ▶

15

said it to me just the other night again, lying in bed with his stories all read:

— When I get bigger, I'm going to have a band …

And me, a selfish attempt to reverse, repair, rearrange our dynamic, alleviate my guilt somehow:

— That's fine baby, so long as you're happy. You can be a garbage man, or a cop, or a writer for all that …

— And what are you going to be, Dad?

— I have no clue, no idea.

And I kissed his cheek and shut out the light, closed his door. One more day in his life gone forever. Never coming back.

When he was one and a half we took him to Shallow Bay in Gros Morne National Park. Miles and miles of fine, hot, golden sand, the salt water warm and tropical from midday on. Wade out for ages and never go over your head. And him, skipping, falling, splashing and squealing in the salt water for near on two hours. Peaceful and wild and happy and pure and absolutely fearless. Dash back to the blanket for a juice box and cheesies. Myself and his mother were drinking O'Doul's non-alcoholic beer, back when my path was a little clearer. I finished my first one and filled the empty bottle with sand from a small mound he'd dumped from a plastic bucket. I put the cap back on the bottle and stuffed it into my duffel bag. Something told me to do that, a little keepsake, because I knew, in some dark pocket of my heart, that it'd never get any better than that day.

> I knew, in some dark pocket of my heart, that it'd never get any better than that day.

16

That bottle of non-alcoholic golden sand sits on my windowsill right now, in my new house where he lives with me part-time, where he sits with me in my office and draws bogeymen and car wrecks and constructs the stairway to Hell.

Yeah. It's the modern way, the new-fashioned *Globe and Mail*-style parenting: go splitsville for the sake of the child rather than slugging it out for too many years and letting him grow up in a house of resentment and stifling anxiety. And who would we all be today if our own parents had been a little less constricted by the opinions of outsiders, if they hadnt been so concerned with keeping up the appearance of the functional family unit? Had they stopped and said:

— You know what? We'd all be a whole lot better off in the long run if we went our separate ways.

I look across the table at him now, his brow scrunched up just so, his little fingers peeling the paper wrapping from the tip of his crayon, and I try to remember him, the bundle of pure innocence that he was just a few short years ago. A lifetime ago. His world passing in a heartbeat. The first time I looked into his eyes he was a minute old. He looked wise. He looked like he'd come a long way and had seen things I could barely comprehend. How suddenly aware I was of the shadows I'd cast on the people who tried to love me. How small I felt for having thought such things, the compulsions I'd acted upon over the years, the dank and dirty suicidal roads I raced down before I was even twenty years old. Cut loose in the world.

Then that shifting inside I hope every new ▶

> **❝** The first time I looked into his eyes he was a minute old. He looked wise. **❞**

A Lifetime in a Heartbeat (*continued*)

parent gets to feel: how I would not hesitate to kill or die for this little human in my arms. How I'd take someone's life in a heartbeat, for him. And for the first time, here is a reason to live on.

A friend of mine once said to me that the best and worst thing about having children is that suicide is no longer an option. Because you have to live on. You cant ever again let yourself fall into those dark holes you've been drawn to. You have to look toward the light from there on in. Or fail your child.

He shows me his new drawing, a snarbled, multi-coloured scramble of scribbles. I study it for a moment and then tell him how it looks like a merry-go-round. He nods and says, *Yes, maybe it's Bowring Park.* My gut tightens, time slipping away. It's been a while since I've taken him for a good romp in Bowring Park. "Real" life comes along and fucks up the best of what you've got.

I remember a day last year when we were breaking the crest of the hill that leads to the Bowring Park swimming pool. It was a sticky summer day. He was running ahead of me in the grass. There was a couple playing with a Frisbee, some picnickers, little people's shouts and whoops from the playground, the roars and screams from the waterslide. He stopped midway and looked back at me, held out his hand for me to catch up. Before I reached it, he was off running again, toddler-mad toward the bottom. And I was struck with the notion that this must be Heaven. That if he were to pass out of this world somehow, and if there really is such a thing as Heaven, such a place to go when we're through with this life, a place of rewards and relaxation and peace and magic, then this is what his would be— merry-go-rounds and swings and Frisbees and waterslides, the sun high in the sky, no wind, fearless in the knowledge that he's loved and watched over. Then, in the blink of an eye, he's constructing the stairway to Hell. And when I tuck him in tonight, this day will be gone and said and done for the rest of time.

He looked up at me today when I picked him up from daycare and asked me when he would be a grown-up. And I said:

— Not for another long, long time.

But I'll lift my head someday soon and he will be twenty. Twenty-five. Thirty. And I'll look back through our days and remember always checking the clock, waiting to drop him at daycare, waiting to put him to bed at night so I can get on with what I'm supposed to be doing with my life. And how each day slips so uselessly into the next, the time come and gone for good, the clock ticking.

Real Heaven, right here and now in the palm of my hand.

His Lego blocks are scattered across his end of my desk. Before I rest my head tonight, I'll build a wall. I'll build a stairway that rises up and up beyond the edge of the wall. I'll stabilize it as best I can. He'll come in the morning and have a look and play with it for a while, try to rearrange it to suit his own tastes. And it'll break, it'll fall, collapse. Because everything does.

Then I'll help him build it back up again.

To receive updates on author events and new books by Joel Thomas Hynes, sign up today at *www.authortracker.ca*.

Soi

cœur/

107/2020 TOA

pas toute sa tête

e arrestation par la

d'Ottawa, le 21 février

subis le prelevement d'un glio
blastome de mon cerveau.

Je m'inscrit par la suite a un plan
de traitement aggresif qui pourrait
mener à une guerison apres 18 mois.

24/07/2020

TOA

Quand on a pas toute sa tête

le 3 mars 2020   un chirurgie fait
le prelevement de 90% d'un tumour
un tum 2000 g.   un glioblastome de

really is such a thing as Heaven, such a place to go when we're through with this life, a place of rewards and relaxation and peace and magic, then this is what his would be— merry-go-rounds and swings and Frisbees and waterslides, the sun high in the sky, no wind, fearless in the knowledge that he's loved and watched over. Then, in the blink of an eye, he's constructing the stairway to Hell. And when I tuck him in tonight, this day will be gone and said and done for the rest of time.

He looked up at me today when I picked him up from daycare and asked me when he would be a grown-up. And I said:

— Not for another long, long time.

But I'll lift my head someday soon and he will be twenty. Twenty-five. Thirty. And I'll look back through our days and remember always checking the clock, waiting to drop him at daycare, waiting to put him to bed at night so I can get on with what I'm supposed to be doing with my life. And how each day slips so uselessly into the next, the time come and gone for good, the clock ticking.

Real Heaven, right here and now in the palm of my hand.

His Lego blocks are scattered across his end of my desk. Before I rest my head tonight, I'll build a wall. I'll build a stairway that rises up and up beyond the edge of the wall. I'll stabilize it as best I can. He'll come in the morning and have a look and play with it for a while, try to rearrange it to suit his own tastes. And it'll break, it'll fall, collapse. Because everything does.

Then I'll help him build it back up again.

To receive updates on author events and new books by Joel Thomas Hynes, sign up today at *www.authortracker.ca*.

19

M'é Prendre pour Soi
et
Relacher par cœur
24/07/2020 TOH

Quand on a pas toute sa tête

Suite a une arrestation par la
police d'Ottawa, le 21 février
de 80%.
Je subis le prelevement d'un glio
blasthome de mon cerveau.
Je m'inscrit par la suite a un plan
de traitement aggressif qui pourrait
mener à une guerison après 18 mois.
24/07/2020
TOH

Quand on a pas toute ça tête

le 3 mars 2020 un chirurgien fait
le prelevement de 80% d'un tumeur
un tum un glioblastome de
2000 g.